It all begins with a letter.

Q **is for Queen.** Penguin Drop Caps is a series of twenty-six collectible hardcover editions of fine works of literature, each featuring on its cover a specially commissioned illustrated letter of the alphabet by type designer Jessica Hische. A collaboration between Jessica Hische and Penguin art director Paul Buckley, whose series design encompasses a rainbow-hued spectrum across all twenty-six books, Penguin Drop Caps debuted with an "A" for Jane Austen's *Pride and Prejudice*, a "B" for Charlotte Brontë's *Jane Eyre,* and a "C" for Willa Cather's *My Ántonia,* and continues with more classics from Penguin.

Penguin Drop Caps is a series inspired by typography—its beauty and its power of expression. A drop cap, or an initial cap, is the first letter of a word when designed and set larger than the surrounding text. It is used to introduce a new idea, paragraph, or chapter. We may recognize such elements from books of our childhood, from sacred and historic texts, and from beautiful early editions of classic literature. Whether they appear in illuminated fifteenth-century manuscripts set by scribes or digitally displayed on Jessica Hische's own *Daily Drop Cap* blog, a drop cap letter impresses upon the reader the arrival of something of which to take note, something unique and special that deserves to be savored.

For the book lover, the series is a nod to the tradition of printing and the distribution of ideas, stories, and opinions—ranging from paper to digital media. For the writer and artist, the series pays homage to the significance of composition, texture, and form. With Penguin Drop Caps, we are inspired by the timeless tradition and craft of letters and their endless capacity to communicate.

—E.R.

Famed New York City art dealer and connoisseur Georg Khalkis is dead, apparently of natural causes. But upon returning to Khalkis's pricey town house after the funeral, his mourners find that the metal box containing his last will and testament has vanished from the library wall safe. Detective Ellery Queen orders for the coffin to be unearthed and searched, and—to the horror of all—a strangled and decaying second corpse is found buried alongside Khalkis instead of the box. Only the brilliant and brash Queen, young master of deduction and son of a New York cop, can solve the complex whodunit. *The Greek Coffin Mystery* is one of the earliest mysteries in the classic Ellery Queen series—also one of the most popular, confounding, and brilliantly plotted—and affirms why the ever-popular Ellery Queen was widely regarded as the stateside successor to Sherlock Holmes and the definitive American detective-hero.

PENGUIN BOOKS

THE GREEK COFFIN MYSTERY

ELLERY QUEEN is the pen name of two cousins from Brooklyn, New York, Frederic Dannay (1905–1982) and Manfred B. Lee (1905–1971), as well as the name of their famous fictional detective. Dannay and Lee created Ellery Queen in 1929 and spent over four decades writing and editing under the pseudonym, spanning radio, television, comics, board games, and film. Leading the Golden Age of "whodunit" mysteries, Dannay and Lee also cofounded *Ellery Queen's Mystery Magazine,* one of the most influential crime publications of all time.

JESSICA HISCHE is a letterer, illustrator, typographer, and web designer. She currently serves on the Type Directors Club board of directors and has been named a *Forbes* magazine "30 under 30" in art and design, as well as an ADC Young Gun and one of *Print* magazine's "New Visual Artists." She has designed for Wes Anderson, *McSweeney's*, Tiffany & Co., Penguin Books, and many others. She resides primarily in San Francisco, occasionally in Brooklyn.

THE
GREEK COFFIN MYSTERY

ELLERY QUEEN

PENGUIN BOOKS

PENGUIN BOOKS
Published by the Penguin Group
Penguin Group (USA) LLC
375 Hudson Street
New York, New York 10014

USA | Canada | UK | Ireland | Australia | New Zealand | India | South Africa | China
penguin.com
A Penguin Random House Company

First published in the United States of America by Frederick A. Stokes Company 1932
Published in Penguin Books (USA) 2014

ISBN 978-0-14-312514-3

Printed in the United States of America
1 3 5 7 9 10 8 6 4 2

Set in LinoLetter Std with Archer
Cover design by Jessica Hische and Paul Buckley
Interior design by Sabrina Bowers

CONTENTS

THE GREEK COFFIN MYSTERY

CHARACTERS

GEORG KHALKIS *art dealer*

GILBERT SLOANE *manager, Khalkis Galleries*

DELPHINA SLOANE *Khalkis's sister*

ALAN CHENEY *son of Delphina Sloane*

DEMMY *Khalkis's cousin*

JOAN BRETT *Khalkis's secretary*

JAN VREELAND *Khalkis's traveling representative*

LUCY VREELAND *Vreeland's wife*

NACIO SUIZA *director of Khalkis's art-gallery*

ALBERT GRIMSHAW *ex-convict*

DR. WARDES *English eye specialist*

MILES WOODRUFF *Khalkis's attorney*

JAMES J. KNOX *millionaire art connoisseur*

DR. DUNCAN FROST *Khalkis's personal physician*

MRS. SUSAN MORSE *a neighbour*

JEREMIAH ODELL *plumbing contractor*

LILY ODELL *Odell's wife*

REV. JOHN HENRY ELDER

SEXTON HONEYWELL

WEEKES *Khalkis's butler*

MRS. SIMMS *Khalkis's housekeeper*

PEPPER *Assistant District Attorney*

SAMPSON *District Attorney*

COHALAN D. A. *detective*

DR. SAMUEL PROUTY *Assistant Medical Examiner*

EDMUND CREWE *architectural expert*

UNA LAMBERT *handwriting expert*

"JIMMY" *fingerprint expert*

TRIKKALA *Greek interpreter*

FLINT, HESSE, JOHNSON, PIGGOTT, HAGSTROM, RITTER *staff detectives*

THOMAS VELIE *detective sergeant*

DJUNA

INSPECTOR RICHARD QUEEN

ELLERY QUEEN

FOREWORD

I find the task of prefacing *The Greek Coffin Mystery* one of especial interest, since its publication was preceded by an extraordinary reluctance on the part of Mr. Ellery Queen to permit its publication at all.

Mr. Queen's readers will perhaps recall, from Forewords in previous Queen novels, that it was sheerest accident which caused these authentic memoirs of Inspector Richard Queen's son to be recast in the mould of fiction and given to the public—and then only after the Queens had retired to Italy to rest, as they say, on their laurels. But after I was able to persuade my friend to permit publication of the first one,* the initial Queen affair to be put between covers, things went very smoothly indeed and we found no difficulty in cajoling this sometimes difficult young man into further fictionizations of his adventures during his father's Inspectorship in the Detective Bureau of the New York Police Department.

Why, then, you ask, Mr. Queen's reluctance with regard to publication of the Khalkis case-history? For an interesting duality of reasons. In the first place, the Khalkis case occurred early in his career as unofficial investigator under the cloak of the Inspector's authority; Ellery had not yet at that time fully crystallized his famous analytico-deductive method. In the

---

* *The Roman Hat Mystery*, Frederick A. Stokes Company, publisher (1929). (The New American Library, P3229.)

second place—and this I am sure is the more powerful reason of the two—Mr. Ellery Queen until the very last suffered a thoroughly humiliating beating in the Khalkis case. No man, however modest—and Ellery Queen, I think he will be the first to agree, is far from that—cares to flaunt his failures to the world. He was put to shame publicly, and the wound has left its mark. "No," he said positively, "I don't relish the notion of castigating myself all over again, even in print."

It was not until we pointed out to him—his publishers and I—that far from being his worst failure, the Khalkis case (published under the present title of *The Greek Coffin Mystery*) was his greatest success, that Mr. Queen began to waver—a human reaction which I am glad to point out to those cynical souls who have accused Ellery Queen of being something less than human. . . . Finally, he threw up his hands and gave in.

It is my earnest belief that it was the amazing barriers of the Khalkis case that set Ellery's feet in the path that was to lead him to such brilliant victories later. Before this case was done, he had been tried by fire, and . . .

But it would be rude to spoil your enjoyment. You may take the word of one who knows the details of every single affair to which—I trust he will forgive my amicable enthusiasm—he applied the singing keenness of his brain, that *The Greek Coffin Mystery* from many angles is Ellery Queen's most distinguished adventure.

Happy hunting!

J. J. McC.
February, 1932

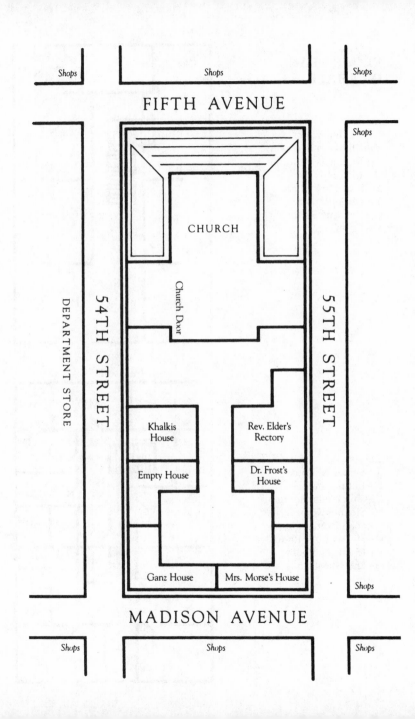

FLOOR PLAN
OF KHALKIS HOUSE

1st floor
A—Khalkis's Library
B—Khalkis's Bedroom
C—Demmy's Bedroom
D—Kitchen
E—Stairs to 2nd Floor
F—Dining Room
G—Drawing Room
H—Foyer

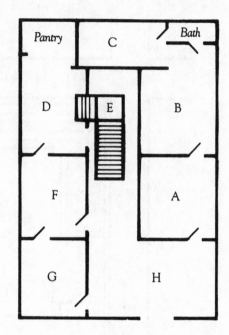

2nd floor
J—Servants' Room
K—Bathrooms
L—Vreelands' Room
M—Sloanes' Room
N—Joan Brett's Room
O—Dr. Warde's Room
P—Cheney's Room
Q—2nd Guest Room

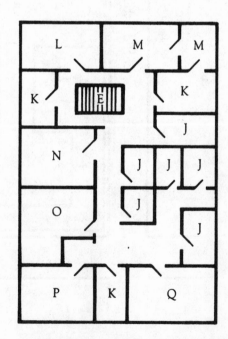

Attic not divided into rooms

THE
GREEK COFFIN
MYSTERY

BOOK ONE

"In science, in history, in psychology, in all manner of pursuits which require an application of thought to the appearance of phenomena, things are very often not what they seem. Lowell, the illustrious American thinker, said: 'A wise scepticism is the first attribute of a good critic.' I think precisely the same theorem can be laid down for the student of criminology. . . .

"The human mind is a fearful and tortuous thing. When any part of it is warped—even if it be so lightly that all the instruments of modern psychiatry cannot detect the warping— the result is apt to be confounding. Who can describe a motive? A passion? A mental process?

"My advice, the gruff dictum of one who has been dipping his hands into the unpredictable vapours of the brain for more years than he cares to recall, is this: Use your eyes, use the little grey cells God has given you, but be ever wary. There is pattern but no logic in criminality. It is your task to cohere confusion, to bring order out of chaos."

—Closing Address by Prof. Florenz Bachmann to Class
in *Applied Criminology* at University of Munich (1920)

CHAPTER 1

Tomb

From the very beginning the Khalkis case struck a sombre note. It began, as was peculiarly harmonious in the light of what was to come, with the death of an old man. The death of this old man wove its way, like a contrapuntal melody, through all the intricate measures of the death march that followed, in which the mournful strain of innocent mortality was conspicuously absent. In the end it swelled into a crescendo of orchestral guilt, a macabre dirge whose echoes rang in the ears of New York long after the last evil note had died away.

It goes without saying that when Georg Khalkis died of heart failure no one, least of all Ellery Queen, suspected that this was the opening motif in a symphony of murder. Indeed, it is to be doubted that Ellery Queen even knew that Georg Khalkis had died until the fact was forcibly brought to his attention three days after the blind old man's clay had been consigned, in a most proper manner, to what everyone had reason to believe was its last resting-place.

What the newspapers failed to make capital of in the first announcement of Khalkis's death—an obituary tribute which Ellery, a violent non-reader of the public prints, did not catch—was the interesting location of the man's grave. It gave a

Georg Khalkis Dead at 67 of Heart Failure

Internationally Famous Art Dealer and Collector Was Stricken Blind 3 Years Ago

Georg Khalkis, prominent art-dealer, connoisseur and collector of this city, founder of the Khalkis Galleries and one of the last survivors of the old New York Khalkis family, died Saturday morning in the private library of his home of heart-failure, at the age of 67.

Death came suddenly, despite the fact that Mr. Khalkis had been confined to his house for several years because of an organic illness which Dr. Duncan Frost, his personal physician, said induced blindness.

He had been a lifelong resident of New York City, and was responsible for bringing to the United States some of its most precious art treasures—now in museums, in the collections of his clients or in his own galleries on Fifth Avenue.

He is survived by an only sister, Delphina, who is the wife of Gilbert Sloane, manager of the Khalkis Galleries; by Alan Cheney, Mrs. Sloane's son by a former marriage; and by Demetrios Khalkis, a cousin—all of whom reside in the home of the deceased, 11 E. 54th Street, New York City.

Services and interment, to be held on Tuesday, October fifth, are to be strictly private out of respect for the deceased's own often expressed wish.

curious sidelight on old New Yorkana. Khalkis's drooping brownstone at 11 East Fifty-fourth Street was situated next to the tradition-mellowed church which fronts Fifth Avenue and consumes half the area of the block between Fifth and Madison Avenues, flanked on the north by Fifty-fifth Street and on the south by Fifty-fourth Street. Between the Khalkis house and the church itself was the church graveyard, one of the oldest private cemeteries in the city. It was in this graveyard that the bones of the dead man were to be interred. The Khalkis family, for almost two hundred years parishioners of this church, were not affected by that article of the Sanitary Code which forbids burial in the heart of the city. Their right to lie in the shadow of Fifth Avenue's skyscrapers was established by their traditional ownership of one of the subterranean vaults in the church graveyard—vaults not visible to passers-by, since their adits were sunken three feet below the surface, leaving the sod of the graveyard unmarred by tombstones.

The funeral was quiet, tearless and private. The dead man, embalmed and rigged out in evening clothes, was laid in a large black lustrous coffin, resting on a bier in the drawing-room on the first floor of the Khalkis house. Services were conducted by the Reverend John Henry Elder, pastor of the adjoining church—that Reverend Elder, it should be noted, whose sermons and practical diatribes were given respectful space in the metropolitan press. There was no excitement, and except for a characteristic swooning entered upon with vigour by Mrs. Simms, the dead man's housekeeper, no hysteria.

Yet, as Joan Brett later remarked, there was something wrong. Something that may be attributed, we may suspect, to that superior quality of feminine intuition which, medical men are prone to say, is sheer nonsense. Nevertheless she described it, in her straight-browed and whimsical English fashion, as "a tightness in the air." Who caused the tightness, what individual or individuals were responsible for the tension—if indeed it existed—she could not or would not say. Everything, on the contrary, seemed to go off smoothly and with just the proper touch of intimate, unexploited grief. When the simple services were concluded, for example, the members of the family and the scattering of friends and employees present filed past the coffin, took their last farewell of the dead clay, and returned decorously to their places. Faded Delphina wept, but she wept in the aristocratic manner—a tear, a dab, a sigh. Demetrios, whom no one would dream of addressing by any other name than Demmy, stared his vacant idiot's stare and seemed fascinated by his cousin's cold placid face in the coffin. Gilbert Sloane patted his wife's pudgy hand. Alan Cheney, his face a little flushed, had jammed his hands into the pockets of his jacket and was scowling at empty air. Nacio Suiza, director of the Khalkis art-gallery, correct to the last detail of funereal attire, stood very languidly in a corner. Woodruff, the dead man's attorney, honked his nose. It was all very natural and innocuous. Then the undertaker, a worried-looking, bankerish sort of man by the name of Sturgess, manipulated his puppets and the coffin-lid was quickly fastened down. Nothing remained but the sordid business of organizing the last procession. Alan, Demmy, Sloane and Suiza took their places by the bier, and after the customary confusion had subsided, hoisted the coffin to their shoulders, passed the critical scrutiny of Undertaker Sturgess, the Reverend Elder murmured a prayer, and the cortège walked firmly out of the house.

Now Joan Brett, as Ellery Queen was later to appreciate, was a very canny young lady. If she had felt a "tightness in the air," a tightness in the air there was. But where—from what direction? It was so difficult to pin it to—*someone*. It might have proceeded from bearded Dr. Wardes, who with Mrs. Vreeland made up the rear of the procession. It might have proceeded from the pallbearers, or from those who came directly after, with Joan. It might, in point of fact, have proceeded from the house itself, arising from just such a simple matter as Mrs. Simms wailing in her bed, or Weekes the butler rubbing his jaw foolishly in the dead man's study.

Certainly it does not seem to have thrust barriers in the way of expedition. The cortège made its way, not through the front door to Fifty-fourth Street, but through the back door into the long garden-court serving as a little private lane for the six residences on Fifty-fourth and Fifty-fifth Streets which enclosed it. They turned to the left and marched through the gate on the west side of the court, and they were in the graveyard. Passers-by and curiosity-seekers, attracted like flies to Fifty-fourth Street, probably felt cheated; which was precisely the reason that the private route to the graveyard had been selected. They clung to the spike-topped fence, peering into the little cemetery through the iron bars; there were reporters among them, and cameramen, and everyone was curiously silent. The actors in the tragedy paid no attention to their audience. As they wound across the bare sod, another little company faced them, surrounding a rectangular cavity in the grass and a mathematically upturned heap of earth. Two gravediggers—Sturgess's assistants—were there, and Honeywell, the church sexton; and by herself, a little old lady wearing a preposterously outmoded black bonnet and wiping her bright rheumy eyes.

The tightness, if we are to give credence to Joan Brett's intuition, persisted.

Yet what followed was as innocent as what had gone before. The customary ritualistic preparations, a gravedigger leaning far forward and grasping the handle of a rusty old iron door embedded horizontally in the earth; a slight rush of dead air; the coffin gently lowered into the old brick-lined crypt beneath; a milling of workmen, some low hurried words, the shifting of the coffin slowly to one side out of sight, where it nudged its way into one of the many niches of the underground vault; the iron door clanging to, the earth and sod replaced above it . . .

And somehow, Joan Brett was positive when she later told of her impressions of that moment, somehow the tightness in the air vanished.

CHAPTER 2

Hunt

V anished, that is to say, until a brief few moments after the funeral party, retracing its route through the garden-court, returned to the house.

Then it materialized again, accompanied by such a horde of ghastly events as made its source very clear indeed much later.

The first warning of what was to come was sounded by Miles Woodruff, the dead man's attorney. The picture seems to be etching-sharp at this point. The Reverend Elder had returned to the Khalkis house to offer consolation, trailing in his wake the dapper, clerical and annoyingly fidgety figure of Sexton Honeywell. The little old lady with the bright rheumy eyes who had met the cortège in the graveyard had expectantly joined the returning procession and was now in the drawing-room, inspecting the barren bier with a hypercritical air, while Undertaker Sturgess and his assistants busied themselves removing the grisly signs of their labour. No one had asked the little old lady in; no one now took cognizance of her presence except perhaps imbecile Demmy, who was eyeing her with a faintly intelligent dislike. The others had taken chairs, or were wandering listlessly about; there was little conversation; no one except the undertaker and his assistants seemed to know what to do.

Miles Woodruff, as restless as the others, seeking to bridge the ugly post-burial gap, had sauntered into the dead man's library quite without purpose, as he said later. Weekes, the butler, clambered to his feet in some confusion; he had been nodding a bit, it appears. Woodruff waved his hand and, still aimlessly, occupied with dismal thoughts, strolled across the room to the stretch of wall between two bookcases where Khalkis's wall-safe was imbedded. Woodruff has stoutly maintained that his act in twirling the dial of the safe and selecting the combination which caused the heavy round little door to swing open was wholly mechanical. Certainly, he averred later, he had not intended to look for it, let alone find it missing. Why, he had seen it, actually handled it only five minutes before the funeral party left the house! However, the fact remains that Woodruff did discover, whether by accident or design, that it was gone, and the steel box too—a discovery which sounded the warning-note that, quite like The House That Jack Built, caused the tightness to reappear that led to all the dire events that followed.

Woodruff's reaction to its disappearance was characteristic. He whirled on Weekes, who must have thought the man had gone insane, and shouted, "Did you touch this safe?" in a terrible voice. Weekes stammered a denial and Woodruff puffed and blew. He was hot on a chase, the goal of which he could not even vaguely see.

"How long have you been sitting here?"

"Ever since the funeral party left the house to go to the graveyard, sir."

"Did anyone come into this room while you were sitting here?"

"Not a living soul, sir." Weekes was frightened now; the ring of cotton-white hair at the back of his pink scalp, puffing over his ears, quivered with earnestness. In the eyes of stuffy old Weekes there was something terrifying in Woodruff's lord-and-master pose. Woodruff, it is to be feared, took advantage of his bulk, his red face and crackling voice to browbeat the old man almost to tears. "You were asleep!" he thundered. "You were dozing when I walked in here!"

Weekes mumbled in a soupy voice, "Just nodding, sir, really, sir, just nodding, sir. I wasn't asleep for an instant. I heard you the instant you came in, didn't I, sir?"

"Well . . ." Woodruff was mollified. "I guess you did at that. Ask Mr. Sloane and Mr. Cheney to come in here at once."

Woodruff was standing before the safe in a Messianic attitude when the two men came in, looking puzzled. He challenged them silently, with his best witness-baiting manner. He noticed at once that something was wrong with Sloane; precisely what he could not make out. As for Alan, the boy was scowling as usual, and when he moved nearer to Woodruff the lawyer caught the pungent odour of whisky on his breath. Woodruff spared no language in his peroration. He chopped at them savagely, pointed to the open safe, eyed each of them with heavy suspicion. Sloane shook his leonine head; he was a powerful man in the prime of life, elegantly attired in the height of foppish fashion. Alan said nothing—shrugged his spare shoulders indifferently.

"All right," said Woodruff. "It's all right with me. But I'm going to get to the bottom of this, gentlemen. Right now."

Woodruff appears to have been in his glory. He had everyone in the house peremptorily summoned to the study. Amazing as it may seem, it is true that within four minutes of the time the funeral party returned to the Khalkis house, Woodruff had them all on the carpet—*all*, including even Undertaker Sturgess and his assistants!—and had the dubious satisfaction of hearing them, to the last man and woman, deny having taken anything out of the safe, or even having gone to the safe that day at all.

It was at this dramatic and slightly ludicrous moment that Joan Brett and Alan Cheney were struck by the same thought. Both plunged for the doorway, colliding, boiling out of the room into the hall, flying down the hall to the foyer. Woodruff, with a hoarse shout, lunged after them, suspecting he knew not what. Alan and Joan assisted each other in unlocking the foyer door, scrambled through the vestibule to the unlocked street-door, flung it open and faced a mildly astonished throng in the street, Woodruff hurrying after them. Joan called out in her clear contralto, "Has anyone come into this house in the past half-hour?" Alan shouted, "*Anybody?*" and Woodruff found himself echoing the word. A hardy young man, one of a group of reporters draped over the latched gate on the sidewalk, distinctly said, "No!," another reporter drawled, "What's up, Doc? Why the hell don't you let us inside?—we won't touch nothin'," and there was a little scattering of applause from the onlookers in the street. Joan blushed, as was natural, and her hand strayed to her auburn hair, patting it for no apparent reason into place. Alan cried, "Did anybody come *out*?" and there was a thunderous chorus of "*No!*" Woodruff coughed, his self-assurance shaken by this public spectacle, irritably herded the young couple back into the house, and carefully locked the doors behind them—both of them, this time.

But Woodruff was not the type of man whose self-assurance can be permanently shaken. He recaptured it immediately upon re-entering the library, where the others sat and stood about looking faintly expectant. He rapped questions at them, pouncing on one after the other, and almost snarled with disappointment when he discovered that most of the household knew the combination of the safe.

"All right," he said. "All right. Somebody here is trying to pull a fast one. Somebody's lying. But we'll find out soon enough, soon enough, I'll promise you that." He prowled back and forth before them. "I can be as smart as the rest of you. It's my duty—my *duty*, you understand," and everybody nodded, like a battery of dolls, "to search every soul in this house. Right now. At once," and everybody stopped nodding. "Oh, I know someone here doesn't like the idea. Do you think *I* like it? But I'm going to do it anyway. It was stolen right under my nose. My nose." At this point, despite the seriousness of the situation, Joan Brett giggled; Woodruff's nose *did* cover a generous strip of territory.

Nacio Suiza, the immaculate, smiled slightly. "Oh, come now, Woodruff. Isn't this a bit melodramatic? There's probably a very simple explanation for the whole thing. You're dramatizing it."

"You think so, Suiza, you think so?" Woodruff transferred his glare from Joan to Suiza. "I see you don't like the idea of a personal search. *Why?*"

Suiza chuckled. "Am I on trial, Woodruff? Get a hold of yourself, man. You're acting like a chicken with its head cut off. Perhaps," he said pointedly, "perhaps you were mistaken when you thought you saw the box in the safe five minutes before the funeral."

"Mistaken? You think so? You'll find I wasn't mistaken when one of you turns out a thief!"

"At any rate," remarked Suiza, showing his white teeth, "*I* won't stand for this high-handed procedure. Try—just try—to search me, old man."

At this point the inevitable occurred; Woodruff completely lost his temper. He raged, and raved, and shook his heavy fist under Suiza's sharp cold nose, and spluttered, "By God, *I'll* show you! By heaven, *I'll* show you what high-handed is!" and concluded by doing what he should have done in the very beginning— he clutched at one of the two telephones on the dead man's desk, feverishly dialled a number, stuttered at an unseen inquisitor, and replaced the instrument with a bang, saying to Suiza with malevolent finality, "We'll see whether you'll be searched or not, my good fellow. Everybody in this house, by order of District Attorney Sampson, is not to stir a foot from the premises until somebody from his office gets here!"

CHAPTER 3

Enigma

Assistant District Attorney Pepper was a personable young man. Matters proceeded very smoothly indeed from the moment he stepped into the Khalkis house a half-hour after Woodruff's telephone call. He possessed the gift of making people talk, for he knew the value of flattery—a talent that Woodruff, a poor trial-lawyer, had never acquired. To Woodruff's surprise, even he himself felt better after a short talk with Pepper. Nobody minded in the least the presence of a moon-faced, cigar-smoking individual who had accompanied Pepper—a detective named Cohalan attached to the District Attorney's office; for Cohalan, on Pepper's warning, merely stood in the doorway to the study and smoked his black weed in complete, self-effacing silence.

Woodruff hurried husky Pepper into a corner and the story of the funeral tumbled out. "Now here's the situation, Pepper. Five minutes before the funeral procession was formed here in the house I went into Khalkis's bedroom"—he pointed vaguely to another door leading out of the library—"got hold of Khalkis's key to his steel box, came back in here, opened the safe, opened the steel box, and there it was, staring me in the face. Now then—"

"There *what* was?"

"Didn't I tell you? I must be excited." Pepper did not say that this was self-evident, and Woodruff swabbed his perspiring face. "Khalkis's new will! The *new* one, mind you! No question about the fact that it was the new will in the steel box; I picked it up and there was my own seal on the thing. I put it back into the box, locked the box, locked the safe, left the room. . . ."

"Just a moment, Mr. Woodruff." From policy Pepper always addressed men from whom he desired information as "Mister." "Did anyone else have a key to the box?"

"Absolutely not, Pepper, absolutely not! That key is the only one to the box, as Khalkis told me himself not long ago; and I found it in Khalkis's clothes in his bedroom, and after I locked the box and the safe, I put the key into my own pocket. On my own key-ring, in fact. Still have it." Woodruff fumbled in his hip-pocket and produced a key-wallet; his fingers were trembling as he selected a small key, detached it, and handed it to Pepper. "I'll swear that it's been in my pocket all the time. Why, nobody could have stolen it from *me!*" Pepper nodded gravely. "There was hardly any time. Right after I left the library, the business of the procession came up, and then we had the funeral. When I got back instinct or something, I guess, made me come in here again, open the safe—and, by God, the box with the will in it was gone!"

Pepper clucked sympathetically. "Any idea who took it?"

"Idea?" Woodruff glared about the room. "I've got plenty of ideas, but no proof! Now get this, Pepper. Here's the situation. Number one: everyone who was in the house at the time I saw the will in the box is still here; nobody permanently left the house. Number two: all those in the funeral party left the house in a group, went in a group through the court to the graveyard, were accounted for all the time they were there, and had no contact with outsiders except the handful of people they met at the grave. Number three: when the original party returned to the house, even these outsiders returned with them, and they're also still here."

Pepper's eyes were gleaming. "Damned interesting set-up. In other words, if someone of the original party has stolen the will, and passed it to one of these outsiders, it will do him no good, because a search of the outsiders will disclose it if it wasn't hidden somewhere along the route or in the graveyard. *Very* interesting, Mr. Woodruff. Now who were these outsiders, as you call them?"

Woodruff pointed to the little old lady in the antiquated black bonnet. "There's one of them. A Mrs. Susan Morse, crazy old loon who lives in one of the six houses surrounding the court. She's a neighbour." Pepper nodded, and Woodruff pointed out the sexton, standing trembling behind Reverend Elder. "Then there was Honeywell, the shrinking little fellow—sexton of the church next door; and those two working men next to him, the gravediggers, are employees of that fellow over there— Sturgess the undertaker. Now, point number four: while we were in the graveyard, no one entered the house or went out—*I* established that from some reporters who've been hanging about outside. And I myself locked the doors after that, so no one has been able to go out or come in since."

"You're making it tougher, Mr. Woodruff," said Pepper, when an angry voice exploded behind them, and he turned to find young Alan Cheney, more flushed than ever, brandishing a forefinger at Woodruff.

"Who's this?" asked Pepper.

Alan was crying, "Look here, Off'cer, don't believe him. *He* didn't ask the reporters! Joan Brett did—Miss Brett over here did. Di'n't you, Joanie?"

Joan had what might be termed the basis for a chilly expression—a tall slender English body, a haughty chin, a pair of very clear blue eyes and a nose susceptible of tilting movement. She looked through young Cheney in the general direction of

Pepper and said with icy, chiming distinctness, "You're potted again, Mr. Cheney. And *please* don't call me 'Joanie.' I detest it."

Alan stared blearily at an interesting shoulder. Woodruff said to Pepper, "He's drunk again, you see—that's Alan Cheney, Khalkis's nephew, and—"

Pepper said, "Excuse me," and walked after Joan. She faced him a little defiantly. "*Was* it you who thought of asking the reporters, Miss Brett?"

"Indeed it was!" Then two little pink spots appeared in her cheeks. "Of course, Mr. Cheney thought of it, too; we went together, and Mr. Woodruff followed us. It's remarkable that that drunken young sot had the *man*liness to give a lady credit for . . ."

"Yes, of course." Pepper smiled—he had a winning smile with the fair sex. "And you are, Miss Brett—?"

"I *was* Mr. Khalkis's secretary."

"Thank you so much." Pepper returned to a wilted Woodruff. "Now, Mr. Woodruff, you were going to tell me—"

"Just going over the whole ground for you, Pepper, that's all." Woodruff cleared his throat. "I was going to say that the only two people *in* the house during the funeral were Mrs. Simms, the housekeeper, who collapsed at Khalkis's death and has been confined to her room ever since; and the butler Weekes. Now Weekes—this is the unbelievable part of it—Weekes was *in* the library all the time we were gone. And he swears that no one came in. He had the safe under observation all the time."

"Good. Now we're getting somewhere," said Pepper briskly. "If Weekes is to be believed, we can now begin to limit the probable time of the theft a bit. It must have occurred during the five minutes between the time you looked at the will and the time the funeral party left the house. Sounds simple enough."

"Simple?" Woodruff was not quite certain.

"Sure. Cohalan, come here." The detective slouched across the room, followed by eyes that were chiefly blank. "Get this. We're looking for a stolen will. It must be one of four places. It's either hidden in the house here; or it's on the person of some-one now in the house; or it's been dropped somewhere along the private court route; or it will be found in the graveyard it-self. We'll eliminate them one by one. Hold up a sec while I get the Chief on the wire."

He dialled the number of the District Attorney's office, spoke briefly to District Attorney Sampson, and returned rubbing his hands. "The D.A. is sending police assistance. After all, we're in-vestigating a felony. Mr. Woodruff, you're appointed a committee of one to hold all persons in this room while Cohalan and I go over the courtyard and graveyard. One moment, please, every-body!" They gaped at him: a stupefaction of indecision, of mys-tery, of bewilderment had crept over them. "Mr. Woodruff is going to stay here in charge and you'll please co-operate with him. Don't leave the room, anyone." He and Cohalan strode out of the room.

Fifteen minutes later they returned, empty-handed, to find four newcomers in the library. They were Sergeant Thomas Ve-lie, black-browed giant attached to Inspector Queen's staff; two of Velie's men, Flint and Johnson; and a broad and ample police matron. Pepper and Velie held earnest colloquy in a corner, Ve-lie noncommittal and cold as usual, while the others sat apa-thetically waiting.

"Covered the court and graveyard, have you?" growled Velie.

"Yes, but it might be a good idea if you and your men go over the ground again," said Pepper. "Just to make sure."

Velie rumbled something to his two men, and Flint and John-son went away. Velie, Pepper and Cohalan began a systematic search of the house. They launched the search from the room they were in, Khalkis's study, and worked through to the dead man's bedroom and bathroom, and Demmy's bedroom beyond. They returned and Velie, without explanation, went over the study again. He ferreted about in the safe, in the drawers of the dead man's desk on which the telephones stood, through the

books and bookshelves lining the walls. . . . Nothing escaped his
attention, not even a small tabouret standing in an alcove, on
which were a percolator and various tea-things; with utter gravity Velie removed the tight lid of the percolator and peered inside.
Grunting, he led the way out of the library into the hall, from
which they spread to search the drawing-room, the dining-room,
and the kitchens, closets and pantry to the rear. The sergeant examined with particular care the dismantled trappings furnished
for the funeral by Undertaker Sturgess; but he discovered nothing. They mounted the stairs and swept through the bedrooms
like Visigoths, avoiding only Mrs. Simms's sanctuary; then they
climbed to the attic and raised clouds of dust rummaging through
old bureaux and trunks.

"Cohalan," said Velie, "tackle the basement." Cohalan sucked
sadly at his cigar, which had gone out, and trudged downstairs.

"Well, Sergeant," said Pepper as the two men leaned, puffing, against a bare attic wall, "it looks as if we'll have to do the
dirty work at that. Damn it, I didn't *want* to have to search those
people."

"After this muck," said Velie, looking down at his dusty fingers, "that'll be a real pleasure."

They went downstairs. Flint and Johnson joined them. "Any
luck, boys?" growled Velie.

Johnson, a small drab-looking creature with dirty-grey hair,
stroked his nose and said, "Nothing doin'. To make it worse, we
got hold of a wench—maid or somethin'—in a house on the
other side of the court. Said she was watchin' the funeral through
a back window, and she's been snoopin' there ever since. Well,
Sarge, this jane says that with the exception of two men—Mr.
Pepper and Cohalan, I guess—nobody's come out of the back of
this house since the funeral party returned from the graveyard.
Nobody's come out of the back of *any* house on the court."

"How about the graveyard itself?"

"No luck there either," said Flint. "Gang of newspaper leg-
men've been hanging around outside the iron fence on the

Fifty-fourth Street side of the graveyard. They say there hasn't been a damn' soul in the graveyard since the funeral."

"Well, Cohalan?"

Cohalan had succeeded in relighting his cigar, and he wore a happier expression. He shook his moon-face vigorously. Velie muttered, "Well, I don't see what there is to laugh about, you dumb ox," and strode into the centre of the room. He raised his head and, quite like a parade-sergeant, roared, " 'Tention!"

They sat up, brightening, some of the weariness fleeing their faces. Alan Cheney crouched in a corner, head between his hands, rocking himself gently. Mrs. Sloane had long since dabbed away the last decorous tear; even Reverend Elder wore an expectant expression. Joan Brett stared at Sergeant Velie with anxious eyes.

"Now get this," said Velie in a hard voice. "I don't want to step on anybody's toes, y'understand, but there's a job to be done and I'm going to do it. I'm going to have everyone in this house searched—down to the skin, if necessary. That will that was stolen can be in only one place—on the person of somebody right here. If you're wise, you'll take it like sports. Cohalan, Flint, Johnson—tackle the men. Matron," he turned to the brawny police-woman, "you take the ladies in the drawing-room, close the doors and get busy. And don't forget! If you don't find it on one of 'em, tackle the housekeeper and her room upstairs."

The study erupted in little conversations, assorted comments, half-hearted protests. Woodruff twiddled his thumbs before the desk and eyed Nacio Suiza benevolently; Suiza thereupon grinned and offered himself to Cohalan as the first victim. The women straggled out of the room; and Velie snatched one of the telephones. "Police Headquarters . . . Gimme Johnny . . . Johnny? Get Edmund Crewe down to Eleven East Fifty-fourth right away. Rush job. Snap into it." He leaned against the desk and watched frostily, Pepper and Woodruff by his side, as the three detectives took the men one by one and explored each male body with a thoroughness and impersonality that was shameless. Velie moved suddenly; Reverend Elder, quite uncomplaining, was due to be the next victim. "Reverend . . . Here, Flint, none o' that! I'll waive a search in your case, Reverend."

"You will do nothing of the kind, Sergeant," replied the minister. "According to your lights I am as much a possibility as any of the others." He smiled as he saw the indecision on Velie's hard face. "Very well. I'll search myself, Sergeant, in your presence." Velie's scruple at laying irreverent hands on the cloth did not prevent him from watching with keen eyes as the pastor turned out all his pockets, loosened his clothes and forced Flint to pass his hands over his body.

The matron trudged back with a laconic grunt of negation. The women—Mrs. Sloane, Mrs. Morse, Mrs. Vreeland, and Joan— were all flushed; they avoided the eyes of the men. "The fat dame upstairs—housekeeper?—she's okay too," said the matron.

There was silence. Velie and Pepper faced each other gloomily; Velie, confronted by an impossibility, was growing angry and Pepper, behind his bright inquisitive eyes, was thinking hard. "There's something screwy somewhere," said Velie in an ugly voice. "You're dead sure, matron?"

The woman merely sniffed.

Pepper grasped Velie's coat-lapel. "Look here, Sergeant," he said softly. "There's something vitally wrong here, as you say, but we can't butt our heads against a stone wall. It's possible that there's a secret closet or something in the house that we didn't find. Crewe, your architectural expert, will certainly locate it if it exists. After all, we've done the best we can, all we can. And we can't keep these people here forever, especially those who don't live in the house. . . ."

Velie scuffed the rug viciously. "Hell, the Inspector'll murder me for this."

Things happened swiftly. He stepped back, and Pepper politely suggested that the outsiders were free to leave, while those who lived in the house were not to quit the premises without official permission and without being searched thoroughly each time. Velie crooked his finger at the matron and Flint, who was a muscular young man, and led the way out into the hall and to the foyer, where he grimly took his stand by the front door. Mrs. Morse uttered a little squeal of terror as she shuffled toward him. "Search this lady again, matron," growled Velie. . . . The Reverend Elder he favoured with a bleak smile; but Honeywell the sexton he examined himself. Meanwhile Flint was again searching Undertaker Sturgess, his two assistants, and a bored Nacio Suiza.

As in all former searches, the result was empty air.

Velie stamped back to the library after the outsiders left, stationing Flint on guard outside the house, where he could watch both the front door and the front basement door below the stone steps. Johnson he dispatched to the back door at the top of a flight of wooden steps leading down into the court; Cohalan he sent to the rear door level with the court, which led out of the rear of the basement.

Pepper was engaged in earnest conversation with Joan Brett. Cheney, a much chastened young man, rumpled his hair and scowled at Pepper's back. Velie swung a horny finger at Woodruff.

CHAPTER 4

Gossip

Edmund Crewe was so perfectly the picture of the absent-minded professor that Joan Brett only with difficulty repressed an alarming impulse to laugh aloud in his horsy lugubrious face, pinched nose and lustreless eyes. Mr. Crewe, however, began to speak, and the impulse died aborning.

"Owner of the house?" His voice was like a wireless spark, pungent and crackling.

"He's the guy that kicked off," said Velie.

"Perhaps," said Joan, a little abashed, "I can be of service."

"How old's the house?"

"Why, I—I don't know."

"Step aside, then. Who does?"

Mrs. Sloane blew her nose daintily in a tiny scrap of lace. "It's—oh, eighty years old if it's a day."

"It's been remodelled," said Alan eagerly. "Sure. Remodelled. Loads of times. Uncle told me."

"Not specific enough." Crewe was annoyed. "Are the plans still in existence?"

They looked doubtfully at each other.

"Well," snapped Crewe, "does anybody know *anything*?"

No one, it seemed, knew anything. That is, until Joan,

pursing two excellent lips, murmured, "Oh, wait a moment. Is it blueprints and things you want?"

"Come, come, young woman. Where are they?"

"I think . . ." said Joan thoughtfully. She nodded like a very pretty bird and went to the dead man's desk. Pepper chuckled appreciatively when she rummaged through the lowest drawer and emerged finally with a battered old cardboard filing-case bursting with yellowed papers. "An old paid-bill file," she said. "I think . . ." She thought clearly, for in no time at all she found a white slip of paper with a folded set of blueprints pinned to it. "Is this what you want?"

Crewe snatched the sheaf from her hand, stalked to the desk and proceeded to burrow his pinched nose into the blueprints. He nodded from time to time, then suddenly rose and without explanation left the room, the plans in his hand.

Apathy settled again, like a palling mist.

"Something you ought to know, Pepper." Velie drew Pepper aside and grasped Woodruff's arm with what he considered gentleness. Woodruff whitened. "Now, listen, Mr. Woodruff. The will's been grabbed off by somebody. There's got to be a reason. You say it was a new will. Well, who lost what by it?"

"Well—"

"On the other hand," said Pepper thoughtfully, "I can't see that the situation, aside from its criminal implications, is very serious. We can always establish intention of testator from your office copy of the new will, Mr. Woodruff."

"The hell you can," said Woodruff. He snorted. "The hell you can. Listen." He drew them closer to him, looking around cautiously. "We *can't* establish the old man's intention! That's the funny part of it. Now get this. Khalkis's old will was in force up to last Friday morning. The provisions of the old will were simple: Gilbert Sloane was to inherit the Khalkis Galleries, which includes the art-and-curio business as well as the private art-gallery. There were two trust-funds mentioned—one for Khalkis's nephew Cheney and one for his cousin Demmy, that half-witted yokel over there. The house and personal effects were bequeathed to his sister, Mrs. Sloane. Then there were the usual things—cash bequests to Mrs. Simms and Weekes, to various employees, a detailed disposition of art-objects to museums and so on."

"Who was named executor?" asked Pepper.

"James J. Knox."

Pepper whistled and Velie looked bored. "You mean Knox the multi-millionaire? The art-bug?"

"That's the one. He was Khalkis's best customer, and I would say something of a friend, too, considering the fact that Khalkis named him executor of his estate."

"One hell of a friend," said Velie. "Why wasn't he at the funeral to-day?"

"My dear Sergeant," said Woodruff, opening his eyes, "don't you read the papers? Mr. Knox is a somebody. He was notified of Khalkis's death and intended to come to the funeral, but at the last minute he was called to Washington. This morning, in fact. Papers said it was at the personal request of the President—something to do with Federal finance."

"When's he get back?" demanded Velie truculently.

"No one seems to know."

"Well, that's unimportant," said Pepper. "Now how about the new will?"

"The new will. Yes." Woodruff looked very cunning. "And here is the mysterious part of it. Last Thursday night, about midnight, I got a telephone call from Khalkis. He told me to bring him on Friday morning—the next morning—the complete draft of a new will. Now get this: the new will was to be an exact duplicate of the existent will except for one change: I was to omit the name of Gilbert Sloane as beneficiary of the Khalkis Galleries and leave the space blank for the insertion of a *new* name."

"Sloane, eh?" Pepper and Velie studied the man surreptitiously. He was standing like a pouter pigeon behind Mrs.

Sloane's chair staring glassily into space, and one of his hands was trembling. "Go on, Mr. Woodruff."

"Well, I had the new will drawn up first thing Friday morning and chased over here with it considerably before noon. I found Khalkis alone. He was always a pretty rocky sort of codger—cold and hard and businesslike as you please—but that morning he was upset about something. Anyway, he made it plain right away that nobody, not even your humble servant, was to know the name of the new beneficiary of his Galleries. I fixed up the will in front of him so that he'd fill in the blank space conveniently—he made me cross over and stand on the other side of the room, mind you!—and then he scribbled a name, I suppose, in the space. He blotted it himself, closed the page quickly, had Miss Brett, Weekes and Mrs. Simms witness his signature, signed the will, sealed it with my assistance, and put it into the small steel box he kept in his safe, locking the box and the safe himself. And there you are—not a soul but Khalkis himself knew who the new beneficiary was!"

They chewed upon that. Then Pepper asked: "Who knew the provisions of the old will?"

"Everybody. It was common gossip about the house. Khalkis himself didn't make any bones about it. As for the new will, Khalkis hadn't specifically made a point of keeping quiet about the fact that he was making a new testament, and I didn't see any reason to hush it up. Naturally, the three witnesses knew it, and I suppose they spread the word around the house."

"The Sloane guy know it?" rasped Velie.

Woodruff nodded. "I should say he did! In fact, that afternoon he called at my office—evidently he'd already heard that Khalkis had signed a new will—and wanted to know if the change affected him in any way. Well, I told him that somebody was taking his place, who exactly nobody knew but Khalkis himself, and he—"

Pepper's eyes flashed. "Damn it all, Mr. Woodruff, you had no right to do that!"

Woodruff said weakly: "Well, now, Pepper, maybe it wasn't the . . . But you see, I figured that maybe Mrs. Sloane was the new beneficiary, and in that case Sloane would get the Galleries through her, so he wouldn't be losing anything anyway."

"Oh, come now," said Pepper with a snap in his voice, "it was an unethical thing to do. Ill-advised. Well, no use crying over spilt milk. When you looked at the new will in the box five minutes before the funeral, did you find out then who the new beneficiary was?"

"No. I didn't mean to open the will until after the funeral."

"You're sure it was the authentic document?"

"Positive."

"Did the new will have a revocation clause?"

"It did."

"What's that?" growled Velie suspiciously. "What's that mean?"

"Plenty to give us a headache," said Pepper. "The inclusion of a revocation clause in a new will is made to establish the intention of testator to revoke all previous testaments. That means that the old will in force up to last Friday morning is voided whether the new will is found or not. And," he added grimly, "if we don't find the new will and can't establish the identity of the new beneficiary for the Galleries, Khalkis will be considered to have died intestate. A rotten mess!"

"That means," said Woodruff gloomily, "that Khalkis's estate will have to be apportioned by law strictly according to the tenets of inheritance."

"I get it," rumbled Velie. "This Sloane guy comes in for his cut no matter what happens, just as long as that new will isn't found. Khalkis's next of kin is his sister, Mrs. Sloane, I reckon . . . Pretty smart!"

Edmund Crewe, who had been slipping in and out of the library like a wraith, hurled the blueprints on the desk and approached the three men. "Well, Eddie?" demanded Velie.

"No can find. No panels or secret closets. No interstices in the walls left by improper mating of two rooms. Ceilings and floors solid—they made 'em that way in the old days."

"Damn!" said Pepper.

"No, sirree," continued the architectural expert. "If the will isn't on any one person in this house, you take it from me that it isn't in the house at all."

"But it must be!" said Pepper with exasperation.

"Well, it isn't, younker." Crewe marched out of the room and they heard the bang of the front door a moment later.

The three men said nothing, eloquently. Velie without explanation thundered out of the study, to return some minutes later harder-jawed than ever. A sour helplessness radiated from his mammoth bulk. "Pepper," he said dourly, "I give up. Just went over that court and graveyard myself. Nothing doing. Must've been destroyed. How do you stand?"

"I have an idea," said Pepper, "but that's all. I'll have to talk it over with the Chief first."

Velie thrust his fists into his pockets, surveying the battle-ground. "Well," he grumbled, "I'm washed up. Listen, folks." They had been listening; but all vitality had been drained out of them by the cloying wait, and they stared at Velie with doggy eyes. "When I leave this house, I'm closing up this room and those two others beyond. Understand? Nobody is to come in here. Nobody is to touch Khalkis's room either, or Demetrios Khalkis's—leave everything exactly as it is. And one more thing. You can come and go in and out of the house as you please, but you'll be searched every single time, so don't anybody try any funny stuff. That's all."

"I say." Someone had spoken in a cavernous voice. Velie turned slowly. Dr. Wardes was coming forward—a man of middle height, bearded like one of the old prophets, but with a physique almost simian. His very bright brown eyes, set closely together, regarded Sergeant Velie almost with humour.

"What do *you* want?" Velie bristled, wide-legged, on the rug.

The physician smiled. "Your orders will not put any of the

regular residents of this house to great inconvenience, don't you know, Sergeant, but they will affect me most unpleasantly. You see, I've been merely a guest here. Must I intrude on the hospitality of this very sad establishment indefinitely?"

"Say, who are you anyway?" Velie moved a ponderous step forward.

"My name is Wardes, and I am a citizen of Great Britain and a humble subject of His Majesty the King," replied the bearded man, twinkling. "I'm a medico—eye specialist. I've been having Mr. Khalkis under observation for some weeks."

Velie grunted. Pepper moved to his side and whispered. Velie nodded, and Pepper said: "Naturally, Dr. Wardes, we don't want to embarrass you or your hosts. You are perfectly free to leave. Of course," he continued smiling, "you won't object to a last formality—a thorough search of your person and luggage on going away?"

"Object? Certainly not, sir." Dr. Wardes played with his shaggy brown beard. "On the other hand—"

"Oh, do stay, Doctor!" shrilled Mrs. Sloane. "Don't leave us in this dreadful time. You've been so kind . . ."

"Yes, do, Doctor." This was a new voice, and it proceeded from the deep chest of a large handsome woman—a dark bold beauty. The physician bowed and murmured something inaudible, and Velie said nastily, "And who are *you*, Madame?"

"Mrs. Vreeland." Her eyes sparked warning; her voice had coarsened, and Joan, perched on the edge of Khalkis's desk in woeful resignation, swallowed a smile bravely; her blue eyes went appraisingly to Dr. Wardes's powerful shoulder-blades. "Mrs. Vreeland. I live here. My husband is—was—Mr. Khalkis's travelling representative."

"I don't get you. What do you mean—travelling representative? Where is your husband, Madame?"

The woman flushed darkly. "I don't like your tone! You have no *right* to speak to me in such a disrespectful tone!"

"Can it, sister. Answer my question." Velie's eyes grew cold, and when Velie's eyes grew cold they grew very cold indeed.

The little mutter of anger sputtered away. "He's—he's in Canada somewhere. On a scouting trip."

"We tried to locate him," said Gilbert Sloane unexpectedly. His pomaded black hair, small mathematical moustache, pounced watery eyes gave him an incongruously dissipated appearance. "We tried to locate him—the last we heard, he was operating from Quebec as a base, on the trail of some old hooked rugs he'd heard about. We haven't heard from him yet, though we left word at his last hotel. Perhaps he'll see the news of Georg's death in the papers."

"And perhaps he won't," said Velie shortly. "Okay. Dr. Wardes, you staying?"

"Since I am requested to do so—yes. I shall be very happy to." Dr. Wardes moved back and contrived to stand near Mrs. Vreeland's stately shape.

Velie looked at him darkly, motioned to Pepper and they walked out into the corridor. Woodruff almost trod on their heels, he followed so quickly. Everyone shuffled out of the library and Pepper shut the door carefully behind him. Velie said to Woodruff, "What's on your mind now, Woodruff?"

They had turned to face him near the foyer door. The lawyer said in a sharp tone, "Look here. Pepper saw fit to accuse me of an error of judgement a while ago. I'm not taking any chances. I want you to search *me* too, Sergeant. Yourself. I wasn't tackled in there, you know."

"Now, don't take it that way, Mr. Woodruff," said Pepper in a soothing voice. "I'm sure it isn't—"

"I think it's a damned good idea," said Velie unpleasantly. Without ceremony he gave Woodruff such a pounding, scraping and pinching as Woodruff, to judge from his expression, had hardly anticipated. And Velie went very carefully indeed through all the papers the lawyer had in his pockets. Finally, he surrendered his victim. "You're clean, Woodruff. Come along, Pepper."

Outside the house they found Flint, the brawny young plain clothesman, bantering with the dwindled group of reporters, a handful clinging tenaciously to the sidewalk gate. Velie promised Flint a relief for himself and Johnson in the rear, and for the matron he had left inside, and doggedly ploughed through the gate. Like a cloud of gnats the reporters swarmed about him and Pepper.

"What's the angle, Sarge?"

"What's up?"

"Give us a break, you mug!"

"Come on, Velie, don't be a thick flattie all your life."

"How much was your cut for keeping quiet?"

Velie shook their hands off his big shoulders; and he and Pepper took refuge in a police car waiting at the curb.

"How'm I gonna tell the Inspector?" groaned Velie, as the car lurched forward. "He'll crown me for this."

"Which Inspector?"

"Richard Queen." The sergeant stared morosely at the back of the chauffeur's crimson neck. "Well, we did what we could. Left the house under a kind of siege. And I'll send one of the boys over to look at the safe for fingerprints."

"Much good that'll do." Pepper's brightness had dissipated; he sat gnawing a fingernail. "The D.A.'ll probably give me hell, too. I think I'll stick pretty close to the Khalkis house. Drop in to-morrow to see what's doing, I will. And if those palookas in the house want to make trouble about our restricting their movements that way—"

"Aw, nuts," said Velie.

CHAPTER 5

Remains

On Thursday morning, which was the seventh of October, and a singularly cheerless day, District Attorney Sampson called a council of war. It was on this day, then, that Ellery Queen was formally introduced to the perplexing riddle that eventually came to be known as "The Khalkis Case." It was a younger and cockier Ellery;[*] and, since his connexion with the policing of New York City was not so firmly established at this time, he was still considered something of an interloper despite his unique position as the son of Inspector Richard Queen. Indeed, it is to be suspected that the good grey Inspector himself had good grey doubts concerning Ellery's convenanted ability to combine pure reason with practical criminology. The few isolated cases to which Ellery had applied his still formative faculties of deduction, however, had established a precedent which accounted for his cool assumption that he too was meant to be a councilman when District Attorney Sampson sounded the tocsin.

---

[*] It should be recalled that *The Greek Coffin Mystery* precedes in point of time those Queen cases which have already been presented to the public. It dates only a short time after Ellery Queen's graduation from college—J. J. McC.

Truth to tell, Ellery had heard nothing whatsoever about Georg Khalkis's death, and considerably less about the stolen will. Consequently, he disturbed the District Attorney by questions to which everyone present, save Ellery himself, knew the answers. The District Attorney, not yet the tolerant colleague he was in later years to become, was distinctly irritated. The Inspector himself was annoyed and said so in no uncertain terms, and Ellery sank back on his spine in one of Sampson's best leather chairs, a trifle abashed.

They were very solemn. There was Sampson, almost at the outset of his prosecutor's career, a thin and deceptively sturdy man in his prime—bright-eyed and eager, and not a little upset by this waspish problem that seemed so ridiculous until it was examined closely. There was Pepper, the intelligent Pepper, one of Sampson's staff of prosecutors, a political appointee, his whole husky healthy body portraying despair. There was old Cronin, Sampson's First Assistant District Attorney, much more mature in criminal wisdom than his two colleagues; a veteran of the office—red-haired, nervous, springy as a colt and wise as an old roan. There was Inspector Richard Queen, already grey, more bird-like than ever, with his little sharp withered face and thick grey hair and moustache—a slender little old man with a quaint taste in cravats, the potential resiliency of a greyhound and a vast knowledge of orthodox criminalism. He was toying in exasperation with his old brown snuff-box.

Then, of course, there was Ellery himself—Ellery the temporarily chastened. When he made a point, he brandished the winking lenses of his *pince-nez* eyeglasses. When he smiled, it was with his whole face—a very good face, it has been said, with long delicate lines and the large limpid eyes of the thinker. Otherwise, he was much like other young men whose memories of their Alma Mater are not yet mildewed: tall and spare and square-shouldered and not unathletic. At the moment he was watching District Attorney Sampson, and District Attorney Sampson felt distinctly uncomfortable.

"Well, gentlemen, we're up against the old story," muttered Sampson. "Lots of leads, but no goal in sight. Well, Pepper, is there anything else you've discovered to confound us?"

"Not a solitary thing of importance," replied Pepper dolefully. "I naturally tackled this Sloane fellow the first chance I got—alone. He's the only baby who stood to lose by the new Khalkis will. Well, Sloane shut up like a Bluepoint—refused to talk at all yesterday. What could I do? We haven't any proof."

"There are ways," said the Inspector darkly.

"Rot, Q.," snapped Sampson. "There's not a shred of evidence against him. You can't browbeat people like Sloane on mere suspicion because theoretically he had motive. What else, Pepper?"

"Well, Velie and I were sunk, and we knew it. We had no earthly right to keep the house segregated from the world, and Velie had to withdraw his two men yesterday. I didn't feel like giving it up so easily, so I stayed overnight last night on a hunch—I don't think most of 'em even knew I was there."

"Catch anything?" asked Cronin curiously.

"Well," Pepper hesitated. "I did see something . . . Not," he continued hastily, "not that I think it means anything. She's a swell kid—isn't capable—"

"Who on earth are you talking about, Pepper?" demanded Sampson.

"Miss Brett. Joan Brett," replied Pepper reluctantly. "I saw her snooping around Khalkis's library at one o'clock this morning. She shouldn't have been there, of course—Velie expressly told them all to keep out . . ."

"The charming amanuensis of our defunct mysterioso, I take it?" inquired Ellery lazily.

"Uh-huh. Well," and Pepper seemed to have difficulty with his usually ready tongue, "well, she messed about the safe a bit—"

"Ha!" said the Inspector.

". . . but I guess she didn't find anything, because she sort of stood still in the centre of the study for a moment, looking very pretty in a *négligé,* then she stamped her foot and beat it."

"Did you question her?" asked Sampson querulously.

"No, I didn't. You see, I don't really think there's anything wrong in that direction," began Pepper, spreading his hand, when Sampson said dryly, "You'll have to get over that predilection for pretty faces, Pepper. *I'll* see that she's questioned, and *I'll* see that she talks, too, damn it all!"

"You'll learn, Pepper," chuckled Cronin. "I remember once when a dame threw her nice softy baby arms around my neck, and—"

Sampson frowned. Pepper started to say something, reddened behind the ears, and decided not to say anything after all.

"Anything else?"

"Just routine stuff. Cohalan's still on duty at the Khalkis house, and so is Velie's matron. They keep on searching everyone that goes out of the house. Cohalan's been keeping a list," said Pepper, fumbling in his breast pocket and producing a ragged slip of paper most unprofessionally scribbled over in smudgy pencil, "a list of everyone from outside who's visited the house since we left it Tuesday. Complete up to last night."

Sampson snatched the scrap and read it aloud. "Reverend Elder. Mrs. Morse—that's the old nut, isn't it? James J. Knox—so he's back. Clintock, Eilers, Jackson, the reporters. And who are these, Pepper?—these two people, Robert Petrie and Mrs. Duke?"

"Two wealthy old clients of the dead man. Called to pay their respects."

Sampson crumpled the list absently. "Well, Pepper, it's your funeral. When the call came in from Woodruff about the lost will you asked for the case and I gave you your chance. I don't want to rub it in, but I'll simply have to switch you if you let considerations like Miss Brett's no doubt gorgeous map sway you from your duty. . . . Well, enough of that. How does it line up to you? Any ideas?"

Pepper swallowed hard. "Don't want to fall down . . . Well,

one idea, Chief. Offhand, the facts make an utterly impossible case. The will must be in the house, and yet it isn't. Poppycock!" He slapped Sampson's desk. "Now there's one fact that makes all the other facts look impossible. And that is—that Woodruff saw the will in the safe five minutes before the funeral. Well, sir—we've got only his word for that fact! You get what I mean."

"You mean," said the Inspector thoughtfully, "that Woodruff was lying when he said he saw the will at that time? In other words, that the will could have been stolen much before that five-minute period, and the person who stole it could have disposed of it outside the house at a time when his movements didn't have to be accounted for?"

"That's the ticket, Inspector. Listen—we have to go by logic, don't we? The will didn't disappear into thin air, did it?"

"How do you know," objected Sampson, "that the will wasn't taken out during that five-minute interval, as Woodruff said, and then burned, or was torn up or something?"

"But Sampson," said Ellery mildly, "you can't very well burn or tear up a steel box, can you?"

"That's right, too," muttered the District Attorney. "Where on earth *is* that box?"

"That's why I say," said Pepper triumphantly, "that Woodruff's lying. That will, and the steel box, too, never *was* in the safe when he said he saw it there!"

"But, heavens," exclaimed the Inspector, "why? Why should he lie?"

Pepper shrugged. Ellery said with amusement, "Gentlemen, none of you is tackling this problem in the proper manner. This is just such a problem as must be analysed, and every possibility taken into consideration."

"*You've* analysed it, I suppose?" said Sampson sourly.

"Ah—yes. Yes indeed. And my analysis leads to an interesting—I might say a *very* interesting—possibility." Ellery sat up now, smiling. The Inspector took a pinch of snuff; he said nothing. Pepper leaned forward, all ears, regarding Ellery with a dawning personality, as if he had just noticed Ellery's existence. "Let me go over the facts to date," continued Ellery briskly. "You will agree that there are two supplementary possibilities: one, that the new will does not exist at this moment; two, that the new will *does* exist at this moment.

"Consider the first. If the will does not now exist, it means that Woodruff lied when he said he saw it in the safe five minutes before the funeral, that the will wasn't there at that time, that the will had been previously destroyed by person or persons unknown. Or Woodruff told the truth, the will *was* stolen after he saw it, in that five-minute interval, and then destroyed. In this last event, it would have been possible for the thief to have burnt or torn up the will, disposing of the remains by slipping them down a bathroom drain, perhaps; but, as I pointed out an instant ago, the fact that the steel box has not turned up at all points to the improbability of this destruction theory. No remains of the steel box were found; then where is the steel box? Presumably taken away. If the steel box were taken away, then plausibly the will also was taken away, not destroyed. But, you say, under the circumstances, if Woodruff was telling the truth, the box *couldn't* have been taken away. We have reached an impasse, therefore, in our first major possibility. In any event, if it is true that the will was destroyed, there is nothing further to be done."

"And that," said Sampson, turning to the Inspector, "that's a help, that is. My God, man," he said irascibly, swinging on Ellery, "we know all that. What are you getting at?"

"Inspector dear," said Ellery mournfully to his father, "do you allow this man to insult your son? Look here, Sampson. You're anticipating me, and that's fatal to logic. Having thrown aside the first theory as so much tenuous vapour, we attack the alternative theory—that the will *does* exist at this moment. But what have we?—ah, a most fascinating state of affairs. Lend ear, gentlemen! Everyone who left the house to attend the funeral returned to the house. The two people in the house remained in the house—one of them, Weekes, actually in the study, where the safe is, all the time. No one entered the house during the funeral. And at no time was there contact between the people of the house and the cortège with outsiders; for everyone in the graveyard to whom the will might have been passed also returned to the house.

"Yet," he continued rapidly, "the will was not found in the house, on the persons of anyone in the house, along the courtyard route, or in the graveyard! I therefore entreat, sue, beg, implore you," concluded Ellery, his eyes mischievous, "to ask me the enlightening question: What is the only thing which *left* the house during the funeral, *didn't* come back and *has never been searched* since the will was found to have disappeared?"

Sampson said, "Tommyrot. Everything was searched, and damned thoroughly as you've been told. You know that, young man."

"Why, of course, son," said the Inspector gently. "Nothing was overlooked—or didn't you understand that when the facts were related?"

"Oh, my living, breathing soul!" groaned Ellery. "'None so blind as those that will not see . . .'" He said softly, "Nothing, my honourable ancestor, nothing but *the coffin itself, with Khalkis's corpse in it!*"

* * *

The Inspector blinked at that, Pepper muttered disgustedly in his throat, Cronin guffawed and Sampson smote his forehead a mighty blow. Ellery grinned shamelessly.

Pepper recovered first, and grinned back at him. "That's smart, Mr. Queen," he said. "That's smart."

Sampson coughed into his handkerchief. "I—well, Q., I take it all back. Go on, young man."

The Inspector said nothing.

"Well, gentlemen," drawled Ellery, "it's gratifying to speak to such an appreciative audience. The argument is arresting. In the excitement of the last-minute preparations for the funeral, it would have been a simple enough matter for the thief to have opened the safe, extracted the small steel box with the will in it and, watching his opportunity in the drawing-room, to have slipped box and will into the coffin beneath the folds of the coffin's lining, or whatever they call Mr. Khalkis's cerements."

"It's a cinch," muttered Inspector Queen, "that burying the will with the body would be as effective as destroying it."

"Precisely, Dad. Why destroy the will if by secreting it in the coffin due for immediate burial the thief would achieve the same end? Certainly he had no reason to believe, since Khalkis died a natural death, that the coffin would ever be looked into again this side of the Judgement Day. *Ergo*—the will is removed from mortal ken as completely as if it had been burnt and its ashes consigned to our sewage system.

"Then there's a psychological justification for this theory. Woodruff had on his person the only key to the steel box. The thief therefore probably could not open the box in the short five-minute interval before the funeral party left the house. He couldn't—or wouldn't—carry the box with the will in it around with him; too bulky, too dangerous. *Alors, messieurs*, box and will are possibly in Khalkis's coffin. If this be information, make the most of it."

Inspector Queen hopped to his tiny feet. "An immediate disinterment seems in order."

"It looks that way, doesn't it?" Sampson coughed again and stared at the Inspector. "As Ellery—ahem!—Ellery has pointed out, it is not at all certain that the will is there. Maybe Woodruff *was* lying. But we've got to open that coffin and make sure. What do you think, Pepper?"

"I think," Pepper smiled, "that Mr. Queen's brilliant analysis hit the nail right square on the head."

"All right. Arrange the disinterment for to-morrow morning. No particular reason for doing it to-day any more."

Pepper looked doubtful. "There may be a hitch, Chief, in

getting it. After all this isn't a disinterment based on suspicion of homicide. How are we going to justify to the judge—?"

"See Bradley. He's liberal about these things, and I'll call him later myself. Won't be any trouble, Pepper. Hop to it." Sampson reached for his telephone and called the number of the Khalkis residence. "Cohalan . . . Cohalan, this is Sampson speaking. Instruct everyone in the house to be present for a confab tomorrow morning. . . . Yes, you can tell 'em that we're disinterring the body of Khalkis. . . . Disin*terr*ing, you idiot! . . . Who? All right, let me speak to him." He burrowed the instrument to his chest and said to the Inspector, "Knox is there—*the* Knox. . . . Hello! Mr. Knox? This is District Attorney Sampson. . . . Yes, too bad. Very sad. . . . Well, something's come up and it will be necessary for us to disinter the body. . . . Oh, it must be done, sir. . . . What? . . . Naturally I'm sorry about *that*, Mr. Knox. . . . Well, don't fret yourself about it. We'll take care of everything."

He hung up softly and said: "Complicated situation. Knox was named executor in a non-producible will, and if that will isn't found and we can't establish identity of the new beneficiary for the Galleries, there won't *be* any executor. Khalkis will be considered to have died intestate. . . . Well, he seems keen about it. We'll have to see that he's appointed administrator if the will isn't found in the coffin to-morrow. Knox is busy right now conferring with Woodruff at the house. Preliminary survey of the estate. Says he'll be there all day. Damned nice of him at that, to take all this interest."

"Will he attend the disinterment?" asked Ellery. "I've always wanted to meet a multi-millionaire."

"He says not. He's got to go out of town again early tomorrow morning."

"Another childhood ambition shattered," said Ellery sadly.

CHAPTER 6

Exhumation

I t was on Friday the eighth of October, then, that Mr. Ellery Queen was first introduced to the actors in the Khalkis tragedy, the scene of operations and, what he considered more interesting at the moment, the "tightness in the air" sensed a few days before by Miss Joan Brett.

They had all congregated in the drawing-room of the Khalkis house Friday morning—a very subdued and apprehensive company; and while they waited for Assistant District Attorney Pepper and Inspector Queen to arrive, Ellery found himself engaged in conversation with a tall pink-and-white young Englishwoman of charming mould.

"You're *the* Miss Brett, I take it?"

"Sir," she said severely, "you have the advantage of me."

There was a tiny smile behind the potential frost of her very lovely blue eyes.

Ellery grinned. "That's not literally true, my dear. Don't you think that if I had the advantage of you my circulatory system would know it?"

"Hmm. And a fresh 'un, too." She folded her white hands primly in her lap and glanced sideways at the door, where Woodruff and Sergeant Velie stood talking. "Are you a bobby?"

"The veriest shadow of one. Ellery Queen, scion of the illustrious Inspector Queen."

"I can't say you're a very convincing shadow, Mr. Queen."

Ellery took in her tallness and straightness and niceness with very masculine eyes. "At any rate," he said, "that's one accusation which will never be directed against *you*."

"Mr. Queen!" She sat up very straight, smiling. "Are you jolly well casting aspersions on my figure?"

"Shades of Astarte!" murmured Ellery. He examined her body critically, and she blushed. "As a matter of fact, I hadn't even noticed it."

They laughed together at that, and she said, "I'm a shade of a different kind, Mr. Queen. I'm really very psychic."

And that was how Ellery learned, most unexpectedly, about the tightness in the air on the day of the funeral. There was a new tightness, too, as he excused himself and rose a moment later to greet his father and Pepper; for young Alan Cheney was glaring at him with homicidal savagery.

Hard on the heels of Pepper and the Inspector came Detective Flint, towing a tubby little old fellow who was perspiring copiously.

"Who's this?" growled Velie, barring entrance to the drawing-room.

"Says he belongs here," said Flint, grasping the tubby one's fat little arm. "What'll I do with him?"

The Inspector strode forward, hurling his coat and hat on a chair. "Who are you, sir?"

The newcomer was bewildered. He was small and portly and Dutch, with billowy white hair and almost artificially rosy cheeks. He puffed them out now, and the expression on his face became more harassed than ever. Gilbert Sloane said, from across the room, "That's all right, Inspector. This is Mr. Jan Vreeland, our scout." His voice was flat and curiously dry.

"Oh!" Queen eyed him shrewdly. "Mr. Vreeland, eh?"

"Yes, yes," panted Vreeland. "That's my name. What's the

trouble here, Sloane? Who are all these people? I thought
Khalkis was . . . Where's Mrs. Vreeland?"

"Here I am, darling," came a floating sugary voice, and Mrs.
Vreeland posed in the doorway. The little man trotted to her
side, kissed her hastily on the forehead—she was compelled to
stoop, and anger flashed for a moment from her bold eyes—
handed his hat and coat to Weekes, and then stood stock still,
looking about him with amazement.

The Inspector said, "How is it you've only just got back, Mr.
Vreeland?"

"Returned to my hotel in Quebec last night," said Vreeland
in a series of rapid little wheezes. "Found the telegram. Didn't
know a word about Khalkis dying. Shocking. What's the con-
gregation for?"

"We're disinterring Mr. Khalkis's body this morning, Mr.
Vreeland."

"So?" The little man looked distressed. "And I missed the
funeral. *Tch, tch!* But why a disinterment? Is—?"

"Don't you think," said Pepper fretfully, "we ought to get
started, Inspector?"

*   *   *

They found Sexton Honeywell fidgeting in the graveyard,
prancing up and down before a raw rectangle in the sod where
the earth had been turned up during the burial of Khalkis. Honeywell indicated the boundaries, and two men spat on their
hands, lifted their spades and began to dig with energy.

No one said a word. The women had been left in the house;
only Sloane, Vreeland and Woodruff of the men connected with
the case were present; Suiza had professed a distaste for the
spectacle, Dr. Wardes had shrugged, and Alan Cheney had doggedly stayed at the trim skirts of Joan Brett. The Queens, Sergeant Velie and a newcomer with a tall lank figure, black jowls,
a hideous ropy cigar clenched in his teeth and a black bag at
his feet, stood nearby watching the mighty heavings of the

gravediggers. Reporters lined the iron fence on Fifty-fourth Street, cameras poised. Police prevented a crowd from massing in the street. Weekes the butler peeped cautiously from behind the courtyard fence. Detectives leaned against the fence. Heads poked out of windows facing the court, necks craning.

At a depth of three feet the men's spades clanked against iron. They scraped vigorously and, like pirate henchmen digging for buried treasure, cleaned the horizontal surface of the iron door leading to the vault beneath almost with enthusiasm. Their labours completed, they leaped from the shallow pit and leaned against their spades.

The iron door was hauled open. Almost at once the large nostrils of the tall lank cigar-chewing man oscillated rapidly, and he muttered something cryptic beneath his breath. He stepped forward, under the puzzled glances of his audience, fell to his knees and leaned far over, sniffing. He raised his hand, scrambled to his feet and snapped at the Inspector: "Something fishy here!"

"What's the matter?"

Now the tall lank cigar-chewing man was not given to alarums and excursions, as Inspector Queen knew from previous experience. He was Dr. Samuel Prouty, assistant to the Chief Medical Examiner of New York County, and he was a very canny gentleman. Ellery found his pulse quickening, and Honeywell looked positively petrified. Dr. Prouty did not reply; he merely said to the gravediggers: "Get in there and pull out that new coffin, so we can hoist it up here."

The men lowered themselves cautiously into the black pit, and for a few moments the confused sounds of their hoarse voices and scraping feet could be heard. Then something large and shiny and black crawled into view, and apparatus was hastily adjusted, instructions given. . . .

Finally, the coffin lay on the surface of the graveyard, a little to one side of the gaping crypt.

"He reminds me of Herr Frankenstein," murmured Ellery to Pepper, looking at Dr. Prouty. But neither of them smiled.

Dr. Prouty was sniffing like a bloodhound. But now they all detected a foul, sickening smell; it grew more malodorous with every passing second. Sloane's face had turned grey; he fumbled for his handkerchief and sneezed violently.

"Was this damned body embalmed?" demanded Dr. Prouty, crouching over the coffin. No one replied. The two gravediggers began to unscrew the lid. On Fifth Avenue, at precisely the dramatic moment, a vast number of automobiles began a cacophony of raucous horn-tooting—an unearthly accompaniment singularly appropriate to the noisome character of the scene. Then the lid came off. . . .

One thing was immediately, horribly, unbelievably evident. And that was the source of the grave-smell.

For, crammed on top of the stiff, dead, embalmed body of Georg Khalkis, its members askew and—where their rotting flesh was naked to the sky—all blue and blotched . . . was the putrescent body of a man. A *second* corpse!

*   *   *

It is at such moments that life becomes an ugly thing, pushed aside by the dreadful urgency of death, and time itself stands still.

For the space of a heart-beat they were puppets in a tableau—unmoving, moveless, stricken dumb, pure terror gleaming in their distended eyes.

Then Sloane made a retching sound, his knees quivering, and he clutched childishly at Woodruff's meaty shoulder for support. Neither Woodruff nor Jan Vreeland so much as sighed—they just glared at the noxious interloper in Khalkis's coffin.

Dr. Prouty and Inspector Queen looked at each other in stupefaction. Then the old man strangled a shout and leaped forward, a handkerchief at his offended nostrils, peering wildly into the coffin.

Dr. Prouty's fingers curved into talons; he grew busy.

Ellery Queen threw back his shoulders and looked at the sky.

"Murdered. Strangled."

Dr. Prouty's brief examination revealed so much. He had managed, with Sergeant Velie's assistance, to turn the body over. The victim had been found lying face down, head cradled against Khalkis's lifeless shoulder. Now they could see the face itself—eyes sunken deeply in the head, open eyes revealing eyeballs incredibly dry and brownish. But the face itself was not so distorted as to be inhuman. Under the irregular livid patch was a dark skin. The nose, a little flaccid now, must nevertheless have been sharp and pointed in life. The lines and creases of the face, softened and puffed by putrefaction, must still have been harsh before decay set in.

Inspector Queen said, in muffled tones, "By heaven, that mug looks familiar!"

Pepper was leaning over his shoulder, staring intently. He muttered: "To me, too, Inspector. I wonder if—"

"Are the will and the steel box in there?" asked Ellery in a dry, cracked voice.

Velie and Dr. Prouty prodded, pulled, felt. . . . "No," said Velie disgustedly. He looked at his hands, and made a surreptitious brushing movement along his thighs.

"Who cares about that now!" snarled the Inspector. He rose, his small body quivering. "Oh, that was a marvellous deduction of yours, Ellery!" he cried. "Marvellous! Open the coffin and you'll find the will. . . . *Faugh!*" He wrinkled his nose. "Thomas!"

Velie lumbered to his side. The Inspector rapped words at him; Velie nodded and plodded away, making for the courtyard gate. The Inspector said sharply, "Sloane, Vreeland, Woodruff. Get back in the house. At once. Not a word to anyone. Ritter!" A burly detective lounging at the fence scrambled across the yard. "Stave off the newspaper men. We don't want them nosing about now. Hurry!" Ritter plunged toward the Fifty-fourth Street gate of the graveyard. "You—Sexton What's-Your-Name. You men there. Put the lid back on and let's get this damned— this thing into the house. Come along, Doc. There's work to do."

CHAPTER 7

Evidence

There was such work as Inspector Queen knew, better perhaps than any other executive of the New York Police Department, how to do.

In five minutes the house was again under siege, the drawing-room converted into a makeshift laboratory, the coffin with its ghastly double burden deposited on the floor. Khalkis's library was commandeered as an assembly-hall and all exits were put under guard. The door to the drawing-room was shut, and Velie's wide back set against its panels. Dr. Prouty, his coat off, was busy on the floor with the second corpse. In the library, Assistant District Attorney Pepper was dialling a telephone number. Men were running mysterious errands in and out of the house.

Ellery Queen faced his father, and they smiled rather wanly at each other. "Well, one thing is sure," said the Inspector, wetting his lips. "That inspiration of yours uncovered a murder that probably would never have been suspected otherwise."

"I'll see that ghastly face in my sleep," muttered Ellery. His eyes were a little bloodshot and he was twirling his *pince-nez* ceaselessly in his fingers.

The Inspector inhaled snuff with grateful breaths. "Fix him

up a little, Doc," he said to Dr. Prouty, steadily enough. "I want to get that crowd in here for a possible identification."

"I've got him about ready now. Where do you want to put him?"

"Better take him out of the coffin and stretch him on the floor. Thomas, get a blanket and cover up everything but his face."

"I've got to get hold of some rosewater or something to drown that awful smell," complained Dr. Prouty facetiously.

* * *

It seemed, when the preliminaries had been taken care of and the corpse of the second man hurriedly made presentable, that not one of the fearful, pallid people who filed in and out of the drawing-room could identify the dead face. Were they certain? Yes. They had never, they said, seen the man before. You, Sloane? Oh, no! — for Sloane was very, very ill; the sight had turned his stomach, and he had a little bottle of smelling-salts in his hand which he applied to his nostrils frequently. Joan Brett had looked, through eyes held steady only by a straining of her will, thoughtful. Mrs. Simms, roused out of her sick-bed, was led in by Weekes and a detective; she had no idea of what was occurring and, after one long horrified glimpse at the face of a strange dead man, promptly screeched and fainted, requiring the combined efforts of Weekes and three detectives to haul her back to her room on the upper floor.

They were all herded back into Khalkis's library. The Inspector and Ellery hurried after, leaving Dr. Prouty alone in the drawing-room with two corpses for company. Pepper, a very excited Pepper, was waiting impatiently for them by the door.

His eyes shone. "Cracked the nut, Inspector!" he said in a low eager voice. "I knew I'd seen that face somewhere before. And I'll tell you where *you* saw it — in the Rogues' Gallery!"

"Seems likely. Who is he?"

"Well, I just called up Jordan, my old law-partner — you know, sir, before I was appointed to Sampson's office. I had an idea I knew who the fellow was. And Jordan refreshed my memory. He was a guy by the name of Albert Grimshaw."

"Grimshaw?" The Inspector stopped short. "Not the forger?"

Pepper smiled. "Good memory, Inspector. But that was only one of his accomplishments. I defended him about five years ago when we were Jordan & Pepper. We lost, and he was sentenced to five years, says Jordan. Say, he must have just got out of the pen!"

"That's so? Sing Sing?"

"Yes!"

They moved into the room; everybody looked at them. The Inspector said to a detective, "Hesse, scoot back to h.q. and go over the files on Albert Grimshaw, forger, in Sing Sing for the past five years." The man disappeared. "Thomas." Velie loomed over him. "Put somebody on the job of tracing Grimshaw's movements since his release from stir. Find out how long ago he was let out—might have got time off for good behaviour."

Pepper said: "I called the Chief, too, and notified him of the new development. Told me to take care of his end down here—he's busy on that bank investigation. Anything on the body to make identification certain?"

"Not a thing. Just a few odds and ends, a couple of coins, an old empty wallet. Not even an identifying mark on his clothing."

Ellery caught Joan Brett's eye. "Miss Brett," he said quietly, "I couldn't help noticing a moment ago, when you looked at the body in the drawing-room, that . . . Do you know the man? Why did you say you had never seen him?"

Joan coloured; she stamped her foot. "Mr. Queen, that's insulting! I shan't—"

The Inspector said coldly: "Do you know him or don't you?"

She bit her lip. "It's a dashed long story, and I didn't see that it would do any good, since I didn't know his name. . . ."

"The police are generally good judges of that," said Pepper with conscientious severity. "If you know anything, Miss Brett, you can be prosecuted for withholding information."

"Can I, indeed?" She tossed her head. "But I'm not withholding anything, Mr. Pepper. I wasn't sure at first glance. His face was—was. . . ." She shivered. "Now that I think it over, I do recall having seen him. Once—no, twice. Although, as I said, I don't know his name."

"Where did you see him?" The Inspector was sharp, and he seemed not at all impressed by the fact that she was a pretty young lady.

"In this very house, Inspector."

"Ha! When?"

"I'm coming to that, sir." She paused deliberately, and something of her self-assurance returned. She favoured Ellery with a friendly smile, and he nodded encouragingly. "The first time I saw him was a week ago Thursday night."

"September the thirtieth?"

"Yes. This man appeared at the door at about nine o'clock in the evening. As I said twice, I don't know—"

"His name was Grimshaw, Albert Grimshaw. Go on, Miss Brett."

"He was admitted by a maid, just as I chanced to be passing through the foyer . . ."

"What maid?" demanded the Inspector. "I haven't seen any maids in this house."

"Oh!" She seemed startled. "But then—how silly of me!—of course you couldn't have known. You see, there were two maids employed in the house, but they were both ignorant, superstitious women and they insisted on making off the day Mr. Khalkis died. We couldn't prevail upon them to stay in what one called 'a house of death, ma'am.'"

"Is that right, Weekes?"

The butler nodded dumbly.

"Go on, Miss Brett. What happened? Did you see anything further?"

Joan sighed. "Not very much, Inspector. I saw the maid go into Mr. Khalkis's study, usher in the man Grimshaw, and then come out again. And that's all that evening."

"Did you see the man leave?" put in Pepper.

"No, Mr. Pepper. . . ." She lingered over the last syllable of his name and Pepper angrily turned his head away, as if to conceal an undesirable, unprosecutorlike emotion.

"And what was the second occasion on which you saw him, Miss Brett?" asked the Inspector. His eyes strayed slyly to the others; they were all listening attentively, straining forward.

"The next time I saw him was the night after—that is, a week ago Friday night."

"By the way, Miss Brett," interrupted Ellery with an odd inflexion, "I believe you acted as Khalkis's secretary?"

"Right you are, Mr. Queen."

"And Khalkis was blind and helpless?"

She made a little *moue* of disapproval. "Blind, but scarcely helpless. Why?"

"Well, didn't Khalkis tell you anything Thursday about his visitor—the man to come in the evening? Didn't he ask you to make the appointment?"

"Oh, I see! . . . No, he did not. Not a word to me about an expected visitor Thursday night. It was a complete surprise to me. In fact, it may have been as complete a surprise to Mr. Khalkis! But please let me continue." She contrived, by the artful twitching of a dark unspoiled eyebrow, to convey maidenly annoyance. "You people *interrupt* so. . . . It was different on Friday. After dinner Friday night—that was the first of October, Inspector Queen—Mr. Khalkis summoned me to the library and gave me some very careful instructions. Some *very* careful instructions indeed, Inspector, and—"

"Come, come, Miss Brett," said the Inspector impatiently. "Let's have it without embroidery."

"If you were on the witness-stand," said Pepper with a trace of bitterness, "you'd make a distinctly undesirable witness, Miss Brett."

"Not really?" she murmured. She heaved herself to a sitting position on Khalkis's desk and crossed her legs, raising her skirt ever so little. "Very well. I shall be the model witness. Is this the correct pose, Mr. Pepper? . . . Mr. Khalkis told me that he expected two visitors that night. Quite late. One of them, he said, was coming incognito, so to speak—he was anxious, Mr. Khalkis said, to keep his identity secret and therefore I was to see that nobody caught a glimpse of him."

"Curious," muttered Ellery. ·

"Wasn't it?" Joan said. "Very well, then. I was also to admit these two persons myself, and to see that the servants were out of the way. After admitting them I was to go to bed—just like that, upon my word! Naturally, when Mr. Khalkis added that the nature of his business with these two gentlemen was extremely private, I asked no questions and followed orders like the perfect secretary I've always been. Charming bit o' fluff, eh, Lord Higginbotham?"

The Inspector frowned, and Joan looked down demurely. "The visitors arrived at eleven," she went on, "and one of them, I saw at once, was the man who had called by himself the previous evening—the man you say was named Grimshaw. The other, the mysterious gentleman, was bundled up to the eyes; I couldn't see his face. I did get the impression that he was middle-aged or older, but that's really all I can tell you about him, Inspector."

Inspector Queen sniffed. "That mysterious gentleman, as you say, may be mighty important from our standpoint, Miss Brett. Can't you give us a better description? How was he dressed?"

Joan swung one leg reflectively. "He was wearing an overcoat and he kept his bowler on his head all the time, but I can't even recall the style or colour of the coat. And that's really all I can tell you about your—" she shuddered, "about your awful Mr. Grimshaw."

The Inspector shook his head; he was distinctly not pleased. "But we're not talking about Grimshaw now, Miss Brett! Come now. There must be something else about this second man. Didn't anything happen that night that might be significant— anything at all that would help us to get to that fellow?"

"Oh, heavens." She laughed and kicked out with her slim feet. "You guardians of law and order are so persistent. Very well—if you consider the incident of Mrs. Simms's cat significant. . . ."

Ellery looked interested. "Mrs. Simms's cat, Miss Brett? There's a fascinating thought! Yes, it might very well be significant. Give us the gory details, Miss Brett."

"Well, Mrs. Simms owns a shameless hussy of a cat. Tootsie, she's called. Tootsie's always poking her cold little nose into places where good little cats should not be poking their cold little noses. Er—you grasp the idea, Mr. Queen?" She saw an ominous glint in the Inspector's eye, sighed and said penitently, "Really, Inspector, I'm—I'm not being a silly boor. I'm just—oh everything's so higgledy-piggledy." She was silent then, and they saw something—fear, nervousness, a suspicion of dread— in her charming blue eyes. "It's my nerves, I suppose," she said wearily. "And when I'm nervous, I become perverse, and I giggle like a callow baggage. . . . This is exactly what happened," she said abruptly. "The unknown man, the man bundled up to the eyes, stepped into the foyer first when I opened the door. Grimshaw was a little behind and to one side of him. Mrs. Simms's cat, which generally remains in Mrs. Simms's bedroom upstairs, had, unnoticed by me, promenaded downstairs into the foyer and had laid down directly in the path of the front door. As I opened the door and the mysterious man started to step in, he stopped suddenly with one foot in mid-air, almost falling in his effort to avoid stepping on the cat, which lay quite cunningly on the rug washing its face, and without making a sound. It wasn't really until I saw the man's almost acrobatic effort to avoid stepping on little Tootsie—typically Simmsian name for a cat, don't you think?—that I noticed Tootsie at all. Then, of course, I prodded her out of the way; Grimshaw stepped in, and he said: 'Khalkis expects us,' and I led the way to the library. And *that's* the incident of Mrs. Simms's cat."

"Not intensely productive," confessed Ellery. "And this bundled man—did he say anything?"

"Do you know, he was the rudest person," said Joan with a little frown. "Not only didn't he say one solitary word—after all, he could have seen that I wasn't a *slavey*—but when I led the way to the library door and was about to knock, he actually jostled me away from the door and opened it himself! He didn't knock, and he and Grimshaw slipped inside and shut the door in my face. I was so angry I could have chewed a tea-cup."

"Shocking," murmured Ellery. "You're sure, then, that he didn't utter a word?"

"Positive, Mr. Queen. As I say, I was angry and began to go upstairs." It was at this moment that Miss Joan Brett betrayed evidences of a very lively temper. Something in what she was about to say touched springs of rancour within her, for her brilliant eyes smouldered and she threw a glance of extreme bitterness in the direction of young Alan Cheney, who slouched against a wall not ten feet away, hands plunged in his pockets. "I heard a key fumbling and scratching against the vestibule door, which is always kept locked. I turned around on the stairs and, lo and behold! whom should I see tottering into the foyer but Mr. Alan Cheney, quite, quite muzzy."

"Joan!" muttered Alan reproachfully.

"Muzzy?" repeated the Inspector in bewilderment.

Joan nodded emphatically. "Yes, Inspector, muzzy. I might say—squiffy. Or pot-valiant. Or maudlin. Obfuscated. I believe there are some three hundred English colloquialisms for the condition in which I saw Mr. Cheney that night. In a word, drunk as a lord!"

"Is this true, Cheney?" demanded the Inspector.

Alan grinned in a feeble way. "Shouldn't be surprised, Inspector. When I'm on a bat I generally forget home and country. I don't remember, but if Joan says it's so—well, then, it's so."

"Oh, it's true enough, Inspector," snapped Joan, tossing her head. "He was foully, disgustingly drunk—slobbering all over himself." She glared at him. "I was afraid that in his despicable condition he would raise a row. Mr. Khalkis had said he wanted no noise, no commotion, so I—well, I had very little choice, don't you see? Mr. Cheney grinned at me in his characteristically muddled fashion, and I ran down, grasped his arm very firmly, and marched him upstairs before he could rouse the household."

Delphina Sloane was sitting very haughtily on the edge of her chair, looking from her son to Joan. "Really, Miss Brett," she said icily, "I see no excuse for this disgraceful . . ."

"Please!" The Inspector focused his sharp eyes on Mrs. Sloane and she promptly shut her mouth. "Go on, Miss Brett." Alan, against the wall, seemed to be praying for the floor to give way and remove him peremptorily from the scene.

Joan twisted the fabric of her skirt. "Perhaps," she said in a less impassioned voice, "I shouldn't have. . . . At any rate," she continued, raising her head and looking defiantly at the Inspector, "I took Mr. Cheney upstairs to his room and—and saw to it that he went to bed."

"Joan Brett!" gasped Mrs. Sloane in an outraged whimper. "Alan Cheney! Do you two mean to admit—"

"I didn't *undress* him, Mrs. Sloane," said Joan coldly, "if that's what you're insinuating. I just scolded him"—her tone implied that this was more properly the province of a mother than of a mere secretary—"and he quieted down, to be sure, almost at once. He quieted down, that is to say, only to become—become very nastily sick after I tucked him in . . ."

"You're straying from the point," said the Inspector sharply. "Did you see anything more of the two visitors?"

Her voice was low now; she seemed absorbed in studying the design of the rug at her feet. "No. I went downstairs to fetch some—some raw eggs; I thought they might jog Mr. Cheney up a bit. On my way to the kitchen, I had to pass by the study here, and I noticed that there was no light from the crack under the door. I assumed that the visitors had left while I'd been upstairs and that Mr. Khalkis had gone to bed."

"When you passed the door, as you say—how long a period had elapsed from the time when you admitted the two men?"

"Difficult to judge, Inspector. Perhaps a half-hour or more."

"And you didn't see the two men again?"

"No, Inspector."

"And you're certain this was last Friday night—that is, the night before Khalkis died?"

"Yes, Inspector Queen."

There was complete silence then of an increasingly embarrassing depth. Joan sat biting her red lips, looking at no one. Alan Cheney, from the expression on his face, was in agony. Mrs. Sloane, her slight figure stiff as the Red Queen's, tightened her faded unattractive features. Nacio Suiza, sprawled in a chair across the room, sighed with *ennui*; his dark vandyke pointed accusingly at the floor. Gilbert Sloane sniffed his salts. Mrs. Vreeland stared Medusa-like at her husband's rosy old cheeks. The atmosphere was anything but cheerful; and Dr. Wardes, buried in a study as deep and brown as his beard, seemed affected by the general moroseness. Even Woodruff looked depressed.

Ellery's cool voice brought their eyes up. "Miss Brett, exactly who was in this house last Friday night?"

"I really can't say, Mr. Queen. The two maids, of course, had been sent to bed, Mrs. Simms had retired, and Weekes was out—his night off, apparently. Aside from Mr.—Mr. Cheney, I can't account for anyone else."

"Well, we'll find out soon enough," grunted the Inspector. "Mr. Sloane!" He raised his voice, and Sloane almost let the tiny coloured bottle slip from his startled fingers. "Where were you last Friday night?"

"Oh, at the Galleries," Sloane replied hastily. "Working late. I work there very often into the small hours."

"Anybody with you?"

"No, no! I was quite alone!"

"Hmm." The old man explored his snuff-box. "And what time did you get into the house?"

"Oh, long past midnight."

"Did *you* know anything about Khalkis's two visitors?"

"I? Certainly not."

"That's funny," said the Inspector, putting his snuff-box away. "Mr. Georg Khalkis seems to have been a sort of mysterious character himself. And you, Mrs. Sloane—where were *you* last Friday night?"

She licked her faded lips, blinking rapidly. "I? I was upstairs asleep. I know nothing about my brother's visitors—nothing."

"Asleep at what hour?"

"I retired about ten o'clock. I—I had a headache."

"A headache. Hmm." The Inspector whirled on Mrs. Vreeland. "And you, Mrs. Vreeland? Where and how did you spend last Friday evening?"

Mrs. Vreeland reared her large, full-curved body and smiled coquettishly. "At the opera, Inspector—at the opera."

Ellery felt an irresistible urge to snap, "What opera?" but caught himself up sternly. There was a scent of perfume about this specimen of the fairer sex—expensive perfume, to be sure, but sprayed on with a hand that knew no restraint.

"Alone?"

"With a friend." She smiled sweetly. "We then had a late supper at the Barbizon and I returned home about one o'clock in the morning."

"Did you notice a light in Khalkis's study when you came in?"

"I don't believe I did."

"Did you see anyone at all downstairs here?"

"It was dark as the grave. I didn't even see a ghost, Inspector." She gurgled far in the recesses of her throat, but no one echoed her laugh. Mrs. Sloane sat up even more stiffly; it was apparent that she considered the jest ill-advised, ill-advised.

The Inspector tugged at his moustache thoughtfully; then he looked up to find Dr. Wardes's bright brown eyes fixed on him. "Ah, yes. Dr. Wardes," he said pleasantly. "And you?"

Dr. Wardes played with his beard. "I spent the evening at the theatre, Inspector."

"The theatre. Quite so. You came in, then, before midnight?"

"No, Inspector. I took a turn about one or two places of entertainment after the theatre. Really, I didn't get back until well after midnight."

"You spent the evening alone?"

"Quite."

The old man's shrewd little eyes glistened over his fingers as he took another pinch of snuff. Mrs. Vreeland was sitting with a frozen smile, her eyes wide open, too wide open. All the others were mildly bored. Now Inspector Queen had questioned thousands of people in his professional career, and he had developed a special policeman's sense—an instinct for detecting falsehood. Something in Dr. Wardes's too smooth replies, in Mrs. Vreeland's strained pose. . . .

"I don't believe you're telling the truth, Doctor," he said easily. "Of course, I understand your scruples. . . . You were with Mrs. Vreeland last Friday night, weren't you?"

The woman gasped, and Dr. Wardes elevated his hairy eyebrows. Jan Vreeland was peering from the physician to his wife in bewilderment, his fat little face puckered with hurt and worry.

Dr. Wardes chuckled suddenly. "An excellent surmise, Inspector. And very true." He bowed lightly to Mrs. Vreeland. "You will permit me, Mrs. Vreeland?" She tossed her head like a nervous mare. "You see, Inspector, I didn't care to put the lady's action in an embarrassing light. Actually, I did escort Mrs. Vreeland to the Metropolitan and later to the Barbizon—"

"See here! I don't think—" interrupted Vreeland in a little flurry of protest.

"My dear Mr. Vreeland. It was the most innocent evening imaginable. And a very delightful one, too, I'm sure." Dr. Wardes studied the old Dutchman's discomforted countenance. "Mrs. Vreeland was much alone because of your protracted absences, sir; I myself have no friends in New York—it was natural for us to drift together, don't you know."

"Well, I don't like it," said Vreeland childishly. "I don't like it at all, Lucy." He waddled over to his wife and shook his fat little forefinger in her face, pouting. She looked faint, clutched the arms of her chair. The Inspector abruptly commanded Vreeland to keep silent, and Mrs. Vreeland sank back, shutting her eyes in mortification. Dr. Wardes shook his broad shoulders lightly. From the other side of the room Gilbert Sloane drew a sharp breath, and Mrs. Sloane's wooden face showed a fleeting anima-tion. The Inspector darted bright glances from one to another. His eyes fixed on the shambling figure of Demetrios Khalkis. . . .

Demmy was, except for his vacant idiotic expression, an ugly, gaunt, sproutlike counterpart of his cousin Georg Khalkis. His large blank eyes were set in a perpetual stare; his bulging lower lip hung heavily, the back of his head was almost flat, and his skull was huge and misshapen. He had been wandering noiselessly about, speaking to no one, peering myopically into the faces of the room's occupants, his enormous hands clench-ing and unclenching with weird regularity.

"Here—you, Mr. Khalkis!" called the Inspector. Demmy continued his shambling circumambulation of the study. "Is he deaf?" asked the old man irritably, of no one in particular.

Joan Brett said: "No, Inspector. He just doesn't understand English. He's a Greek, you know."

"Khalkis's cousin, isn't he?"

"That's right," said Alan Cheney unexpectedly. "But he's shy up here." He touched his own well-shaped head significantly. "Mentally, he rates as an idiot."

"That's extremely interesting," said Ellery Queen mildly. "For the word 'idiot' is of Greek derivation, and etymologically indi-cated merely a private ignorant person in the Hellenic social organization—*idiotes* in Greek. Not an imbecile at all."

"Well, *he's* an idiot in the modern English sense," said Alan wearily. "Uncle brought him over from Athens about ten years ago—he was the last of the family strain over there. Most of the Khalkis family have been American for at least six generations. Demmy never could grasp the English language—mother says he's illiterate even in Greek."

"Well, I've got to talk to him," said the Inspector in a sort of desperation. "Mrs. Sloane, this man is your cousin also, isn't he?"

"Yes, Inspector. Poor dear Georg. . . . " Her lips quivered; she seemed about to cry.

"Now, now," said the Inspector hastily. "Do you know this lingo? I mean, can you talk Greek, or whatever it is he gabbles?"

"Enough to converse with him."

"Please question him about his movements last Friday night."

Mrs. Sloane sighed, rose, smoothed her gown and caught the tall, gaunt idiot by the arm, shaking him vigorously. He wheeled slowly, puzzled; he searched her face anxiously; then he smiled and took her hand in his. She said sharply, "Demetrios!" He smiled again, and she began to speak in a foreign tongue, in halting guttural accents. He laughed aloud at this, tightening his powerful grasp on her hand; his reaction was as transparent as a child's—he was filled with glee at hearing his native language. He replied to her, in the same alien syllables, speaking with a slight lisp; but his voice was deep and grating.

Mrs. Sloane turned to the Inspector. "He says that Georg sent him to bed that night about ten o'clock."

"His bedroom is off Khalkis's there?"

"Yes."

"Ask him if he heard anything from the library here after he went to bed."

Another interchange of strange sounds. "No, he says he heard nothing. He fell asleep at once and slept soundly all night. He sleeps like a child, Inspector."

"And he saw no one in the library?"

"But how could he, Inspector, if he was asleep?"

Demmy was peering from his cousin to the Inspector in a pleased, yet confused sort of way. The old man nodded. "Thanks, Mrs. Sloane. That's all right now."

The Inspector went to the desk, picked up the dial telephone, and dialled a number. "Hello! Queen speaking. . . . Listen, Fred, what's the name of that Greek interpreter who hangs around the Criminal Courts Building?...What? Trikkala? T-r-i-k-k-a-l-a?...Okay. Locate him right away and send him over to Eleven East Fifty-fourth Street. Tell him to ask for me."

He banged the instrument back on the desk. "Please wait for me here, all of you," he said, beckoned to Ellery and Pepper, nodded laconically to Sergeant Velie, and strode to the door. Demmy's staring eyes followed the figures of the three men in a childishly astonished way.

* * *

They mounted the carpeted stairs, and at Pepper's gesture turned to the right. He indicated a door not far from the head of the stairs, and the Inspector knocked. A woman's voice, fat with tears, gurgled: "Who's *there*?" in frightened tones.

"Mrs. Simms? This is Inspector Queen. May I come in a minute?"

"Who? Who? Oh, yes! Just a moment, sir, just a moment!" They heard a hasty bed-creak, a rustling accompanied by lusty feminine exhalations of breath, and a weak panting. "Come in, sir. Come in."

The Inspector sighed, opened the door, and the three men entered the room to find themselves confronted by an awesome apparition. An old shawl was draped about Mrs. Simms's bulging shoulders. Her grey hair was dishevelled—stiff strands stuck out all over her head, so that it faintly resembled the crowned head of the Statue of Liberty. Her face was puffy and red, and blotched with tears, and her matronly bosoms were heaving energetically as she rocked herself in an old-fashioned rocker. Carpet slippers covered her large swollen feet. And at those battered feet reposed an ancient Persian cat—evidently the adventurous Tootsie.

The three men walked in solemnly, and Mrs. Simms looked at them with such affrighted bovine eyes that Ellery gulped.

"How do you feel now, Mrs. Simms?" asked the Inspector amiably.

"Oh, terrible, sir, terrible." Mrs. Simms rocked faster. "Who *was* that dreadful creature in the drawing-room, sir? He—it gave me the unholy creeps!"

"Oh, then you never saw that man before?"

"*I?*" she shrieked. "Heaven above! I? Mother of God, no!"

"All right, all right," said the Inspector hurriedly. "Now, Mrs. Simms, do you recall last Friday night?"

Her damp handkerchief paused at her nose and a saner look came into her eye. "Last Friday night? The night before—before Mr. Khalkis died? I do, sir."

"That's very good, Mrs. Simms, very good. I understand you went to bed early—is that correct?"

"Indeed it is, sir. Mr. Khalkis himself told me to."

"Did he tell you anything else?"

"Why, nothing important, sir, if that's what you're driving at." Mrs. Simms blew her nose. "He just called me into the study and—"

"He *called* you in?"

"Well, I mean he rang for me. There's a buzzer on his desk which leads to the kitchen downstairs."

"What time was this?"

"Time? Let me see." She puckered her old lips thoughtfully. "I'd say about a quarter to eleven."

"At night, of course?"

"Well, of all things! Of course. And when I came in he told me to fetch him at once a percolator of water, three cups and saucers, some tea-balls, cream, lemon and sugar. At once, he said."

"Was he alone when you entered the library?"

"Oh, yes, sir. All alone, the poor creature sitting at his desk so nice and straight. . . . To think—just to think that—"

"Now, don't think, Mrs. Simms," said the Inspector. "And then what happened?"

She dabbed at her eyes. "I brought the tea-things right away and set them down on the tabouret by his desk. He asked me if I had brought *everything* he'd ordered—"

"Now, that's queer," muttered Ellery.

"Not at all, sir. He couldn't see, you see. So he said in a sharper voice—he looked a mite nervous, it seemed to me, if you ask, sir, which you didn't—he said to me, 'Mrs. Simms, I want you to go to bed at once. Do you understand?' So I said, 'Yes, Mr. Khalkis,' and I went right up to my room and to bed. And that's all, sir."

"He said nothing to you about having guests that night?"

"Me, sir? Oh, no, sir." Mrs. Simms blew her nose again and then thrashed it about vigorously with her handkerchief. "Although I *did* think he might be having company of sorts, considering the three cups and all. But it wasn't *my* place to ask, you see."

"Of course not. So you didn't see any visitors that night?"

"No, sir. I went right up to my room and to bed, as I said. I was that tired, sir, having had a bad day with rheumatics. My rheumatics—"

Tootsie rose, yawned, and began to wash her face.

"Yes, yes. We quite understand. That's all for now, Mrs. Simms, and thank you very much," said the Inspector, and they hastily left the room. Ellery was thoughtful as they descended the stairs; Pepper looked at him curiously and said, "You think . . ."

"My dear Pepper," said Ellery, "that is the curse of my composition. I'm always thinking. I'm pursued by what Byron in *Childe Harold*—you recall that magnificent first canto?—saw fit to call, 'The blight of life—the demon Thought.'"

"Well," said Pepper dubiously, "there's something in that."

CHAPTER 8

Killed?

A s they were about to re-enter the study downstairs, they heard voices from the drawing-room across the hall. The Inspector inquisitively trotted over and opened the door to peer in. His eyes sharpened and he strode inside without ceremony, Pepper and Ellery following meekly. They found Dr. Prouty chewing his cigar and looking out of the window into the graveyard, while another man—a man none of them had seen before—poked about the odorous corpse of Grimshaw. He straightened immediately, looking inquiry at Dr. Prouty. The Assistant Medical Examiner introduced the Queens and Pepper tersely, said: "This is Dr. Frost, Khalkis's personal physician. Just came in," and turned back to his window.

Dr. Duncan Frost was a handsome cleanly man, of fifty or more—the typical smart solid society physician with whom upper Fifth Avenue, Madison Avenue and the West Side commune for the preservation of their health. He murmured something polite and backed away, looking down at the swollen corpse with keen interest.

"I see you've been examining our find," remarked the Inspector.

"Yes. Very interesting. Very interesting indeed," replied Dr. Frost, "and quite incomprehensible to me. How on earth did this cadaver ever get into Khalkis's coffin?"

"If we knew that, Doctor, we'd breathe easier."

"Well, it's a cinch it wasn't in there when Khalkis was buried!" said Pepper dryly.

"Naturally! That's what makes it so amazing."

"I believe Dr. Prouty said you were Khalkis's personal physician?" asked the Inspector abruptly.

"That's correct, sir."

"Have you ever seen this man before? Treated him?"

Dr. Frost shook his head. "An absolute stranger to me, Inspector. And I was associated with Khalkis for ever so many years. In fact, I live just across the court back here—on Fifty-fifth Street."

"How long," asked Ellery, "has the man been dead?"

The Assistant Medical Examiner turned his back on the window, smiled glumly, and the two physicians exchanged glances. "Matter of fact," growled Dr. Prouty, "Frost and I were discussing that just before you men came in. Hard to tell from superficial examination. I'd want to examine the nude cadaver and his insides before I said definitely."

"A good deal may depend," said Dr. Frost, "upon where the body was kept before burial in Khalkis's coffin."

"Oh," said Ellery quickly, "then he has been dead more than three days? He died before Tuesday, the day of Khalkis's funeral?"

"I should say so," replied Dr. Frost, and Dr. Prouty nodded carelessly. "The external cadaveric changes certainly indicate a minimum period of three days."

"The *rigor* passed off long ago. Secondary flaccidity marked. Lividity seems to be complete," said Dr. Prouty in a grumpy voice, "as far as we can tell without taking the clothes off. Anterior surfaces especially so—body was lying face down in the coffin. Points of clothing pressure and parts in contact with certain sharp edges and hard sides have lightened the lividity in spots. But that's a detail."

"All of which means—" prompted Ellery.

"The things I've mentioned don't mean much," replied the Assistant Medical Examiner, "as far as fixing the strict time of death, although the lividity certainly points to putrefaction of at least three days, with a possibility of double that. Can't tell until I conduct an autopsy. You see, the other things I touched on merely establish certain minima. Passing off of *rigor mortis* in itself indicates a lapse of a day to a day and a half, sometimes two days. Secondary flaccidity is the third stage—normally, immediately after death you have a state of primary flaccidity—everything relaxed. Then *rigor* sets in. When *rigor* passes off secondary flaccidity sets in—a return to relaxation of the muscles."

"Yes, but that doesn't—" began the Inspector.

"Of course," remarked Dr. Frost, "there are other things. For example, the abdomen shows a formative green 'spot'—one of the first phenomena of putrefaction—and is distended characteristically by gases."

"That helps to fix the time, all right," said Dr. Prouty. "But there's always a raft of things to keep in mind. If the body were kept before burial in the coffin in a dry place comparatively free of air currents, it wouldn't putrefy as rapidly as it would normally. Three days as a minimum, absolutely, as I said."

"Well, well," said the Inspector impatiently, "you dig into his belly, Doc, and let us know as exactly as you can how long he's been dead."

"Say," said Pepper suddenly, "how about Khalkis's body? Is *that* all right? I mean, there's nothing funny about Khalkis's death, is there?"

The Inspector stared at Pepper; then he smote his small thigh and exclaimed, "Bully, Pepper! There's a real idea. . . . Dr. Frost, you were the attending physician on Khalkis's death, weren't you?"

"I was."

"You made out the death-certificate, then."

"That's correct, sir."

"Anything queer about his death?"

Dr. Frost stiffened. "My dear sir," he said coldly, "do you think I would have officially ascribed his death to heart-disease unless it were true?"

"Complications?" growled Dr. Prouty.

"Not at the time of death. But Khalkis had been a very sick man for years; it's at least twelve years that he'd had a bad case of compensatory hypertrophy—enlargement of the heart as a result of a defective mitral valve. Then to make matters worse, about three years ago he contracted some nasty stomach ulcers. His heart condition forbade surgery, and I treated intravenously. But haemorrhages set in, and they brought on his blindness."

"Is that a common result of such a condition?" asked Ellery curiously.

Dr. Prouty said: "Our much-vaunted medical science knows very little about it, Queen. It isn't common, but it happens every once in a while after haemorrhages caused by stomach ulcers or stomach cancer. Why, no one can tell you."

"At any rate," continued Dr. Frost, nodding, "the specialist I called in, and I, hoped that the blindness would prove only temporary. Sometimes such blindness clears spontaneously, as mysteriously as it comes on. However, the condition remained and Khalkis never regained his sight."

"That's all very interesting, I'm sure," said the Inspector, "but we're more concerned with the possibility that Khalkis died, not as a result of a bad heart, but—"

"If you entertain any doubt as to the authenticity of the stated cause of death," snapped Dr. Frost, "you can ask Dr. Wardes, who was present when I officially pronounced Khalkis dead. There was no violence, nothing quite so melodramatic, Inspector Queen. The intravenous-injection treatments for the ulcers, complicated by the rigorous diet he was naturally compelled to follow, taxed his heart. Besides, against my specific instructions, he insisted on continuing the supervision of his Galleries, even if only through the instrumentality of Mr. Sloane and Mr. Suiza. His heart simply collapsed."

"But—poison?" persisted the Inspector.

"I assure you there wasn't the slightest evidence of toxication."

The Inspector beckoned Dr. Prouty. "You'd better perform an autopsy on Khalkis, too," he said. "I want to be sure. There's been one murder here—how do we know, with all respect to Dr. Frost, that there weren't two?"

"Can you perform an autopsy all right on Khalkis?" asked Pepper anxiously. "After all, he was embalmed."

"Doesn't make a particle of difference," said the Assistant Medical Examiner. "They don't remove any vital organs in embalming. If there's anything wrong, I'll find it. Matter of fact, the embalming helps matters. It's served to preserve the body— there isn't the slightest sign of putrefaction."

"I think," said the Inspector, "we'll find out a little more about the circumstances surrounding Khalkis's death. There may be a clue to this feller Grimshaw there. Doc, you'll see that the bodies are taken care of?"

"Sure thing."

Dr. Frost put on his hat and coat and, somewhat coldly, took his leave. In Khalkis's study the Inspector found a headquarters fingerprint expert busily going over the room. His eyes lighted at sight of the Inspector, and he hurried over.

"Find anything, Jimmy?" asked the Inspector in a low tone.

"Lots, but none of it means anything. This place is lousy with prints. All over the place. I understand there've been a million people tramping in and out of here all week."

"Well," sighed the Inspector, "do what you can. Suppose you go into that drawing-room across the hall and take prints of the little corpse. The man we think is Grimshaw. Bring the file set from h.q.?"

"Yeah." Jimmy hurried from the room.

Flint came in and said to the Inspector, "Morgue bus is here."

"Get the boys in. But tell 'em to wait until Jimmy is finished across the hall."

Five minutes later the fingerprint expert entered the study wearing a look of satisfaction. "That's Grimshaw, all right," he said. "The prints match the gallery set." His face fell. "Sort of went over that coffin, too," he said disgustedly. "But it's chockful o'prints. Won't get anything out of it. I'll bet every dick in town's had his mitts on it."

Photographers were filling the room with silent flashes. The library became a miniature battlefield. Dr. Prouty came in to say good-bye; the two bodies and the coffin were carted out of the house; Jimmy and the photographers departed; and the Inspector, smacking his lips, shooed Ellery and Pepper into the library and shut the door.

CHAPTER 9

Chronicles

A loud knock on the door, and Sergeant Velie opened it an inch. He nodded, admitted a man, and closed the door again.

The newcomer was a roly-poly, greasy individual; Inspector Queen discovered that he was Trikkala, the Greek interpreter, and at once set him to questioning Demmy concerning the imbecile's movements on Friday night of the previous week.

Alan Cheney contrived to slip into a seat near Joan Brett. He gulped, then whispered shyly, "Evidently my mother's talent for interpreting Greek isn't trusted by the Inspector"—obviously as an excuse for speaking to Joan; but she turned her head to give him a frigid stare and he smiled weakly.

Demmy's eyes took on a flicker of intelligence. He was apparently unaccustomed to being the object of public interest, and some amorphous emotion of vanity stirred within him, for his dull face became wreathed in smiles and his Greek stuttered faster than before.

"He says," reported Trikkala, in a voice as greasy as himself, "he says that his cousin sent him to bed that night, and that he saw and he heard nothing."

The Inspector peered curiously at the tall shambling

caricature of a man standing by the interpreter. "Now ask him what happened the next morning when he awoke—Saturday, last Saturday, the day his cousin died."

Trikkala fired a mouthful of harsh syllables at Demmy; Demmy, blinking, replied in a more halting version of the same language. The interpreter turned to the Inspector. "He says his cousin Georg's voice woke him up that morning, calling to him from his bedroom next door. He says he got up, he dressed, he went into his cousin's bedroom, he helped his cousin to rise and dress."

"Ask him what time that was," directed he old man.

A brief colloquy. "He says it was half past eight in the morning."

"How is it," inquired Ellery sharply, "that this man Demmy had to dress Georg Khalkis? Miss Brett, didn't you say before that Khalkis was not helpless, despite his blindness?"

Joan shrugged her cleanly curved shoulders. "You see, Mr. Queen, Mr. Khalkis took his blindness very hard. He was always an energetic person, and he would never admit, even to himself, that the loss of his sight made any difference in his normal life. That's why he insisted on keeping a tight rein on the welfare of his Galleries. That's why, too, he insisted that no one ever touch a single article in his room or his bedroom. Nobody has ever so much as moved a chair out of its accustomed place in here during Mr. Khalkis's life as a blind man. In this way he always knew where everything was and could get about his own little series of rooms with perfect facility, just as if he could see."

"But you're not answering my question, Miss Brett," said Ellery gently. "It would seem, from what you've just said, that he would refuse assistance in such a simple matter as getting out of bed and dressing. Surely he could dress himself?"

"You're so terribly keen, aren't you, Mr. Queen?" Joan smiled and Alan Cheney rose suddenly and returned to his old place by the wall. "It would seem so. I don't think that Demmy meant to convey the idea that he actually assisted Mr. Khalkis out of bed, or even helped him physically to dress. You see, there was one thing Mr. Khalkis *couldn't* do, and *had* to have help in doing."

"And what was that?" Ellery was toying with his *pince-nez*, his eyes alert.

"Selecting his clothes!" she said triumphantly. "He was an extremely fastidious person. His clothes had to be top-hole. And, being blind, he could not select his day's wardrobe. So Demmy always did that for him."

Demmy, who had been gawping at this incomprehensible interlude in his questioning, must have felt neglected, for he suddenly erupted in a shower of Greek. Trikkala said: "He wants to proceed with his story. He says he dressed his cousin Georg according to schedule. He—"

The Queens interrupted simultaneously: "According to schedule?"

Joan laughed. "It's a pity I can't speak Greek.... You see, Inspector, Demmy has never been able to assimilate the intricacies of Mr. Khalkis's wardrobe. As I said, Mr. Khalkis was very finical about his clothes—he had many suits and always wore something different every day. A completely new ensemble. If Demmy had been a valet of ordinary intelligence, the problem would have been simple. But Demmy is naturally feeble-minded and, to save himself the bother of commanding a new ensemble each morning, Mr. Khalkis had cleverly arranged a written schedule, in Greek, prescribing for Demmy's edification a definite ensemble for each day in the week. This put no tax on poor Demmy's stunted brain. The schedule was flexible. If Mr. Khalkis desired to alter any day's prescribed ensemble, he gave Demmy oral instructions in their native language."

"The schedule was used over and over again?" asked the Inspector. "I mean, did Khalkis make out a new schedule every week?"

"Oh, no! It was a seven-day schedule, repeated each week. When his suits showed signs of wear—or what Mr. Khalkis thought were signs of wear from his sense of touch; he was very stubborn about those things and wouldn't take anyone's word— he merely had the worn garment exactly duplicated by his tailor. He followed the same plan with his haberdasher, booter, and so on. In this way, the schedule has remained the same ever since Mr. Khalkis's blindness."

"Interesting," murmured Ellery. "I suppose it prescribed evening ensembles also?"

"No indeed. Mr. Khalkis religiously wore strict evening clothes every night; this was something which didn't strain Demmy's memory, and so it wasn't in the schedule."

"All right," growled the Inspector. "Trikkala, you ask this halfwit what happened next."

Trikkala's hands described a few heated arcs, and the words flew out of his mouth. Demmy's face became almost animated. He held forth at length, quite amiably, and Trikkala finally stopped him, wiping his forehead desperately. "He says he dressed his cousin Georg according to schedule. It was about nine o'clock when he and his cousin left the bedroom and went into the library."

Joan said: "It was Mr. Khalkis's custom to confer with Mr. Sloane in the study at nine each morning. When he was finished talking over the day's affairs with Mr. Sloane, I used to take his dictation."

Trikkala continued: "This man says nothing about that. He says he left his cousin sitting at the desk here and went away from the house. I cannot exactly make out what he tries to say, Inspector Queen. It is something about a doctor, but his speech is mixed up. He is not all there, hey?"

"No, he isn't," grumbled the Inspector, "darn the luck. Miss Brett, do you know what he's trying to tell the interpreter?"

"I fancy he meant to say that he went to visit Dr. Bellows, the psychiatrist. You see, Mr. Khalkis tried always to improve Demmy's mental condition, although he'd been told repeatedly that Demmy's case was quite hopeless. Dr. Bellows became interested, secured someone who knew how to speak Greek, and he has kept Demmy under observation at his office, a few squares away. Demmy visits Dr. Bellows twice a month, on Saturdays. He must have gone to Dr. Bellow's office. At any rate, he returned at about five in the afternoon. Mr. Khalkis had died meanwhile, and nobody had thought in the confusion of the afternoon to notify Demmy. So when he reached home he knew nothing about his cousin's death."

"It was very sad," sighed Mrs. Sloane. "Poor Demmy! I told him, and he took on dreadfully. He whimpered like a child. In his own poor feeble-minded way, he was very fond of Georg."

"All right, Trikkala. Tell him to stay here, and stand by, yourself. We may need him again." The Inspector turned to Gilbert Sloane. "Evidently you were the next after Demmy to see Khalkis last Saturday morning, Mr. Sloane. Did you meet him here at nine, as usual?"

Sloane cleared his throat nervously. "Not exactly," he said in his slightly simpering voice. "You see, while I met Georg in the study here every morning strictly at nine, last Saturday I overslept—I'd worked particularly late at the Galleries the night before. So I didn't get downstairs until a quarter after nine. Georg seemed a little—well, put out because I had kept him waiting. He was very cross and grumpy; he'd become unusually so in late months, probably because of his growing feeling of helplessness."

Inspector Queen applied snuff to his thin nostrils, sneezed, and said very deliberately, "Was there anything amiss in this room when you came in that morning?"

"I don't see . . . Why, of course not. Everything was as usual. Normal, I should say."

"Was he alone?"

"Oh, yes. He did remark that Demmy had gone out."

"Tell me exactly what happened while you were with him."

"Nothing important, Inspector, I assure you—"

The Inspector snapped: "Everything, I said. *I'll* judge what's important and what isn't, Mr. Sloane!"

"As a matter of fact," commented Pepper, "nobody here seems to consider anything important, Inspector."

Ellery murmured, in a jingly rhythm: "*'Wie machen wir's, dass alles frisch und neu—Und mit Bedeutung auch gefällig sei?'*"*

Pepper blinked. "Eh?"

"Goethe in a twinkling mood," said Ellery gravely.

"Oh, don't mind him. . . . Well, we'll change their attitude about *that*, Pepper!" The Inspector glared at Sloane. "Go on, Mr. Sloane. Go on. Spill it all. Even if it's a matter of Khalkis having cleared his throat."

Sloane looked bewildered. "But . . . Well, sir, we went through the business of the day quickly. Georg seemed to have something on his mind aside from sales and collections."

"Good!"

"He was brusque with me, very brusque. I was quite put out, I assure you, Inspector. I didn't like his tone, and I told him so. Yes. He half-apologized in the growl he used when he was angry. Perhaps he felt that he'd overstepped himself, because he changed the subject abruptly. He was fingering the red tie he was wearing, and he said, in a much calmer tone: 'I think this tie is losing its shape, Gilbert.' Of course, he was just making conversation. I reassured him, saying: 'Oh, no, Georg, it looks quite all right.' He said, 'Well, it's flabby—I can feel it's flabby, Gilbert. Before you leave remind me to call Barrett's and order some new ties like the one I'm wearing.' Barrett's is his haberdasher—I should say 'was'. . . . Well, that was Georg's way; there was nothing wrong with the necktie, but he was very fussy about his appearance. I don't know if all this—" he said doubtfully.

---

* "How shall we plan, that all be fresh and new—Important matter yet attractive too?"—Goethe's *Faust. Vorspiel auf dem Theater*, 1.15.

Before the Inspector could speak, Ellery said sharply: "Go on, Mr. Sloane. And did you remind him before you left?"

Sloane blinked. "Naturally. I think Miss Brett will bear me out. You remember, don't you, Miss Brett?" he asked anxiously, turning to the girl. "You had come into the room just before Georg and I finished talking over the day's affairs—you were waiting to take some dictation." Joan nodded emphatically. "There, you see?" said Sloane in a triumphant voice. "That's just what I was about to say. Before I left, I said to Georg: 'You asked me to remind you, Georg, about the ties.' He nodded, and I left the house."

"And that's all that happened between you and Khalkis that morning?" demanded the Inspector.

"That's all, sir. Everything exactly as I've told you—our exact words. I didn't go to the Galleries at once—I had a business appointment downtown—so it wasn't until I got to the Galleries two hours later that I was informed by one of our employees, Miss Bohm, that Georg had died not long after I'd left the house. Mr. Suiza here had already gone to the house. I went back at once—the Galleries are only a few blocks away, you know, on Madison Avenue."

Pepper whispered to the Inspector, Ellery stuck his head into the circle, and the three men had a hurried conference. The Inspector nodded and turned to Sloane with a gleam in his eye. "I asked you before, Mr. Sloane, whether you noticed anything amiss in his room last Saturday morning and you said no. A few minutes ago you heard Miss Brett testify that the man we found murdered, Albert Grimshaw, called upon Khalkis the night before Khalkis died, with a mysterious fellow who tried hard to keep his identity secret. Now what I'm getting at is this: That mysterious fellow may be an important lead. Think hard: Was there anything in the library here, on the desk perhaps, that shouldn't have been here? Something that this secretive man may have left—something that might give us a clue to his identity?"

Sloane shook his head. "I don't recall anything like that. And I was seated right by the desk. I'm sure that if there was something there which didn't belong to Georg I should have noticed it."

"Did Khalkis say anything to you about his having had visitors the night before?"

"Not a word, Inspector."

"All right, Mr. Sloane. Stick around." Sloane sank into a chair beside his wife with a relieved sigh. The Inspector beckoned familiarly to Joan Brett, a little smile of benevolence on his grey face. "Now, my dear," he said in a fatherly voice, "you've been very helpful thus far—you're a witness after my own heart. I'm really interested in you. Tell me something about yourself."

Her blue eyes sparkled. "Inspector, you're transparent! I assure you I haven't a *dossier*. I'm just a poor menial, what we call in England 'lady help.'"

"Dear, dear, and such a nice young lady," murmured the old man. "Nevertheless—"

"Nevertheless you want to know all about me," she smiled. "Very well, Inspector Queen." She arranged her skirt primly over her round knees. "My name is Joan Brett. I worked for Mr. Khalkis for slightly over a year. I am, as perhaps my British accent, now a little blurred by your hideous New Yorkese, had already told you—I am a lady, a *lady*, Inspector!—of English extraction. Shabby gentility, you know. I came to Mr. Khalkis with a recommendation from Sir Arthur Ewing, the British art-dealer and expert, for whom I had worked in London. Sir Arthur knew Mr. Khalkis by reputation and gave me a very nice character indeed. I arrived at an opportune time; Mr. Khalkis required assistance badly; and he engaged me, at a jolly honorarium, I assure you, to act as his confidential secretary. My knowledge of the business swayed him, I fancy."

"Hmm. That's not quite what I wanted—"

"Oh! More personal details?" She pursed her lips. "Let me

see, now. I'm twenty-two—past the marrying age, you see, Inspector—I have a strawberry on my right hip, I've a perfectly *frightful* passion for Ernest Hemingway, I think your politics are stuffy, and I just adore your undergrounds. *Cela suffit?*"

"Now, Miss Brett," said the Inspector in a feeble voice, "you're taking advantage of an old man. I want to know what happened last Saturday morning. Did *you* notice anything in this room that morning that might have indicated the identity of the previous night's mysterious visitor?"

She shook her head soberly. "No, Inspector, I did not. Everything seemed quite in order."

"Tell us just what occurred."

"Let me see." She placed her forefinger on her pink lower lip. "I entered the study, as Mr. Sloane has told you, before he and Mr. Khalkis had finished talking. I heard Mr. Sloane remind Mr. Khalkis about the cravats. Mr. Sloane then left and I took Mr. Khalkis's dictation for about fifteen minutes. When he had finished, I said to him: 'Mr. Khalkis, shall I telephone Barrett's and order the new cravats for you?' He said: 'No, I'll do that myself.' Then he handed me an envelope, sealed and stamped, and asked me to post it at once. I was a bit surprised at this—I generally attended to all his correspondence . . ."

"A letter?" mused the Inspector. "To whom was it addressed?"

Joan frowned. "I'm so sorry, Inspector. I really don't know. You see, I didn't examine it very closely. I do seem to recall that the address was in pen-and-ink, not typewriting—that would be natural, anyway, for there's no typewriter down here—but . . ." She shrugged. "At any rate, just as I was leaving the room with the letter, I saw Mr. Khalkis pick up his telephone—he always used the old-fashioned instrument by which the operator gets your number; the dial telephone was for my convenience—and I heard him give the number of Barrett's, his haberdasher. Then I went out to post the letter."

"What time was this?"

"I should say a quarter to ten."

"Did you see Khalkis alive again?"

"No, Inspector. I was upstairs in my own room a half-hour later when I heard someone scream from below. I dashed down and found Mrs. Simms in the study, in a faint, and Mr. Khalkis dead at his desk."

"Then he died between a quarter to ten and ten-fifteen?"

"I fancy so. Mrs. Vreeland and Mrs. Sloane both rushed downstairs after me, spied the dead body and began to bellow. I tried to bring them to their senses, finally persuaded them to look to poor Simmsy, and at once telephoned Dr. Frost and the Galleries. Weekes came in then from the rear of the house, Dr. Frost appeared in a remarkably short time—just as Dr. Wardes appeared; he'd slept late, I believe—and Dr. Frost pronounced Mr. Khalkis dead. There was really nothing for us to do but drag Mrs. Simms upstairs and revive her."

"I see. Hold up a moment, Miss Brett." The Inspector drew Pepper and Ellery aside.

"What do you think, boys?" asked the Inspector guardedly.

"I think we're going somewhere," murmured Ellery.

"How do you figure that out?"

Ellery looked at the old ceiling. Pepper scratched his head. "I'm blamed if I can see anything in what we've learned so far," he said. "I got all these facts about what happened Saturday long ago, when we were digging into that will business, but I couldn't see . . ."

"Well, Pepper," chuckled Ellery, "perhaps, being American, you're classed in the last category of the Chinese adage which Burton in his *Anatomy of Melancholy* mentions: to wit, 'The Chinese say that we Europeans have one eye, they themselves two, all the world else is blind.'"

"Quit being fancy," growled the Inspector. "Listen, you two." He said something very decisive. Pepper lost a little of his colour, looked uncomfortable, but squared his shoulders and made, to judge from his expression, a mental decision. Joan, perched on the edge of the desk, waited patiently. If she knew what was coming, she gave no sign. Alan Cheney grew tense.

"We'll see," concluded the Inspector aloud. He turned back to the others and said to Joan, dryly, "Miss Brett, let me ask you a peculiar question. Exactly what were your movements this past Wednesday night—two nights ago?"

A veritable silence of the tomb descended on the study. Even Suiza, long legs sprawled to their full length along the rug, cocked his ears. A jury of eyes sat in judgement on Joan as she hesitated. At the instant of Queen's question, her slim leg ceased its pendulum movement, and she grew very still indeed. Then it resumed its swing, and she replied in a casual tone: "Really, Inspector, it's *not* a peculiar question at all. The events of the preceding few days—Mr. Khalkis's death, the confusion in the house, the details of the funeral and the funeral itself— had left me rather worn out. Wednesday afternoon I ambled about Central Park for a breath of air, had an early dinner, and retired immediately after. I read in bed for an hour or so, and turned in at about ten o'clock. That's quite all."

"Are you a sound sleeper, Miss Brett?"

She said with a little laugh: "Oh, very."

"And you slept soundly all that night?"

"Of course."

The Inspector placed his hand on Pepper's rigid arm and said: "Then how do you account for the fact, Miss Brett, that at one o'clock in the morning—an hour after Wednesday midnight—Mr. Pepper saw you prowling about this room, and tampering with Khalkis's safe?"

If the silence had been thunderous before, it was earth-shaking now. For a long moment no one drew a normal breath. Cheney was staring wildly from Joan to the Inspector; he blinked and then focused an unholy glare on Pepper's white face. Dr. Wardes had allowed a paperknife, with which he had been playing, to slip from his fingers; and his fingers remained in a clutching position.

Joan herself seemed the least disturbed of them all. She
smiled and addressed Pepper directly. "You saw *me* prowling
about the study, Mr. Pepper—you saw *me* poking in the safe?
Are you sure?"

"My dear Miss Brett," said Inspector Queen, patting her
shoulder, "it won't do you the slightest good to stall for time.
And don't place Mr. Pepper in the embarrassing position of
calling you a liar. What were you doing down here at that hour?
What were you looking for?"

Joan shook her head with a bewildered little grin. "But, my
dear Inspector, I don't know what either of you is talking about,
really!"

The Inspector eyed Pepper slyly. "Only I was talking, Miss
Brett. . . . Well, Pepper, were you seeing a ghost or was it the
young lady here?"

Pepper kicked the rug. "It was Miss Brett, all right," he muttered.

"You see, my dear," continued the Inspector genially, "Mr.
Pepper seems to know what he's talking about. Pepper, what
was Miss Brett wearing, do you recall?"

"I certainly do. Pyjamas and a *négligé*."

"What colour was the *négligé*?"

"Black. I was sitting, dozing, in the big chair there, across
the room; I suppose I wasn't visible. Miss Brett stole in, very
cautiously, closed the door and turned the switch on that small
lamp on the desk. It gave me light enough to see what she was
wearing and what she did. She rifled the safe. She went through
every paper there." The last sentence came out in a torrent, as
if Pepper were very glad indeed to get his recital over.

The girl had grown perceptibly paler with each successive
word. She sat biting her lip with vexation; tears had sprung into
her eyes.

"Is that true, Miss Brett?" asked the Inspector evenly.

"I—I—no, it isn't!" she cried, and, covering her face with her
hand, she began to weep convulsively. With a strangled oath

young Alan sprang forward and laid muscular hands on Pepper's clean collar. "Why, you rotten liar!" he shouted, "implicating an innocent girl—!" Pepper, his face crimson, shook himself out of Cheney's grip; Sergeant Velie, for all his bulk, was at Cheney's side in a flash and had grasped that young man's arm so sternly as to make him wince.

"Now, now, my boy," said the Inspector in a gentle voice, "control yourself. This isn't—"

"It's a frame-up!" yelled Alan, twisting in Velie's hand.

"Sit down, you young whelp!" thundered the Inspector. "Thomas, you park that hellion in a corner and stand over him." Velie grunted with as close an expression of joy as he ever exhibited, and herded Alan effortlessly into a chair on the farther side of the room. Cheney subsided, muttering.

"Alan, don't." Joan's words, low and choked, startled them. "Mr. Pepper is telling the truth." Her voice caught on a little sob. "I—I *was* in the study late Wednesday night."

"That's more sensible, my dear," said the Inspector cheerfully. "Always tell the truth. Now, what were you looking for?"

She spoke rapidly, without raising her voice. "I—I thought it might be difficult to explain if I admitted . . . It *is* difficult. I—oh, I awoke at one o'clock and suddenly remembered that Mr. Knox, the executor or whatever he is, would probably want an itemization of certain—well, bonds that Mr. Khalkis owned. So I—I went downstairs to list them and—"

"At one o'clock in the morning, Miss Brett?" asked the old man dryly.

"Yes, yes. But when I saw them in the safe I realized, yes, I realized how foolish it was to do that at such an unearthly hour, so I put them back and went upstairs to bed again. That's it, Inspector." Rosy blotches appeared in her cheeks; she kept her eyes steadfastly on the rug. Cheney stared at her with horror; Pepper sighed.

The Inspector found Ellery at his elbow, tugging at his arm. "Well, son?" he asked in a low tone.

But Ellery spoke aloud, a little smile on his lips. "That sounds reasonable enough," he said heartily.

His father stood very still for an instant. "Yes," he said, "so it does. Ah—Miss Brett, you're a trifle upset; you need a little diversion. Suppose you go upstairs and ask Mrs. Simms to come down at once?"

"I'll be—very glad to," replied Joan in the tiniest voice imaginable. She slid off the edge of the desk, flashed a damply grateful look at Ellery, and hurried out of the library.

Dr. Wardes was examining Ellery's face in a very pensive way.

*   *   *

Mrs. Simms appeared in state, attired in a shrieking wrapper, Tootsie padding at her worn heels. Joan slipped into a chair near the door—and near young Alan, who did not look at her but studied the grey corona of Mrs. Simms's head with fierce concentration.

"Ah, Mrs. Simms. Come in. Have a seat," exclaimed the Inspector. She nodded regally and flounced into a chair. "Now, Mrs. Simms, do you remember the events of last Saturday morning, the morning Mr. Khalkis died?"

"I do," she said, with a shudder that set in motion a vast number of fleshy ripples. "I do, sir, and I'll remember them to my dying day."

"I'm sure of that. Now, Mrs. Simms, tell us what happened that morning."

Mrs. Simms raised and lowered her beefy shoulders several times, like an old rooster mustering the energy for a rousing cockadoodledoo. "I came into this room at a quarter past ten, sir, to clean up, take away the tea-things of the night before, and so on—my usual morning chores, sir. As I came through the door—"

"Er—Mrs. Simms." Ellery's voice was gently deferential; a little smile immediately wreathed her puffy lips. This was a nice young man! "You've been doing the chores *yourself*?" His tone implied incredulity that such an important person as Mrs. Simms should be required to do menial labour.

"Only in Mr. Khalkis's private rooms, sir," she hastened to explain. "You see, Mr. Khalkis had a holy horror of young maids— snippy young idiots, he used to call them. He always insisted that I straighten out his personal quarters myself."

"Oh, then you usually put Mr. Khalkis's bedroom in order also?"

"Yes, sir, and Mr. Demmy's too. So I meant to be doing these chores last Saturday morning. But when I came in I—" her bosoms heaved like the sea—"I saw poor Mr. Khalkis a-lying on his desk; which is to say, sir, his *head* was a-lying on the desk. I thought he was asleep. So—God have mercy on me!—I touched his poor hand, and it was cold, so cold, and I tried to shake him, and then I screamed and that's all I remember, sir, on the Book." She regarded Ellery anxiously, as if he doubted the facts as she had stated them. "The very next thing I knew, there was Weekes here and one of the maids a-slapping and a-pummelling my face and giving me smelling-salts and whatnot, and I saw I was upstairs in my very own bed."

"In other words, Mrs. Simms," said Ellery in the same deferential tone, "you really didn't touch anything either in the library here or in the bedrooms."

"No, sir, that I did not."

Ellery whispered to the Inspector, and the Inspector nodded. The old man said, "Did anyone in this household other than Miss Brett, Mr. Sloane, and Demetrios Khalkis see Khalkis alive last Saturday morning before he died?"

All heads shook vigorously; there was no hesitation anywhere.

"Weekes," said the Inspector, "you're sure you didn't enter these rooms between nine and nine-fifteen last Saturday morning?"

The cotton-balls above Weekes's ears trembled. "I, sir? No, sir!"

"A matter of possible moment," murmured Ellery. "Mrs. Simms, have you touched any of these rooms since Khalkis's death seven days ago?"

"I haven't laid finger to them," quavered the housekeeper. "I've been ill, sir."

"And the maids who left?"

Joan said in a subdued voice: "I think I told you before, Mr. Queen, that they left the day of Mr. Khalkis's death. They refused even to step into these rooms."

"You, Weekes?"

"No, sir. Nothing was touched up to Tuesday, the day of the funeral, sir, and after that we were told *not* to touch anything."

"Oh, admirable! Miss Brett, how about you?"

"I've had other things to do, Mr. Queen," she murmured.

Ellery encompassed them all with a sweeping glance. "Has anybody at all touched these rooms since last Saturday?" No response. "Doubly admirable. In other words, this seems to be the situation. The immediate resignation of the maids left the *ménage* shorthanded; Mrs. Simms was confined to her bed and touched nothing; the house being in an uproar, there was no one to clean up. And after the funeral on Tuesday, with the will discovered stolen, nothing was disturbed in these rooms by Mr. Pepper's orders, I believe."

"The undertakers worked in Mr. Khalkis's bedroom," ventured Joan timidly, "fixing—fixing up the body for burial."

"And during the will search, Mr. Queen," put in Pepper, "although we ransacked the rooms, I can assure you personally that nothing was taken away or radically disturbed."

"I think we may discount the undertakers," said Ellery. "Mr. Trikkala, will you check up with Mr. Khalkis here?"

"Yes, sir." Trikkala and Demmy went into frenzied conference again, Trikkala's questions sharp and explosive. A visible pallor spread over the imbecile's sagging face, and he began to stammer and splutter in Greek. "He is not clear, Mr. Queen," reported Trikkala with a frown. "He is trying to say he did not so much as set foot in either bedroom after his cousin's death, but there is something else . . ."

"If I may presume to interrupt, sir," put in Weekes, "I think I know what Mr. Demmy is trying to say. You see, he was so put out by Mr. Khalkis's death, so upset, I might say, sort of like a child fearing the dead, that he refused to sleep in his old room next to Mr. Khalkis's inside, and by Mrs. Sloane's order we prepared one of the empty maids' rooms upstairs."

"He's been staying there," sighed Mrs. Sloane, "like a fish out of water ever since. Poor Demmy *is* a problem sometimes."

"Please make sure," said Ellery in quite a different voice. "Mr. Trikkala, ask him if he has been in the bedrooms since Saturday."

It was not necessary for Trikkala to translate Demmy's horrified negative. The imbecile shrank within himself and shambled to a corner, standing there, biting his nails, looking about him with the uneasy glare of a wild animal. Ellery studied him thoughtfully.

The Inspector turned to the brown-bearded English physician. "Dr. Wardes, I was speaking to Dr. Duncan Frost a few moments ago and he said that you had examined the body of Khalkis immediately after death. Is that correct?"

"Quite right."

"What is your professional opinion as to cause of death?"

Dr. Wardes raised his full brown brows. "Exactly what Dr. Frost ascribed it to in the death-certificate."

"Fine. Now, a few personal questions, Doctor." The Inspector took snuff and smiled benignly. "Would you mind relating the circumstances which find you in this house?"

"I believe," replied Dr. Wardes indifferently, "that I touched upon that not long ago. I am a London specialist on diseases of the eye. I had been visiting New York on a sorely needed sabbatical. Miss Brett visited me at my hotel—"

"Miss Brett again." Queen shot a shrewd glance at the girl. "How is that—were you acquainted?"

"Yes, through Sir Arthur Ewing, Miss Brett's former employer. I treated Sir Arthur for a mild *trachoma* and made the young lady's acquaintance in that way," said the physician. "When she learned through the newspapers of my arrival in New York, she visited me at my hotel to renew our acquaintance and broached the possibility of getting me to look at Khalkis's eyes."

"You see," said Joan in a breathless little rush, "when I saw the announcement of Dr. Wardes's arrival in the ship news, I spoke to Mr. Khalkis about him and suggested that he might be induced to examine Mr. Khalkis's eyes."

"Of course," continued Dr. Wardes, "I was properly in blighty— my nerves aren't up to snuff at present—and at first I didn't feel like turning my vacation into a busman's holiday. But Miss Brett was hard to refuse and I finally consented. Mr. Khalkis was very kind—insisted I be his guest during my stay in the States. I had the man under observation for a little more than a fortnight when he died."

"Did you agree with the diagnosis of Dr. Frost and the specialist on the nature of Khalkis's blindness?"

"Oh, yes, as I think I told the good Sergeant here and Mr. Pepper a few days ago. We know very little about the phenomenon of *amaurosis*—complete blindness—when it is induced by haemorrhage from ulcerous or cancerous stomach. Nevertheless, it was a fascinating problem from the medical standpoint, and I tried a few experiments of my own in an effort to stimulate a possible spontaneous recovery of sight. But I met with no success—my last rigorous examination was a week ago Thursday, and his condition remained unchanged."

"You're certain, Doctor, that you've never seen the man Grimshaw—the second man in the coffin?"

"No, Inspector, I have not," replied Dr. Wardes impatiently. "Furthermore, I know nothing about Khalkis's private affairs, his visitors, or anything else you may consider pertinent to your investigation. My only concern at the moment is to return to England."

"Well," said the Inspector dryly, "you didn't feel that way, I understand, the other day. . . . It isn't going to be so easy, Doctor, to leave. This is a murder inquiry now."

He cut short a protest on the physician's bearded lips and turned aside to Alan Cheney. Cheney's replies were curt. No, he could add nothing to the testimony given so far. No, he had never seen Grimshaw before, and what was more, he added viciously, he didn't care a hoot if Grimshaw's murderer were never found. The Inspector raised a mildly humourous eyebrow and questioned Mrs. Sloane. The result was disappointing—like her son, she knew nothing and cared less. Her only concern was to have the household restored to at least a semblance of propriety and peace. Mrs. Vreeland, her husband, Nacio Suiza, Woodruff were equally unproductive of information. None of them had known or even seen Grimshaw before, it seemed. The Inspector pressed the butler Weekes particularly on this point; but Weekes was positive, despite his eight years' service in the Khalkis house, that Grimshaw had never appeared on the premises prior to the visits of the week before, and even then he, Weekes, had not seen him.

The Inspector, a Napoleonic little figure of despair, stood in the centre of the room as if it were his Elba. There was an almost frantic glitter in his eye. The questions rattled out of his grey-moustached mouth. Had anyone seen possibly suspicious activity in the house after the funeral? No. Had any of them visited the graveyard since the funeral? No. Had any of them *seen* anyone go into the graveyard since the funeral? And again, a climax of thunderous negation—no!

Inspector Queen's fingers curled in an impatient little gesture and Sergeant Velie tramped over. The Inspector was very short-tempered now. Velie was to foray out into the silence of the graveyard and personally question Sexton Honeywell, Reverend Elder and other *attachés* of the church. He was to discover if possible someone who might have witnessed something of interest in the graveyard since the funeral. He was to quiz neighbours and servants in the Rectory across the court and in the four other private residences which gave rear exit to the court. He was to be *mighty* sure that he missed no possible witness to a possible visit by a possible suspect to the graveyard, particularly at night.

Velie, accustomed to his superior's tantrums, grinned a frozen grin and barged out of the library.

The Inspector bit his moustache. "Ellery!" he said with a paternal irritation. "What the devil are you doing now?"

His son made no immediate reply. His son, it might be said, had discovered something of piquant interest. His son, it should be concluded, was for no sensible reason—and it seemed most inappropriately—whistling the thematic tune of Beethoven's Fifth Symphony over a very ordinary-looking percolator perched on a tabouret in a slight alcove across the room.

CHAPTER 10

Omen

Now Ellery Queen's was a curious young soul. He had for hours been disturbed by the merest mental twinge—the vaguest sense of impending events—a dream-like feeling that had no form; in short, an intuition that he was on the verge of a brilliant discovery. He prowled about the library, getting into people's way, prodding furniture and poking books about and generally making a nuisance of himself. He had passed the tabouret with the percolator on it twice without more than a cursory glance; the third time his nostrils quivered ever so slightly—agitated not by a palpable odour but by the less tangible scent of discord. He stared at it for a moment with wrinkled brow, and then he lifted the lid of the percolator to look inside. Whatever he expected to see there, it was at least nothing bizarre; for all that met his eyes was water.

Nevertheless, his eyes were sparkling when he looked up, and he began the musical accompaniment to his thoughts that was to annoy his father. The Inspector's question was doomed to go unanswered; instead, Ellery addressed Mrs. Simms in his old incisive accents. "Where was this tabouret with the tea-things when you found Khalkis dead last Saturday morning?"

"Where? By the desk, sir, not where it is now. By the desk, where I'd set it down the night before at Mr. Khalkis's command."

"Well then," and Ellery swung about to take them all in, "who moved this tabouret to the alcove after Saturday morning?"

Again it was Joan Brett who replied, and again glances now coloured by the purple of suspicion were directed at her tall slender figure. "I did, Mr. Queen."

The Inspector was frowning, but Ellery smiled at his father and said: "You did, Miss Brett. When and why, pray?"

Her laughter was a little helpless. "I seem to have done nearly everything . . . You see, there was so much confusion here the afternoon of the funeral, with everyone searching and running about the library looking for the will. The tabouret was in the way, standing by the desk here, and I merely moved it *out* of the way into the alcove. Surely there's nothing sinister in that?"

"Surely not," said Ellery indulgently, and turned to the housekeeper again. "Mrs. Simms, when you fetched the tea-things last Friday night, how many tea-bags did you provide?"

"A handful, sir. There were six, as I recall."

The Inspector moved quietly forward, as did Pepper, and both men eyed the tabouret with puzzled interest. The tabouret itself was small and old—there was nothing distinguished about it that either could see. On it there was a large silver tray; and on the tray, beside the electric percolator, were three cups and saucers, with spoons; a silver sugar-bowl; a plate with three desiccated, unsqueezed pieces of old lemon; a second plate with three unused tea-bags; and a silver pitcher of curdled, yellowed sweet-cream. In each of the cups there was a dried sediment of tea-fluid, and in each cup a tannic ring near the inside of the rim. Each of the three silver spoons was dull and stained. In each of the three saucers, too, dropped a stained yellowish tea-bag and a dried, squeezed piece of lemon. And nothing more, so far as either the Inspector or Pepper could see.

It was too much for the Inspector, accustomed though he was to his son's whimsical vagaries. "I don't see what—"

"Be loyal to your Ovid," chuckled Ellery. "'Have patience and endure; this unhappiness will one day be beneficial.'" He raised the lid of the percolator again, stared inside, then, removing from his inseparable pocket-kit[*] a tiny glass vial, he drained a few drops of the stale cold water from the percolator-tap, replaced the lid, stoppered the vial and tucked it away in a bulging pocket, whereupon, under an assault of eyes growing more and more bewildered, he lifted the entire tray from the tabouret and carried it to the desk, setting it down with a sigh of satisfaction. A thought struck him; he said sharply to Joan Brett: "When you moved the tabouret last Tuesday, did you touch or change anything on this tray?"

"No, Mr. Queen," she said submissively.

"Excellent. In fact, I might say perfect." He rubbed his hands briskly together. "Now, ladies and gentlemen, we have all had a somewhat fatiguing morning. Perhaps some liquid refreshment . . . ?"

"Ellery!" said the Inspector coldly. "After all there's a limit to everything. This is no time for anything so—so—"

Ellery transfixed him with a mournful eye. "Father! Do you spurn what Colley Cibber took a whole speech to eulogize? 'Tea! thou soft, thou sober, sage, and venerable liquid, thou female tongue-running, smile-soothing, heart-opening, wink-tippling cordial!'" Joan giggled, and Ellery made her a little bow. One of Inspector Queen's detectives, standing in a corner, whispered behind a horny hand to a confederate, "This is one hell of a murder investigation." The glances of the Queens crossed above the percolator, and the Inspector lost his ill-humour. He retreated very quietly, as if to say, "My son, the world is yours. Do with it what you will."

---

[*] See *The French Powder Mystery,* by Ellery Queen. (The New American Library, T4083).

Ellery's ideas seemed definite. He said to Mrs. Simms almost brusquely: "Please fetch three new tea-bags, six clean
cups and saucers with spoons, and some fresh lemon and
cream. *Vitement, Madame la gouvernante!* Get a move on!"

The housekeeper gasped, sniffed and sailed out of the
room. Ellery cheerfully grappled with the electric attachment
of the percolator, walked around the desk looking for something, found it, and plugged the attachment into a socket in the
side of the desk. By the time Mrs. Simms returned from the
kitchen, the water was bubbling in the glass top of the percolator. In a deathly silence to which he was merrily oblivious, Ellery, without placing tea-bags in the six cups Mrs. Simms had
brought, opened the tap and began to fill the cups with boiling
water. The percolator ran dry when the fifth cup was almost
full, and Pepper, in a puzzled way, said: "But Mr. Queen, that
water is stale. It must have been standing there for over a week.
You can't be intending to *drink* it . . ."

Ellery smiled. "Stupid of me. Of course. Mrs. Simms," he
murmured, "I'll trouble you to take the percolator away, fill it
with fresh water and bring it back with six clean cups."

Mrs. Simms had quite openly changed her mind about this
young man; the glare she directed at his bent head was annihi-
lating. He picked up the percolator and thrust it at her. While
she was gone, Ellery with perfect gravity dipped the three yellowed, used tea-bags into three of the cups of steaming stale
water. Mrs. Sloane uttered a little exclamation of disgust; surely
this amazing young pagan was not intending to—! Ellery proceeded with his mysterious ritual. He allowed the three used
tea-bags to soak in their stale-water hot baths, then prodded
each one vigorously with one of the stained spoons. Mrs. Simms
sallied back into the library, bearing a new tray with a full
dozen clean cups and saucers, and the percolator. "I trust and
pray," she said cuttingly, "that these are sufficient, Mr. Queen.
I've quite run out of cups, you know!"

"Perfect, Mrs. Simms. You're a jewel of the first water. Happy phrase, eh?" Ellery left off his pushing and prodding long enough to insert the electric attachment into the desk-socket. Then he returned to his pummelling rite. Despite all his efforts the old tea-bags produced no more than the ghost of a tea-solution in the stale hot water. Ellery smiled, nodding his head as if this proved something to him, waited patiently for the fresh water in the percolator to boil, then proceeded to fill the fresh cups Mrs. Simms had furnished. He sighed when the percolator ran dry after the sixth cup, murmuring, "My dear Mrs. Simms, it looks as if you'll have to refill the percolator *again*—we're a goodly company here," but everyone disdained to join him in a frivolous cup of tea—the Britishers, Joan Brett and Dr. Wardes, included—and Ellery sipped alone, ruefully surveying the top of the desk, which was positively cluttered with tea-cups.

As a matter of cold fact, the glances directed at his composed features told, more eloquently than words, that most of those present considered that he had suddenly sunk to Demmy's stratum of intelligence.

CHAPTER 11

Foresight

Having daintily dabbed at his lips with his handkerchief, Ellery set his empty tea-cup down and, still smiling, disappeared into Khalkis's bedroom. The Inspector and
Pepper, both wearing looks of resignation, followed him.

Khalkis's bedroom was large and dark and windowless—
the chamber of a blind man. Ellery switched on a light and
surveyed this new field of exploration. The room was in considerable confusion; the bed was soiled and unmade; a heap of
men's clothing lay on a chair near the bed; there was a faintly
nauseating odour in the air.

"Probably," remarked Ellery, moving toward an old highboy
across the room, "essence of embalming, or something. This
may be an old and solidly built house, as Edmund Crewe said,
but it certainly neglects the ventilative necessities." He looked
the highboy over, critically, without touching anything. Then,
with a sigh, he made a search of the drawers. In the top drawer
he seemed to discover something of interest; for his hand
emerged bearing two pieces of paper, and he began to read one
of them with relish. The Inspector growled, "What have you
found now?" and he and Pepper craned over Ellery's shoulders.

"Merely the clothes schedule that our friend the idiot used

in caparisoning his cousin," murmured Ellery. They saw that one of the papers was written in a foreign language, the other— its physical counterpart—in English. "I have sufficient knowledge of philology," Ellery went on, "to identify this hocus-pocus as the degenerate modern Greek written language. What a marvellous thing education is!" Neither Pepper nor the Inspector smiled; and Ellery, sighing, began to read the English schedule aloud. It read:

MONDAY: Grey tweed suit, black brogans, grey socks, light grey shirt, attached collar, grey checked necktie.

TUESDAY: Dark brown double-breasted suit, brown cordovan shoes, brown socks, white shirt, red moiré tie, wing collar, tan gaiters.

WEDNESDAY: Light grey single-breasted suit with black pinstripe, pointed black shoes, black silk socks, white shirt, black bow-tie, grey gaiters.

THURSDAY: Blue rough worsted single-breasted suit, black brogans, blue silk socks, white shirt with blue pinstripe, blue polka-dot tie, soft collar to match.

FRIDAY: Tan tweed one-button suit, brown Scotch-grain shoes, tan socks, tan shirt, collar attached, tan-brown striped tie.

SATURDAY: Dark grey three-button suit, black pointed shoes, black silk socks, white shirt, green moiré tie, wing collar, grey gaiters.

SUNDAY: Blue serge double-breasted suit, black square-toed shoes, black silk socks, dark blue tie, wing collar, white shirt with semi-stiff bosom, grey gaiters.

"Well, what of it?" demanded the Inspector.

"What of it?" echoed Ellery. "What of it indeed." He went to the door and peeped out into the study. "Mr. Trikkala! Will you come in here a moment." The Greek interpreter shuffled obediently into the bedroom. "Trikkala," said Ellery, offering the man the paper with the Greek script on it, "what does this say? Read it aloud."

Trikkala did so. It was a word-for-word translation of the English schedule Ellery had just read to the Inspector and Pepper.

Ellery sent the man back to the library and became very busy going through the other drawers of the highboy. Nothing seemed to interest him until he came to the third drawer and found a long flat packet, sealed and unopened. It was addressed to *Mr. Georg Khalkis, 11 E. 54th Street, New York City.* It bore the imprint of *Barrett's, Haberdasher,* in the left upper corner, and a stamped line, *Delivered by Messenger,* in the left lower corner. Ellery tore open the packet. Inside he found six red moiré neckties, all alike. He tossed the packet to the top of the highboy and, finding nothing that seemed to pique him further in the drawers, went into Demmy's bedroom next door. This was a small cubicle, with a single window overlooking the court in the rear. It was eremitic in its furnishings—a bare cell, with a high pallet like a hospital cot, a dresser, a wardrobe closet, and a chair. The room possessed not a vestige of personality.

Ellery shivered a little, but the arid atmosphere did not deter him from going through the drawers of Demmy's dresser with thorough fingers. The only item that aroused his curiosity was a sheet of paper identical with the Greek schedule he had found in Khalkis's highboy—a carbon copy, as he ascertained by an immediate comparison.

He returned to Khalkis's bedroom; the Inspector and Pepper had gone back to the library. He worked swiftly now, going directly to the chair with the clothing heaped upon it. He looked each article over—a dark grey suit, white shirt, red tie, wing collar; on the floor beneath the chair were a pair of grey gaiters and a pair of black pointed shoes with black socks stuffed into them. He looked thoughtful, tapped his *pince-nez* for a moment against his lips, then went to the large wardrobe across the room. He opened it and fussed about its interior. There were twelve ordinary suits of clothing on the rack besides three tuxedos and a formal swallow-tail. A tie-rack with dozens of ties indiscriminately intermingled hung on the back of the wardrobe door. There were numerous pairs of shoes, all fitted with shoe-trees, on the floor; and a few pairs of carpet-slippers were scattered among them. Ellery observed that the shelf above the suits held remarkably few hats—three, in fact: a felt, a derby, and a silk-topper.

He closed the wardrobe door, plucked the packet of neckties from the top of the highboy and returned to the study to find Velie in guarded conference with the Inspector. The Inspector looked up inquiringly; Ellery smiled a reassuring smile and proceeded directly to one of the telephones on the desk. He asked for Information, engaged in a short conversation, repeated a number and promptly dialled it. A rapid-fire series of questions with someone on the other end of the wire, and Ellery hung up, smiling broadly. He had discovered from Undertaker Sturgess that the raiment he had found on the chair in Khalkis's bedroom had been left there, as described piece by piece, by Sturgess's assistants after undressing the dead man; it was the clothing Khalkis had been wearing when he died, and was removed from the body in order to embalm and redress it for the funeral in one of Khalkis's two swallow-tail suits.

Ellery flourished the packet in his hand and said cheerfully: "Does this look familiar to anyone?"

Two people responded—Weekes and, inevitably, Joan Brett. Ellery smiled sympathetically at the girl, but turned to the butler first. "And what do you know about this, Weekes?"

"Is that a package from Barrett's, sir?"

"It is."

"It was delivered late Saturday afternoon, sir, several hours after Mr. Khalkis died."

"Did you accept it yourself?"

"Yes, sir."

"What did you do with it?"

"I—" Weekes looked startled. "Why, I placed it on the foyer-table, sir, as I recall."

Ellery's smile vanished. "On the foyer-table, Weekes? You're certain? You didn't take it from there and put it somewhere else later on?"

"No, sir, I'm sure I did not." Weekes was frightened. "As a matter of fact, sir, in the excitement of the death and all, I completely forgot about the package until I just saw it in your hand."

"Strange . . . And you, Miss Brett? What is your connexion with this ubiquitous packet?"

"I saw it on the foyer-table last Saturday afternoon, Mr. Queen. That's really all I know about it."

"Did you touch it?"

"No."

Ellery became abruptly serious. "Come now," he said in a quiet voice to the assembled company. "Somebody here surely took this packet from the foyer-table and placed it in the third drawer of Khalkis's highboy in the bedroom, where I just found it. Who was it?"

No one answered.

"Does anybody besides Miss Brett recall *seeing* it on the foyer-table?"

There was no reply.

"Very well," snapped Ellery. He crossed the room and handed the parcel to the Inspector. "Dad, it might be important to take this package of neckties over to Barrett's and check with them—who ordered it, who delivered it, and so on."

The Inspector nodded absently, crooking his finger at one of his detectives. "You heard Mr. Queen, Piggott. Get going."

"Check up on these here ties, Chief?" asked Piggott, rasping his jaw.

Velie glared at him and, clutching the packet to his thin

bosom, Piggott coughed apologetically and beat a hasty retreat from the room.

The Inspector whispered: "Anything else here you're interested in, son?" Ellery shook his head; there were worried lines now at the corners of his mouth. The old man clapped his hands together sharply, and everybody moved and sat up straight. "That's all for to-day. I want you people to understand one thing. Last week you were annoyed by a search for a stolen will—it wasn't very important, all things considered, so your freedom wasn't restricted much. But now you're all up to your necks in a juicy murder investigation. I'll tell you frankly we don't know what it's all about yet. All we do know is that the murdered man, who has a criminal record, made two mighty mysterious visits to this house, the second time in the company of a man who tried very hard to keep his identity secret—and succeeded."

He glared at them. "The crime is complicated by the fact that this murdered man was found buried in the coffin of a man who died of natural causes. And, I might add, buried right next door to this house.

"Under the circumstances, you're all potentially under suspicion. Of what, and how, the Lord alone knows. But get me straight—every mother's son and daughter of you stays right under my eye until we see daylight. Those of you, like Sloane and Vreeland, who have business to attend to, may go about it as usual; but both of you gentlemen will be very careful to stay within reach and call. Mr. Suiza, you may go home—but you're also to keep within call. Woodruff, you're of course excused. The others, until I say so, leave this house only with permission and with a specific accounting of where they're going."

The Inspector, very grumpily indeed, struggled into his overcoat. No one said a word. The old man snapped orders at his men, stationing a number of them, headed by Flint and Johnson, in the house. Pepper sent word to Cohalan to stay where he was—a representative of the District Attorney's office guarding the prosecutor's interests. Pepper, Velie and Ellery donned their coats; the four men went to the door.

The Inspector turned at the last moment and looked them over. "And I'll tell all of you right here and now," he said in a most unpleasant way, "you can like it or lump it—it's all the same to me! Good day!" He clumped out, and Ellery followed the others, chuckling to himself.

CHAPTER 12

Facts

Dinner at the Queen *ménage* that evening was a lugubrious affair. The apartment on the third floor of the West Eighty-seventh Street brownstone was a little newer then, the foyer a little haughtier, the living-room not quite so aged in the wood of time; and, with young Djuna, the Queens' boy-of-all-work, being very young indeed and consequently a little less restrained than he was to become years later, one would have called the apartment cosy and the atmosphere bright. Not so, however; the Inspector's *Weltschmerz* hung over the rooms like a pall; he dipped into his snuff-box more frequently and more savagely; he replied to Ellery in fierce monosyllables, ordered a very bewildered Djuna about almost with passion, and trotted from the living-room to the bedroom in an ecstasy of restlessness. Nor did the old man's temper improve with the arrival of his guests; Ellery had asked them to dinner, and the sight of Pepper's thoughtful face and District Attorney Sampson's wearily inquiring eyes did not effect a chemical change in the prevailing indigo mood.

Consequently, Djuna served an appetizing repast in silence, and in silence it was received and consumed. Ellery, alone of the four men, was placid. He ate with his customary relish, complimented Djuna on the quality of the roast, quoted Dickens over the pudding and Voltaire over the coffee. . . .

Sampson had no sooner wiped his lips with his napkin than he said: "Well, Q., the old story. Buffaloed, baffled and beaten. One of those rotten puzzles. How does it stack up?"

The Inspector raised haggard eyes. "Ask my son here." He buried his old nose in his coffee-cup. "He seems pleased enough with the way things are going."

"You take these things too seriously, Dad," said Ellery, puffing comfortably on a cigarette. "The problem has its points, but I shouldn't say—" he drew a lungful of smoke and expelled it—"I shouldn't say it's insoluble."

"Hey?" All three of them stared at him; the Inspector's eyes were wide with astonishment.

"Don't press me, I beg of you," murmured Ellery. "It's at moments like these that I become classically antique in my language, and I know Sampson, for one, abhors the practice. Besides, I dislike ratiocination on a full stomach. Djuna, more coffee, like a good boy."

Sampson said decisively: "But if you know anything, Ellery, spill it! What's up?"

Ellery accepted the mug from Djuna. "Much too premature, Sampson. I'd rather not just now."

Sampson jumped up and began to pace the rug excitedly. "That's the way it always is! The old story! 'Much too premature'!" He snorted like a stallion. "Pepper, let me in on this thing. What's the latest dope?"

"Well, Chief," said Pepper, "Velie found out a lot of things, but none of it does us much good, as I see it. For instance, Honeywell—the sexton of the church—maintains that the graveyard is never locked, but that neither he nor his assistants have seen anything suspicious at any time after the funeral."

"Doesn't mean a curse," growled the Inspector. "The graveyard and court aren't patrolled. Somebody could have come in and out a dozen times without being seen. Especially at night. Bah!"

"How about the neighbours?"

"More nothing," replied Pepper. "Velie's report was complete. You see, all the houses on both the south side of Fifty-fifth and the north side of Fifty-fourth have their rears to the court. On Fifty-fifth Street, east to west, the houses in order are: Number Fourteen, on the corner of Madison Avenue, owned by Mrs. Susan Morse, that daffy old dame who attended the funeral. Number Twelve, Dr. Frost's house—that's the physician who took care of Khalkis. Number Ten, the Rectory next to the church, where Reverend Elder lives. On Fifty-fourth Street, east to west, you've got: Number Fifteen, corner of Madison Avenue, Mr. and Mrs. Rudolph Ganz . . ."

"The retired meat-packer?"

"Yes. And between the Ganz place and the Khalkis house, which is Number Eleven, you've got Number Thirteen—an empty house boarded up."

"Who owns it?"

"Don't get excited. It's in the family," grumbled the Inspector. "It belongs to our celebrated multi-millionaire, Mr. James J. Knox, the one Khalkis named executor in that stolen will. Nobody lives there—it's an old piece of property. Knox used to live there years ago, but he moved uptown a way and the place is standing idle."

"I looked up the title," explained Pepper. "It's free and clear, of course, and not offered for sale. I guess he's holding on to it for sentimental reasons. It's a sort of ancestral home—as old as the Khalkis shack—built at the same time.

"Well, anyway, nobody in any of these houses—either owners, servants or in one case guests—could give Velie any information. You see, the court is accessible from the rear of all the houses on both streets; it's not accessible from Madison Avenue unless you go through the basement of the Morse or Ganz house, the only two on the block; and there are no alleys on Fifty-fourth, Madison, or Fifty-fifth Street leading to the court."

"In other words," said Sampson impatiently, "you couldn't get into the court except through the houses themselves, the church or the graveyard—is that right?"

"Right. As for the graveyard, there are only three ways of getting into it—through the rear of the church itself; through the gate at the western end of the court; and through that single door in the fence—really a high gate—on the Fifty-fourth Street side of the graveyard."

"Still doesn't mean a thing," said the Inspector disagreeably. "That's not the important point. The important point is that everybody questioned by Velie denied visiting the graveyard at night or any other time since Khalkis's funeral."

"Except," put in Ellery gently, "Mrs. Morse, Dad. You've forgotten her. Remember Velie said she confessed her pleasant habit of wandering over the heads of the dead in the graveyard each afternoon."

"Yes," said Pepper, "but she denied visiting it at night. At any rate, Chief, all the neighbours are members of the church parish except, of course, Knox. He isn't properly a neighbour."

"He's Catholic," growled the Inspector. "Belongs to a high-toned cathedral on the West Side."

"Where is Knox, by the way?" asked the District Attorney.

"Well, he went out of town this morning. I don't know exactly where," said the old man. "I'm having Thomas get a search-warrant—we can't wait for Knox to get back and I'm dead set on looking over that empty house of his next door to the Khalkis place."

"You see, Chief," explained Pepper, "the Inspector has an idea that the empty Knox house might have been the place where Grimshaw's body was hidden until it could be buried in the Khalkis coffin after the funeral."

"Good hunch, Q."

"Anyway," continued Pepper, "Knox's secretary refused to

disclose the mogul's whereabouts, and we've got to have the warrant."

"It may not be important," remarked the Inspector, "but blast my soul if I let anything go."

"An excellent *principio operandi*," chuckled Ellery.

His father turned on him a very cold and disapproving scowl. "You—you think you're smart," he said weakly. "Well. . . . Look here, gentlemen. As far as that empty house is concerned, we've got a problem. We still don't know exactly when Grimshaw was bumped off—how long he's been dead. All right, the autopsy ought to show that pretty conclusively. In the meanwhile, we've got a basis of figuring. Because if Khalkis died *before* Grimshaw was murdered, it certainly means—considering where we found the body—that burial of Grimshaw in Khalkis's coffin was pre-planned. Get me? In that case, the empty house would be a fine place for the murderer to keep Grimshaw's body until after the Khalkis funeral, when the buried coffin would become available for use."

"Yes, but look at it the other way, Q.," objected Sampson. "It's just as tenable a theory, in the absence of the autopsy-findings, that Khalkis died *after* Grimshaw was murdered. This would mean that the killer couldn't figure on Khalkis's unexpected death and the opportunity to bury the victim in Khalkis's coffin, so that the body must have been hidden wherever the murder took place—and we've no reason to expect that the murder took place in that empty house next door. In any event, I don't see that the line of attack does us any good until we discover how long Grimshaw has been a stiff."

"You mean," said Pepper thoughtfully, "that if Grimshaw was strangled before Khalkis died, his body was probably kept wherever he was killed? Then when Khalkis died, the opportunity to bury the body in Khalkis's coffin flashed on the murderer's mind, and he lugged the body into the graveyard, probably through the Fifty-fourth Street fence-gate?"

"Exactly," snapped Sampson. "The chances are ten to one

that the house next to Khalkis's had nothing to do with the crime. I think all this is irrelevant conjecture."

"Perhaps not so irrelevant," said Ellery gently. "On the other hand, it seems to my feeble intellect that you gentlemen are cooking a stew before buying your ingredients. Why not wait patiently for the autopsy report?"

"Wait—wait," grumbled the Inspector. "I've grown old waiting."

Ellery chuckled. "If we are to believe Chaucer, your age is a distinct advantage, *padre*. Remember *The Parlement of Fowles*? 'For oute of olde feldys, as men sey, Comyth al this newe corn from yere to yere.'"

"Anything else, Pepper?" growled Sampson. He ignored Ellery completely.

"The routine stuff. Velie questioned the doorman of the department store across the street from the Khalkis house and graveyard. The man stands all day at the Fifty-fourth Street entrance to the store. Quizzed the cop on the beat, too. But neither of them has seen suspicious activity in the daytime since the funeral. The cop on night-duty didn't see anything either, but he admits the body could have been hauled into the graveyard without his knowledge. And there's no one on duty at the department store at night who was in a position to observe the graveyard; the nightwatchmen stay inside at all hours. And there you are."

"I'll go daffy with this damnable sitting around," muttered the Inspector, plumping his straight little body before the fire in the grate.

"*La patience est amère, mais son fruit est doux*," murmured Ellery. "I feel in a quotational mood."

"That's what I get," groaned the Inspector, "for having sent my boy to college. He talks down at me. What's that mean?"

"'Patience is bitter, but its fruit is sweet,'" grinned Ellery, "and a frog said it."

"A—what? A *frog*?"

"Oh, he's just trying to be funny," said Sampson wearily. "I suppose he means a Frenchman. It sounds like Rousseau."

"Do you know, Sampson," said Ellery enthusiastically, "sometimes you exhibit positively startling signs of intelligence?"

CHAPTER 13

Inquiries

The next morning, Saturday—a day of brilliant October sunshine—found Inspector Queen's sagging spirits considerably bolstered. The immediate cause of his spiritual elevation was the delivery in person by Dr. Samuel Prouty of the autopsy-findings on both Khalkis and the murdered man.

District Attorney Sampson, chained to his office by a case which demanded his personal attention, had sent his lieutenant Pepper to the Inspector's office at Police Headquarters. When Dr. Prouty slouched in, chewing his first cigar of the day, he found the Inspector, Pepper, Sergeant Velie, and a curiously expectant Ellery awaiting him.

"Well, Doc? Well, well?" cried the Inspector. "What's the news?"

Dr. Prouty jack-knifed his lank length into the most comfortable chair in the room, with sardonic deliberation. "S'pose you want to be sure about the Khalkis stiff? Everything's jake in that direction. Dr. Frost's certificate told the exact truth. No indications of foul play. He was a rotten cardiac and his pumper gave out on him."

"Not a sign of poison, eh?"

"Nary a pinpoint. All okay. Now, as to the second stiff." Dr.

Prouty champed his teeth vigorously. "All the signs point to death prior to Khalkis's. It's a long story." He grinned. "There are a raft of conditions which make a definite finding risky. Loss of body heat in this case doesn't get us very far. But we got something from cadaveric muscular changes and that business of complete lividity. Green spots on surface and in middle of abdomen, due to chemical-bacterial action, well developed; number and position of livid putrefactive patches internally as well as externally check for about a seven-day period up to last night. Gas pressure, forced mucous discharge from mouth and nostrils, internal decay of the windpipe, certain signs in the stomach, intestines and spleen—all check for the period I've mentioned. Skin tense, but beginning to loosen in area of most distention—abdomen; odorous gases, specific gravity down—yep, I'd say that Mr. Albert Grimshaw was killed six and a half days before the disinterment yesterday morning."

"In other words," said the Inspector, "Grimshaw was strangled somewhere in the wee hours—late last Friday night or early last Saturday morning."

"That's right. I'd say, everything considered, that there was a slight retardation of the natural process of putrefaction. Shouldn't be surprised if you find that the body was kept in a dry, fairly airless place before burial in Khalkis's coffin."

Ellery looked uncomfortable. "Not a very pleasant business. Our immortal souls seem to be housed in very treacherous bodies."

"Why, because decay sets in so rapidly?" Dr. Prouty looked amused. "Well, I'll offer a word of consolation. The uterus of a woman sometimes remains intact for seven months after death."

"If that's your idea of consolation—"

The Inspector said hurriedly, "There's no question, Doc, but that Grimshaw died of strangulation?"

"Nope. Someone choked him with bare hands. The marks of the fingers are very pronounced."

"Doctor." Ellery sat well back in his chair, smoking lazily. "What did you find in that sample of stale water I gave you?"

"Oh, that!" The Assistant Medical Examiner looked bored. "You see, there are certain salts—calcium salts chiefly—present in all hard water. Our drinking water's hard, y'know. Well, boiling precipitates these salts. It's easy to make a chemical analysis and by the precipitated content determine whether the water was boiled or not. I'd say absolutely that the sample you gave me from the stale water you found in that percolator indicates boiling, and moreover that no unboiled water had been added after the original water was heated."

"Blessings on your scientific head, Doctor," murmured Ellery.

"Pipe down. Anything else?"

"No, and thanks a lot, Doc," said the Inspector.

Dr. Prouty uncoiled himself like a cobra and smoked his way out of the Inspector's office.

"Now, let's see where we stand," began the old man, briskly rubbing his hands. He consulted a memorandum. "This Vreeland chap. His Quebec trip substantiated by train officials, ticket-stub, hotel records, time of departure, etcetera. Hmm . . . Demetrios Khalkis. Spent the whole day in the office of Dr. Bellows—that's last Saturday . . . Fingerprint report on Khalkis house—nothing doing; Grimshaw's prints found on the desk in the library with a bunch of others. Probably everybody in the house had his hands on that desk at some time or other, especially during that preliminary search for the will. Prints on the coffin—nothing either; a lot of smudges and clear prints, but everyone in the house was around the coffin as it lay in the drawing-room, and the presence of any specific prints would not incriminate their owners . . . Thomas, what did Piggott find out at Barrett's?"

"Everything checks," replied Velie. "Piggott found the clerk who took the telephoned order. Clerk says that Khalkis himself—he was damn' sure it was Khalkis; had spoken to him many times on the phone, he said—called up last Saturday morning, ordering half a dozen red moiré ties; the time checks, and so does the style ordered. Barrett's delivery-man's receipt shows Weekes's signature as receiver of the parcel. All in order."

"Well, that ought to satisfy *you*," said the Inspector maliciously to Ellery, "although what good it does you is beyond me."

"How about that empty house, Sergeant?" asked Pepper. "Get the warrant all right?"

"Whole thing fell flat," grumbled the Inspector.

"We got the warrant okay but Ritter, one of our men, reports searching the dump and says there's nothing to be found there," boomed Velie. "Place is stripped—no furniture except an old broken-down trunk in the basement. Ritter says he couldn't find a thing."

"Ritter, eh?" murmured Ellery, blinking through smoke.

"Well, now," said the Inspector, picking up another sheet of paper, "there's Grimshaw himself."

"Yes, the Chief asked me especially to find out what you've dug up on him," said Pepper.

"Dug up plenty," replied the old man grimly. "Released from Sing Sing on the Tuesday prior to his murder—that is, September twenty-eighth. No time off for good behaviour—of course you know he was in for forgery on a five-year stretch. He wasn't jailed until three years after his crime—couldn't be found. Previous record shows a two-year stretch in the pen about fifteen years ago on an unsuccessful attempt to steal a painting of some kind from the Chicago Museum, where he had a job as attendant."

"That's what I was referring to," remarked Pepper, "when I said forgery was only one of his accomplishments."

Ellery had pricked up his ears. "Museum theft? Doesn't that strike you as rather a too felicitous coincidence? Here we have a great art-dealer, and a museum thief. . . ."

"Something in that," muttered the Inspector. "Anyway, as far as his movements since September twenty-eighth are concerned, he was traced from Sing Sing to a hotel on West Forty-ninth Street, in the city here—Hotel Benedict, third-rate sort of dump—where he registered under his own name of Grimshaw."

"He doesn't seem to have used an alias," commented Pepper. "Brazen crook."

"Have you questioned the hotel people?" asked Ellery.

Velie said: "Nothing to be got out of the day-clerk at the desk, or the manager. But I've put in a call for the night-clerk— he ought to be here soon. Maybe he'll know something."

"Anything else on his movements, Inspector?" asked Pepper.

"Yes, sirree. He was seen with a woman in a speakeasy on West Forty-fifth Street—one of his old hangouts—a week ago Wednesday night, the day after his release. Got Schick here, Thomas?"

"Outside." Velie rose and went out.

"Who's Schick?" demanded Ellery.

"Proprietor of the speakeasy. Old-timer."

Velie returned with a large, robust, red-faced man in tow— a man with "ex-bartender" written all over his hail-fellow-well-met face. He was very nervous. "M-mornin', Inspector. Nice day, ain't it?"

"So-so," grunted the old man. "Sit down, Barney. Want to ask you a few questions."

Schick mopped his dripping face. "Nothin' personal about this here confab, Inspector, is there?"

"Hey? You mean the booze? Hell, no." The Inspector rapped on his desk. "Now, you listen to me, Barney. We know that a 'pen' named Albert Grimshaw who'd just been let out of stir visited your dive a week ago Wednesday night. Right?"

"Guess so, Inspector." Schick stirred uneasily. "The guy that was bumped, hey?"

"You heard me the first time. Now, he was seen with a woman that night. What about it?"

"Well, Inspector, I'll tell you." Schick became hoarsely confidential. "This is the straight boloney. I don't know the broad—never saw her before."

"What's she look like?"

"Hefty dame. Big blonde. Runnin' to beef. I'd say about thirty-five on a guess. Crow's-feet under her lamps."

"Go on. What happened?"

"Well, they came in around nine bells—pretty early; there ain't much doin' round that hour—" Schick coughed—"an' they sets down an' Grimshaw, he orders a shot. The dame, she don't want nothin'. Pretty soon they start jawin' at each other—reg'lar battle, I'd say. Couldn't make out what they was sayin', though I did catch the dame's front handle—Lily, he calls her. Seems like he was tryin' to get her to do somethin', an' she's balky. Anyways, she ups and beats it all of a sudden and leaves the little squirt flat. He was all worked up—talkin' to himself. He sets there another five, ten minutes; then he faded. 'S'all I know, Inspector."

"Lily, big blonde, hey?" The Inspector grasped his small chin and thought deeply. "Okay, Barney. Did Grimshaw come in again, after Wednesday night?"

"Naw. Take me oath, Inspector," said Schick at once.

"All right. Beat it."

Schick rose with alacrity and fairly trotted from the office.

"Want me to tackle the big-blonde lead?" rumbled Velie.

"Hop to it, Thomas. She's probably some moll he was tied up with before he was sent up. If they were quarrelling it's a cinch she wasn't somebody he picked up after only one day out of stir. Look up his record."

Velie left the room. When he returned, he was herding before him a white-faced young man with shrinking eyes bleared by fright. "This is Bell, the Benedict night-clerk, Chief. Go on, go on, mug; nobody's gonna bite you." He shoved Bell into a chair, and towered over him.

The Inspector motioned Velie away. "All right, Bell," he said kindly. "You're among friends. We just want a little information. How long have you been on night-duty at the Hotel Benedict?"

"Four and a half years, sir." The man sat twisting his felt hat between his fingers.

"Were you on duty from September twenty-eighth on?"

"Yes, sir. Haven't missed a night in—"

"Did you know a guest by the name of Albert Grimshaw?"

"Yes, sir, I did. The man the papers say was f-found murdered in that church graveyard on Fifty-fourth Street."

"Fine, Bell. Glad to see you're on your toes. Did you check him in?"

"No, sir. The day-clerk did that."

"Then how do you know him?"

"It's a funny story, sir." Bell had lost some of his nervousness. "There was one night in that week during his stay when something—well, fishy-looking happened, and that made me remember him."

"What night was that?" asked the Inspector eagerly. "And what was it?"

"Two nights after he checked in. Thursday night a week ago . . ."

"Ha!"

"Well, sir, this man Grimshaw had *five* people come in that night to see him! All within a half-hour or so."

The Inspector was admirable. He leaned back and took a pinch of snuff as if Bell's statement was of no importance. "Go on, Bell."

"Around ten o'clock that Thursday night I saw this Grimshaw walk into the lobby from the street with a man. They were together—talking fast, in a hurry, it seemed like. I couldn't hear what they said."

"What did Grimshaw's companion look like?" asked Pepper.

"Can't say, sir. He was all bundled up—"

"Ha!" said the Inspector for the second time.

"—all bundled up. Seemed as if he didn't want to be recognized, I'd say. Might recognize him if I saw him again, but I won't swear to it. Anyway, they went to the elevator and that's the last I saw of 'em."

"Just a minute, Bell." The Inspector turned to the sergeant. "Thomas, round up the night elevator-man."

"Pulled him in already, Chief," said Velie. "Hesse ought to be here with him any minute."

"Fine. Go ahead, Bell."

"Well, as I say, this was around ten o'clock. Practically right away—in fact, while Grimshaw and his pal were still standing there by the elevator, waiting—a man walked up to the desk and asked for Grimshaw. Wanted to know his room-number. I said: 'There he goes right now, sir,' just as they were getting into the elevator; I said: 'His room-number is 314,' I said, because that was his room-number, you see. This man looked a little funny—seemed nervous; anyway, he went and waited for the elevator to come down. We've only got one," added Bell ungrammatically. "The Benedict's a small place."

"And?"

"Well, sir, for a minute or so I'd sort of noticed a woman hanging round the lobby, looking nervous, too. She comes up to the desk now and says: 'Have you a vacant room next to Room 314?' Must have heard the man before her asking, I'd guess. Sort of funny, I thought, and I began to smell a rat somewhere. 'Specially since she had no luggage. As luck would have it, Room 316 next door to Grimshaw's was vacant. I got the key and yelled, 'Front!' but no—she doesn't want a bell-hop, she says, she wants to go up all by herself. I give her the key and she takes the elevator up. By this time the man'd already gone up."

"What did she look like?"

"Uh—I guess I could recognize her if I saw her. Little dumpy kind of woman, middle-aged."

"What name did she register under?"

"Mrs. J. Stone. I'd say she was trying to disguise her hand-writing. Wrote crooked, as if she was doing it on purpose."

"Was she a blonde?"

"No, sir. Black hair getting grey. Anyway, she paid in ad-vance for one night—room without bath—so I said to myself: 'I should worry. Business is rotten enough these days without—'"

"Here, here, stick to your story. You said there were five all told. How about the other two?"

"Well, sir, within about fifteen or twenty minutes two more men came up to the desk and asked whether there was an Albert Grimshaw registered. And if so what his room-number was."

"Were they together?"

"No, sir. They came about five or ten minutes apart."

"Do you think you could identify these two men if you saw them?"

"Sure thing. You know," and Bell became confidential, "what struck me funny was how all of 'em acted so nervous, as if they didn't want to be seen. Even the guy that came in with Grim-shaw originally acted queer."

"Did you see any of these people leave the hotel?"

Bell's pimply face fell. "I guess I ought to be kicked, sir. I should have been on watch. But I got a sort of rush after that— bunch of show girls checked out—and they must have beat it while I was busy."

"How about the woman? When did she check out?"

"That's another funny thing. The day-man told me, when I came on duty the next night, that the chamber-maid had re-ported the bed in 316 hadn't been slept in. Matter of fact, the key was sticking in the door. She must've changed her mind. It was all right, because she'd paid in advance."

"Now about times other than Thursday night—Wednesday night? Friday night? Did Grimshaw have any visitors?"

"That I couldn't say, sir," replied the night-clerk apologeti-cally. "All I know is, nobody asked for him at the desk. He checked out Friday night around nine o'clock, leaving no forwarding address. He didn't have any baggage either—that's another thing that made me remember him."

"Might take a look at that room," muttered the Inspector. "Did anybody occupy 314 after Grimshaw left?"

"Yes, sir. It's been occupied by three different guests since he checked out."

"Cleaned every day?"

"Oh, yes."

Pepper shook his head disconsolately. "If anything was there, Inspector, it's gone by now. You'll never find it."

"Not after a week, we won't."

"Er—Bell," came Ellery's drawl, "did Grimshaw's room have a private bath?"

"Yes, sir."

The Inspector leaned back. "Something tells me," he said genially, "that we're in for some lively doings. Thomas, round up all the people connected with the case so far and have 'em at Eleven East Fifty-fourth within an hour."

As Velie left, Pepper muttered: "Good Lord, Inspector, if we find that some of those five Grimshaw visitors are people already connected with the case so far, we're in some sweet mess. Especially after everybody who looked at the body said they'd never seen Grimshaw before."

"Complicated, hey?" The Inspector grinned without humour. "Well, that's life."

"Good God, Dad!" groaned Ellery. Bell was looking from face to face in bewilderment.

Velie tramped back. "All set. And Hesse's outside with a 'shine'—the night elevator-man at the Benedict."

"Get him in here."

The night elevator-man at the Benedict proved to be a young Negro violet with fear. "What's your name, son?"

"White, suh. W—White."

"Oh, heavens," said the Inspector. "Well, White, do you remember a man named Grimshaw at the Benedict last week?"

"The—the choked gen'man, suh?"

"Yes."

"Y-yassuh, I do," chattered White. " 'Member him plain."

"Do you remember a week ago Thursday night—when he came into your elevator in the company of another man about ten o'clock?"

"Yassuh. Sure do."

"What did the other man look like?"

"Ain't got no idea, Cap'n. Nosuh. Don't 'member whut he looked like."

"Do you remember anything? Taking up other people who got off at Grimshaw's floor?"

"Took up a passel o' folks, Cap'n. Millions, seems like. Always takin' up folks, suh. On'y thing I rec'lects is takin' up Mistuh Grimshaw an' his friend, an' they gets off at the thu'd floor an' I sees 'em go into 314, closin' the door behind 'em. 314's right near th' elevatuh, suh."

"What did they talk about in the elevator?"

The Negro groaned. "I got jus' an empty haid, suh. Can't 'member nothin'."

"What was the second man's voice like?"

"I—I don't know, suh."

"All right, White. You're excused."

White simply vanished. The Inspector rose, put on his coat, and said to Bell: "You wait here for me. I'll be back soon—want you to identify some people for me, if you can." He left the room.

Pepper was staring at the wall. "You know, Mr. Queen," he said to Ellery, "I'm in this thing up to my neck. The Chief has shoved it all on my shoulders. My angle's the will, but it looks as if we'll never—Where in hell *is* that will?"

"Pepper, my lad," said Ellery, "the will, I fear, has passed into the limbo of inconsequential things. I refuse to repudiate my own clever—if I do say so myself—my own clever deduction that the will was slipped into the coffin and buried with Khalkis."

"It certainly looked that way when you explained it."

"I'm convinced of it." Ellery lit another cigarette and inhaled deeply. "In which case I can tell you who has the will, if indeed it still exists."

"You *can*?" Pepper was incredulous. "I don't get you—who?"

"Pepper," sighed Ellery, "it's a problem of almost infantile simplicity. Who but the man who buried Grimshaw?"

CHAPTER 14

Note

Inspector Queen had reason to remember that fine bright shining October morning. It was also, in a manner of speaking, a gala day for young Bell, a hotel clerk with no delusions of—but a strong yen for—grandeur. To Mrs. Sloane it brought only anxiety. What it meant to the others may be only vaguely conjectured—the others, that is, with the exception of Miss Joan Brett.

Miss Joan Brett experienced, all things considered, a horrible morning. That she was resentful, that resentment ultimately dissolved into pearly tears, is not to be wondered at. Fate had been hard, and it seemed determined, in its customary aimless manner, to become harder still. The soil, paradoxically because of its pleasant watering of tears, was scarcely adapted for the sowing of the seeds of gentle passion.

It was more, in a word, than even a daughter of doughty British character could be expected to endure.

And it all began with the disappearance of young Alan Cheney.

Cheney's absence did not strike the Inspector at first when he marshalled his forces and commanded, as he sat in the library of the Khalkis house, that his victims be brought before him. He was too absorbed in watching individual reactions. Bell—a very bright-eyed and important Bell now—stood by the Inspector's chair, the picture of judicial righteousness. They trailed in one by one—Gilbert Sloane and Nacio Suiza, the immaculate director of the private Khalkis art-gallery; Mrs. Sloane, Demmy, the Vreelands, Dr. Wardes, and Joan. Woodruff arrived a little later. Weekes and Mrs. Simms stood against a wall as far from the Inspector as they could get. . . . And as each one came in, Bell's sharp little eyes narrowed, and he made a great to-do with his hands and a fierce lip-quivering, and several times he wagged his head solemnly, as inexorable as a son of the Furies.

No one said a word. They all glanced at Bell—and away.

The Inspector grimly smacked his lips. "Sit down, please. Well, Bell, my lad, do you see anyone in this room who visited Albert Grimshaw on the night of Thursday, September thirtieth, in the Hotel Benedict?"

Someone gasped. The Inspector moved his head as quickly as a snake, but the author of the gasp had recovered himself instantly. Some looked indifferent, others interested, others weary.

Bell made the most of his opportunity. He slapped his hands behind his back and began to promenade about the room before the seated company—eyeing them critically, very critically. Finally, he pointed a victorious finger at the foppish figure of . . . Gilbert Sloane.

"There's one of 'em," he said briskly.

"So." The Inspector sniffed snuff; he was quite collected at this time. "I thought as much. Well, Mr. Gilbert Sloane, we've caught you in a little white lie. You said yesterday that you'd never seen the face of Albert Grimshaw before. Now the night-clerk at the hotel where Grimshaw stayed identifies you as a visitor to Grimshaw the night before he was murdered. What have you got to say for yourself?"

Sloane moved his head feebly, like a fish on a grassy bank. "I—" His voice caught on some tracheal obstruction, and he

paused to clear it very, very carefully. "I don't know what the
man's talking about, Inspector. Surely there's some mistake. . . ."

"Mistake? So." The Inspector considered that. His eyes
twinkled sardonically. "Sure you're not taking a leaf out of Miss
Brett's notebook, Sloane? You'll recall *she* made the same remark yesterday . . ." Sloane mumbled something, and colour
flared into Joan's cheeks. But she kept sitting motionless, staring before her. "Bell, is there a mistake or did you see this man
that night?"

"I saw *him,* sir," said Bell. "*Him.*"

"Well, Sloane?"

Sloane crossed his legs suddenly. "It's—why, it's ridiculous.
I don't know anything about it."

Inspector Queen smiled and turned to Bell. "Which one
was he, Bell?"

Bell looked confused. "I don't exactly recall which one he
was. But I'm sure he was one of them, sir! Absolutely sure!"

"You see—" began Sloane eagerly.

"I'll attend to you some other time, *Mr.* Sloane." The Inspector waved his hand. "Go on, Bell. Anybody else?"

Bell began his hunter's stalk again. His chest swelled again.
"Well," he said, "there's one thing I'll *swear* to." He pounced so
suddenly across the room that Mrs. Vreeland uttered a little
scream. "*This,*" cried Bell, "was the lady!"

He was pointing to Delphina Sloane.

"Hmm." The Inspector folded his arms. "Well, Mrs. Sloane, I
suppose you don't know what we're talking about either, eh?"

A rich slow flush began to invade the woman's chalky
cheeks. Her tongue flicked out over her lips several times.
"Why . . . no, Inspector. I do not."

"And *you* said you'd never seen Grimshaw before, either."

"I hadn't!" she cried wildly. "I hadn't!"

The Inspector shook his head sadly, as if in philosophic
commentary on the mendaciousness of the Khalkis witnesses
in general. "Anybody else, Bell?"

"Yes, sir." There was no hesitancy in Bell's step as he crossed the room and tapped Dr. Wardes's shoulder. "I'd recognize this gentleman anywhere, sir. It isn't easy to forget that bushy brown beard."

The Inspector seemed genuinely astonished. He stared at the English physician, and the English physician stared back— quite without expression. "Which one was he, Bell?"

"The very last one," said Bell positively.

"Of course," said Dr. Wardes in his cool voice, "you must realize, Inspector, that this is tommyrot. Rank nonsense. What possible connexion could I have had with your American jail-bird? What possible motive could I have had in visiting such a man, even if I did know him?"

"Are you asking *me,* Dr. Wardes?" The old man smiled. "I'm asking *you.* You've been identified by a man who meets thousands of people—a man trained by his job to remember faces. And, as Bell says, you're not particularly hard to remember. Well, sir?"

Dr. Wardes sighed. "It seems to me, Inspector, that the very—ah, singularity of this poor hirsute countenance of mine gives me a potent point of refutation. Dash it all, sir, don't you realize that it would be the simplest thing in the world to impersonate me, with this beard of mine?"

"Bravo," murmured Ellery, to Pepper. "Our good leech has a quick mind, Pepper."

"Too damned quick."

"That's very clever, Doctor, very clever indeed," said the Inspector appreciatively. "And quite true. Very well, we accept your word and we agree that you were impersonated by someone. All you have to do now, sir, is to account for your movements on the night of September thirtieth, in the interval during which this impersonation was taking place. Eh?"

Dr. Wardes frowned. "Thursday night last . . . Let me see." He mused, then shrugged. "Oh, come now, Inspector, that's not quite cricket. How can you expect me to recall where I was at a certain hour more than a week ago?"

"Well, you remembered where you were a week ago *Friday* night," remarked the Inspector dryly, "now that I come to think of it. It's true, though, that your memory had to be jogged a bit—"

He turned about at the sound of Joan's voice; everyone looked at her. She was sitting on the edge of her chair; and smiling fixedly. "My dear Doctor," she said, "I must say you're hardly the gallant, or else . . . You defended Mrs. Vreeland in the most cavalier manner yesterday—are you trying to preserve my poor tarnished reputation or have you really forgotten?"

"By Jove!" exclaimed Dr. Wardes instantly, his brown eyes lighting up. "Stupid—dashed stupid of me, Joan. I say, Inspector—curious what a man's mind is, eh?—I say, sir, I was with Miss Brett during that hour a week ago Thursday night!"

"You were." The Inspector looked slowly from the physician to Joan. "How nice."

"Yes," said Joan quickly, "it was after I had seen Grimshaw being admitted to the house by the maid. I returned to my room, and Dr. Wardes knocked at my door and asked if I shouldn't enjoy a spot somewhere in town . . ."

"Of course," murmured the Englishman, "and we left the house soon after, trotted to some little café or other on Fifty-seventh Street—I can't recollect which—had the jolliest evening, in fact. I believe it was midnight when we returned, wasn't it, Joan?"

"I believe it was, Doctor."

The old man grunted. "Very nice. *Very* nice . . . Well, Bell, do you still think that's the last man sitting over there?"

Bell said doggedly, "I know he is."

Dr. Wardes chuckled, and the Inspector rose with a little jump. His good-nature had vanished. "Bell," he snarled, "that accounts—we'll call it 'accounts'—for three; Sloane, Mrs. Sloane, Dr. Wardes. How about the other two men? Do you see either of them here?"

Bell shook his head. "I'm sure neither of them is among these gentlemen sitting about, sir. One of the two was a very big man—a giant, almost. His hair was getting grey, he had a red face all tanned up, sort of, and he spoke like an Irishman. I don't recall now whether he was the one who came between this lady and that gentleman—" he pointed to Mrs. Sloane and Dr. Wardes—"or whether he was one of the first two men."

"Big Irisher, hey?" muttered the Inspector. "By Christopher, where does *he* come in? We haven't run across a man of that description in this case! . . . All right, now, Bell. Here's the situation. Grimshaw came in with a man—a man all bundled up. Another man followed. Then came Mrs. Sloane. Then another man, and then Dr. Wardes. Two of the three men remaining are Sloane here and a big Irishman. How about the third man? Isn't there anybody here who might be that one?"

"I really can't say, sir," replied Bell regretfully. "I'm all mixed up on it. Maybe it's this Mr. Sloane who was the bundled up man, and maybe the other one—the missing one—came later. I—I . . ."

"Bell!" thundered the Inspector. Bell jumped. "You can't let it go that way! Can't you be sure?"

"I—Well, sir, no."

The Inspector looked around grumpily, weighing his audience in the scale of his sharp old eyes. It was evident that he was searching the room for someone who might have been the man whose description Bell did not recall. And then a wild light leaped into his eyes and he roared, "Damnation! I *knew* there was someone missing! I *felt* it!—Cheney! Where's that young whelp Cheney?"

Blank stares.

"Thomas! Who's been on duty at the front door?"

Velie started guiltily and said in a very small voice, "Flint, Inspector—Queen." Ellery quickly suppressed a smile; this was the first time he had ever heard the grizzled veteran address the old man by his formal title. Velie was frankly scared; he looked sick.

"*Get him!*"

Velie went away so quickly that even the Inspector, growling in his tiny throat, was slightly mollified. He brought in a quaking Flint—a Flint, almost as burly as the sergeant, and at the moment just as frightened-looking.

"Well, Flint," said the Inspector in a dangerous voice, "come in. *Come in!*"

Flint mumbled, "Yes, Chief. Yes, Chief."

"Flint, did you see Alan Cheney leave this house?"

Flint swallowed convulsively. "Yes, sir. Yes, Chief."

"When?"

"Last night, Chief. Eleven-fifteen, Chief."

"Where did he go?"

"He said somethin' about goin' down to his club."

The Inspector said calmly: "Mrs. Sloane, does your son belong to a club?"

Delphina Sloane was wringing her fingers; her eyes were tragic. "Why—no, Inspector, no. I can't understand—"

"When did he come back, Flint?"

"He—he didn't come back, Chief."

"He didn't come back?" The Inspector's voice became very quiet indeed. "Why didn't you report this to Sergeant Velie?"

Flint was in agony. "I—I was just goin' to report it, Chief. I came on at eleven last night and I'm—I'm due to be relieved in a coupla minutes. I was gonna report it, Chief. I thought maybe he was on a bat somewhere. Besides, Chief, he wasn't carryin' any luggage or anything. . . ."

"Wait for me outside. I'll attend to you later," said the old man in the same terrible, calm voice. Flint walked out like a man sentenced to death.*

---

* For the information of Mr. Queen's readers who have met Inspector Queen's men in previously published novels, it should be related that Detective Flint, as a result of his defection, was demoted from the detective force, but was later restored to his position because of thwarting a daring robbery; the present case being the earliest so far presented to the public.—J. J. McC.

Sergeant Velie's blue jowls trembled; he muttered: "Not Flint's fault, Inspector Queen. My fault. You told me to round up everybody. I should have done it myself—would've caught it sooner . . ."

"Shut up, Thomas. Mrs. Sloane, has your son a bank account?"

She quavered: "Yes. Yes, Inspector. The Mercantile National."

"Thomas, call the Mercantile National and find out if Alan Cheney withdrew any money this morning."

It was necessary for Sergeant Velie to brush by Joan Brett in order to reach the desk. He muttered an apology, but she did not move. And even Velie, immersed in his own private misery, was shocked by the horror and despair in the girl's eyes. Her hands were clenched in her lap; she barely breathed. Velie fumbled with his big jaw and walked completely around her chair. As he picked up the telephone his eyes were still upon her—the old hard eyes now.

"Haven't you any idea," the Inspector was snapping at Mrs. Sloane, "where your son went, Madame?"

"No. I—You don't think—?"

"How about you, Sloane? Did the boy say anything to you last night about going away?"

"Not a word. I can't—"

"Well, Thomas?" the old man asked impatiently. "What's the answer?"

"Getting it now." Velie spoke briefly to someone, nodded ponderously several times, and finally hung up. He jammed his hands into his pockets and said quietly: "Flew the coop, Chief. Cleaned out his bank account this morning at nine o'clock."

"By God," said the Inspector. Delphina Sloane slipped out of her chair, hesitated, looked about wildly and sat down again when Gilbert Sloane touched her arm. "Any details?"

"He had forty-two hundred in his account. Closed it, took

the money in small bills. Carried a small suitcase; looked new. Gave no explanation."

The Inspector went to the door. "Hagstrom!" A detective with Scandinavian features trotted up—he was jumpy, on the quivering alert. "Alan Cheney's gone. Withdrew forty-two hundred dollars from the Mercantile National at nine this morning. Find him. Find out where he spent the night, as a starter. Get a warrant and take it along with you. Camp on his trail. Take help. He may try to get out of the State. Make tracks, Hagstrom."

Hagstrom disappeared, and Velie followed him quickly.

The Inspector confronted them again; this time there was no benevolence in his glance as he pointed to Joan Brett. "You've had a hand in most everything so far, Miss Brett. Do you know anything about young Cheney's run-out?"

"Nothing, Inspector." Her voice was low.

"Well—anybody!" snarled the old man. "Why did he skip? What's behind all this?"

Questions. Steel-tipped words. Hidden wounds that bled internally. . . . And the minutes ticked by.

Delphina Sloane was sobbing. "Surely—Inspector—you aren't—you can't be thinking of . . . My Alan's a child, Inspector. Oh, he can't be—! There's something wrong, Inspector! Something wrong!"

"You said a mouthful there, Mrs. Sloane," said the Inspector with a ghastly grin. He wheeled—Sergeant Velie stood, like Nemesis, in the doorway. "What's up, Thomas?"

Velie extended his gargantuan arm. In his hand there was a small sheet of notepaper. The Inspector snatched it from him. "What's this?" Ellery and Pepper moved forward quickly; the three men read the few hurriedly scribbled lines on the sheet. The Inspector looked at Velie; Velie stalked over, and they went into a corner. The old man asked a single question, and Velie replied laconically. They came back to the centre of the room.

"Let me read you something, ladies and gentlemen." They

strained forward, breathing hard. The Inspector said: "I hold in my hand a message Sergeant Velie has just found in this house. It is signed by Alan Cheney." He raised the paper and began to read, slowly, and distinctly. "The message reads: 'I am going away. Perhaps forever. Under the circumstances—Oh, what's the use? Everything is all in a tangle, and I just can't say what. . . . Good-bye. I shouldn't be writing this at all. It's dangerous for you. Please—for your own sake—burn this. Alan.'"

Mrs. Sloane half-rose from her chair, her face saffron, screamed once, and fainted. Sloane caught her limp body as she sagged forward. The room burst into sound—cries, exclamations. The Inspector watched it all with calmness, quiet as a cat.

They managed, finally, to revive the woman. Then the Inspector went up to her and, very smoothly, slipped the paper under the woman's tear-swollen eyes. "Is this your son's handwriting, Mrs. Sloane?"

Her mouth was hideously wide. "Yes. Poor Alan. Poor Alan. Yes."

The Inspector's voice said clearly: "Sergeant Velie, where did you find this note?"

Velie growled, "Upstairs in one of the bedrooms. It was stuck under a mattress."

"And whose bedroom was it?"

"Miss Brett's."

*   *   *

It was too much—too much for everybody. Joan closed her eyes to shut out the hostile stares, the unspoken accusation, the Inspector's expressionless triumph.

"Well, Miss Brett?" That was all he said.

She opened her eyes, then, and he saw that they were filled with tears. "I—found it this morning. It had been slipped under the door of my room."

"Why didn't you report it at once?"

No reply.

"Why didn't you tell me about it when we discovered Cheney's absence?"

Silence.

"More important—what did Alan Cheney mean when he wrote: 'It's dangerous for you'?"

Whereupon the floodgates that are an anatomical adjunct of womankind's delicate structure opened with a rush, and Miss Joan Brett dissolved in those pearly tears before noted. She sat shaking, sobbing, gasping, sniffling—as forlorn a young lady as Manhattan encompassed that sunshiny October morning. It was a spectacle so naked that it embarrassed the others. Mrs. Simms, after an instinctive step toward the girl, feebly retreated. Dr. Wardes looked, for once, violently angry; brown lightnings flashed from his eyes as he glared at the Inspector. Ellery was shaking his head in disapproval. Only the Inspector remained unmoved.

"Well, Miss Brett?"

For answer she sprang from her chair, still not looking at them, one arm shielding her eyes, and ran blindly from the room. They heard her stumbling up the stairs.

"Sergeant Velie," said the Inspector coldly, "you'll see that Miss Brett's movements are carefully watched from this moment on."

Ellery touched his father's arm. The old man peered at him slyly. Ellery murmured, so that the others could not hear, "My dear, respected, even venerated father, you are probably the world's most competent policeman—but as a psychologist. . . ." He shook his head sadly.

CHAPTER 15

Maze

Now it will be seen that, while Ellery Queen until October the ninth was little more than a wraith haunting the fringes of the Khalkis case, that memorable Saturday afternoon found him, through the mercurial chemistry of his unpredictable nature, plunged very solidly into the heart of the problem—no longer an observer, now a prime mover.

The time was ripe for revelations; the stage was so faultlessly set that he could not resist the temptation to leap into the spotlight. It will be remembered always that this was a younger Ellery than has heretofore been encountered—an Ellery with a cosmic egotism that is commonly associated with sophomores. Life was sweet, there was a knotty problem to solve, a tortuous maze to stride confidently through, and, to add a pinch of drama, a very superior sort of District Attorney to bait.

It began, as so many portentous events have since begun, in the inviolacy of Inspector Queen's office in Center Street. Sampson was there, thrashing about like a suspicious tiger; Pepper was there, looking very thoughtful; the Inspector was there, slumped in his chair, seething fires in his grey old eyes and his lips as tight as a purse's mouth. Who could resist, indeed? Especially since, in the midst of an aimless Sampsonian summation of the case, Inspector Queen's secretary scurried in, out of breath with excitement, to announce that Mr. James J. Knox, *the* James J. Knox—possessor of more millions than it was decent for any man to amass—Knox the banker, Knox the Wall Street king, Knox the-friend-of-the-President—was outside demanding to see Inspector Richard Queen. Resistance after that would have been superhuman.

Knox was really a legend. He used his millions and the power which accompanied them to keep himself out of, rather than in, the public eye. It was his name, not himself, that people knew. It was only human, therefore, for Messieurs the Queens, Sampson and Pepper to rise as one man when Knox was ushered into the office, and to exhibit more deference and fluster than the strict conventions of democracy prescribe. The great man shook their hands limply and sat down without being asked.

He was the drying hulk of a giant—nearly sixty at this time and visibly drained of his fabulous physical vigour. The hair of his head, brows, and moustache was completely white; the trap of his mouth was a little slack now; only his marbly grey eyes were young.

"Conference?" he asked. His voice was unexpectedly soft— a deceptive voice, low-pitched, and hesitant.

"Ah—yes, yes," said Sampson hastily. "We've been discussing the Khalkis case. A very sad affair, Mr. Knox."

"Yes." Knox looked squarely at the Inspector. "Progress?"

"Some." Inspector Queen was unhappy. "It's all mixed up, Mr. Knox. A great many threads to untangle. I can't say we see daylight yet."

This was the moment. The moment, perhaps, which a still younger Ellery may have envisioned in his day-dreams—the baffled representatives of the law, the presence of mighty personality. . . . "You're being modest, Dad," said Ellery Queen. Nothing more at the moment. Just the gently chiding tone, the little gesture of deprecation, the precise quarter-smile. "You're being modest, Dad," as if the Inspector knew what he was talking about.

Inspector Queen sat very quietly indeed, and Sampson's lips parted. The great one looked from Ellery to his father with judicious inquiry. Pepper was staring open-mouthed.

"You see, Mr. Knox," Ellery went on in the same humble tone—oh, it was perfect! he thought; "you see, sir, while some odds and ends are still strewn about the landscape, my father neglects to say that the main body of the case has taken definitely solid shape."

"Don't quite understand," said Knox encouragingly.

"Ellery," began the Inspector, in a tremulous voice . . .

"It seems clear enough, Mr. Knox," said Ellery with whimsical sadness. Heavens, what a moment! he thought. "The case is solved."

It is at such instants snatched out of the racing mill-stream of time that egotists achieve their noblest riches. Ellery was magnificent—he studied the changing expression on the faces of the Inspector, Sampson, Pepper like a scientist watching an unfamiliar but anticipated test-tube reaction. Knox, of course, grasped nothing of the by-play. He was merely interested.

"The murderer of Grimshaw—" choked the District Attorney.

"Who is he, Mr. Queen?" asked Knox mildly.

Ellery sighed and lit a cigarette before replying. It would never do to hurry the *dénouement*. This must be cherished to the last precious moment. Then he allowed the words to trickle through a cloud of smoke. "Georg Khalkis," he said.

*   *   *

District Attorney Sampson confessed long afterward that, had James J. Knox not been present during this drama, he would have picked up one of the telephones on the Inspector's desk and hurled it at Ellery's head. He did not believe. He *could* not believe. A dead man—a man, moreover, blind before he had

died—as the murderer! It defied all the laws of credibility. It
was more than that—the smug vapourings of a clown, the chi-
mera of a heated brain, the . . . Sampson, it will be noted, felt
very strongly about it.

Restrained, however, by the Presence, he merely shifted in
his chair, looking ill, his busy brain already wrestling with the
problem of covering up this statement of utter lunacy.

Knox spoke first, because Knox required no emotional recovery. Ellery's *pronunciamiento* made him blink, it is true, but
an instant after he said, in his soft voice, "Khalkis. . . . Now, I
wonder."

The Inspector then found his tongue. "I think," he said, lick-
ing his old red lips quickly, "I think *we* owe Mr. Knox an
explanation—eh, son?" His tone belied his glance; his glance
was furious.

Ellery leaped from his chair. "We certainly do," he said
heartily. "Especially since Mr. Knox is personally interested in
the case." He perched on the edge of the Inspector's desk. "Really a unique problem, this one," he said. "It has some positively
inspired points:

"Please attend. There were two principal clues: the first re-
volving about the necktie Georg Khalkis was wearing on the
morning of his collapse from heart-failure; the second concerning the percolator and tea-cups in Khalkis's study."

Knox looked slightly blank. Ellery said: "I beg your pardon,
Mr. Knox. Of course you're unfamiliar with these things," and
rapidly outlined the facts surrounding the investigation. When
Knox nodded his comprehension, Ellery continued. "Now let
me explain what we were able to glean from this business of
Khalkis's neckties." He was careful to pluralize himself; Ellery,
although this had been questioned by malicious persons, possessed a strong family pride. "On Saturday morning a week ago,
the morning of Khalkis's death, you will observe that Khalkis's
imbecile valet Demmy prepared his cousin's raiment, by his
own testimony, *according to schedule*. It was to be expected,

therefore, that Khalkis should have been wearing the precise items of clothing specified in the regular Saturday schedule. Refer to the Saturday schedule, and what do you find? You find that, among other articles, Khalkis should have been wearing a *green* moiré necktie.

"So far, so good. Demmy, concluding his morning ritual of assisting his cousin to dress, or at least of laying out the scheduled clothing, leaves at nine o'clock. Fifteen minutes elapse, an interval during which Khalkis, fully attired, is alone in his study. At nine-fifteen Gilbert Sloane enters to confer with Khalkis about the day's projects. And what do we find? We find, according to Sloane's testimony—not emphasized, of course, but there nevertheless—that at nine-fifteen Khalkis is wearing a *red* tie."

He had his audience now; his feeling of satisfaction manifested itself in a bawdy chuckle. "An interesting situation, eh? Now, if Demmy told the truth, we are confronted with a curious discrepancy which pules for explanation. If Demmy told the truth—and his mental condition obviates mendaciousness— Khalkis therefore must have been wearing the scheduled, or *green,* tie at nine o'clock, the time Demmy left him.

"How explain the discrepancy, then? Well, this is the inevitable explanation: in the fifteen-minute period in which he was alone, Khalkis, for some reason we shall probably never know, went into his bedroom and *changed* his tie, discarding the green one given him by Demmy for one of the red ties hanging on the rack in his bedroom wardrobe.

"Now we also know from Sloane's testimony that, during his confabulation with Khalkis some time after nine-fifteen that morning, Khalkis fingered the tie he was wearing—which Sloane had already noticed, on originally entering the room, to be red—and said, in these exact words: 'Before you leave remind me to call Barrett's and order some new ties *like the one I'm wearing.*'" His eyes were bright. "The verbal italicization is mine. Now observe. Just as Miss Brett was leaving Khalkis's study much later, she heard Khalkis call the number of Barrett's, his haberdasher. Barrett's, as a check-up later established, delivered—according to the testimony of the clerk who spoke to Khalkis—*exactly what Khalkis ordered*. But what was it that Khalkis had ordered? Obviously, what had been delivered. But what had been delivered? Six *red* ties!"

Ellery leaned forward, pounding the desk. "To sum up: Khalkis, to have said he was going to order neckties like the one he was wearing, and then to have ordered red ties, must therefore have *known* that he was wearing a red tie. Fundamental. In other words, Khalkis knew the colour of the necktie that was draped around his neck at the time Sloane conferred with him.

"But how could he, a blind man, have known the colour, since it was *not* the colour called for by the Saturday schedule? Well, he might have been told the colour by someone. But by whom? Only three people saw him that morning before he put in the call to Barrett's—Demmy, who dressed him according to schedule; Sloane, whose word-for-word conversation concerning the ties did not once refer to them by colour; and Joan Brett, whose one reference to the ties that morning, addressed to Khalkis, also omitted mention of its colour.

"In other words, Khalkis wasn't *told* the colour of the changed tie. Was it mere accident, then, if he himself had changed from the scheduled green to the red one he later wore—was it mere accident that he picked a red tie from the rack? Yes, that's possible—for remember that the cravats on the rack in the wardrobe were not arranged by colours—they were mingled in a confusion of colours. But how account for the fact that, whether he picked the red tie by accident or not, he *knew*—as his subsequent actions proved—that he had picked a red tie?"

Ellery ground his cigarette slowly against the bottom of an ashtray on the desk. "Gentlemen, there is only one way in which Khalkis could have *known* he was wearing a red tie. And that is—he could distinguish its colour visually—*he could see*!

"But he was blind, you say?

"And here is the crux of my first series of deductions. For, as Dr. Frost testified and Dr. Wardes corroborated, Georg Khalkis was afflicted by a peculiar type of blindness in which sight might return spontaneously at any time!

"What is the conclusion, then? That last Saturday morning, at least, Mr. Georg Khalkis was no more blind than you or I."

Ellery smiled. "Questions arise at once. If he could suddenly see after an authentic period of blindness, why didn't he excitedly inform his household—his sister, Sloane, Demmy, Joan Brett? Why didn't he telephone his doctor—in fact, why didn't he inform Dr. Wardes, the eye-specialist then visiting in his house? For only one possible psychological reason: he did not want it known that he could see again; it suited some purpose of his own to continue leading people to believe that he was *still* blind. What could this purpose have been?"

Ellery paused and drew a deep breath. Knox was leaning forward, his hard eyes unwavering; the others were stiff with attentiveness.

"Let's leave it there for the moment," said Ellery quietly, "and tackle the clue of the percolator and the tea-cups.

"Observe the superficial evidence. The tea-things found on the tabouret indicated clearly that three persons had drunk tea. Why doubt it? Three cups showed the usual signs of usage by their dried dregs and the ring-stains just below the rims inside; three dried tea-bags were in evidence and prodding them in fresh water elicited only a weak tea-solution, proving that these bags had actually been employed in making tea; three desiccated, squeezed pieces of lemon were there; and three silver spoons with a cloudy film, indicating use—you see, everything tended to show that three persons had drunk tea. Furthermore, this substantiated what we had already learned; for Khalkis had told Joan Brett on Friday night that he expected two visitors, the two visitors had been seen arriving and entering the study—and this made, with Khalkis himself, three people. Again—superficial corroboration.

"But—and it's a leviathan 'but,' gentlemen—" grinned Ellery, "how superficial the indications were was at once revealed when we looked into the percolator. What did we see there? A percolator, to put it tersely, with too much water. We set about proving our surmise that there was too much water. By draining the water from the percolator we discovered that it filled five cups—the fifth not quite full, to be sure, since we had previously drawn off a tiny sample of the stale water in a vial for later chemical analysis. Five cupfuls, then. Later, when we *refilled* the percolator with fresh water, we drained off exactly six cupfuls when the tap ran dry. This meant, then, a six-cup percolator—and the stale water had filled five cups. But how was this possible if *three* cupfuls had been used for tea by Khalkis and his two visitors, as all the superficial signs indicated? According to our test, only *one* cupful had been taken from the percolator, not three. Does this mean that only a third of a cup of water had been used for each of the three men? Impossible—there was a circular tea-stain around the inner *rim* of the cup, indicating that each cup had been *full*. Well, then, was it possible that three cupfuls actually had been drained from the percolator, but that later somebody had added water to the water already in the percolator to make up the difference of the two missing cupfuls? But no—an analysis of the stale water from the little vialful I had taken indicated by a simple chemical test that no fresh water was present in the percolator.

"There was only one conclusion: the water in the percolator was authentic but the evidences on the three cups were *not*. Someone had deliberately tampered with the tea-things—the cups, the spoons, the lemon—*to make it appear that three people had drunk tea*. Whoever tampered with the tea-things had made just one mistake—he had used the same cupful of water for each cup, instead of taking three separate cupfuls out of the percolator. But why go to all this trouble to *make it appear* that three people were there when it was *accepted* that three were there—from the two visitors and Khalkis's own instructions?

For only one possible reason—emphasis. But if three people were there, why emphasize what is established?

"Only because three people, strange as it seems, were *not* there."

He fixed them with the feverish glittering eye of triumph. Someone—Ellery was amused to see that it was Sampson—sighed appreciatively. Pepper was profoundly absorbed in the discourse, and the Inspector was nodding his head sadly. James Knox began to rub his chin.

"You see," continued Ellery in his sharpest lecture-voice, "if three people had been present and all had drunk tea, there would have been three cupfuls of water missing from the percolator. Suppose now, that all had not drunk—people sometimes refuse such mild refreshment in these days of American prohibition. Very well. What's wrong in that? Why go through this tortuous rigmarole of making it *appear* that all had drunk? Again, only to substantiate the accepted belief, fostered by Khalkis himself, please note, that three were present in that study a week ago Friday night—the night Grimshaw was murdered."

He went on rapidly. "We are therefore faced with this interesting problem: if three were not present, how many were? Well, there might have been more than three: four, five, six, any number of people might have slipped into that study without being seen after Joan Brett admitted the two visitors and went upstairs to tuck the bibulous Alan in his little bed. But, since the number cannot by any means at our disposal be fixed, the theory of more than three leads nowhere. On the other hand, if we examine the theory that there were fewer than three present, we find ourselves on a heated trail.

"It couldn't have been one, for two were actually seen entering the study. We have shown that, whatever it was, it was not three. Then, according to the only alternative in the second theory—the theory of fewer than three—it must have been two.

"If two people were there, what are our difficulties? We

know that Albert Grimshaw was one—he was seen and later identified by Miss Brett. Khalkis himself was, by all the laws of probability, the second of the two. If this is true, then, the man who accompanied Grimshaw into the house—the man 'all bundled up,' as Miss Brett described him—must have been Khalkis! But is this possible?"

Ellery lit another cigarette. "It is possible, decidedly. One curious circumstance seems to bear it out. You will recall that when the two visitors entered the study, Miss Brett was not in a position to see into it; in fact, Grimshaw's companion had shoved her out of the way, as if to prevent her from catching a glimpse of what was—or what was not—in the interior of the room. There may be many explanations for this action, but certainly its implication is in tune with the theory of Khalkis being the companion, for he naturally would not want Miss Brett to look into the study and notice that he was not there when he should have been there. . . . What else? Very well—what are the characteristics of Grimshaw's companion? Physically he approximated Khalkis's size and build. That's one thing. For another, from the incident of Mrs. Simms's precious puss, Tootsie, Grimshaw's companion could *see*. For the cat, perfectly still, lay on a rug before the door and the bundled man checked himself with one foot in the air and then deliberately walked around it; if he were blind, he could not have avoided stepping on the tabby. This checks, too; for from the necktie deductions we have demonstrated that Khalkis was not blind the following morning, but was pretending to be—and we have every reason to postulate the theory that his sight may have returned to him at any time after a week ago Thursday, on the basis of the fact that the last time Dr. Wardes examined Khalkis's eyes was on that day—the day *before* the incident of the two visitors.

"But this provides the answer to my former question, which was: Why did Khalkis keep silent about his recovery of sight? The answer is: If Grimshaw were discovered murdered, if

suspicion pointed in Khalkis's direction, he would have the al-
ibi of blindness to support his innocence—for it would be said
that Khalkis, blind, could not have been the unknown man, the
murderer of Grimshaw. The explanation of how Khalkis engineered the physical elements of his deception is simple: after
he had ordered the tea-things that Friday night and Mrs. Simms
had retired, he must have slipped into his overcoat and derby
and stolen out of the house, met Grimshaw probably by prearrangement, and re-entered with Grimshaw as if he were one of
the two expected visitors."

Knox had not stirred in his chair; he seemed about to speak,
then blinked and maintained his silence.

"What confirmations have we of Khalkis's plot and decep-
tions?" continued Ellery blithely. "For one thing, he himself fostered the idea of three people—by his instructions to Miss
Brett—deliberately saying that two visitors were expected, that
one of them wished to keep his identity secret. For another, he
deliberately withheld the information that he had recovered
his sight—a damning circumstance. For another, we know positively that Grimshaw was strangled from six to twelve hours
before Khalkis died."

"Damned funny mistake to make!" muttered the District
Attorney.

"What was that?" asked Ellery pleasantly.

"I mean this business of Khalkis using the same water to
fill each of the faked cups. Pretty dumb, I'd say, considering
how clever the rest of it was."

Pepper interrupted with a boyish eagerness. "It seems to
me, Chief," he said, "with due respect for Mr. Queen's opinion,
that it may not have been a mistake after all."

"And how do you figure that, Pepper?" asked Ellery with interest.

"Well, suppose Khalkis didn't *know* that the percolator was
full. Suppose he took it for granted that it was only half-full or

something. Or suppose he didn't know it was a percolator that normally held six cups when full. Either one of these suppositions would account for his seeming stupidity."

"There's something in that." Ellery smiled. "Very well. Now this solution does leave certain loose ends, none of which we can settle conclusively, although we can hazard reasonable inferences. For one thing, if Khalkis killed Grimshaw, what was his motive? Well, we know that Grimshaw visited him, alone, the night before. And that this visit gave rise to Khalkis's instructions to Woodruff, his attorney, to draw up a new will—in fact, he telephoned Woodruff late that night. Urgency, then—pressure. The new will changed the legatee of the Khalkis Galleries, a considerable inheritance, and nothing else; who this new legatee was Khalkis took scrupulous pains to keep secret—not even his attorney was to know. It isn't far-fetched, I think, to say that Grimshaw, or possibly someone Grimshaw represented, was the new legatee. But why should Khalkis do this amazing thing? The obvious answer is blackmail, considering the character of Grimshaw and his criminal record. Don't forget, too, that Grimshaw was connected with the profession; he had been a museum attendant, he had been jailed for the unsuccessful theft of a painting. Blackmail by Grimshaw would mean a hold on Khalkis, who is also in the profession. That to me seems the probable motive; Grimshaw had something on Khalkis, something in all likelihood connected with a shady phase of the art-business or some nefarious transaction involving an art-object.

"Now let me reconstruct the crime with this admittedly suppositional motive as a foundation. Grimshaw visited Khalkis Thursday night—during which visit we may assume that the ultimatum, or the blackmail project, was launched by the jailbird. Khalkis, either for Grimshaw or Grimshaw's factor, agreed to alter his will in payment—you will probably find Khalkis to have been in straitened financial circumstances, unable to pay cash. Khalkis, after instructing his lawyer to draw up a new will, either felt that the change of will would still leave him open to future blackmail, or suffered a complete change of heart: in any event, he decided to kill Grimshaw rather than pay—and this decision, incidentally, points strongly to the fact that Grimshaw was acting for himself and not for someone else, otherwise Grimshaw's death would be of little avail to Khalkis, since there would still be someone in the background to take up the blackmail cudgels for the murdered man. At any rate, Grimshaw returned the next night, Friday, to see the new will for himself, fell into Khalkis's trap as indicated, and was killed; Khalkis hid his body somewhere in the vicinity, perhaps, until he could permanently dispose of it. But then fate stepped in and Khalkis, from the excitement of the racking events, died of heart-failure the following morning before he was able to finish the job of permanently getting rid of the body."

"But look here—" began Sampson.

Ellery grinned. "I know. You want to ask me: If Khalkis killed Grimshaw and then died himself, who buried Grimshaw in Khalkis's coffin, after the Khalkis funeral?

"Obviously, it must have been someone who discovered Grimshaw's body and utilized Khalkis's grave as a permanent hiding-place. Very well—why didn't this unknown gravedigger produce the body instead of burying it secretly, why didn't he announce his discovery? We may suppose that he suspected where the guilt lay, or perhaps had an erroneous suspicion, and took this means of disposing of the body to close the case forever—either to protect the name of a dead man or the life of a living one. Whatever the true explanation is, there is at least one person in our roster of suspects who fits the theory: the man who drew all his money from his bank and disappeared when he was specifically instructed to keep available; the man who, when the grave was unexpectedly opened and Grimshaw's corpse found, must have seen that the jig was up, took fright, lost his nerve and fled. I refer, of course, to Khalkis's nephew, Alan Cheney.

"And I think, gentlemen," concluded Ellery with a smile of

satisfaction that bordered on smugness, "I think that when you find Cheney you will have cleared up the case."

Knox had the queerest look on his face. The Inspector spoke for the first time since Ellery had begun his recital. He said querulously: "But who stole the new will from Khalkis's wall-safe? Khalkis was dead by that time—*he* couldn't have done it. Was it Cheney?"

"Probably not. You see, Gilbert Sloane had the strongest motive for the theft of the will in the first place, since he was the only one of our suspects affected by it. This means that the *theft* of the will by Sloane has nothing to do with the crime itself—it's merely a fortuitous detail. And naturally we have no evidence with which to pin the theft to Sloane. On the other hand, when you find Cheney you will probably discover that *he* destroyed the will. When he buried Grimshaw, he must have found the new will hidden in the coffin—where Sloane had put it—read it, saw that Grimshaw was the new beneficiary, and took it away, box and all, to destroy it. The destruction of the will would mean that Khalkis died intestate, and Cheney's mother, Khalkis's next of kin, would inherit most of the estate through later apportionment by the Surrogate."

Sampson looked worried. "And how about all those visitors to Grimshaw's hotel room the night before the murder? Where do they fit?"

Ellery waved his hand. "Mere froth, Sampson. They aren't important. You see—"

Someone rapped on the door and the Inspector said with irritation, "Come!" It opened to admit the small, drab detective named Johnson. "Well, well, Johnson?"

Johnson quickly crossed the room and bent over the Inspector's chair. "Got the Brett gal outside, Chief," he whispered. "She insisted on coming down here."

"To see me?"

Johnson said apologetically, "She did say she wanted to see Mr. *Ellery* Queen, Chief. . . ."

"Show her in."

Johnson opened the door for her. The men rose. Joan was looking especially lovely in something grey-and-blue, but her eyes were tragic and she faltered at the door.

"You wanted to see Mr. Queen?" the Inspector asked crisply. "We're engaged at the moment, Miss Brett."

"It's—I think it may be important, Inspector Queen."

Ellery said swiftly: "You've heard from Cheney!" but she shook her head. Ellery frowned. "Stupid of me. Miss Brett, may I present Mr. Knox, Mr. Sampson. . . ." The District Attorney nodded briefly; Knox said: "Had the pleasure." There was a little awkward silence. Ellery offered the girl a chair, and they all sat down.

"I—I scarcely know where or how to begin," Joan said, fumbling with her gloves. "You will think I'm silly. It seems so *ridiculously* petty. And yet . . ."

Ellery said encouragingly, "Something you've discovered, Miss Brett? Or something you forgot to tell us?"

"Yes. I mean—something I forgot to tell you." She spoke in a very small voice, a ghost of her full voice. "Something—something about the tea-cups."

"The *tea-cups!*" The words shot out of Ellery's mouth like a missile.

"Why—yes. You see, when I was originally questioned, I really didn't recall. . . . It's only just come to me. I've been—I've been thinking things over, you see."

"Go on, please," said Ellery sharply.

"It was the—the day when I moved the tabouret with the tea-things from the desk to the alcove. I moved it out of the way—"

"You told us that once before, Miss Brett."

"But I didn't tell you everything, Mr. Queen. I remember now that there was something *different* about those tea-cups."

Ellery sat on his father's desk like a Buddha perched on a mountain-top. Grotesquely still. . . . All his poise had fled. He was staring at Joan idiotically.

She went on with a little rush. "You see, when *you* found the tea-cups in the study there were *three* dirty cups—" Ellery's lips moved soundlessly. "And now I recall that when I moved the tabouret out of the way, the afternoon of the funeral, there was only one dirty cup. . . ."

Ellery rose abruptly. All the humour had fled his face, and its lines were harsh, almost unpleasant. "Be very careful, Miss Brett." His voice cracked. "This is extremely important. You say now that last Tuesday, when you shifted the tabouret from the desk to the alcove, there were *two clean cups* on the tray—that only one showed signs of having been used?"

"Exactly. I'm frightfully sure. In fact, I remember now that one cup was nearly full of stale cold tea; there was a piece of dried lemon in the saucer, and a dirty spoon. Everything else on the tray was perfectly clean—unused."

"How many pieces of lemon were there in the lemon-plate?"

"I'm sorry, Mr. Queen, I can't recall that. We Britishers don't use lemon, you know. That's a filthy Russian habit. And tea-balls!" She shuddered. "But I'm positive about the cups."

Ellery asked doggedly: "This was *after* Khalkis's death?"

"Yes, indeed," sighed Joan. "Not only after his death, but after his funeral. Tuesday, as I said."

Ellery's teeth dug into his lower lip; his eyes were like stone. "Thank you a thousand times, Miss Brett." His voice was low. "You have saved us from a most embarrassing situation. . . . Please go now."

She smiled timidly, looked about as if for warm commendation, a word of praise. Nobody paid the slightest attention to her; they were all looking quizzically at Ellery. She rose without another word and left the room; Johnson followed her and closed the door softly behind him.

Sampson was the first to speak. "Well, my boy, that *was* a fiasco." He said kindly, "Come now, Ellery, don't take it so hard. We all make mistakes. And yours was a brilliant one."

Ellery waved one limp hand; his head was on his chest and his voice was muffled. "Mistake, Sampson? This is utterly inexcusable. I should be whipped and sent home with my tail between my legs. . . ."

James Knox rose suddenly. He examined Ellery shrewdly, with a glint of humour. "Mr. Queen. Your solution depended upon two major elements—"

"I know, sir, I know," groaned Ellery. "Please don't rub it in."

"You'll learn, young man," said the great one, "that there can be no success without failure. . . . Two elements. One was the tea-cups. Ingenious, very ingenious explanation, Mr. Queen, but Miss Brett has exploded it. You now have no reason to claim that only two people were present. You said from the tea-cups that only two were involved from first to last, Khalkis and Grimshaw; that a deliberate attempt had been made to make it appear that three were involved; that there never was a third man, but that Khalkis himself was the second."

"That's right," said Ellery sadly, "but now—"

"That's wrong," said Knox in his soft voice, "because there *was* a third man. And I can prove it by direction, not inference."

"What's that?" Ellery's head snapped up as if it were set on springs. "What's that, sir? There was? You can prove it? How do you know?"

Knox chuckled. "I know," he said, "because I was the third man!"

CHAPTER 16

Yeast

Years later Ellery Queen was to go back in memory to this moment with the sad remark: "I date my maturity from Knox's revelation. It changed my entire conception of myself and my faculties."

The whole delicate structure of his reasoning, so glibly outlined, toppled and shivered into fragments at his feet. This in itself would not have been so disastrous to his ego had it not been coupled with a strong element of personal mortification. He had been "smart" about it. He had been so clever and subtle.... The very phenomenon—of Knox's august presence—that originally inspired him to make a show of himself now faced about to leer at him and burn his cheeks with shame.

His mind was working furiously, trying to put down the rebellion of the facts, trying to forget what a sophomoric young fool he had been. Little waves of panic slapped against his brain, filming the clarity of his thoughts. But one thing he knew—he must work on Knox. Knox's extraordinary statement. Knox the third man. Khalkis—the case against Khalkis based on the tea-cups, the third man—in ruins.... The blindness! Was that too composed of the same thin air? Must come back to that, find another explanation....

Mercifully, they ignored him as he crouched in his chair. The Inspector, with feverish questions, held the great man's attention. What happened that night? How had Knox come to be in Grimshaw's company? What did it all mean? . . .

Knox explained, his hard grey eyes appraising the Inspector and Sampson. Three years before, it seemed, Khalkis had approached Knox, one of his best clients, with a strange proposition. Khalkis had claimed to have in his possession an almost priceless painting which he was willing to sell to Knox provided Knox promised never to exhibit it. Peculiar request! Knox had been cautious. What was it? And why this secrecy? Khalkis had been apparently honest. The painting, he had said, had been in the possession of the Victoria Museum in London. It was valued by the Museum at a million dollars. . . .

"A million dollars, Mr. Knox?" asked the District Attorney. "I don't know much about art-objects, but I'd say that was a whale of a lot of money even for a masterpiece."

Knox smiled briefly. "Not for this masterpiece, Sampson. It was a Leonardo."

"Leonardo Da Vinci?"

"Yes."

"But I thought all his great paintings are—"

"This one was a discovery of the Victoria Museum's some years ago. A detail in oils from Leonardo's uncompleted fresco project for the Hall of the Palazzo Vecchio at Florence in the early part of the sixteenth century. It's a long story I won't go into now. A precious find the Victoria called, 'Detail from the Battle of the Standard.' A new Leonardo take my word for it, is cheap at a million."

"Go on, sir."

"Naturally I wanted to know how Khalkis had got his hooks on it. Hadn't heard anything about its being on the market. Khalkis was vague—led me to believe he was acting as American agent for the Museum. Museum wanted no publicity, he said—might be a storm of British protest if it was found the

painting had left England. Beautiful thing, it was. He hauled it
out. Couldn't resist it. I bought at Khalkis's price—seven hundred and fifty thousand, a bargain."

The Inspector nodded. "I think I see what's coming."

"Yes. Week ago Friday a man calling himself Albert Grimshaw called on me—ordinarily wouldn't be allowed in—but he
sent in a scribbled note with the words, 'Battle of the Standard,'
and I had to see him. Small dark man, eyes of a rat. Shrewd—
hard bargainer. Told me an amazing story. Gist of it was that the
Leonardo I'd purchased from Khalkis in good faith wasn't offered for sale by the Museum at all—it was stolen goods. Stolen
from the Museum five years ago. He, Grimshaw, had been the
thief, and he made no bones about it."

District Attorney Sampson was completely absorbed now;
the Inspector and Pepper leaned forward. Ellery did not move;
but his eyes were on Knox unblinkingly.

Knox went on, unhurried, coldly precise. Grimshaw, working under the alias of Graham as an attendant in the Victoria
Museum, had contrived five years before to steal the Leonardo
and make his escape with it to the United States. Daring theft,
undiscovered until Grimshaw had left the country. He had
come to Khalkis in New York to sell it under cover. Khalkis was
honest, but he was a passionate art-lover and he could not resist the temptation to own one of the world's great master-
pieces. He wanted it for himself: Grimshaw turned it over to
him for a half-million dollars. Before the money could be paid,
Grimshaw was arrested in New York on an old forgery charge
and sent to Sing Sing for five years. In the meantime, two years
after Grimshaw was imprisoned, it seemed that Khalkis through
disastrous investments had lost most of his negotiable fortune;
he was desperately in need of cash and had sold the painting to
Knox, as already related, for three quarters of a million dollars,
Knox purchasing it on the basis of Khalkis's fictitious story, ignorant of the fact that it had been stolen.

"When Grimshaw was released from Sing Sing a week ago

Tuesday," continued Knox, "his first thought was to collect the half-million Khalkis owed him. Thursday night, he told me, he had called on Khalkis demanding payment. Khalkis, it seemed, had continued to make bad investments; claimed to have no money. Grimshaw demanded the painting, Khalkis ultimately had to confess that he'd resold it to me. Grimshaw threatened Khalkis—said he'd kill him if payment wasn't made. He left and the next day came to me, as I've said.

"Now Grimshaw's purpose was evident. He wanted *me* to pay him the half-million Khalkis owed him. Naturally I refused. Grimshaw was ugly, threatened to make public my illegal possession of the stolen Leonardo unless I paid. I became angry, thoroughly aroused." Knox's jaws snapped like the jaws of a trap; his eyes shot grey fire. "Angry at Khalkis for having duped me, put me into this horrible position. Telephoned Khalkis, arranged an appointment with him for me and Grimshaw. For that very night—last Friday night. Deal was shady; I demanded protection. Khalkis, broken up, promised over the phone that he would have everybody away, that his own secretary, Miss Brett, who knew nothing about the affair and could be depended upon to be discreet, would admit me and Grimshaw. Wasn't taking any chances. Nasty business. That night Grimshaw and I went to Khalkis's house. Admitted by Miss Brett. Found Khalkis alone in his study. Talked turkey."

The blush, the burn had left Ellery's cheeks and ears; he was intent now, like the others, on Knox's recital.

Knox had at once made it clear to Khalkis, he said, that he expected the dealer to appease Grimshaw, at least to the extent of extricating Knox from the tangled situation into which Khalkis had forced him. Nervous and desperate, Khalkis claimed to have no money at all; but the night before, Khalkis had said, after Grimshaw's first visit, he had thought things over and decided to offer Grimshaw the only payment in his power. Khalkis had then produced a new will which he had had drawn up the same morning, and which he had signed; the new will made Grimshaw legatee of Khalkis's galleries and establishment, worth considerably more than the half-million he owed Grimshaw.

"Grimshaw was no fool," said Knox grimly. "Flatly refused. Said he wouldn't have a chance to collect if the will were contested by relatives—even then he'd have to wait for Khalkis to 'kick off,' as he said graphically. No, he said, he wanted his money in negotiable securities or cash—on the spot. He said he wasn't 'the only one' in on the deal. He had one partner, he said, the only other person in the world who knew about the business of the stolen painting and Khalkis's purchase of it; he said that the night before, after seeing Khalkis, he had met his partner and they had gone to Grimshaw's room at the Hotel Benedict, and he had told his partner that Khalkis had resold the Leonardo to me. They wanted no will, or truck like that. If Khalkis couldn't pay on the spot, they were willing to take his promissory note, made out to bearer—"

"To protect the partner," muttered the Inspector.

"Yes. Made out to bearer. Note for five hundred thousand to be met within one month, even if Khalkis had to sell out his business under the hammer to get the money. Grimshaw laughed in his nasty way and said it wouldn't do either of us any good to kill him, because his partner knew everything and would hound us both if anything happened to him. And he wasn't telling us who the partner was, either, he said with a significant wink. . . . The man was odious."

"Certainly," said Sampson, frowning, "this story changes the complexion of things, Mr. Knox. . . . Smart of Grimshaw, or his partner, who probably engineered the business. Keeping the partner's identity secret was a protection to Grimshaw as well as the partner."

"Obvious, Sampson," said Knox. "To get on. Khalkis, blind as he was, made out the promissory note, to bearer, signed it and gave it to Grimshaw, who took it and stowed it away in a tattered old wallet he carried."

"We found the wallet," put in the Inspector severely, "and nothing in it."

"So I understand from the papers. I then told Khalkis I washed my hands of the entire affair. Told him to take his medicine. Khalkis was a broken, blind old man when we left. Over-reached himself. Bad business. We left the house together, Grimshaw and I; didn't meet anyone on the way out, fortunately for me. Told Grimshaw on the steps outside that so long as he steered clear of me I'd forget everything. Bamboozle me, would they! Mad clear through."

"When did you see Grimshaw last, Mr. Knox?" asked the Inspector.

"At that time. Glad to be rid of him. Crossed over to the corner of Fifth Avenue, hailed a cab and went home."

"Where was Grimshaw?"

"Last I saw of him he was standing on the sidewalk looking at me. Swear I saw a malicious grin on his face."

"Directly in front of the Khalkis house?"

"Yes. There's more. Next afternoon, after I'd already heard of Khalkis's death—that was last Saturday—I received a personal note from Khalkis. By the postmark it was mailed that morning, before Khalkis died. Must have written it just after Grimshaw and I left the house Friday night and had it mailed in the morning. Got it with me." Knox dug into one of his pockets and produced an envelope. He handed it to the Inspector, who took a single sheet of notepaper from it and read the scrawled message aloud:

Dear J. J. K.: What happened to-night must put me in a bad light. But I could not help it. I lost money and my hand was forced. I didn't mean to involve you, didn't think this rascal Grimshaw would approach you and try to blackmail you. I can assure you that from now on you will be in no way implicated. I shall try to shut up Grimshaw and this partner of his, although it will mean I shall probably have to sell my business, auctioning off the items in my own galleries and if necessary borrowing against my insurance. At any rate you are safe, because the only ones who know of your possession of the painting are ourselves and Grimshaw—and of course his partner, and I'll shut those two up as they ask. I've never told a soul of this Leonardo business, not even Sloane, who runs things for me . . . K.

"This must be the letter," growled the Inspector, "that Khalkis gave the Brett girl to mail last Saturday morning. Scrawly sort of writing. Pretty good for a blind man."

Ellery asked quietly: "You've never told anyone about this affair, Mr. Knox?"

Knox grunted: "No indeed. Up to last Friday naturally I thought Khalkis's yarn gilt-edged—no publicity on the Museum end, so on. My private collection at home is visited very often—friends, collectors, connoisseurs. So I've always kept the Leonardo hidden. And never told a soul. Since last Friday I've naturally had even less reason to talk. Nobody on my end knows about the Leonardo, or my possession of it."

Sampson looked worried. "Of course, Mr. Knox, you realize that you're in a peculiar position . . ."

"Eh? What's that?"

"What I meant to say," Sampson went on lamely, "was that your possession of stolen property is in the nature of—"

"What Mr. Sampson meant to say," explained the Inspector, "is that technically you've compounded a felony."

"Nonsense." Knox chuckled suddenly. "What proof have you?"

"Your own admission that you have the painting."

"Pshaw! And suppose I chose to deny this story of mine?"

"Now, you wouldn't do that," said the Inspector steadily, "I'm sure."

"The painting would prove the story," said Sampson; he was gnawing his lips nervously.

Knox did not lose his good humour. "Could you produce the painting, gentlemen? Without that Leonardo you haven't a leg to stand on. Not a wooden leg."

The Inspector's eyes narrowed. "You mean, Mr. Knox, that you would deliberately secrete that painting—refuse to hand it over, refuse to admit your possession of it?"

Knox massaged his jaw, looking from Sampson to the Inspector. "Look here. You're tackling this the wrong way. What is this—a murder or a felony you're investigating?" He was smiling.

"It seems to me, Mr. Knox," said the Inspector, rising, "that you are adopting a very peculiar attitude. It's our province to investigate any criminal aspect of public relations. If you feel this way about it, why have you told us all this?"

"Now you're talking, Inspector," said Knox briskly. "Two reasons. One, I want to help solve the murder. Two, I've my own axe to grind."

"What do you mean?"

"I've been buffaloed, that's what I mean. That Leonardo I paid three quarters of a million for *isn't a Leonardo at all!*"

"So." The Inspector eyed him shrewdly. "That's the angle, is it? When did you find this out?"

"Yesterday. Last night. Had the painting examined by my own expert. Guarantee his discretion—he won't talk; only one knows I have it; and he didn't know until late yesterday. He thinks the painting is by a pupil of Leonardo's, or maybe by Lorenzo di Credi, one of Leonardo's contemporaries—they were both pupils of Verrocchio. His words I'm quoting. Perfect Leonardo technique, he says—but bases his opinion on certain internal evidence I won't go into now. Damned thing isn't worth more than a few thousand . . . I've been stuck. That's the one I bought."

"In any event, it belongs to the Victoria Museum, Mr. Knox," said the District Attorney defensively. "It should be returned—"

"How do I know it belongs to the Victoria Museum? How do I know that the one I bought isn't a copy someone dug up?

Suppose the Victoria's Leonardo *was* stolen. Doesn't mean that that's the one offered to me. Maybe Grimshaw pulled a fast one—believe he did. Maybe it was Khalkis. Who knows? And what are you going to do about it?"

Ellery said, "I suggest everyone here keep perfectly quiet about the whole story."

They let it go at that. Knox was master of the situation. The District Attorney was a most uncomfortable man; he whispered heatedly to the Inspector, and the Inspector shrugged his shoulders.

"Forgive me if I return to the scene of my ignominy." Ellery spoke with unfamiliar humility. "Mr. Knox, what actually occurred last Friday night with regard to the will?"

"When Grimshaw refused it, Khalkis mechanically went back to his wall-safe and, locking the will in a steel box there, closed the safe."

"And the tea-things?"

Knox said abruptly, "Grimshaw and I entered the library. The tea-things were on the tabouret near the desk. Khalkis asked us if we would have tea—he had already, I noticed, started the water in the percolator to boiling. We both refused. As we talked, Khalkis poured himself a cup of tea—"

"Using a tea-bag and a slice of lemon?"

"Yes. Took the tea-bag out again, though. But in the excitement of the conversation that followed, he did not drink. Tea got cold. He didn't drink all the time we were there."

"There were three cups and saucers all told, on the tray?"

"Yes. Other two remained clean. No water was poured into them."

*   *   *

Ellery said in a bitter-cold voice, "It is necessary for me to adjust certain misconceptions. I seem to be, plainly speaking, the goat of a clever adversary. I have been toyed with in Machiavellian fashion. Made to appear ridiculous.

"On the other hand we must not permit personal considerations to befog the greater issue. Please attend carefully—you, Mr. Knox; you, Dad; you, Sampson; you, Pepper. If I slip anywhere, catch me up.

"I have been the dupe of an astute criminal who, giving me credit for a laborious mentality, has deliberately concocted such false clues for my edification as I would seize upon in the construction of a 'clever' solution—that is, a solution which tended to reveal Khalkis as the murderer. Since we know that for a period of several days after Khalkis's death there was only one dirty tea-cup, the fixing of the three tea-cups must have been a 'plant' left by the murderer. The criminal deliberately used only the water from Khalkis's full but untouched tea-cup in his process of dirtying the two clean cups, and then poured the tea-water out somewhere, leaving the original water-content of the percolator to provide me with the basis for a false deduction. Miss Brett's story establishing the time when she saw the cups in their original condition completely absolves Khalkis from having himself left the three-dirty-cups false clue; for at the time Miss Brett saw the cups in their original condition Khalkis was already dead and buried. There is only one person who had the motive for planting such a false clue, and that is the murderer himself—the person who was furnishing me with a made-to-order suspect leading away from himself.

"Now," continued Ellery in the same bleak voice, "the clue which tended to show that Khalkis was not blind . . . The criminal must have taken advantage of a fortuitous circumstance; he discovered or knew what Khalkis's schedule called for, and he found the packet from Barrett's on the foyer-table, probably at the same general time when he fixed the tea-cups, and, taking advantage of the discrepancy in the colours, put the packet in the highboy drawer in Khalkis's bedroom to make sure I would find it there and use it as part of my deductive framework. The question arises: Was Khalkis really blind, despite the 'plant,' or

was he not? How much did the criminal know? I'll leave this
last consideration for the moment.

"One thing, however, is important. The criminal could not
have so arranged matters that Khalkis wore the wrong tie the
Saturday morning of his death. The whole chain of reasoning
on which I based the deduction that Khalkis had regained his
sight is fallacious somewhere, provided we work on the theory
now that Khalkis really was blind, although it is still possible
that he was not . . ."

"Possible but not probable," commented Sampson, "since,
as you pointed out, why did he keep quiet if he suddenly regained his sight?"

"That's perfectly right, Sampson. It would seem that Khalkis *was* blind. So my logic was wrong. How account, then, for
the fact that Khalkis knew he was wearing a red tie, and yet
was blind? Is it possible that Demmy, Sloane or Miss Brett *did*
tell Khalkis he was wearing a red tie? This would explain the
facts; on the other hand, if all told the truth, the explanation is
still floating about somewhere. If we cannot discover a satisfactory alternative explanation, we shall be forced to conclude
that one of the three lied in his or her testimony."

"That Brett girl," growled the Inspector, "isn't my idea of a
reliable witness."

"We'll get nowhere with unsupported inspirations, Dad."
Ellery shook his head. "Unless we are to confess the inade-
quacy of reasoning, which I am loath to do . . . I have been going over the possibilities mentally during Mr. Knox's recital. I
see now that my original logic overlooked one possibility—a
possibility rather amazing, if true. For there is one way in which
Khalkis could have known he wore a red tie without having
been told and without having been able to *see* the colour. . . .
Easy enough to prove or disprove. Excuse me a moment."

Ellery went to the telephone and put in a call to the Khalkis
house; they watched him in silence. This was somehow, they
felt, a test. "Mrs. Sloane. . . . Mrs. Sloane? This is Ellery Queen.

Is Mr. Demetrios Khalkis there? . . . Excellent. Please have him come to Police Headquarters in Center Street at once—to Inspector Queen's office . . . Yes, I understand. Very well, have Weekes bring him, then . . . Mrs. Sloane. Tell your cousin to bring with him one of your brother's green ties. This is important. . . . No, please don't tell Weekes what Demmy is bringing. Thank you."

He joggled the receiver and spoke to the central police operator. "Please locate Trikkala, the Greek interpreter, and have him come to Inspector Queen's office."

"I don't quite see—" began Sampson.

"Please." Ellery lit another cigarette with steady fingers. "Let me continue. Where do we stand? Here—the entire solution, it must be plain now, with Khalkis as the murderer, collapses. For the solution was based on two points: one, that Khalkis really wasn't blind and, two, that only two people were in the study last Friday night. The second Mr. Knox and Miss Brett have already exploded; I have every reason to believe that I shall be able to explode the first myself in a few moments. In other words, provided we can demonstrate that Khalkis was really blind that night, we no longer have any more reason for suspecting Khalkis of Grimshaw's murder than anyone else. In fact, we can eliminate Khalkis as a suspect; the only one who had reason to leave the false clues was the murderer; the clues were left after Khalkis's death; and moreover were designed to make Khalkis appear as the criminal. So, Khalkis at least was innocent of Grimshaw's murder.

"Now, from Mr. Knox's story, it is evident that Grimshaw was murdered for a motive connected with the stolen Leonardo— not a far cry from my former inference," continued Ellery. "One thing that tends to bear out this stolen-painting motive is: that when Grimshaw was found in the coffin, the promissory note which Khalkis had given him, as Mr. Knox related, was missing from his wallet and clothes—obviously appropriated by his murderer at the time he strangled Grimshaw. The murderer would then be able to hold this promissory note over Khalkis's head, for remember that Grimshaw was killed before Khalkis died. When Khalkis died unexpectedly, however, the note became virtually valueless to the murderer; for such a document presented for payment to anyone but Khalkis himself, now dead, would be so suspicious as to cause an investigation necessarily perilous to the murderer. When he stole the promissory note from Grimshaw, then, the murderer did it on the basis of Khalkis's remaining alive. In a way, Khalkis by dying did his rightful heirs a good turn, saving his dwindling estate the considerable sum of half a million dollars.

"But an even more important fact arises." Ellery paused and looked about the office. The door to the Inspector's room was shut; he crossed over, opened it, peered about, closed it again and returned. "This is so important," he explained bitterly, "that I don't want even a clerk to hear it.

"Attend. The only person, as I said a moment ago, who had reason to divert guilt on to the head of the dead man, Khalkis, was naturally the murderer. Whereupon there are two characteristics which the murderer must possess: one, to have been able to plant the false tea-cup clue, the murderer *must* have had access to the Khalkis house after the funeral, between Tuesday afternoon when Miss Brett saw the two clean cups and Friday when we found the three dirty cups; two, the whole deception of the dirty tea-cups, to make it appear that only two people were involved, absolutely *depended*—mark this point—absolutely depended on Mr. Knox's remaining silent about the fact that he was the third man, the fact obviously that there was a third man at all.

"Let me enlarge on this latter point. There were, as we now know, three people present that night. Whoever later made it appear by the tea-cups that only two had been present, obviously knew that three had been present, and who they were. But observe. He wanted the police to believe that only two had been present; therefore each of the three men actually there must be made to preserve silence, or the deception would be unsuccessful. Now the planter of the two-present idea could depend, at the time he laid the false trail between Tuesday and Friday, on the silence of two of the three men—Grimshaw, murdered, and Khalkis, dead of natural causes. That left only the third man, Mr. Knox, as a potential informer whose information would break down the two-present deception. Yet, despite Mr. Knox's remaining alive, healthy and unmolested, the plotter deliberately went ahead with his deception. In other words, he felt that he could *depend* on Mr. Knox's remaining silent. Is this clear so far?"

They nodded, alert to every syllable. Knox was watching Ellery's lips with a curious intentness. "But how could the planner have been *able* to depend on Mr. Knox's silence?" continued Ellery crisply. "Only if he knew the whole story of the Leonardo, *only if he knew that Mr. Knox possesses the painting under circumstances of an illicit nature*. Then, and then only, could he be certain that Mr. Knox in self-protection would keep quiet about having been the third man in the Khalkis house last Friday night."

"Smart, young man," said Knox.

"For once." Ellery did not smile. "But the most significant feature of this analysis is still to come. For who could know the whole story of the stolen Leonardo and your connexion with it, Mr. Knox?

"Let us eliminate.

"Khalkis, by his own letter, had told no one, and he is now dead.

"You, Mr. Knox, have told no one except a single person— and we can eliminate him by pure logic: you told your expert— the expert who yesterday examined the painting for you and pronounced it the work of someone other than Leonardo Da Vinci; but you told him only last night—too late for him to have planted the clues! The clues were planted *before* last night, since I found them yesterday morning. This eliminates your expert, the only one who knows of your possession of the painting through you, Mr. Knox. . . . This may seem unnecessary analysis; your expert scarcely enters the picture; certainly it is beyond reason that he is the criminal; yet I choose to be very careful to make my point on the basis of irrefutable logic."

He stared glumly at the wall. "Who is left? Only Grimshaw, and he is dead. *But*—according to your related story of Grimshaw's own words that night at Khalkis's, Mr. Knox, Grimshaw said he had told *only one person*—the only other person 'in the world,' I believe was your transmission of Grimshaw's statement, whom he had told about the stolen painting. That single person was Grimshaw's partner, by his own admission. And that single person is therefore the only outsider who knew enough about the story of the stolen painting and your possession of it to have planted the false clue of the three used teacups, for one thing, and to have been able to depend upon your silence, for another!"

"Right, right," muttered Knox.

"What is the conclusion from this?" went on Ellery in colourless tones. "Grimshaw's partner being the only individual who *could* have planted the false clues, and the murderer being the only individual who had *reason* to plant the false clues—Grimshaw's partner then must be the murderer. And, according to Grimshaw's own story, Grimshaw's partner was the man who accompanied him to his Hotel Benedict room the night before the fatal events—and the man who, we may presume, met Grimshaw after you and Grimshaw emerged from the Khalkis house last Friday night, at which time he could have learned all about the offer of the new will, the promissory note, and everything else that had transpired during the visit to Khalkis."

"Of course," said the Inspector reflectively, "that's progress, but it really doesn't get us anywhere at this time. The man who accompanied Grimshaw last Thursday night might have been anyone. We have no description of him, son."

"True. But at least we have clarified certain issues. We know where we are going." Ellery ground out his cigarette, looking at them wearily. "One significant point I have thus far deliberately omitted to discuss. And that is—that the murderer was fooled: Mr. Knox *didn't* keep silent. Now, why didn't you keep silent, Mr. Knox?"

"Told you that," said the banker. "The Leonardo I have isn't a Leonardo at all. Practically worthless."

"Precisely. Mr. Knox talked because he had discovered that the painting is practically worthless—to put it crudely, he has an 'out' for himself and feels free to confess the entire story. But he has told his story only to ourselves, gentlemen! In other words, the murderer, Grimshaw's partner, still believes we know nothing about the painting, still believes that the Khalkis solution, if we snatch at his false clues, is acceptable to us. Very well—we shall oblige him in one thing and disoblige him in another. We cannot publicly accept the Khalkis solution—we know it to be wrong. But we want to feed our murderer, give him rope, see what he will do next, perhaps trap him in some way by forcing him to continue—how shall I put it?—to continue doing things. Therefore, let us give out the Khalkis solution, then publicize Miss Brett's testimony which burst the bubble of the Khalkis solution; in all this, let us say nothing about Mr. Knox's coming forward with his story—not one word. The murderer will believe then that Mr. Knox has kept silent, will continue to depend upon his silence, as it were, having no inkling that the painting is not a genuine Leonardo worth a million dollars."

"He'll be forced to cover himself up," muttered the District Attorney. "He'll know we're still hunting a murderer. Good idea, Ellery."

"We run no risk of frightening our quarry," continued Ellery, "by exposing the Khalkis solution as false on the basis of Miss

Brett's new testimony. The murderer will be constrained to accept this, because after all he took the risk from the beginning
that someone would observe the discrepancy in the appearance of the tea-cups. The fact that someone did observe the
discrepancy will appear to him an unlucky but not necessarily
disastrous circumstance."

"How about Cheney's disappearance?" asked Pepper.

Ellery sighed. "Of course, my very brilliant inference that
Alan Cheney buried Grimshaw's body was based entirely on
the hypothesis that Khalkis, his uncle, was the murderer. We
now have reason to believe, with the new facts, that Grimshaw
was buried by the same person who murdered him. In any
event, we cannot ascribe any reason, on the basis of available
data, to Cheney's disappearance. That will have to wait."

An inter-office communicator buzzed and the Inspector
rose to answer it. "Send him in. Keep the other outside." He
turned to Ellery. "Well, there's your man, son," he said. "Weekes
brought him."

Ellery nodded. A man opened the door to admit the tall
shambling figure of Demetrios Khalkis, decently and soberly
attired; but the hideous vacant grin distorted his lips and he
looked more idiotic than ever. They could see Weekes, the butler, his derby clutched to his old chest, sitting uneasily in the
Inspector's anteroom; the outer door opened and greasy Trikkala shuffled in with an inquiring look on his face; someone
shut the door of the office from the anteroom.

"Trikkala," said Ellery, "ask this imbecile if he has brought
what he was told to bring."

Trikkala, at whose entrance Demmy's face had lighted,
fired a clatter of words at the grinning idiot. Demmy nodded
vigorously, holding up the packet.

"Very well." Ellery was subdued, watchful. "Now ask him,
Trikkala, *what* he was told to bring."

A short interchange of the fiery syllables, and Trikkala said:

"He says he was to bring a green necktie, one of the green neckties from his cousin Georg's wardrobe at home."

"Admirable. Ask him to produce this green necktie."

Trikkala said something sharp to Demmy, who nodded again and with clumsy fingers began to undo the strings about his packet. It took him a long time—an interval during which all eyes were silently concentrated on those large fumbling digits. Finally he was victorious over a stubborn knot, carefully coiled the string and put it into one of his pockets, then undid the folds of the packet. The paper fell away—and Demmy held up a *red* necktie. . . .

Ellery silenced the hubbub that ensued, the excited exclamation of the two lawyers, the mild curse of the Inspector. Demmy stared at them with his vacant grin, mutely seeking approval. Ellery turned and pulled open the top drawer of his father's desk, rummaging. Finally he straightened up, holding a blotter—a green blotter.

"Trikkala," said Ellery steadily, "ask him what the colour of this blotter is."

Trikkala complied. Demmy's response in Greek was decisive. "He says," reported the interpreter in a wondering tone, "he says the blotter is red."

"Excellent. Thank you, Trikkala. Take him out and tell the man waiting in the anteroom that they may go home."

Trikkala grasped the imbecile's arm and piloted him from the office; Ellery closed the door behind them.

"That, I think," he said, "explains how I misled myself in my cocksure logic. I did not take into account the remote possibility that Demmy was—colour-blind!"

They nodded. "You see," he continued, "I presumed that if Khalkis had not been *told* the tie he was wearing was red, and if Demmy had dressed him according to schedule, that Khalkis knew the colour of the tie because he could see it. I did not take into consideration the fact that the schedule itself might have been misleading. According to schedule, Demmy should have handed Khalkis a green tie last Saturday morning. Yet we now find that to Demmy the word 'green' means red—that he is colour-blind. In other words, Demmy is afflicted with a common case of partial colour-blindness in which he consistently sees red as green and green as red; Khalkis knew that Demmy was so afflicted, and arranged the schedule on that basis, as far as these two colours were concerned. When he wanted a red tie, he knew he must ask Demmy to fetch a 'green' one. The schedule served exactly the same end. To sum up—that morning, despite the fact that Khalkis was wearing a tie whose colour differed from the physical colour prescribed by the Saturday schedule, he knew without having to be told and without being able to see for himself that he was wearing a red tie. He didn't 'change' his tie—he was wearing the red one when Demmy left the house at nine o'clock."

"Well," said Pepper, "that means Demmy, Sloane and Miss Brett told the truth. That's something."

"Very true. We should also discuss the delayed question of whether the plotter-murderer knew that Khalkis was blind, or actually believed, from the data on which I myself went astray, that Khalkis wasn't blind. It's rather a fruitless conjecture now; although the probabilities lie in the direction of the latter; he probably did not know that Demmy is colour-blind; probably believed, and still believes, that at the time Khalkis died he could see. In any event, we can get nothing out of it." Ellery turned to his father. "Has anyone kept a list of all visitors to the Khalkis house between Tuesday and Friday?"

Sampson replied: "Cohalan. My man stationed there. Got it, Pepper?"

Pepper produced a typewritten sheet of paper. Ellery scanned it quickly. "I see he's brought it up to date." The list included those visitors to the house mentioned in the list the Queens had seen on Thursday, the day before the disinterment, plus the additional names of all persons who had visited the house from that time until the investigation directly after the disinterment. This addendum included all members of the Khalkis household and the following: Nacio Suiza, Miles Woodruff, James J. Knox, Dr. Duncan Frost, Honeywell, the Reverend Elder, Mrs. Susan Morse; and several old clients of the dead man besides the Robert Petrie and Mrs. Duke already listed—one Reuben Goldberg, one Mrs. Timothy Walker, one Robert Acton. Several employees of the Khalkis Galleries had also called at the house: Simon Broecken, Jenny Bohm, Parker Insull. The list was concluded with the names of a number of accredited newspaper reporters.

Ellery returned the paper to Pepper. "Everybody in the city seems to have visited the place. . . . Mr. Knox, you'll be certain to keep the entire story of the Leonardo and your possession of it a secret?"

"Shan't breathe a word," said Knox.

"And you'll keep alert, sir—report to the Inspector any new circumstance the instant it develops?"

"Glad to." Knox rose; Pepper hastened to help him on with his coat. "Working with Woodruff," said Knox as he struggled into his coat. "Retained him to take care of the legal details of the estate. All messy, with Khalkis apparently intestate. Hope that new will doesn't turn up anywhere—Woodruff says it will complicate matters. Got permission of Mrs. Sloane, as nearest of kin, to allow me to assume the job of administrator if the new will isn't found."

"Damn that stolen will," said Sampson pettishly. "Although I do think we have sufficient grounds to base a plea of duress. We'd probably be able to break it after a hell of a fuss. Wonder if Grimshaw had any kin?"

Knox grunted, waved his hand, and was gone. Sampson and Pepper rose, and they looked at each other. "I see what you're thinking, Chief," said Pepper softly. "You think Knox's story about the painting he has not being a Leonardo—is just a story, eh?"

"Well, I shouldn't be surprised," confessed Sampson.

"Nor I," snapped the Inspector. "Big bug or no big bug, he's playing with fire."

"Quite likely," agreed Ellery, "although not particularly important as far as I'm concerned. But the man is a notoriously rabid collector, and he evidently means to keep that painting at all costs."

"Well," sighed the old man, "it's a rotten mess." Sampson and Pepper nodded to Ellery, and left the office. The Inspector followed them, headed for a conference with police reporters.

They left Ellery alone—an idle young man with a busy brain. He consumed cigarette after cigarette, wincing repeatedly at some memory. When the Inspector returned, alone, Ellery was contemplating his shoes with an absent frown.

"Spilled it," growled the old man, sinking into his chair. "Told the boys the Khalkis solution and then Joan Brett's testimony that upset the apple-cart. It'll be all over the city in a few hours, and our friend the murderer ought to be getting busy."

He barked into his communicator, and a moment later his secretary hurried in. The Inspector dictated a cablegram to be marked *Confidential,* addressed to the director of the Victoria Museum in London. The secretary went away.

"Well, we'll see," said the old man judiciously, his hand straying to his snuff-box. "Find out where we stand on this painting business. Just talked it over with Sampson outside. We can't drop it on Knox's say-so. . . ." He studied his silent son quizzically. "Come now, El, snap out of it. The world hasn't come to an end. What if your Khalkis solution was a flop? Forget it."

Ellery looked up slowly. "Forget it? Not for a long time, Dad." He clenched one fist and regarded it blankly. "If this affair has taught me one thing above all others, it's taught me this—and if ever you catch me breaking this pledge put a bullet through my conk: Never again will I advance a solution of any case in which I may be interested until I have tenoned into the whole every single element of the crime, explained every particle of a loose end."[*]

The Inspector looked concerned. "Come now, boy—"

"When I think of what a fool I've made of myself—what a swollen, unmitigated, egotistical jackass of a fool. . . ."

"I think your solution, false as it was, was darned brilliant," said the Inspector defensively.

Ellery did not reply. He began to polish the lenses of his *pince-nez*, staring bitterly at the wall above his father's head.

---

[*] This goes far to explain a situation concerning which much conjecture and even criticism has arisen. It has been remarked that, from Ellery's method as shown in the three novels already given to the public, he has always seemed inconsiderate of his father's feelings, tightly suppressing what he knew or had reasoned concerning a crime until the last gasp of the solution. When it is recalled that this vow of Ellery's came in a case preceding those others already published, his strange conduct is understandable. —J. J. McC.

CHAPTER 17

Stigma

The proverbial arm stretched forth and plucked young Mr. Alan Cheney out of limbo into the light of day. To be exact, its fingers descended upon him out of the darkness above a Buffalo flying-field on the night of Sunday, October the tenth, as he was about to step unsteadily into the cabin of a Chicago airplane. The fingers, attached to the hand of Detective Hagstrom—an American gentleman with latent centuries of exploratory Norse blood in his veins—were very sure, and they saw to it that young Mr. Alan Cheney, bleared and sodden and surly and exceedingly drunk, was deposited on the next Pullman express bound across the State for New York City.

The Queens, apprised by telegram of the capture after a Sunday in which hymns were conspicuously absent and gloom seemed the order of the day, were on hand early Monday morning in the Inspector's office to welcome the homecoming recalcitrant and his justly jubilant captor. District Attorney Sampson and Assistant District Attorney Pepper joined the reception committee. The atmosphere of that fragment of Center Street was gay indeed.

"Well, Mr. Alan Cheney," began the Inspector genially, as young Alan, seedier and surlier than ever now that his tipple had worn off, flung himself into a chair, "what have you got to say for yourself?"

Alan's voice was hoarse through cracked lips. "I refuse to talk."

Sampson snapped: "You realize what your flight implies, Cheney?"

"My flight?" His eyes were sullen.

"Oh, then it wasn't flight. Just a jaunt—a little holiday, eh, young man?" The Inspector chuckled. "Well, well," he said suddenly, with that change of front so characteristic of him, "this isn't a joke and we aren't kids. You ran away. Why?"

Young Alan folded his arms across his chest and stared defiantly at the floor.

"It wasn't—" the Inspector groped in the top drawer of his desk—"it wasn't because you were *afraid* to stay, was it?" His hand emerged from the drawer flourishing the scribbled note Sergeant Velie had found in Joan Brett's bedroom.

Alan paled all at once and he glared at the slip of paper as if it were an animate enemy. "Where on earth did you get that?" he whispered.

"Gets a rise out of you, does it? We found it under Miss Brett's mattress, if you'd like to know!"

"She—she didn't burn it . . . ?"

"She did not. Cut the comedy, son. Are you going to talk or do we have to apply a little pressure?"

Alan blinked rapidly. "What's happened?"

The Inspector turned to the others. "*He* wants information, the whelp!"

"Miss Brett . . . Is she—all right?"

"She's all right *now.*"

"What do you mean?" Alan leaped from his chair. "You haven't—?"

"Haven't what?"

He shook his head and sat down again, pressing his knuckles wearily into his eyes.

"Q." Sampson tossed his head. The Inspector cast a peculiar glance at the young man's dishevelled hair and joined the District Attorney in a corner. "If he refuses to talk," said Sampson in a low voice, "we can't very well hang on to him. We might hold him on a technical charge, but I can't see that it will do us any good. After all, we haven't a thing on him."

"True. But there's one thing I want to satisfy myself about before we let this cub slip through our fingers again." The old man went to the door. "Thomas!"

Sergeant Velie appeared, bestriding the sill like a Colossus. "Want him now?"

"Yes. Get him in here."

Velie barged out. A moment later he returned escorting the slight figure of Bell, the night-clerk at the Hotel Benedict. Alan Cheney sat very still concealing his uneasiness beneath a mask of stubborn silence; his eyes leaped to Bell as if anxious to come to grips with something tangible.

The Inspector jerked his thumb at the victim. "Bell, do you recognize this man as one of Albert Grimshaw's visitors a week ago Thursday night?"

Bell examined the grim figure of the boy scrupulously. Alan met his eye in a sort of defiant bewilderment. Then Bell shook his head with energy. "No, sir. He wasn't one of 'em. Never saw the gentleman before."

The Inspector grunted his disgust; and Alan, ignorant of the meaning of the inspection but sensible of its failure, sank back with a sigh of relief. "All right, Bell. Wait outside." Bell retreated hastily, and Sergeant Velie set his back against the door. "Well, Cheney, still refuse to explain your little skip-out?"

Alan moistened his lips. "I want to see my lawyer."

The Inspector threw up his hands. "Heavens, how many times I've heard *that*! And who is your lawyer, Cheney?"

"Why—Miles Woodruff."

"Family mouth-piece, hey?" said the Inspector nastily. "Well, it isn't necessary." The Inspector plumped himself into his chair and consulted his snuff-box. "We're going to let you go, young man," he said, gesturing with the old brown box as if he begrudged the necessity of releasing his prisoner. Alan's features lightened by magic. "You may go home. But," and the old man leaned forward, "I can promise you this. One more monkey-shine like the one you pulled Saturday, my boy, and I'll put you behind the bars if I have to go to the Commissioner to do it. Understand?"

"Yes," muttered Alan.

"Furthermore," continued the Inspector, "I make no bones about telling you that you're going to be watched. Every move. So it won't do you any good to try a skip again, because there'll be a man on your fanny every second of the time you're out of the Khalkis house. Hagstrom!" The detective jumped. "Take Mr. Cheney home. Stay in the Khalkis house with him. Don't bother him. But stick to him like a brother every time he leaves the place."

"I got you. Come on, Mr. Cheney." Hagstrom grinned and grasped the young man's arm. Alan rose with alacrity, shook off the detective's grip, squared his shoulders in sorry defiance, and stalked out of the room with Hagstrom at his elbow.

Now it will be observed that Ellery Queen had not so much as uttered a syllable during the scene. He had examined his perfect fingernails, held his *pince-nez* up to the light as if he had never seen it before, sighed several times, consumed several cigarettes, and generally composed himself as if he were wearied to tears. The only flicker of interest he had exhibited was when Cheney had been confronted with Bell; but the flicker died away as soon as Bell failed to identify him.

Ellery pricked up his ears when Pepper said, as the door closed behind Cheney and Hagstrom: "Seems to me, Chief, he's getting away with murder."

Sampson said quietly: "And what does that massive brain of yours think we have on him, Pepper?"

"Well, he ran away, didn't he?"

"How true! But are you going to be able to convince a jury that a man is a criminal merely because he runs away?"

"It's been done," said Pepper stubbornly.

"Tommyrot," snapped the Inspector. "Not a shred of evidence, and well you ought to know it, Pepper. He'll keep. If there's anything fishy about that young man, we'll find it. . . . Thomas, what's on *your* mind? You seem bursting with news."

In truth, Sergeant Velie had been turning from one to another, opening his mouth and closing it again as he failed to find a crevice in the conversation. Now he drew a Brobdingnagian breath and said: "I've got two of 'em outside!"

"Two of whom?"

"The dame Grimshaw scrapped with in Barney Schick's dive, and her husband."

"No!" The Inspector drew himself up sharply. "That's good news, Thomas. How'd you find her?"

"Traced her through Grimshaw's record," rumbled Velie. "She's a certain Lily Morrison—ran around with Grimshaw in the old days. Got married while Grimshaw was in stir."

"Get Barney Schick."

"Got him waiting, too."

"Great. Bring 'em all in."

Velie tramped out and the Inspector settled back expectantly in his swivel-chair. The sergeant returned in a moment with the redfaced speakeasy proprietor, whom the Inspector commanded to silence as Velie at once departed by another door. Velie returned shortly with a man and a woman.

They came in hesitantly. The woman was a veritable Brünnehilde, large and blonde and Amazonian. The man was a fitting mate—a grizzled giant in his forties with an Irish nose and hard black eyes.

Velie said: "Mr. and Mrs. Jeremiah Odell, Inspector."

The Inspector indicated chairs, and they sat down stiffly. The old man began to fuss with some papers on his desk—a purely mechanistic exhibition performed for its effect. They were properly impressed, and their eyes ceased twitching about the office and concentrated on the old man's thin hands.

"Now, Mrs. Odell," began the Inspector, "please don't be frightened; this is just a formality. D'ye know Albert Grimshaw?"

Their eyes touched, and hers drew away. "Why—you mean the man that was found choked to death in that coffin?" she asked. She possessed a throaty voice at the base of which something constantly churned. Ellery felt his own throat ache.

"Yes. Know him?"

"I—No, I don't. Only through the newspapers."

"I see." The Inspector turned to Barney Schick, sitting motionless across the room. "Barney, do you recognize this lady?"

The Odells shifted quickly, and the woman gasped. Her husband's hairy hand clamped on her arm, and she turned about with a pale effort at composure.

"I sure do," said Schick. His face was wet with perspiration.

"Where did you see her last?"

"In my place on Forty-fifth Street. Week ago—near two weeks ago. A Wednesday night."

"Under what circumstances?"

"Huh? Oh. With the guy that was croaked—Grimshaw."

"Mrs. Odell was quarrelling with the dead man?"

"Yep," Schick guffawed. "On'y he wasn't dead then, Inspector—not by a long shot."

"Cut the comedy, Barney. You're sure this is the woman you saw with Grimshaw?"

"Nothin' else but."

The Inspector turned to Mrs. Odell. "And you say you never saw Albert Grimshaw, didn't know him?"

Her full over-ripe lips began to quiver. Odell leaned forward, scowling. "If my wife says no," he growled, "it's no—get me?"

The Inspector considered that. "Hmm," he murmured. "There's

something in *that* . . . Barney, my boy, have you ever seen this fighting Mick here?" He flung his thumb at the Irish giant.

"Nope. Can't say I have."

"All right, Barney. Go back to your customers." Schick creaked to his feet and went out. "Mrs. Odell, what was your maiden name?"

The lip-quivering redoubled. "Morrison."

"Lily Morrison?"

"Yes."

"How long have you been married to Odell?"

"Two and a half years."

"So." The old man again consulted a fictitious *dossier*. "Now listen to me, Mrs. Lily Morrison Odell. I have before me a clear record. Five years ago one Albert Grimshaw was arrested and sent to Sing Sing. At the time he was arrested there is no record of your connexion with him—true. But several years before that you were living with him at . . . What was the address, Sergeant Velie?"

"One-o-four-five Tenth Avenue," said Velie.

Odell had leaped to his feet, his face surcharged with purple. "*Livin'* with him, was she?" he snarled. "There ain't a skunk breathin' can say that about my wife and get away with it! Put up your mitts, you old wind-bag! I'll knock—"

He was crouching forward, huge fists flailing the air. Then his head jerked backward with a viciousness that almost snapped his vertebrae; it had moved in that direction under the iron urging of Sergeant Velie's fingers, now clamped in the man's collar. Velie shook Odell twice, as a baby shakes a rattle, and Odell, mouth open, found himself slammed back in his chair.

"Be good, you mug," said Velie gently. "Don't you know you're threatening an officer?" He did not release his grip on Odell's collar; the man sat choking.

"Oh, I'm sure he'll be good, Thomas," remarked the Inspector, as if nothing untoward had occurred. "Now, Mrs. Odell, as I was saying—"

The woman, who had watched the manhandling of her leviathan husband with horror-struck eyes, gulped. "I don't know anything. I don't know what you're talking about. I never knew a man named Grimshaw. I never saw—"

"A lot of 'nevers,' Mrs. Odell. Why did Grimshaw look you up as soon as he got out of prison two weeks ago?"

"Don't answer," gurgled the giant.

"I won't. I won't."

The Inspector turned his sharp eyes on the man. "Do you realize that I can arrest you on a charge of refusing assistance to the police in a murder investigation?"

"Go ahead and try it," muttered Odell. "I've got influence, I have. You'll never get away with it. I know Ollivant at the Hall . . ."

"Hear that, Mr. District Attorney? He knows Ollivant at the Hall," said the Inspector with a sigh. "This man suggests bringing undue influence to bear . . . Odell, what's your racket?"

"Got no racket."

"Oh! You make an honest living. What's your business?"

"I'm a plumbing contractor."

"That explains your pull . . . Where do you live, Irish?"

"Brooklyn—Flatbush section."

"Anything on this bird, Thomas?"

Sergeant Velie released Odell's collar. "Clean record, Chief," he said regretfully.

"How about the woman?"

"Seems to have gone straight."

"There!" flared Mrs. Odell triumphantly.

"Oh, so you admit you had something to go straight about?"

Her eyes, large as a cow's, opened wider; but she stubbornly kept silent.

"I suggest," drawled Ellery from the depths of his chair, "that the omniscient Mr. Bell be summoned."

The Inspector nodded to Velie, who went out and reappeared almost at once with the night-clerk. "Take a look at this man, Bell," said the Inspector.

Bell's Adam's-apple joggled prominently. He pointed a trembling finger at the suspicious, glowering face of Jeremiah Odell. "That's the man! That's the man!" he cried.

"Ha!" The Inspector was on his feet. "Which one was he, Bell?"

Bell looked blank for an instant. "Gee," he muttered, "don't seem to remember exactly—by God, I do! This man came next to last, just before that doctor with the beard!" His voice rose confidently. "He was the Irishman—the big fellow I told you about, Inspector. I remember now."

"Positive?"

"I'd swear to it."

"All right, Bell. Go on home now."

Bell went away. Odell's mammoth jaw had fallen; there was desperation in his black eyes.

"Well, what about it, Odell?"

He shook his head like a groggy prize-fighter. "About what?"

"Ever see that man who just went out?"

"No!"

"Do you know who he is?"

"No!"

"He's the night-clerk," said the Inspector pleasantly, "at the Hotel Benedict. Ever been there?"

"No!"

"He says he saw you there at his desk between ten and ten-thirty on the night of Thursday, September thirtieth."

"It's a damn lie!"

"You asked at the desk whether there was an Albert Grimshaw registered."

"I didn't!"

"You asked Bell for his room-number and then went up. Room 314, Odell. Remember? It's an easy number to remember . . . *Well?*"

Odell pulled himself to his feet. "Listen. I'm a taxpayer and an honest citizen. I don't know what any of you guys are ravin' about. This ain't Russia!" he shouted. "I've got my rights! Come on, Lily, let's go—they can't keep us here!"

The woman rose obediently; Velie stepped behind Odell and for a moment it seemed as if the two men must clash; but the Inspector motioned Velie aside and watched the Odells, slowly at first, and then with ludicrous acceleration, make for the doorway. They sped through it out of sight.

"Get somebody on them," said Inspector Queen in the glummest of voices. Velie followed the Odells out.

"Most pig-headed bunch of witnesses I've ever seen," muttered Sampson. "What's behind all this?"

Ellery murmured: "You heard Mr. Jeremiah Odell, didn't you, Sampson? It's Soviet Russia. Some of that good old Red propaganda. Good old Russia! What would our noble citizenry do without it?"

No one paid attention. "It's something screwy, I'll tell you that," said Pepper. "This guy Grimshaw was tangled up in a lot of darned shady affairs."

The Inspector spread his hands helplessly, and they were silent for a long moment.

But as Pepper and the District Attorney rose to go, Ellery said brightly: "Say with Terence: 'Whatever chance shall bring, we will bear with equanimity.'"

* * *

Until late Monday afternoon the Khalkis case remained in a *status quo* that was drearily persistent. The Inspector went about his business, which was multifarious; and Ellery went about his—which consisted largely in consuming cigarettes, wolfing random chunks from a tiny volume of Sapphics in his pocket, and between-whiles slumping in the leather chair in his father's office immersed in furious reflections. It was easier, it appeared, to quote Terence than to follow his advice.

The bomb burst just before Inspector Queen, having concluded his routine work for the day, was about to gather in his son and depart for the scarcely more cheerful destination of the Queen household. The Inspector was already getting into his overcoat, in fact, when Pepper flew into the office, his face crimson with excitement and a strange exultation. He was waving an envelope over his head.

"Inspector! Mr. Queen! Look at this." He flung the envelope on the desk, began to pace up and down restlessly. "Just arrived in the mail. Addressed to Sampson, as you can see. Chief's out—his secretary opened it and gave it to me. Too good to keep. Read it!"

Ellery rose quickly and went to his father's side. Together they stared at the envelope. It was of cheap quality; the address was typewritten; the postmark indicated that it had been cancelled through the Grand Central post office that very morning.

"Well, well, what's this?" muttered the Inspector. Carefully he drew from the envelope a slip of notepaper as cheap as its container. He flipped it open. It bore a few lines of typewriting—and no date, salutation or signature. The old man read it aloud, slowly:

The writer (it ran) has found out something hot—good and hot—about the Grimshaw case. The District Attorney ought to be interested.

Here it is. Look up the ancient history of Albert Grimshaw and you will find that he had a brother. What you may *not* find out, though, is that his brother is actively involved in the investigation. In fact, the name he goes by now is Mr. Gilbert Sloane.

"What," cried Pepper, "do you think of *that*?"

The Queens regarded each other, and then Pepper. "Interesting, if true," remarked the Inspector. "It may be just a crank letter, though."

Ellery said calmly: "Even if it is true, I fail to see its significance."

Pepper's face fell. "Well, darn it!" he said. "Sloane denied ever having seen Grimshaw, didn't he? That's significant if they're brothers, isn't it?"

Ellery shook his head. "Significant of what, Pepper? Of the fact that Sloane was ashamed to admit his brother was a gaol-bird? Especially in the face of his brother's murder? No, I'm afraid Mr. Sloane's silence was animated by nothing more sinister than a fear of social degradation."

"Well, I'm not so sure," said Pepper doggedly. "I'll bet the Chief thinks I'm right, too. What are you going to do about it, Inspector?"

"The first thing, after you two spalpeens get through arguing," remarked the Inspector dryly, "is to see if we can find anything in this letter of internal significance." He went to his inter-office communicator. "Miss Lambert? Inspector Queen. Come up to my office a minute." He turned back with a grim smile. "We'll see what the expert has to say."

Una Lambert turned out to be a sharp-featured young woman with a sleek dash of grey running through her blackish hair. "What is it, Inspector Queen?"

The old man tossed the letter across the desk. "What do you make of this?"

Unfortunately, she made little of it. Beyond the fact that it had been typed on a well-used Underwood machine of fairly recent model, and that the characters had clearly distinguishable if microscopic defects in certain instances, she was unable to offer much of value. She felt sure, however, that she would be able to identify any other specimen which might be typed on the same machine.

"Well," grumbled the Inspector, when Una Lambert had been dismissed, "I suppose we can't expect miracles even from an expert." He dispatched Sergeant Velie to the police laboratories with the letter for photographing and fingerprint tests.

"I'll have to locate the D.A.," said Pepper disconsolately, "and tell him about this letter."

"Do that," said Ellery, "and you might inform him at the same time that my father and I are going to go over Number Thirteen East Fifty-fourth Street at once—ourselves."

The Inspector was as much surprised as Pepper. "What d'ye mean, you idiot? Ritter went over that empty Knox house—you know that. What's the idea?"

"The idea," replied Ellery, "is misty, but the purpose surely is self-evident. In a word, I have implicit faith in the honesty of your precious Ritter, but I have vague misgivings about his power of observation."

"Sounds like a good hunch," said Pepper. "After all, there may be something that Ritter missed."

"Nonsense!" said the Inspector sharply. "Ritter's one of my most reliable men."

"I have been sitting here all the long afternoon," said Ellery with a bitter sigh, "contemplating, among my sins, the complexities of the ever-snarling problem. It occurred to me with force that, as you say, Your Reverence, Ritter is one of your most reliable men. Ergo: my decision to go over the ground myself."

"You don't mean to stand there and say you think Ritter is—" The Inspector was shocked.

"By my faith, as the Christians used to say—no," replied Ellery. "Ritter is honest, trustworthy, valiant, conscientious and a credit to his guild. Except that—henceforth I trust nothing but my own two eyes and the dizzy cerebrum that the Immanent Will, in Its autonomous, aimless, unconscious, and indestructible wisdom has seen fit to bestow upon me."[*]

---

[*] Mr. Queen was undoubtedly referring here to the Schopenhauerian conception of God.—The Editor.

CHAPTER 18

Testament

E vening found the Inspector, Ellery and Sergeant Velie standing before the gloomy façade of Number Thirteen.

The empty Knox house was a twin of the Khalkis house next door. Crumbling brownstone streaked with age, large old-fashioned window-spaces blinded with grey boards—a forbidding edifice. There were lights in the Khalkis house at its side, and the restless figures of detectives prowled about it—by comparison the Khalkis house was a cheerful place.

"Have you got the key, Thomas?" Even the Inspector felt the dreary spell, and his voice was subdued.

Velie silently produced a key.

"*En avant!*" muttered Ellery, and the three men pushed through the creaking gate on the sidewalk.

"Upstairs first?" demanded the sergeant.

"Yes."

They mounted the chipped stone steps. Velie brought out a large flashlight, tucked it under his arm, and unlocked the front door. They stepped into the crypt of a vestibule; Velie twitched his torch about, located the lock of the inner door, and opened it. The three men marched in in close formation, and found themselves in a black cavern which, on being illuminated by the flickering rays of the sergeant's flash, revealed itself as an exact replica in shape and size of the Khalkis foyer next door.

"Well, let's go," said the Inspector. "This was your idea, Ellery. Lead the way."

Ellery's eyes were queerly luminous in the jumping light. He hesitated, looked about, and then made for a dark open doorway up the hall. The Inspector and Velie followed patiently, Velie's flashlight held high.

The rooms were utterly bare—dismantled, it was clear, by the owner when he had vacated the premises. On the lower floor, at least, there was nothing—literally nothing—to be found. Empty rooms, dust-laden, here and there revealing men's footprints in the dust where Detective Ritter and his colleagues had tramped in their original search. The walls were yellow, the ceilings cracked, the floors warped and noisy.

"I hope you're satisfied," growled the old man, when they had completed a tour of all the rooms on the lower floor. He sneezed violently as he inhaled some dust—choked and gasped and cursed.

"Not yet," said Ellery. He led the way up the bare wooden stairs. Their footsteps thundered through the empty house.

But—there was nothing to be found on the second floor either. As in the Khalkis house, the second floor contained only bedrooms and bathrooms; but these had neither beds nor carpets to make them habitable, and the old man grew increasingly irritable, Ellery poked about in old wardrobe-closets. It was a labour of love; he found nothing, not so much as a scrap of paper.

"Satisfied yet?"

"No."

They made their way up groaning stairs to the attic.

Nothing.

"Well, that's that," said the Inspector as they descended to the foyer floor. "Now that the nonsense is over, we can go home and have something to eat."

Ellery did not reply; he was twirling his *pince-nez* thought-fully. Then he looked at Sergeant Velie. "Wasn't something said about a broken-down trunk in the basement, Velie?"

"Yep. Ritter reported that, Mr. Queen."

Ellery made for the rear of the foyer. Beneath the staircase which led to the upper floors there was a door. He opened it, borrowed Velie's torch, and flashed its beams downward. A sagging flight of steps sprang up at them.

"Basement," he said. "Come on."

They descended the precarious stairs and found them-selves in a large chamber which ran the entire length and width of the house. It was a ghostly place, full of shadows called into being by the flashlight; and it was even dustier than the rooms upstairs. Ellery proceeded at once to a spot a dozen feet from the steps. He focused the light of Velie's torch upon it. A large battered old trunk lay there—a hulking iron-bound cube, its lid down, its shattered lock protruding dismally.

"You won't find anything in that," said the Inspector. "Ritter reported looking into it, Ellery."

"Of course he did," murmured Ellery, and raised the lid with a gloved hand. He sprayed beams of light about the trunk's shabby interior. Empty.

As he was about to drop the lid, however, his nostrils con-tracted, then quivered, and he leaned forward swiftly, sniffing. "Eureka," he said softly. "Dad, Velie, get a whiff of this perfume."

The two men sniffed. They straightened, and the Inspector muttered: "By gosh, the same smell we got when the coffin was opened! Only fainter, much fainter."

"That's right," came Velie's *basso profundo*.

"Yes." Ellery released the lid and it crashed back into place. "Yes. We have discovered the first resting-place, so to speak, of Mr. Albert Grimshaw's corporeal remains."

"Thank goodness for something," said the Inspector pi-ously. "Although how that fool of a Ritter—"

Ellery continued, more to himself than to his companions.

"Grimshaw was probably strangled in here, or near here. That was Friday night, late—October the first. His body was crammed into this trunk and left here. I shouldn't be surprised to learn that there was no primary intention on the part of the murderer to dispose of the body elsewhere. This empty old house would make an ideal hiding-place for a corpse."

"And then Khalkis died," mused the old man.

"Exactly. Then Khalkis died—the following day, Saturday the second. The murderer saw a splendid opportunity to provide an even more permanent hiding-place for his victim's body. He waited for the funeral, therefore, and on the night of Tuesday or Wednesday stole in here, lugged the body out—" Ellery paused and went swiftly to the rear of the dark basement, nodding when he saw a weatherbeaten old door—"out through this door into the court, then through the gate into the graveyard. Dug down three feet to the vault . . . Very simple under cover of darkness, provided you have a complete indifference to such things as cemeteries, dead bodies, grave-smells, and the ghost of ghosts. Our murderer must be a gentleman of practical imagination. This means that Grimshaw's decaying body lay here for four or five days and nights. That should be sufficient," he said grimly, "to account for the odour of putrefactive mortality."

He swept the torch about. The floor of the basement, cement in spots and wood in others, was utterly bare except for dust and the trunk. But nearby loomed a monstrous shape, a grisly bulk that towered to the ceiling . . . The torch flashed frantically, and the monster turned into a large furnace—the central heating-plant of the house. Ellery strode over to it, grappled with the rusty handle of the firedoor, pulled it open and thrust his hand, with the torch, inside. At once he exclaimed: "Something here! Dad, Velie, quickly!"

The three men bent over and peered through the rusty shutter into the interior of the furnace. On its floor, in a corner, nestled a neat little heap of ashes; and protruding from the ashes was a small—a very small—fragment of thickish white paper.

Ellery snatched a glass from the depths of one of his pockets, trained the beams of the torch on the paper, and peered earnestly. "Well?" demanded the Inspector.

"I think," said Ellery slowly, standing straight again and lowering his glass, "I think we have finally found the last will and testament of Georg Khalkis."

* * *

It took the good sergeant all of ten minutes to solve the problem of how to retrieve the fragment from its inaccessible hiding-place. He was too huge to creep through the ash-pit orifice, and neither the Inspector nor Ellery felt inclined to wriggle their slighter bodies through the accumulated muck of years. Ellery for the solution of *this* problem was useless; and it took the more mechanically minded sergeant to discover the process whereby the scrap might be rescued. He manufactured a makeshift javelin by jamming a needle from Ellery's pocket-kit into the ferrule of Ellery's walking-stick; whereupon, on hands and knees, he managed to spear the fragment without great difficulty. He prodded the ashes, but nothing could be made of them—they were thoroughly charred and useless for examination.

The fragment, as Ellery had predicted, seemed indubitably part of Khalkis's last will. Fortunately, that portion of it which was untouched by fire contained the name of the legatee of the Khalkis Galleries. It was, in a scrawly script which the Inspector at once recognized as Georg Khalkis's, the name: *Albert Grimshaw*.

"This corroborates Knox's story, all right," said the Inspector. "And clearly shows that Sloane was the one cut out by the new will."

"So it does," murmured Ellery. "And very stupid and bungling indeed is the person who burnt this document. . . . A vexing problem. A very vexing problem." He rapped his *pince-nez* sharply against his teeth, staring at the char-edged fragment, but he did not explain what the problem was nor why it was vexing.

"One thing is sure," said the Inspector with satisfaction. "Mr. Sloane has some tall explaining to do, what with that anonymous letter about his being Grimshaw's brother and this will. All set, son?"

Ellery nodded, sweeping the basement once more with his glance. "Yes. I imagine that's quite all."

"Come on, then." The Inspector tucked the burnt fragment tenderly into a fold of his wallet and led the way to the front door of the basement. Ellery followed, deep in thought; and Velie brought up the rear, not unhurriedly, it should be noted, since not even his broad substantial back was impervious to the deathly blackness pressing upon it.

CHAPTER 19

Exposé

Weekes reported at once, as the Queens and Sergeant Velie stood in the foyer of the Khalkis house, that everyone in the Khalkis household was at home. The Inspector gruffly commanded the presence of Gilbert Sloane, Weekes hurried away toward the staircase at the rear of the hall, and the three men went into the Khalkis library.

The Inspector immediately proceeded to one of the telephones on the desk, called the District Attorney's office, and spoke to Pepper briefly, explaining the discovery of what seemed to be the missing Khalkis will. Pepper shouted that he was on his way. The old man then called Police Headquarters, roared a few questions, listened to a few replies, and hung up fuming. "No results on that anonymous letter. No fingerprints at all. Jimmy thinks the writer was damned careful—Come in, Sloane, come in. Want to talk to you."

Sloane hesitated in the doorway. "Something new, Inspector?"

"Come in, man! I shan't bite you."

Sloane walked in and sat down on the edge of a chair, white trim hands folded tensely in his lap. Velie lumbered off to a corner and flung his overcoat on the back of a chair; Ellery lit a cigarette and studied Sloane's profile through the curling smoke.

"Sloane," began the Inspector abruptly, "we've caught you in a number of downright lies."

Sloane paled. "What is it now? I'm sure I—"

"You've claimed from the beginning that the first time you ever laid eyes on Albert Grimshaw was when Khalkis's coffin was hauled up in the graveyard outside," said the Inspector. "You maintained that obviously false stand even after Bell, the night-clerk at the Hotel Benedict, identified you as one of a number of persons who visited Grimshaw on the night of September thirtieth."

Sloane muttered: "Of course. Of course. It wasn't true."

"It wasn't, eh?" The Inspector leaned forward and rapped him on the knee. "Well, Mr. Gilbert Grimshaw, suppose I tell you that we have found out you were Albert Grimshaw's brother?"

Sloane was not a pretty sight. His jaw dropped foolishly, his eyes popped, his tongue crept over his lips, beads of perspiration sprang into moist life on his forehead, and his hands twitched uncontrollably. He tried twice to find his tongue, and each time succeeded only in emitting an unintelligible splutter.

"Nipped you that time, eh, Sloane? Now, you come clean, Mister." The Inspector glowered. "What's it all about?"

Sloane finally discovered how to co-ordinate thought with larynx. "How—how on earth did you find out?"

"Never mind how. It's true, isn't it?"

"Yes." Sloane's hand went to his brow and came away greasy. "Yes, but I don't see yet how you—"

"Start talking, Sloane."

"Albert was—was my brother, as you say. When our mother and father died, many years ago, we were left alone. Albert—he was always in trouble. We quarrelled and separated."

"And you changed your name."

"Yes. My name was Gilbert Grimshaw, of course." He gulped; his eyes were watery. "Albert was sent to prison—some petty offence. I—well, I couldn't stand the shame and notoriety. I took my mother's maiden name of Sloane and started all over again. I told Albert at the time that I wanted nothing further to do with him . . ." Sloane squirmed; his words came slowly, pressed out by some inner piston of necessity. "He didn't know—I didn't tell him I had changed my name. I got as far away from him as I could. Came to New York, got into business here . . . But I always kept an eye on him, afraid he'd find out what I was doing, make more trouble, extort money from me, proclaim publicly his relationship . . . He was my brother, but he was an incorrigible rascal. Our father was a schoolteacher—taught drawing, painted himself; we grew up in a refined, a cultural atmosphere. I can't understand why Albert should have turned out so badly—"

"I don't want ancient history; I want immediate facts. You did visit Grimshaw that Thursday night at the hotel, didn't you?"

Sloane sighed. "I suppose it won't do any good to deny it now . . . Yes. I had kept an eye on him all during his rotten career, saw him go from bad to worse—although he didn't know I was watching. I knew he was in Sing Sing, and I waited for his release. When he got out that Tuesday, I found where he was stopping and Thursday night went to the Benedict to talk to him. I didn't like the idea of having him in New York. I wanted him—well, to go away . . ."

"He went away, all right," interrupted Ellery. Sloane jerked his head sideways, startled as an owl. "When was the last time you saw your brother before that Thursday night visit to his room?"

"Face to face, you mean?"

"Yes."

"I hadn't actually met and talked to him during the entire period in which my name has been Sloane."

"Admirable," murmured Ellery, applying himself to his cigarette again.

"What happened between you that night?" demanded Inspector Queen.

"Nothing, I swear! I asked him, pleaded with him to leave town. I offered him money. . . . He was surprised and I could see maliciously glad to see me, as if seeing me were the last thing in the world he had dreamed of, and it wasn't so unpleasant after all. . . . I realized at once I'd made a mistake in coming, that I should have been better off to have let sleeping dogs lie. Because he told me himself he hadn't even *thought* of me for years—had nearly forgotten he had a brother—his exact words, mind you!

"But it was too late. I offered him five thousand dollars to get out of town and stay out. I'd brought the money with me in small bills. He promised, snatched the money, and I left."

"Did you see him alive after that at any time?"

"No, no! I thought he'd gone away. When the coffin was opened and I saw him there . . ."

Ellery drawled: "And during your conversation with the ubiquitous Albert, did you tell him the name you now go by?"

Sloane seemed horrified. "Why, no. Of course not. I was keeping that as a kind of—well, self-protection. I don't think he even suspected that I wasn't still calling myself Gilbert Grimshaw. That's why I'm so surprised—the Inspector saying he had discovered we were brothers—I can't understand how on earth . . ."

"You mean," said Ellery swiftly, "no one knew that Gilbert *Sloane* was Albert Grimshaw's brother?"

"Exactly." Sloane wiped his forehead again. "In the first place, I've never told a soul about having a brother, not even my wife. And Albert couldn't have told anyone, because while he knew he had a brother somewhere, he didn't know that I was called Gilbert Sloane. Didn't know *that,* in fact, even after I went to his room that night."

"Funny," muttered the Inspector.

"Isn't it," said Ellery. "Mr. Sloane, did your brother know you were connected with Georg Khalkis?"

"Oh, no! I'm sure he didn't. In fact, he even asked me what

I was doing, in a jeering sort of way, and I naturally put him off. I didn't want him looking me up."

"One thing more. Did you meet your brother somewhere that Thursday night and enter the hotel with him?"

"No. I was alone. I got into the lobby almost in the wake of Albert and another man who was bundled up . . ."

The Inspector uttered a little exclamation.

". . . bundled up. I didn't see this man's face. I wasn't following Albert all night, and didn't know where he was coming from. But seeing him, I asked at the desk for his room-number, got it, and followed Albert and his companion up. I waited in a branching corridor on the third floor for a while, hoping the other fellow would go away so that I could go in, talk to Albert, and get away from the place. . . ."

"Did you have the door of Room 314 under observation?" asked Ellery sharply.

"Well, yes and no. But I suppose Albert's companion slipped out when I wasn't looking. I waited for a few moments; then I went to the door of 314 and knocked. Albert opened the door for me after a few moments—"

"And the room was empty?"

"Yes. Albert didn't mention having a previous visitor, and I assumed it must have been a hotel acquaintance of his who had left before I came in, while I was waiting." Sloane sighed. "I was too anxious to get the hideous business over and to get away, to ask questions. Then we said what I told you, and I left. I was very much relieved."

The Inspector said suddenly: "That's all."

Sloane jumped to his feet. "Thank you, Inspector, thank you for your splendid consideration. You too, Mr. Queen. Not what I've been led to believe—these third degrees and things . . ." He touched his necktie and Velie's shoulders quivered like the slope of Mount Vesuvius during an eruption. "I guess I—I'll be getting along," he said feebly. "Catch up on some work at the Galleries. Well . . ."

They kept silent, looking at him; Sloane muttered something, gave birth to a sound astonishingly like a giggle, and
slipped out of the library. A few moments later they heard the
slam of the front door.

"Thomas," said Inspector Queen, "I want you to get me a
complete transcript of the hotel register of the Benedict, showing who was stopping there on Thursday and Friday, the thirtieth and the first."

"Then you think," asked Ellery with amusement, as Velie
left the study, "you think there's something in that business of
Grimshaw's companion having been a guest at the hotel, as
Sloane suggested?"

The Inspector's pale face reddened. "And why not? Don't you?"
Ellery sighed.

It was at this moment that Pepper, coat tails flying, burst in
upon them, ruddy face made ruddier by the wind, eyes bright,
demanding to see the fragment of the will they had fished from
the furnace next door. Ellery sat by, musing, as Pepper and the
Inspector examined the scrap by a stronger light over the desk.
"Hard to tell," said Pepper. "Offhand, I see no reason why this
shouldn't be the remains of the authentic document. The handwriting seems to be the same."

"We'll check that."

"Of course." Pepper took off his coat. "If we do establish this
as a fragment of the last Khalkis testament," he continued reflectively, "and couple that with Mr. Knox's story, we're going to
find ourselves involved, I'm afraid, in one of those deuced testamentary tangles that make life so interesting for the Surrogate."

"What do you mean?"

"Well, unless we can prove that this will was signed by the
testator under circumstances indicating duress, the Khalkis
Galleries will go to the estate of Albert Grimshaw, deceased!"

They stared at each other. The Inspector said slowly: "I see.
And with Sloane probably the nearest of Grimshaw's kin . . ."

"Under suspicious circumstances," murmured Ellery.

"You mean you think Sloane would feel safer inheriting through his wife?" asked Pepper.

"Wouldn't you, Pepper, if you were in Sloane's place?"

"There's something in that," muttered the Inspector. He shrugged his shoulders and related the substance of Sloane's testimony a few moments before; and Pepper nodded. They looked again at the small burnt scrap in a sort of helplessness.

Pepper said: "The first thing to do is to see Woodruff and compare this fragment with his office copy. That ought to establish, with a comparison of handwritings . . ."

They all turned swiftly at the sound of a light step in the hall outside the study-door. Mrs. Vreeland, attired in a shimmering black gown, stood in the doorway in an attitude suggestive of pose. As Pepper hastily thrust the scrap into his pocket, the Inspector said easily: "Come in, Mrs. Vreeland. Did you want to see me?"

She replied in almost a whisper, "Yes," peering up and down the hall outside. Then she came in quickly and shut the door behind her. There was something furtive in her manner—a repressed emotion the men could not define, but which heightened the colour of her cheeks and the sparkle in her large eyes, and set her breast to rising and falling in long surges of breath. Somehow, there was malice in that handsome face— little dagger-points in those bold eyes.

The Inspector offered her a chair, but she refused, choosing to stand straight against the closed door, her manner openly cautious—as if she were straining to catch sounds from the hall outside. The Inspector's eyes narrowed, Pepper frowned, and even Ellery watched her with interest.

"Well, what is it, Mrs. Vreeland?"

"Just this, Inspector Queen," she whispered. "I've been withholding something . . ."

"Yes?"

"I have a story to tell—a story that ought to prove *very*

interesting to you." Her moist black lashes swept down over her eyes, concealed them; when they swept up again, the eyes were hard as ebony. "On Wednesday night, a week ago—"

"The day after the funeral?" asked the Inspector swiftly.

"Yes. On Wednesday night last, very late, I couldn't sleep," she murmured. "Insomnia—I suffer often from insomnia, you know. I got out of bed and went to my window. My bedroom window overlooks the court at the rear of the house. And I happened to see a man sneaking down the court to the gate of the graveyard. He went into the graveyard, Inspector Queen!"

"Indeed," said the Inspector gently. "This is very interesting, Mrs. Vreeland. Who was the man?"

"Gilbert Sloane!"

It came out with an intensity that was—unquestionably—venomous. She held them with her staring black eyes, something that was almost a voluptuous leer curving her lips. In that moment the woman was horrible—and earnest. The Inspector blinked, and Pepper clenched one fist exultantly. Only Ellery was unmoved—studying the woman as if she were a bacterium under the lens of a microscope.

"Gilbert Sloane. You're sure of this, Mrs. Vreeland?"

"Positive." The word lashed out like a whip.

The Inspector drew his thin shoulders up. "Now this is, as you say, a very serious matter, Mrs. Vreeland. You must be careful to give exact information. Tell me just what you saw—no more and no less. When you looked out of the window, did you see where Mr. Sloane was coming from?"

"He appeared from the shadows below my window. I couldn't tell whether he walked out of the shadows of this house or not, but I suppose he came from the Khalkis basement. At least, I got that impression."

"How was he dressed?"

"In a felt hat and overcoat."

"Mrs. Vreeland." Ellery's voice twisted her head about. "This was very late?"

"Yes. I don't know exactly what hour. But it must have been a good deal past midnight."

"The courtyard is extremely dark," said Ellery gently, "in the wee hours."

Two cords in her neck strained outward. "Oh, I see what you think! You think I really didn't know him! But it was he, I tell you!"

"Did you actually catch a glimpse of his face, Mrs. Vreeland?"

"No, I didn't. But it was Gilbert—I'd know him anywhere, any time, under any circumstances . . ." She bit her lip, Pepper nodded sagely, and the Inspector looked grim.

"Then, if it became necessary, you would swear," said the old man, "that you saw Gilbert Sloane that night in the court, going into the graveyard."

"Yes. I would." She glared sideways at Ellery.

"Did you stay by the window after he disappeared into the graveyard?" asked Pepper.

"Yes. He reappeared in about twenty minutes. He walked quickly, looking about him as if he didn't want to be seen, and jumped into the shadows directly under my window. I'm sure he went into this house."

"You saw nothing else?" persisted Pepper.

"My God," she said bitterly, "wasn't that enough?"

The Inspector stirred, his sharp nose aimed squarely at her breast. "When you first saw him going into the graveyard, Mrs. Vreeland—was he carrying anything?"

"No."

The Inspector turned away to conceal his disappointment. Ellery drawled: "Why haven't you come forward with this pretty tale before, Mrs. Vreeland?"

Again she glared at him, detecting in his detached, judicious, and slightly acid attitude a note of suspicion. "I don't see that that's important!"

"Ah, but it is, Mrs. Vreeland."

"Well—I didn't recall it until just now."

"Hmm," said the Inspector. "That's all, Mrs. Vreeland?"

"Yes."

"Then, please don't repeat the story to anyone, *anyone*. You may go now."

Some iron skeleton within her rusted and crumbled on the instant—her tension collapsed and suddenly she looked old. Going slowly to the door, she whispered: "But aren't you going to do anything about it?"

"Please go now, Mrs. Vreeland."

She turned the knob of the door in a tired way and went out without a backward glance. The Inspector closed the door after her and rubbed his hands together in a curious washing motion. "Well," he said briskly, "that's a horse of a different colour. The wench was telling the truth, by heaven! And it's beginning to look as if—"

"You will observe," said Ellery, "that the lady did not actually see the gentleman's physiognomy."

"You think she's lying?" asked Pepper.

"I think she told what she conceives to be the truth. Feminine psychology is a subtle thing."

"But you'll admit," said the Inspector, "that there's a good chance it *was* Sloane?"

"Oh, yes," said Ellery wearily, waving his hand.

"There's one thing we ought to do right this minute," said Pepper, clicking his jaws together. "And that's to go through Mr. Sloane's rooms upstairs."

"I quite agree with you," replied the Inspector grimly. "Coming, El?"

Ellery sighed and followed the Inspector and Pepper from the room, without too much hope on his features. As they emerged into the corridor, they caught sight of Delphina Sloane's slight figure hurrying along, at the front of the hall, looking back with flushed face and feverish eyes. She disappeared through the door leading into the drawing-room.

The Inspector stopped in his tracks. "I hope she wasn't

listening," he said in alarm. Then, shaking his head, he led the way along the corridor to the staircase, and they mounted to the upper floor. At the head of the stairs the old man paused, looked about, then skirted the stairway railing to his left. He knocked upon a door. Mrs. Vreeland appeared at once. "You'd oblige me, Madame," whispered the Inspector, "if you'd go downstairs to the drawing-room and keep Mrs. Sloane busy until we come back." He winked and nodded breathlessly. She closed the door of her room and ran down the stairs. "At least," said the old man contentedly, "we shan't be interrupted. Come along, boys."

*   *   *

The private apartment of the Sloanes on the upper floor was divided into two rooms—a sitting-room and a bedroom.

Ellery refused to participate in the search; he stood idly by watching the Inspector and Pepper go through the bedroom—through drawers, wardrobe, and closets. The Inspector was very circumspect; he allowed nothing to escape him; he dropped to his old knees and probed beneath the rug, tapped the walls, explored the interior of the closet. But all for nothing. There was no scrap of anything which either he or Pepper considered worth looking at twice.

Whereupon they returned to the sitting-room and began all over again. Ellery leaned against a wall, watching; he took a cigarette from his case, stuck it between his thin lips, struck a match—and shook the light out without igniting the cigarette. This was no place to smoke. He put cigarette and burnt match carefully into a pocket.

It was not until failure loomed imminent that the discovery was made. It was made by a very inquisitive Pepper poking about the carved old desk in a corner of the room. He had rifled every drawer without finding anything of moment; but, on standing over the desk and staring hypnotically down at it, a large tobacco-humidor seemed to draw his eye, and he lifted the lid. The jar was filled with pipe-tobacco. "This would be a good place," he muttered . . . and stopped short as his hands, dipping and sifting in the moist tobacco, met some cold metallic object.

"By God!" he exclaimed softly. The Inspector, fussing about the fireplace, raised his head, wiped a soot-smudge from his cheek and ran over to the desk. Ellery's nonchalance vanished, and he hurried over in the Inspector's wake.

In Pepper's trembling hand, to which clung a few shreds of tobacco, reposed a key.

The Inspector snatched it from the Assistant District Attorney. "This looks—" he began. His lips clamped together and he tucked the key into a vest pocket. "I think this is plenty, Pepper. Let's get out of here. If this key fits where I think it does, by heaven, there'll be merry hell popping!"

They left the sitting-room quickly and cautiously. Downstairs they found Sergeant Velie.

"Sent a man for that Hotel Benedict register," rumbled Velie, "and it ought to be here—"

"Never mind that now, Thomas," said the Inspector, grasping Velie's paw. The old man peered about; the corridor was empty. He extracted the key from his vest pocket and pressed it into Velie's hand, whispering something into the sergeant's ear. Velie nodded and strode down the hall toward the foyer; a moment later they heard him leave the house.

"Well, gentlemen," said the Inspector gleefully, inhaling snuff with gusty vigour, "well, gentlemen"—sniff! sneeze!—"it looks like the good old McCoy. Here, let's go into the library and out of the way."

He herded Pepper and Ellery into the study and stood by the door, which he had left open to the tiniest crack. They were silent, waiting; and there was a look of tired expectancy on Ellery's lean face. Suddenly the old man opened the door and tugged; and Sergeant Velie materialized at the end of the Inspector's arm.

He closed the door at once. Velie's sardonic lineaments

showed distinct evidences of excitement. "Well, Thomas—well, well?"

"It's the one, sure enough!"

"Jerusalem!" cried the Inspector. "That key from Sloane's humidor fits the basement door of the empty Knox house!" The old man was chirping like an aged robin. Velie, standing guard against the closed door, resembled a condor with glittering eyes. Pepper was a hopping sparrow. And Ellery, as might be expected, was the lugubrious raven of black plumage and un-uttered croakings.

"This key business means two things," the Inspector was saying, with a grin that split his taut face in two. "Taking a leaf out of your book, my son. . . . It indicates that Gilbert Sloane, who had the strongest motive for stealing the will in the first place, owns a duplicate key to the basement in which the will-scrap was found. This means that he must have been the one who attempted to destroy the will there in the furnace. You see, when he stole the will originally from the wall-safe in this room the day of the funeral, he slipped it into the coffin—with the box still unopened probably—and retrieved it either Wednesday or Thursday night.

"The second indication is confirmation. The smelly old trunk, the key to the basement—confirmation that the body of Grimshaw was kept there before burial in Khalkis's coffin. That empty basement next door would be a safe place. . . . By God, I'll have Ritter's hide for incompetence! Imagine missing that scrap in the furnace!"

"It begins to look interesting," said Pepper, rubbing his jaw. "Damned interesting. My job's clear—I'll have to see Woodruff at once and compare the burnt remnant with his office copy. Got to make sure the scrap is genuine." He went to the desk and dialled a number. "Busy line," he said, hanging up for a moment. "Inspector, it looks to me as if somebody bit off more than he could chew. If we can only establish. . . ." He dialled again and succeeded in getting Woodruff's house on the wire. Woodruff's

valet regretted that the lawyer was out, but he was expected
back within a half-hour it seemed. Pepper instructed the valet
to have Woodruff wait for him, and clamped down the dumbbell
instrument with a bang.

"You'd better make it snappy," twinkled the Inspector. "Or
you'll miss the fireworks. Anyway, it's necessary for us to be
sure the scrap is genuine. We'll wait here a while, and then—
You let me know as soon as you find out, Pepper."

"Right. We'll probably have to go down to Woodruff's office
and snag the copy, but I'll come back here as soon as I can."
Pepper snatched up his hat and coat and hurried out.

"Pretty smug about this thing, Inspector," remarked Ellery.
The humour was gone from his face; he looked worried.

"And why not?" The old man sank into Khalkis's swivel-
chair with a luxurious little sigh. "It looks like the end of the
trail—for us and for Mr. Gilbert Sloane."

Ellery grunted.

"Here's one case," chuckled the Inspector, "in which your
high-falutin methods of deduction aren't worth a tinker's dam.
Just good old-fashioned straight thinking—no fancy stuff,
my son."

Ellery grunted again.

"The trouble with you is," continued the Inspector slyly,
"you think every case has to be a mental wrestling-match. You
won't give your old man credit for a little common-sense. Heck,
that's all a detective needs, anyway—common-sense. You're
beyond your depth, boy."

Ellery said nothing.

"Now you take this case against Gilbert Sloane," went on the
old man. "It's open-and-shut. Motive? A-plenty. Sloane bumped
Grimshaw for two reasons: one, Grimshaw was dangerous to
him, maybe even tried to blackmail him for all we know. But that
isn't the important motive. Because Grimshaw, as beneficiary of
the Khalkis Galleries by Khalkis's new will, was doing Sloane
out of his inheritance. With Grimshaw out of the way, the will

destroyed for the reason you pointed out—that Sloane wouldn't want it known he was Grimshaw's brother, wouldn't want to inherit in a dangerous way—well, with the will destroyed Khalkis would be considered to have died intestate and Sloane would get his cut through his wife anyway. Slick!"

"Oh, very."

The Inspector smiled. "Don't take it so hard, younker. . . . I'll bet you an investigation of Sloane's personal affairs will show he has money troubles. He needs the old do-re-mi. All right. That takes care of motive. Now for another tack.

"As you pointed out before, in your analysis about Khalkis as the criminal, it's dead certain that whoever choked Grimshaw must have planted those false clues against Khalkis later, and therefore must have known of Knox's possession of the painting to have depended on his silence. All right. Yet the only outsider, as you also showed, who could have planted the false clues and known of Knox's possession of the Leonardo was Grimshaw's phantom 'partner.' Right?"

"Gospel."

"Now then," continued the old man with a judicious frown, placing the tips of his fingers together, " — Thomas, stop fidgeting! — now then, that being the case, Sloane to be the murderer must also have been Grimshaw's 'unknown' partner—something I find it easy to believe, in the light of the fact that they were brothers."

Ellery groaned.

"Yes, I know," said his father indulgently, "it means that Sloane therefore was lying in two important points of his spiel a while ago. First, if he was Grimshaw's partner, then Grimshaw must have known that Sloane, as Sloane, was his brother, and therefore knew Sloane's position in the Khalkis business. Second, Sloane must have been the one who came into the Benedict with Grimshaw, not the man who followed directly after, as he claimed to us. This means that Sloane having been Grimshaw's unknown companion, the single unidentified visitor must have been the second—and where he fits in the Lord alone knows, if he fits in at all."

"Everything should fit," said Ellery.

"And well you know it, eh?" grinned the Inspector. "But this satisfies *me*, my boy. In any event, if Sloane is the murderer and Grimshaw's partner, the will motive was the vital one, getting rid of Grimshaw as a personal menace was a contributing motive, and clearing the field for realizing by blackmail on Knox's illegal possession of the Leonardo, still a third motive."

"An important point," remarked Ellery. "We must watch for that particularly. Now that you have arranged everything to your satisfaction, I should appreciate a reconstruction of the crime. This seems to be an object-lesson for me, and I crave further instruction."

"Why not? It's as simple as a,b,c. Sloane buried Grimshaw in Khalkis's coffin last Wednesday night—the night Mrs. Vreeland saw him snooping about the court. I suppose she saw him on a second trip, which would account for the fact that she didn't see him carrying the body. He must've already lugged it into the graveyard."

Ellery shook his head. "I have no argument at my command to refute anything you say, Dad, but—it doesn't ring true."

"Fiddlesticks. Sometimes you're as stubborn as a mule. Rings true to me. Naturally Sloane buried Grimshaw before he had any reason to believe the coffin would be opened by the law. When he dug it up to put the body inside he probably took out the will at the same time to make sure of destroying it. No extra risk to himself—the coffin was open already—get the idea? Sloane must also have taken the promissory note from Grimshaw's body at the time he murdered him, and destroyed it later to protect the estate, which he was going to inherit indirectly anyway, against any claim if the note were found and presented for payment by someone else. Boy, it fits like a glove!"

"You think so?"

"I know so, darn it! Why, that basement duplicate key in

Sloane's tobacco-jar—that's *evidence*. The burnt scrap of will in the furnace next door—that's *evidence*. And then on top of that— the fact that Grimshaw and Sloane were brothers. . . . Son, wake up. You can't shut your eyes to a case like that."

"Sad, but true," sighed Ellery. "But please leave me out of this, Dad. Take all the credit for this solution, I want none of it. I've had my fingers burnt once by clues which turned out to be deliberate plants."

"Plants!" The Inspector snorted derisively. "You mean you think that key was stuck in Sloane's humidor by somebody in order to frame the man?"

"My reply must be cryptic. Please observe, however, that my eyes are as wide open as nature permits," said Ellery, rising. "And although I can't see clearly what lies ahead, I pray *le bon dieu* to grant me that 'double pleasure' of which La Fontaine speaks so eloquently: the pleasure of deceiving the deceiver . . . *de tromper le trompeur.*"

"Stuff and nonsense!" cried the Inspector, springing from Khalkis's swivel-chair. "Thomas, get on your hat and coat and collect some of the boys. We're going to pay a little visit to the Khalkis Galleries."

"You mean you're going to confront Sloane with what you've found?" asked Ellery slowly.

"Yes, sirree," said the Inspector. "And if Pepper brings an authentification of the will-scrap, Mr. Sloane will be behind nice shiny bars in the Tombs to-night charged with murder!"

"Only," rumbled Sergeant Velie, "they ain't so shiny."

CHAPTER 20

Reckoning

Madison Avenue in the vicinity of the Khalkis Galleries was a dark and quiet region when Inspector Queen, Ellery Queen, Sergeant Velie and a number of detectives descended upon it from several directions later that evening. They worked without clamour. The shop itself, as they could see through the wide front pane, was dark; and the entrance to the shop was barred, protected by familiar electrically wired lattice-work. A separate entrance, however, to one side of the shop door held their attention; and the Inspector and Velie whispered together for a moment. Then the sergeant pressed his big thumb on a button above which appeared the words: *Night Bell,* and they waited in silence. There was no response, and Velie rang again. Five minutes passing without a sound or a light from within, Velie grunted, waved several of his men to join him, and together they broke down the door. It gave with a grinding and screaming of wood and steel hinges, and they tumbled in a heap in the blackness of the hall beyond.

They swarmed up a flight of steps, came to another door which they found in the rays of their flashlights to be protected by another burglar-alarm device, attacked this door with callous vehemence and no apparent fear of the alarm they were setting off in the central bureau of the protective agency, and crashed through.

They found themselves in a long black gallery, extending the entire length of the floor. Their torches revealed in flitting glimpses the unmoved features of numerous painted faces on the walls, the gleam of floor-cases containing *objets d'art,* and many pieces of pale statuary. Everything seemed quite in order, and no one appeared to challenge their coming.

Almost at the end of the gallery, to their left, a stream of light gashed across the floor, emanating from an open doorway. The Inspector cried: "Sloane! Mr. Sloane!" but there was no answer. They hurried in a body to the source of the illumination and found themselves in a doorway, steel door gaping open and on it lettered the legend:

Mr. Gilbert Sloane, *Private*

But their eyes were not long occupied with such fleeting details. For, as one man, they sucked in their breaths, thronging the doorway, now still as death . . . still, in fact, as the figure of death that was sprawled at a desk in the room, the light of a desk-lamp pitilessly revealing the stark body of Gilbert Sloane.

* * *

There was little material for speculation. They stood about the room—someone had snapped on the electric switch—and gazed down at the shattered, bloody head of what had been Gilbert Sloane.

The desk at which he sat, head lying on its left side on a green desk blotter, was in the centre of the private office. One end of the desk was squarely facing the doorway, so that the view of Sloane's body from the gallery outside was a sideways view. He sat slumped forward in a leather chair, his left arm extended along the top of the blotter, his right arm dangling to the floor along the side of his chair. And a revolver lay on the floor directly under his right hand, a few inches below the tips of his dead fingers, as if it had slipped from his hand. The Inspector leaned over and, without touching the body, examined the dead man's right temple, which lay exposed to the glare of the office lights. There was a deep, torn, crimson hole in the temple, spattered with blackish powder marks—unquestionably the point of the bullet's entry. The old man knelt and, very carefully, broke open the revolver. It was fully loaded except for one chamber. He sniffed the muzzle and nodded.

"If this isn't suicide," he announced, getting to his feet, "I'm a monkey's uncle."

Ellery looked about the room. It was a small, neat office; everything in it seemed precisely in its accustomed place. There was no slightest sign of a scuffle anywhere.

Meanwhile, the Inspector had sent a detective off with the revolver, wrapped in tissue, to determine its ownership. He turned back to Ellery as the man went out. "Well, isn't this enough for you? Still think it's a frame-up?"

Ellery's eyes sought some far-off place beyond the confines of the room. He murmured: "No, it looks genuine enough. But what I cannot grasp is the pressing necessity for suicide. After all, there was nothing in our talk with Sloane earlier this evening which might have made him suspect you had a case against him. Nothing was said about the will at that time, the key had not been found, Mrs. Vreeland had not yet told her story. I began to suspect . . ."

They stared at each other. "Mrs. Sloane!" they cried together, and Ellery jumped for the telephone on Sloane's desk. He became very busy interrogating the operator, was switched to a central office. . . .

The Inspector's attention was diverted. The wail of a siren reached his ears faintly from Madison Avenue; brakes screeched in the street, and he heard the pounding of heavy feet on the stairs. The Inspector peered into the gallery. Sergeant Velie's ruthless destruction of the electrical alarm had borne fruit. A squad of grim men dashed in, automatics levelled. It took the Inspector several minutes to convince them that he was in truth the well-known Inspector Queen of the Detective Bureau, and that the men scattered about were detectives, not thieves, and that nothing had apparently been stolen from the Khalkis Galleries. By the time he had placated them, sent them packing, and returned to the office, he found Ellery smoking in a chair and looking more disturbed than ever.

"Find out anything?"

"It's incredible. . . . It's taken me some time, but I finally managed to get the information. There was one incoming call on this instrument to-night," said Ellery morosely. "Within the hour. We traced the incoming call. It emanated from the Khalkis house."

"As I thought. So that's how he knew the jig was up! Somebody overheard us talking the case over in the library, and tipped Sloane off by phone from the house."

"On the other hand," said Ellery wearily, "there was no way of discovering who put the call through to this office or what the conversation was. You'll have to be satisfied with the bare facts."

"They're plenty sufficient, believe me. Thomas!" Velie appeared in the doorway. "Scoot back to the Khalkis house and question everybody there. Find out who was in the house this evening during the time we searched Sloane's room, questioned Sloane and Mrs. Vreeland, and talked over the Sloane business in the library downstairs. Find out if you can who used one of the phones in the house to-night—and be mighty sure you put Mrs. Sloane on the pan. Understand?"

"Spill the news to the Khalkis bunch?" growled Velie.

"You bet. Take some of the boys with you. Nobody is to put a foot out of the place until I say so."

Velie left. The telephone rang; the Inspector answered. It was a call from the detective whom he had dispatched with the revolver. He had succeeded in tracing the weapon; it was registered under an official permit which had been issued to Gilbert Sloane. The old man, chuckling, telephoned headquarters for Dr. Samuel Prouty, the Assistant Medical Examiner.

He turned away from the telephone to find Ellery exploring a small safe set in the wall behind Sloane's desk, its round steel door wide open.

"Anything there?"

"I don't know yet. . . . Hullo!" Ellery adjusted his *pince-nez* more firmly on his nose and bent over. Beneath several documents strewn on the floor of the little safe there was a metallic object. The Inspector took it away from him at once.

It was a heavy, old-fashioned gold watch, worn with age. There was no tick of life within it.

The old man turned it over. "If this isn't the darnedest—!" He waved the watch aloft, and executed a little impromptu war-dance. "Ellery," he cried, "this clinches it! By the Lord Harry, the whole messy business is finished!"

Ellery sharply examined the watch. There, on the reverse side of the open face, etched in tiny script on the gold case-back, appeared the almost obliterated letters of the name: *Albert Grimshaw*. The engraving was genuinely aged.

Ellery looked more dissatisfied than ever. His misery increased when the Inspector, tucking the watch into one of his vest pockets, said: "No question about it. This is corroboration. Sloane evidently took Grimshaw's watch from the body at the same time he swiped the promissory note. This coupled with Sloane's suicide is as much proof of Sloane's guilt as any man could want."

"There," said Ellery dolefully, "I thoroughly agree with you." Miles Woodruff and Assistant District Attorney Pepper put in an appearance on the scene of the suicide some time later. They looked soberly down at the remains of Gilbert Sloane.

"So it was Sloane all the time," said Woodruff. His normally ruddy face was ridged with pallid muscle. "I knew he must have been the one who stole the will in the first place.... Well, Inspector, it's finished, eh?"

"Thank goodness, yes."

"Darned rotten way for a man to go out," said Pepper. "Coward's way. But then from what I hear Sloane was almost a pansy.... Woodruff and I were going back to the Khalkis house when we bumped into Sergeant Velie. Told us what had happened, and we hurried over here. Woodruff, suppose you tell 'em about the will."

Woodruff sat down heavily on a modernistic divan in a corner, wiping his face. "Not much to tell. That scrap is genuine. I think Pepper will confirm this; it exactly matches the corresponding portion of my office copy—exactly. And the handwriting—the written name of Grimshaw—that's Khalkis's fist, all right, all right."

"Fine. But we might as well be sure. Did you bring the scrap and copy back with you?"

"Certainly." Woodruff handed the Inspector a large manila envelope. "I've put in some other samples of Khalkis's writing you'll find."

The old man looked into the envelope, nodded, and beckoned one of the men standing about. "Johnson, you go down and locate Una Lambert, the handwriting expert. You'll find her home address at Headquarters. Tell her to examine all samples of handwriting in this envelope. Also the typewriting of the burnt scrap. Want an immediate check-up."

Johnson went away just as the tall, lank figure of Dr. Prouty, the inevitable cigar in his mouth, slouched into the room.

"Come in, Doc!" said the Inspector genially. "Got another stiff for you. Looks like the last."

"In *this* case," said Dr. Prouty cheerfully. He set down his black bag and looked at the dead man's shattered head. "Hmph! So it's you, hey? Never thought I'd meet you again under *these* circumstances, Mr. Sloane." And he dropped his hat and coat and became busy.

Five minutes later he rose from his knees. "Plain case of suicide, and that's my verdict unless somebody here knows different," he growled. "Where's the gat?"

"Sent it off with a man," said the Inspector. "The gun checks."

"A .38, I suppose?"

"Right."

"Reason I say that," continued the Assistant Medical Examiner, chewing away on his cigar, "is that the bullet isn't here."

"What do you mean?" asked Ellery swiftly.

"Keep your shirt on, Queen. Come over here." Ellery and the others crowded about the desk as Dr. Prouty leaned over the dead man, gripped the thin disordered hair and raised the head. On the left side of the head, which had been lying against the green blotter, there was a welter of stiff blood and a distinguishable hole; the blotter where the head had been resting was stained with blood. "Bullet went clean through his dome. Must be about here somewhere."

He pulled the body to a sitting position in the chair, as calmly as if he were handling a sack of wet wash. He jerked the head straight, holding it by the slippery hair, and squinted in the direction the bullet must have taken if Sloane had shot himself as he sat in his chair.

"Right out through the open door," said the Inspector. "Easy to tell from the general direction and the body's position. Door was open when we found him, so the bullet must be out in the gallery there."

The Inspector trotted through the doorway into the now brilliantly lighted gallery. He gauged the probable trajectory of the bullet with his eye, nodded, and proceeded directly to the wall opposite the doorway. A thick antique Persian rug hung there. A moment's careful scrutiny, a moment's prodding with the point of his pen-knife, and the old man returned triumphantly carrying a slightly smashed and flattened bullet.

Dr. Prouty grunted in approval, and restored the dead man to his original position. The Inspector turned the deadly pellet over in his fingers. "Nothing to it. He shot himself, the bullet went clean through his head and out through the left side of the skull, flew through the doorway, most of its force spent, and landed in that rug on the wall opposite, outside. Not in very deep, either. Checks all around."

Ellery examined the bullet, then returned it to his father with an exasperated shrug that was eloquent of a queer and tenacious puzzlement. He retired to a corner to sit beside Woodruff and Pepper while the Inspector and Dr. Prouty superintended the removal of the body for autopsy purposes—a precaution the old man insisted upon.

While the corpse was being carted through the long gallery, Sergeant Velie toiled up the stairs, strode by the stretcher with no more than a passing glance, and marched into the office like a grenadier on parade. Disdaining to remove his great felt hat, which was jammed like a busby on his head, he growled to the Inspector: "No luck."

"Well, it doesn't really matter. Just what did you find?"

"Nobody telephoned to-night—at least, that's what *they* say."

"Naturally, whoever phoned won't admit it. Point probably never will be cleared up," remarked the Inspector, feeling for his snuff-box. "Dollars to doughnuts it was Mrs. Sloane who tipped Sloane off. Probably eavesdropped when we were gabbing in the library, waited until she could ditch Mrs. Vreeland, and then called Sloane in a hurry. Either she was an accomplice of Sloane's or she was innocent and realized, when she heard us talking, where the guilt lay and called to dig the truth out of her hubby. . . . Hard to tell. What Sloane said, or what she said, is a question, but at least the call served to show Sloane that he was through. So he committed suicide as the only way out."

"I'd say," rumbled Velie, "that she's not guilty. When she heard the news, she fainted clear away—and believe me, Chief, that wasn't a phoney. That was a *faint*."

Ellery had risen restlessly, barely listening, and was again prowling about. He went through the safe again—nothing there seemed to interest him and he sauntered over to the desk, which was littered with papers, studiously avoiding with the eyes the dark splotch on the blotter where Sloane's blood had oozed from his head. He began to rummage among the papers. A book-like object caught his fancy; it was a Morocco-bound diary, as he saw by the gilt letters: *Diary*, 192—, stamped on the cover. It was half-hidden beneath some papers, and he plucked it from the desk with avidity. The Inspector went to his side and inquisitively peeped over his son's shoulder. Ellery flipped through the yearbook—there was page after page of neat, precise, voluminous writing. He picked up several sheets of paper from the desk on which were samples of Sloane's handwriting, and compared them with the handwriting in the diary; they all matched exactly. He read snatches in the yearbook, shook his head angrily, shut the book and—slipped it into the side pocket of his jacket.

"Anything there?" asked the Inspector.

"If there is," said Ellery, "it wouldn't interest *you*, Dad. I thought you said the case was closed?"

The old man grinned and turned away. Men's hoarse voices were echoing through the main gallery outside. Sergeant Velie appeared in the midst of a yelling group of reporters. Somehow cameramen managed to slip in, and before long the room was filled with flashes and smoke. The Inspector began an indulgent recital of the facts; men were busy scribbling, and Sergeant Velie was cornered for *his* story, and Assistant District Attorney Pepper became the centre of a cynically admiring group; and Miles Woodruff expanded his chest and began to talk, rapidly and personally, the gist of his remarks being that he, Attorney Woodruff, had known all along where the guilt lay, but the—well, you know, boys, how these official investigations creep along; the police and the Detective Bureau. . . .

In the midst of the turmoil, Ellery Queen managed to slip out of the office unobserved. He picked his way past the statuary in the gallery, beneath the rich paintings on the walls; trod lightly down the stairs and past the shattered front door, and emerged with a vast sigh of relief into the dark cold air of Madison Avenue.

The Inspector found him there, fifteen minutes later, leaning against a shadowy shop-window, communing with whatever of darkling thoughts swirled about each other in his aching head.

CHAPTER 21

Yearbook

The cheerless mood persisted until far—very far—into the bleak hours of the early morning. In vain the Inspector endeavoured, by every paternal artifice known to him, to persuade his gloomy scion to abandon thought and seek solace in the depths of bed. Ellery, clad in dressing-gown and slippers, crouched in an armchair before a weak fire in the living-room, intent on every word of the leather-bound yearbook he had filched from Sloane's desk, did not deign even to reply to the old man's blandishments.

Finally in despair the Inspector shuffled into the kitchen, brewed a pot of coffee—young Djuna was fast asleep in his cubicle—and in silence drank a lonely toast. The aroma titillated Ellery's olfactory just as he concluded his study of the diary; he rubbed his eyes sleepily, went into the kitchen, poured himself a cup of coffee and the two drank together, still in a silence that offended the eardrums.

The old man set his mug down with a bang. "Tell papa. What the devil's eating you, son?"

"Well," said Ellery, "may you ask. I've been awaiting that question with the impatience of Lady Macbeth. You postulate Gilbert Sloane as the murderer of his brother, Albert

Grimshaw—the result of admittedly confessional circumstances and what seem to you a sharp, clear case. Now I ask you: who sent the anonymous letter which disclosed Sloane as Grimshaw's brother?"

The old man sucked at his old teeth. "Go on," he said. "Get it off your chest. There's an answer for everything."

"Oh, and is there?" retorted Ellery. "Very well—let me expatiate. Sloane himself didn't send that letter, obviously—would he give the police an item of damning information against himself if he were guilty? Naturally not. Who then did write the letter? Remember that Sloane said no one in the world except himself—not even Grimshaw, mind you, his own brother—knew that Gilbert Sloane, *as Gilbert Sloane,* was the brother of the murdered man. So I ask again: who wrote the letter? For whoever wrote it did know, and yet it seems that no one except the single individual who *wouldn't* write the letter *did* write it. Doesn't follow."

"Ah, my son, if all questions were as easy to answer as that," grinned the Inspector. "Of course Sloane didn't write the letter! And I don't care a hoot who did. It isn't important. Because—" he brandished his thin forefinger affectionately—"because we have only Sloane's word for it that no one but he knew. You see? Certainly, if Sloane had told the truth the question would be a poser, but with Sloane himself the criminal, anything he said is open to doubt, especially if he said it—as he did—at a time when he thought he was safe and when lies might tangle up the trail for the police. So—it's quite likely that someone else *did* know that Sloane as Sloane was Grimshaw's brother. Sloane himself must have spilled it to someone. The best possibility is Mrs. Sloane, although it's true that there doesn't seem to be any reason why she should inform against her own husband—"

"An acute parenthesis," drawled Ellery. "Because, according to your own case against Sloane, you postulated Mrs. Sloane as the person who warned Sloane by telephone. Certainly that isn't consistent with the indigenous malice of the anonymous letter-writer."

"All right," said the Inspector instantly, "look at it this way. Did Sloane have an enemy? Darned right he did—the one who told against him in another instance: Mrs. Vreeland! So maybe she's the one who wrote the letter. How she came to know of the brothership, of course, is a matter of guesswork, but I'll bet—"

"And you'd lose your money. There's something so rotten in Denmark that it makes my head ache—a flaw, a flaw! I'm hanged if . . ." He did not finish; his face grew longer, if that were possible, and he flung a matchstick into the dying fire with viciousness.

The shrill br-r-ring of the telephone startled them. "Who on earth could that be at this hour?" exclaimed the old man. "Hello! . . . Oh. Good *morning.* . . . Quite all right. What did you find? . . . I see. That's fine. Now run along to bed—late hours are mighty bad for a nice young girl's complexion. Ha, ha! . . . Very well. Good night, my dear." He hung up, smiling. Ellery asked a question with his eyebrows. "Una Lambert. Says there's no question about the authenticity of the written name on that burnt scrap of will. It's Khalkis's fist, without a doubt. And she says that everything else tends to show that the fragment is part of the original document."

"Indeed." The information depressed Ellery for no reason imaginable to the Inspector.

The old man's good humour was swallowed in a little storm of temper. "By heaven, it seems to me you don't *want* this blasted case to end!"

Ellery shook his head gently. "Don't scold, Dad. I can think of no consummation more devoutly to be wished. But it must be a consummation which is satisfactory to me."

"Well, it's satisfactory to *me.* The case against Sloane is perfect. And with Sloane dead, Grimshaw's partner is wiped off the map and everything is cleaned up. Because, as you said, Grimshaw's partner was the only outsider who knew that Knox had that Leonardo thingamajig, and now that he's a stiff—although the painting business might still have been one of the contributing motives in Sloane's original plot—the whole thing remains a police secret. That means," continued the Inspector with a little smack of his lips, "that we can go to work on Mr. James J. Knox. We've got to get that painting back, if it's really the one that was stolen by Grimshaw from the Victoria Museum."

"Have you had a reply to your cablegram?"

"Nary a word." The Inspector frowned. "Can't understand why the Museum doesn't answer. Anyway, if that British crowd try to get the painting back from Knox, there'll be a cat-fight. Knox with his money and pull will keep himself in the clear. I think Sampson and I had better work this problem out slowly—don't want to scare our rich bird into getting his hackles up."

"You'll have ample opportunity to settle the affair. It's doubtful if the Museum would want the story publicized that the painting which their experts had pronounced a genuine Leonardo and which was exhibited publicly as such is an almost valueless copy. That is, always provided it *is* a copy. We have only Knox's word for that, you know."

The Inspector spat thoughtfully into the fire. "Gets more and more complicated. Anyway, to come back to the Sloane case. Thomas got his report on the list of people registered at the Hotel Benedict on the Thursday and Friday of Grimshaw's stay. Well, there's no name on the list which corresponds or is connected with anyone in the case. I suppose that was to be expected. Sloane said he thought the fellow was a hotel acquaintance of Grimshaw's—he must have lied, and this mysterious baby must be someone else, maybe not in the case at all, who came after Sloane. . . ."

The Inspector chattered on, carried away by a soothing virtuous contentment. Ellery said nothing in reply to these calm verbal wanderings; he extended his long arm and picked up the Sloane diary, flipping its pages, studying it again with gloomy mien.

"Look here, Dad," he said at last, without raising his eyes, "it is true that on the surface everything matches glossily with the

hypothesis of Sloane as the *deus ex machina* of these events.
But that's just the trouble with it; it's all occurred much too for-
tuitously to lull my restless sensibilities. Don't forget, please,
that once before we—I—have been tricked into accepting a
solution ... a solution which might have been accepted and
publicized and forgotten by this time had it not been pricked
by the sheerest accident. This one seems, so to speak, unprick-
able. ..." He shook his head. "I can't put my finger on it. But I
feel there's something wrong."

"But it won't do you any good to bat your head against a
stone wall, son."

Ellery grinned feebly. "Such a procedure might knock an
inspiration into being," he said, and bit his lip. "Follow me for a
moment." He held up the diary, and the Inspector flapped over
in his carpet-slippers to look at it. Ellery had opened the book
at the point of its last written entry—a wordy report in neat,
small script under the printed date: *Sunday Oct.* 10. The opposite page was headed by: *Monday Oct.* 11. That page was blank.

"Now, you see," said Ellery with a sigh, "I have been poring
over this personalized and therefore interesting yearbook, and I
could not escape noting that Sloane made no entry to-night—
the night of his, as you say, suicide. Allow me for a moment to
epitomize the spirit-content of this diary. We brush aside at once,
of course, the fact that nowhere in these pages is mention made
of the incidents surrounding Grimshaw's strangling; and the fact
that merely conventional reference is made to Khalkis's death:
for naturally, were Sloane a murderer, he would avoid commit-
ting to paper anything which might incriminate him. On the
other hand, certain observations are self-evident: for one thing,
Sloane wrote in this diary religiously each night of the week at
the same approximate hour, setting down before his day's notation the time of writing; as you can see, it has been for months
the hour of eleven P.M. or thereabout. For another thing, this diary reveals Sloane to have been a gentleman of overwhelming
ego, a man of enormous preoccupation with himself; a reading

elicits lurid details, for example—painfully lurid—of a sexual affair with some woman cautiously unnamed."

Ellery slammed the book shut, flung it on the table, leaped to his feet and began to pace the rug before the hearth, his forehead creased in scores of tiny lines. The old man peered up at him unhappily. "Now I ask you, in the name of all the knowledge of modern psychology," cried Ellery, "would such a man as this—a man who dramatized everything about himself, as this diary copiously illustrates, a man who found in the expression of his ego the obviously morbid satisfaction that is so characteristic of his type—would such a man pass up the unexampled, the unique, the cosmic opportunity of writing dramatically about the greatest event of his life: his coming death?"

"Thoughts of that very death may have pushed everything else from his mind," suggested the Inspector.

"I doubt it," said Ellery bitterly. "Sloane, if he had been informed by the tenuous telephone call of police suspicion, realizing that he could no longer evade punishment for his crime having besides even a brief interval during which he might work unmolested, would have been impelled by every crying fibre of his personality to make that last heroic entry in his diary . . . an argument supported, moreover, by the circumstance that all this occurred around the general period—eleven o'clock—when he was accustomed to confiding in his little yearbook. And yet," he cried, "no entry at all was made for this night, of all nights!"

His eyes were fevered, and the Inspector rose and placed his small thin hand on Ellery's arm, shaking him with almost womanish sympathy. "Come, don't take on so. It sounds good, but it doesn't prove anything, son. . . . Come to bed."

Ellery allowed himself to be led into their bedroom. "Yes," he said, "it proves nothing."

And a half-hour later in the darkness, addressed to his father's soft snores, "But it is just such a psychological indication as this that makes me question whether Gilbert Sloane committed suicide after all."

The chill darkness of the bedroom providing little comfort and no response, Ellery proved himself a philosopher and went to sleep. He dreamed all night of animated diaries astride curiously human coffins brandishing revolvers and shooting at the man in the moon—a lunar countenance whose features were unmistakably those of Albert Grimshaw.

BOOK TWO

"Most of the epic discoveries of modern science have been made possible fundamentally by their discoverers' persistence in applying cold logic to a set of actions and reactions. . . .

"Lavoisier's simple explanation—it seems simple to us now—of what happens to pure lead when it is 'burned'—an explanation which exposed the centuries-old fallacy of that horrific creation of the medieval mind, phlogiston—was the result of what seems to us in our atmosphere of modern scientific thoroughness an absurdly basic principle, as indeed it is; that if a substance weighs one ounce before burning in the air, and weighs one ounce point o seven after burning in the air, then some substance from the air has been added to the original ore to account for the extra weight. . . . It took some sixteen centuries for man to realize this, and to name the new product lead oxide!

"No phenomenon in a crime is impossible of explanation. Persistence and simple logic are the cardiac requisites of the detective. What to the unthinking is a mystery, to the calculating is self-evident truth. . . . The detection of crime is no longer a matter of medieval mutterings over a crystal; it is one of the most exact of modern sciences. And at its root lies logic."

—from *Byways of Modern Science* (pp. 147–48)
by Dr. George Hinchcliffe

CHAPTER 22

Bottom

Ellery Queen discovered with a growing sense of futility that one of his innumerable ancient sources for wisdom, Pittacus of Mitylene, had not made provision for the human margin of frailty. Time, Ellery found, was not to be seized by the forelock. The days went by, and it was not in his power to stay them. A week passed, and he had succeeded in wringing from its fleeing hours only a few drops of bitterness, and not any mental sap at all—an empty beaker, all things considered, into whose arid bottom he stared with increasing unhappiness.

For others, however, the week had been full to the brim. Sloane's suicide and funeral had undammed a flood. The newspapers wallowed in copious details. They splashed about in the backwaters of Gilbert Sloane's personal history. They sluiced the dead man with streams of subtle vituperation, managed without singular effort to soak and soften the outer shell of his life, so that it warped and split and curled off, a spoiled and loggy reputation. Those who survived him were caught up in the backwash, and of these Delphina Sloane became of inexorable necessity the most prominent. Waves of words lapped at the shores of her grief. The Khalkis house had been converted into an impregnable lighthouse toward whose beacon the not-to-be-daunted representatives of the press directed their barques.

One miniature newspaper which might well have been named *The Enterprise*—but was not—offered the widow a rajah's ransom in return for her permission to sanction a series of articles, to be printed below a line-cut of her signature, and to be titled with editorial restraint: *Delphina Sloane's Own Story of Life With a Murderer.* And although the magnanimous offer was spurned with outraged silence, this glowing model of journalistic impudence succeeded in excavating some precious personal items from Mrs. Sloane's first marriage and exhibited them to their readers with the zest and pride of victorious archaeology. Young Alan Cheney punched a reporter attached to the tabloid, sending him back to his City Editor with a bruised eye and a scarlet nose; and it took a grand pulling of wires to keep the paper from having Alan arrested on a charge of assault.

During this buzzing interim in which the scavengers croaked about their carrion, Police Headquarters remained singularly peaceful. The Inspector returned to the less perplexing problems of routine, content merely with clearing up an odd point here and there in order to satisfy the official records of the Khalkis-Grimshaw-Sloane Case, as the newspapers virtuously called it. Dr. Prouty's autopsy on the body of Gilbert Sloane, performed in a manner thorough although perfunctory, elicited not the barest indication of foul play: there was no poison, no tell-tale marks of violence; the bullet-wound was just such a bullet-wound as a man inflicts when he commits suicide by shooting himself in the temple; and Sloane's cadaver, as has been signified, was released by the Medical Examiner's office for consignment to a flowery grave in a suburban cemetery.

The sole morsel of information which seemed to Ellery Queen to possess even a modicum of digestibility was this: that Gilbert Sloane had died instantly. But how this fact was to assist him Ellery confessed to himself, in the thickening fog, he could not see.

The fog, although he did not in this period of darkness realize it, was to be dispelled very shortly; and the fact of Gilbert Sloane's instantaneous death was to become a brightly visible signpost indeed.

CHAPTER 23

Yarns

I t began innocently enough, on Tuesday, October the nineteenth, a little before noon.

How Mrs. Sloane had contrived to elude the keen eyes of her tormentors she did not explain, but the fact remained that, unescorted and unpursued, she appeared at Police Headquarters—dressed, to be sure, in unostentatious black and lightly veiled—asking in a timid voice if she might see Inspector Richard Queen on a matter of importance. Inspector Richard Queen, it appeared, would have preferred to isolate the lady on the isles of her sorrow, but being a gentleman and something of a fatalist in feminine matters, he resigned himself to the inevitable and consented to see her.

The Inspector was alone when she was brought in—a slight frail middle-aged woman with eyes burning fiercely even through their filmy covering. He handed her into a chair after murmuring a few words of practiced sympathy, and stood by his desk waiting—as if by standing he might subtly suggest to her that the life of a detective-inspector was a busy one indeed and she would be serving her city well to come directly to the point.

She did so, disconcertingly. Speaking in a voice tinged by

the merest hysteria, she said: "My husband was not a murderer, Inspector."

The Inspector sighed. "But the facts, Mrs. Sloane."

She was prone to ignore, it seemed, those precious facts. "I've told reporters all week," she cried, "that Gilbert was an innocent man. I want justice, do you hear, Inspector? The scandal will follow me—all of us—my son—to the grave!"

"But, my dear lady, your husband took justice into his own hands. Please remember that his suicide was practically a confession of guilt."

"Suicide!" she said scornfully; she snatched at her veil with an impatient hand and her eyes blazed at him. "Are you all blind? Suicide!" Tears blurred her voice. "My poor Gilbert was murdered, and no one—no one . . ." She began to sob.

It was very distressing, and the Inspector stared out of his window uncomfortably. "That's a statement which calls for proof, Mrs. Sloane. Have you any?"

She jumped out of the chair. "A woman doesn't need proof," she cried. "*Proof!* Of course I haven't any. But what of it? I know—"

"My dear Mrs. Sloane," said the Inspector dryly, "that's where the law and womenfolk differ. I'm sorry, but if you can't offer new evidence pointing directly to someone else as the murderer of Albert Grimshaw, my hands are tied. The case is closed on our records."

She left without a word.

*   *   *

Now surely this short, unhappy, sterile incident was on the surface no matter of great moment. And yet it was to set in motion an entirely new and related series of events. The case would in all probability—Ellery has maintained this with conviction for many years—have remained a dead issue in the burdened police archives had not the Inspector, shrewdly gauging his son's sour expression at the dinner table that evening, recounted the incident of Mrs. Sloane's visit over the coffee-cups—in the pathetic paternal hope that news, any news, would sweeten that grim unhappy face.

To his astonishment—for it had been after all a forlorn hope—the ruse worked perfectly. Ellery became interested at once. The restless lines vanished, to be replaced by others characteristically thoughtful. "So she thinks Sloane was murdered, too," he said with faint surprise. "Interesting."

"Isn't it?" The Inspector winked at skinny Djuna, who had grasped his mug in two thin hands and was staring with large black gypsy eyes over its rim at Ellery. "Interesting how women's minds work. Won't be convinced. Like you, by heaven." He chuckled, but his eyes awaited a responsive twinkle.

It failed to appear. Ellery said quietly: "I think you're taking this thing much too flippantly, Dad. I've lolled about too long, sucking my thumbs and sulking like a child. I'm going to get busy."

The Inspector was alarmed. "What are you going to do—rake up the old coals, El? Why don't you let well enough alone?"

"The attitude of *laissez faire*," remarked Ellery, "has operated much to the detriment of others than the French, and in other fields than physiocratic economics. Do I sound didactic? I'm afraid many a poor devil is buried in the unhallowed soil of a homicide's grave who has no more right to be known to posterity as a murderer than you or I."

"Talk sense, son," said the old man uneasily. "You're still convinced, against all reason, that Sloane was innocent?"

"Not precisely. I don't say that in so many words." Ellery tapped a cigarette against a fingernail. "I do say this: Many elements of this case which you, Sampson, Pepper, the Commissioner and God knows how many others consider irrelevant and unimportant remain unexplained. I mean to pursue them just so long as there is the feeblest hope of satisfying my admittedly vague convictions."

"Anything clear in your mind?" asked the Inspector shrewdly.

"Got any notions of who did do it, since you suspect Sloane didn't?"

"I haven't the shadow of an idea who might be behind these little excursions into crime." Ellery expelled a gloomy lungful of smoke. "But one thing I'm as certain of as that all's wrong with the world. And that is that Gilbert Sloane did *not* kill Albert Grimshaw—or himself."

* * *

It was bravado, but bravado with stern intent. The next morning, after a fitful night, Ellery betook himself immediately after breakfast to East Fifty-fourth Street. The Khalkis house was shuttered—unguarded outwardly, but as lifeless as a tomb. He mounted the steps and rang the bell. The vestibule door did not open; instead he heard a grouchy, most unbutlerlike voice grunt: "Who is it?" It required patience and much conversation to induce the owner of the voice to unlatch the door. It did not open so much as it twitched aside a bit; and through the crack Ellery saw the pink cranium and harassed eyes of Weekes. After that, there was no difficulty; and Ellery did not even smile as Weekes pulled the door quickly open, thrust his rosy skull out in a hasty reconnaissance of Fifty-fourth Street, as hastily shut the door behind Ellery, and after latching it led the way to the drawing-room.

Mrs. Sloane, it appeared, was barricaded in her rooms upstairs. The name of Queen, Weekes coughingly reported a few moments later, had flushed the widow's face, caused her eyes to flash, and brought bitter invective to her lips. Weekes was sorry, but Mrs. Sloane—cough!—could not, should not, or would not see Mr. Queen.

Mr. Queen, however, was not to be denied. He thanked Weekes gravely and instead of turning south in the corridor, in which direction lay exit, he turned north and made for the staircase leading to the upper floor. Weekes looked shocked and wrung his hands.

Ellery's plan for gaining admittance was simplicity itself. He knocked on the Sloane door and when the widow's harsh, "Who is it now?" grated in his ears, said: "Someone who doesn't believe Gilbert Sloane was a murderer." Her response was immediate. The door flew open and Mrs. Sloane stood there, breathing fast, searching the face of this Delphic oracle with hungry eyes. When she saw who her visitor was, however, the hunger changed into hate. "It's a trick!" she said angrily. "I don't want to see any of you fools!"

"Mrs. Sloane," said Ellery gently, "you're doing me grave injustice. It wasn't a trick, and I believe what I said."

The hatred drained away, and in its place appeared cold speculation. She was silent as she studied him. Then the coldness melted, she sighed, held the door wide, and said: "I'm sorry, Mr. Queen. I'm a—a little upset. Do come in."

Ellery did not sit down. He placed his hat and stick on the desk—Sloane's fateful humidor was still there—and said: "Let's come to the point, Mrs. Sloane. Evidently you want to help. Certainly you possess the greatest animus for desiring to clear your husband's name."

"God, yes, Mr. Queen."

"Very well, then. We'll get nowhere with evasions. I am going to comb every crevice of this case, see what's lurking in each dark unexplored cranny. I want your confidence, Mrs. Sloane."

"You mean . . ."

"I mean," said Ellery firmly, "I want you to tell me why you visited Albert Grimshaw at the Benedict several weeks ago."

She hugged her thoughts to her breast then, and Ellery waited without too much hope. But when she looked up, he saw that he had won the first skirmish. "I'll tell you everything," she said simply. "And I pray to God it may help you . . . Mr. Queen, I was telling the truth in a way when I said that time that I didn't go to the Benedict to see Albert Grimshaw." Ellery nodded encouragingly. "I didn't know *where* I was going. For you see," she paused and stared at the floor, "I was following my husband all that evening . . ."

The story came out slowly. For many months before the death of her brother Georg, Mrs. Sloane had suspected that her husband was conducting a clandestine affair with Mrs. Vreeland, whose bold beauty and tempting proximity in the house, coupled with Jan Vreeland's long absences and Sloane's self-centred susceptibility, made the affair almost inevitable. Mrs. Sloane, nursing the worm of jealousy in her breast, could find nothing material with which to feed it. Unable to verify her suspicions she had kept silent, deliberately pretending to be ignorant of what she sensed was going on. But always she kept her eyes open for signs and her ears alert for sounds of possible assignations.

For weeks Sloane had made it a habit to return to the Khalkis house at late hours. He gave varying excuses—a rigorous diet for the worm. Unable to endure the gnawing agony, Mrs. Sloane had succumbed to her canker for verification. On Thursday evening, the thirtieth of September, she had followed her husband; he had offered an obviously mythical "conference" as a pretext for leaving the Khalkis house some time after dinner.

Sloane's movements had been apparently aimless; certainly there was no conference; and of contacts that entire evening there were none until ten o'clock. Then he had turned off Broadway and made for the shabby exterior of the Hotel Benedict. She had pursued him into the lobby, the worm whispering that here was to be enacted the Gethsemane of her marital life; that Sloane, acting in a strange and furtive manner, was about to meet Mrs. Vreeland in some dingy room at the Hotel Benedict for purposes to which Mrs. Sloane shut her mind with horror. She had seen him go to the desk and speak to the clerk; whereupon, in the same peculiar manner, he went on to the elevator. She had managed to overhear, while Sloane was conversing with the clerk, the words: "Room 314." Consequently, she approached the desk, certain that Room 314 was to be the scene of the assignation, and demanded the room adjoining. This action was born of impulse; nothing tangible was in her mind, except perhaps some wild notion of eavesdropping on the guilty pair and bursting in upon them when they were locked in each other's lustful arms.

The woman's eyes were burning with the recollection of those heated moments, and Ellery gently fed her regurgitated passions. What had she done? Her face flamed; she had gone directly to the room she had rented and paid for, Room 316, had pressed her ear to the wall . . . But she could hear nothing: the masonry of the Hotel Benedict, if nothing else, was aristocratic. Baffled, trembling, she had leaned against the silent wall, almost weeping; when suddenly she heard the door of the next room open. She had flown to her own door and opened it cautiously. Just in time to see the object of her suspicions, her husband, leave Room 314 and stride down the corridor to the elevator. . . . She did not know what to make of it. She left the room stealthily and ran down the three flights of emergency stairs to the lobby. She caught sight of Sloane hurrying out. She followed him; to her astonishment he headed for the Khalkis house. When she arrived there herself, she discovered by an adroit question directed at Mrs. Simms that Mrs. Vreeland had been home all evening. For the night, at least, then she knew that Sloane had been innocent of adultery. No, she did not remember what time it was when Sloane emerged from Room 314. She did not remember *any* times.

That, it seemed, was all.

She challenged him anxiously with her eyes, as if to ask whether this recital had furnished a clue, any clue. . . .

Ellery was thoughtful. "While you were in Room 316, Mrs. Sloane, did you hear anyone else enter Room 314?"

"No. I saw Gilbert enter, then leave, and I followed him away at once. I'm sure that if anyone had opened or closed that door while I was in the next room I should have heard."

"I see. That's helpful, Mrs. Sloane. And since you've been so completely candid, tell me one thing more: did you telephone your husband from this house last Monday evening, the night of his death?"

"I did not, as I told Sergeant Velie when he questioned me that same night. I know I'm suspected of having warned my husband, but I didn't, Mr. Queen, I didn't—I hadn't any idea that the police intended to arrest him."

Ellery studied her face; she seemed sincere enough. "You will recall that that evening, as my father, Mr. Pepper and I left the study downstairs, we saw you hurrying down the corridor to the drawing-room. Please pardon this question, Mrs. Sloane, but I must know—did you listen at the study door before we came out?"

She flushed darkly. "I may be—oh, vile in many other respects, Mr. Queen, and perhaps my conduct in connexion with my husband doesn't bear this out . . . but I swear I didn't eavesdrop."

"Can you suggest someone who might have eavesdropped."

Spite crept into her voice. "Yes, I can! Mrs. Vreeland. She—she was close enough to Gilbert, close enough . . ."

"But that doesn't follow from her action in relating to us that evening the story of having seen Mr. Sloane go into the graveyard," said Ellery gently. "She seems to have been more inclined to malice than to defence of a lover."

She sighed uncertainly. "Perhaps I'm wrong . . . I didn't know that Mrs. Vreeland had told you anything that night, you see; I learned about *that* only after my husband's death, and then it was from the newspapers."

"One last question, Mrs. Sloane. Did Mr. Sloane ever tell you that he had a brother?"

She shook her head. "He never so much as suggested it. In fact, he was always reticent about his family. He had told me about his father and mother—they seemed nice enough people in a middle-class sort of way—but never about a brother. I was always under the impression that he had been an only child, and that he was the last of his family."

Ellery picked up his hat and stick, said: "Be patient, Mrs. Sloane, and above all say nothing about these things to anyone," smiled and quickly left the room.

*   *   *

From Weekes downstairs Ellery received a bit of news which momentarily staggered him.

Dr. Wardes was gone.

Ellery gnawed at his leash. This looked like something! But Weekes was a barren source of information. It seemed that, with the publicity following the solution of the Grimshaw case, Dr. Wardes had retired into his hard British shell, beginning to cast about for escape from this brilliantly illuminated household. The police ban having been lifted with the suicide of Sloane, he had commandeered his luggage, hastily taken leave of his hostess—who was, it appeared, in no mood for the proprieties—expressed his regrets and departed with dispatch for regions unknown. He had left on Friday last, and Weekes was certain no one in the house knew where he had gone.

"And Miss Joan Brett, too—" Weekes added.

Ellery paled. "What about Miss Joan Brett? Has she gone, too? For heaven's sake, man, find your tongue!"

Weekes found it. "No, sir, no indeed, she hasn't gone yet, but I venture to say, sir, that she's *going* to go, if you get my meaning, sir. She—"

"Weekes," said Ellery savagely, "speak English. What's up?"

"Miss Brett is preparing to leave, sir," said Weekes with a polite little cough. "Her employment, it's terminated, so to speak. And Mrs. Sloane—" he looked pained—"Mrs. Sloane, she informed Miss Brett that her services would not be required any longer. So—"

"Where is she now?"

"In her room upstairs, sir. Packing, I believe. First door to your right from the head of the stairs. . . ."

But Ellery was off like the wind, coat tails flying. He took the steps three at a time. As he reached the upper landing, however, he halted in his tracks. There were voices; and, unless his ears deceived him, one of the voices emanated from the larynx of Miss Joan Brett. So, unabashed, he stood still, stick clutched in his hand, head cocked a little toward the right . . . and was rewarded with hearing a man's voice, thickened with what is popularly known as passion, cry: "Joan! Dearest! I love—"

"Tippling," came Joan's voice, frigidly—not the voice of a young woman listening to a gentleman's avowal of undying affection.

"No! Joan, don't make a joke of it. I'm deadly serious. I love you, love you, darling. Really, I—"

There were certain noises indicative of scuffle. Presumably the owner of the masculine voice was pressing his suit physically. A little outraged gasp, quite distinct, then a sharp *smack!* at which even Ellery, outside the range of Miss Brett's vigorous arm, winced.

Silence. The two combatants, Ellery felt certain, were now staring at each other with hostility, perhaps circling each other in that feline manner which human beings adopt under the surge of the choleric passions. He listened placidly and grinned when he heard the man murmur: "You shouldn't have done that, Joan. I didn't mean to frighten you—"

"Frighten me? Heavens! I assure you I wasn't the least bit frightened," came Joan's voice, dripping with amused hauteur.

"Well, damn it all!" cried the man with exasperation, "is that a way to receive a fellow's proposal of marriage? By—"

Another gasp. "How *dare* you swear at me, you—you oaf!" cried Joan. "I should horsewhip you. Oh, I've never been so humiliated in my life. Leave my room at once!"

Ellery shrank against his wall. A bitter strangled roar of

rage, the violent sound of a door being torn open, a slam which shook the house—and Ellery peeped around the corner in time to see a wildly gesticulating Mr. Alan Cheney thunder up the corridor, fists clenched and head jerking up and down. . . .

When Mr. Alan Cheney had disappeared into his own room, agitating the old house for the second time with the vehemence with which he shut his door, Mr. Ellery Queen complacently adjusted his necktie and without hesitation went to the door of Miss Joan Brett's room. He raised his stick and knocked, gently. Silence. He knocked again. He heard then a most unmannerly sniffle, a choked sob and Joan's voice: "Don't you *dare* come in here again, you—you—you . . ."

Ellery said: "It's Ellery Queen, Miss Brett," in the most un-ruffled voice in the world, as if a maiden's sobs were fitting reply to a visitor's knock. The sniffles ceased instantly. Ellery waited with patience. Then a very small voice: "Do come in, Mr. Queen. The—the door is open," and he pushed the door in and entered.

Miss Joan Brett, he found, was standing by her bed, a white-knuckled little hand grasping a damp handkerchief, two geometrically round dabs of colour in her cheeks. About the pleasant room, on the floor, chairs, the bed itself, were strewn feminine garments of various descriptions. Two portmanteaux lay open on chairs, and a small steamer-trunk yawned on the floor. On the dressing-table, Ellery noticed without seeming to do so a framed photograph—lying face down, as if it had hastily been upset.

Now Ellery was—when he wanted to be—a most diplomatic young man. The occasion seemed to call for finesse and a conversational myopia. Whereupon he smiled in a rather vacuous fashion and said: "What was that you said when I first knocked, Miss Brett? I'm afraid I didn't quite catch it."

"Oh!"—a very small *oh* it was, too. Joan indicated a chair and sat down herself in another. "It—I often talk to myself. Silly habit, isn't it?"

"Not at all," said Ellery heartily, sitting down. "Not at all. Some of our best people are addicted to the habit. It's supposed to mean that the ego conversationalist has money in the bank. Have you money in the bank, Miss Brett?"

She smiled weakly at that. "Not so *very* much, and besides I'm having it transferred, you know. . . ." The colour had left her cheeks, and she sighed a little. "I'm leaving the United States, Mr. Queen."

"So Weekes told me. We shall be desolated, Miss Brett."

"La!" She laughed aloud. "You speak like a Frenchman, Mr. Queen." She reached to the bed and snared her purse. "This box of mine—my luggage . . . How depressing sea-journeys are." Her hand emerged from the purse with a sheaf of steamship tickets. "Is this a professional call? I'm really leaving, Mr. Queen. Here are the visible evidences of my intention to take passage. You're not going to tell me that I mayn't go?"

"I? Horrors, no! And do you want to go, Miss Brett?"

"At the moment," she said, with a savage champing of her small teeth, "I want to go very much indeed."

Ellery became obtuse. "I see. This business of murders and suicides—naturally depressing. . . . Well, I shan't keep you a moment. The object of my visit is the very opposite of sinister." He regarded her gravely. "As you know, the case is closed. Nevertheless, there are a few points, obscure and probably unimportant, which my tenacious mind persists in worrying. . . . Miss Brett, just what was your mission that night when Pepper saw you prowling about the study downstairs?"

She weighed him quietly with her cool blue eyes. "You weren't impressed with my explanation, then . . . Have a cigarette, Mr. Queen." He refused, and she touched a match to one for herself with steady fingers. "Very well, sir—*Absconding Secretary Tells All*, as your tabloids would have it. I shall confess, and I dare say you're in for a whopping surprise, Mr. Queen."

"I haven't the remotest doubt about *that*."

"Prepare yourself." She took a deep breath, and the smoke

dribbled out of her lovely mouth like punctuation marks as she talked. "You see before you, Mr. Queen, a lady-sleuth."

"No!"

"*Mais oui*. I am an employee of the Victoria Museum of London—not the Yard, sir, no, not that. That would be too much. Merely the Museum, Mr. Queen."

"Well, I'll be drawn, quartered, eviscerated, and boiled in oil," murmured Ellery. "You speak in riddles. The Victoria Museum, eh? My dear, this is such news as detectives dream of. Elucidate."

Joan tapped ashes from her cigarette. "The story is quite melodramatic. While I applied to Georg Khalkis for employment, I was a paid investigator for the Victoria Museum. I was operating along a trail which led to Khalkis—a confused bit of information which seemed to indicate that he was mixed up, probably as the receiver, in the theft of a painting from the Museum—"

The grin faded from Ellery's lips. "A painting by whom, Miss Brett?"

She shrugged. "A mere detail. It was valuable enough—a genuine Leonardo Da Vinci—a masterpiece discovered not long ago by one of the Museum's field-workers—a detail from some fresco or other on which Leonardo worked in Florence during the first decade of the sixteenth century. This seems to have been an oils canvas Leonardo executed after the original fresco project was abandoned: 'Detail from the Battle of the Standard,' it's catalogued. . . ."

"Such luck," murmured Ellery. "Go on, Miss Brett. You have my passionate attention. In what way was Khalkis involved?"

She sighed. "Except that we thought he might have been the receiver, as I said, it wasn't very clear. More of a 'hunch,' as you Americans persist in saying, than the result of definite information. But let me begin in the proper place.

"My recommendations to Khalkis were genuine enough—Sir Arthur Ewing, who gave me the character, is quite the legitimate toff—one of the directors of the Victoria as well as a famous London art-dealer; he naturally was in the secret, and the character was the least of it. I have done investigatory work of this nature for the Museum before, but never in this country; chiefly on the Continent. The directors demanded absolute secrecy—I was to work under cover, you see, trace the painting and attempt to locate it. Meanwhile, the theft was kept from public knowledge by a series of 'restoration' announcements."

"I begin to see."

"You have keen eyesight then, Mr. Queen," said Joan severely. "*Will* you allow me to proceed with my story, or *won't* you? . . . All the time I spent in this house as Mr. Khalkis's secretary, I endeavoured to find a clue to the whereabouts of the Leonardo; but I have never been able to find the tiniest lead to it, either from his papers or conversation. I was really becoming discouraged, despite the fact that our information seemed authentic.

"Which brings me to Mr. Albert Grimshaw. Now the painting had originally been stolen by one of the Museum attendants, a man who called himself Graham and whose real name we later discovered was Albert Grimshaw. The first hope, the first tangible indication that I was on the scent came when the man Grimshaw presented himself at the front door on the evening of September thirtieth. I saw at once, from descriptions with which I was provided, that this man was the thieving Graham who had disappeared from England without a trace and who had never been found in the five years which had elapsed from the time of the theft."

"Oh, excellent!"

"Quite. I endeavoured to listen at the study door, but I could hear nothing of his conversation with Mr. Khalkis. Nor did I learn anything the next evening, when Grimshaw appeared with the unknown man—the man whose face I could not see. To complicate matters—" her face darkened—"Mr. Alan Cheney chose that moment to lurch into the house in a disgustingly bibulous condition, and by the time I had attended to *him* the two men had gone. But of one thing I was certain—that somewhere between Grimshaw and Khalkis lay the secret of the Leonardo's hiding-place."

"I take it, then, that your search in the study was inspired by a hope that there might be some new record among Khalkis's effects—a new clue to the painting's whereabouts?"

"Exactly. But that search, like the others, was unsuccessful. You see, from time to time I had personally ransacked the house, the shop, and the Galleries; and I was certain that the Leonardo was not concealed anywhere about the Khalkis premises. On the other hand, this unknown who accompanied Grimshaw appeared to me to be someone interested—the secrecy, Mr. Khalkis's nervous manner—interested, as I say, in the painting. I'm positive that this unknown is a vital clue to the fate of the Leonardo."

"And you were never able to discover the identity of this man?"

She smashed her cigarette flat in an ashtray. "No." Then she regarded Ellery suspiciously. "Why—do *you* know who he is?"

Ellery did not reply. His eyes were abstracted. "And now a feeble question, Miss Brett . . . Why, if matters came to a head so dramatically, are you returning to your bailiwick?"

"For the very good reason that the case has become too unwieldy for me." She rummaged in her purse and produced a letter bearing a London postmark. She handed it to Ellery, and he read it without comment; it was on the stationery of the Victoria Museum and was signed by the Director. "You see, I have kept London informed of my progress—or rather, my lack of progress. This note is in reply to my last report concerning the unknown man. You can see for yourself that we are at an impasse. The Museum writes that since the original inquiry by cable from Inspector Queen some time ago a considerable correspondence has sprung up—I suppose you know that—between the Director and the New York police. Of course, at first they didn't know whether to answer or not, as it would have meant relating the whole story.

"This letter authorizes me, as you can see, to confide in the New York police and use my own discretion about future activity." She sighed. "My own discretion dictates the distinct conviction that the case is now beyond my humble capacities; I was about to call on the Inspector, relate my story, and then return to London."

Ellery returned the letter, which she replaced carefully in her purse. "Yes," he said, "I'm inclined to agree that the trail to the painting has grown excessively tangled, and that it is now more the job of professionals than of a lone—and amateur—investigator. On the other hand . . ." He paused thoughtfully. "It's barely possible that I may be able to assist you soon in your apparently hopeless quest."

"Mr. Queen!" Her eyes were shining.

"Would the Museum consent to keep you in New York if there was still a chance of recovering the Leonardo without fanfare?"

"Oh, yes! I'm sure of that, Mr. Queen! I'll cable the Director at once."

"Do that. And Miss Brett—" he smiled—"I shouldn't go to the police quite yet, if I were you. Not even to my father, bless him. You may be more useful if you are still—to put it politely—under suspicion."

Joan rose swiftly. "I should love that. Orders, Commandant?" She stood at mock-attention, right hand raised in stiff salute.

Ellery grinned. "You're going to make an admirable *espionne*, I can see that now. Very well, Miss Joan Brett, henceforth and forever we are allies, you and I—a private *entente*."

"*Cordiale*, I hope?" She sighed happily. "It will be thrilling!"

"And perhaps dangerous," said Ellery. "Yet, despite our secret understanding, Lieutenant Brett, there are certain things it is better that I keep from you—for your own safety." Her face fell, and he patted her hand. "Not from suspicion of you—word of honour, my dear. But you must take me on faith for the present."

"Very well, Mr. Queen," said Joan soberly. "I'm entirely in your hands."

"No," said Ellery hastily, "that's too much of a temptation. You're far too handsome a wench . . . Here, here!" He averted his head to avoid her amused stare and began to ruminate aloud. "Let's see what course is open. Hmm. . . . Must have a good excuse to keep you around—I suppose everyone knows your employment has ceased here. . . . Can't stay in New York without a job—might be suspicious . . . Can't stay here at Khalkis's . . . I have it!" He caught her hands excitedly. "There's one place where you could stay—and legitimately, so that no one's suspicions would be aroused."

"And where is that?"

He drew her to the bed and they sat down, heads close together. "You are familiar with all of Khalkis's personal and business affairs, of course. There's one gentleman who has obligingly involved himself in a mess relating to these tangled affairs. And that's James Knox!"

"Oh, splendid," she whispered.

"Now you see," continued Ellery rapidly, "with Knox dabbling in this headachey business, he would welcome expert assistance. I heard just last night from Woodruff that Knox's secretary has become ill. I'll arrange it in such a way that Knox himself will make the offer, lulling all possible suspicions. And you're to keep mum about this, my dear—please understand that. You're to pretend the job is a real one by working faithfully at it—*no one* is to know you're not what you seem to be."

"You needn't have any fears on that score," she said grimly.

"I'm sure I needn't." He rose and grabbed his hat and stick. "Glory to Moses! there's work to do . . . Good day, *ma lieutenante*! Remain in this house until you get word from the Omnipotent Knox."

He clucked aside Joan's breathless words of thanks and

dashed out of her room. The door closed slowly behind him. He caught himself up in the hall and fell to musing. Then, with a malicious little grin on his lips, he strode up the corridor and knocked at Alan Cheney's door.

*　*　*

Alan Cheney's bedroom resembled the ruins of a chamber caught in the heart of a Kansas twister. Things were thrown about, as if the young man had been indulging in a hurling contest with his own shadow. Cigarette butts lay about the floor where they had fallen, like little dead soldiers. Mr. Cheney's hair looked as if it had gone through a threshing-machine, and his eyes darted about in pinkish angry pools.

He was patrolling the floor—pacing it, measuring it, eating it up with hungry strides, over and over. A very restless young man, and Ellery stood wide-eyed in the doorway after Cheney's muttered, "Come, damn you, whoever you are!" and surveyed the débris-strewn battlefield before him.

"Well, and what do *you* want?" growled the young man, halting abruptly in his career as he saw who his visitor was.

"A word with you." Ellery closed the door. "I seem to find you," he continued with a grin, "in a more or less turbulent mood. But I shan't consume a moment of your no doubt precious time. May I sit down, or is this to be a conversation conducted with all the punctilio of a duel?"

Some vestige of decency remained in young Alan, it appeared, for he mumbled: "Certainly. Do sit down. Sorry. Here, have this one," and he swept a chairful of cigarette-stubs to the already frowsy floor.

Ellery sat down and straightway began to polish the lenses of his *pince-nez.* Alan watched him in a sort of absent irritation. "Now, Mr. Alan Cheney," began Ellery, setting the glasses firmly on his straight nose, "to business. I've been pottering about tying up loose ends on this sad business of Grimshaw's murder and your step-father's suicide."

"Suicide my left eyebrow," retorted Alan. "Wasn't anything of the sort."

"Indeed? So your mother suggested a few moments ago. Have you anything concrete on which to base this belief?"

"No. I suppose not. Well, it doesn't matter. He's dead and six feet under, and *that* can't be rectified." Alan threw himself on his bed. "What's on your mind, Queen?"

Ellery smiled: "A useless question to which surely you no longer have reason to withhold the answer . . . Why did you run away a week and a half ago?"

Alan lay still on the bed, smoking, his eyes fixed on a battered old assegai hanging on the wall. "My old man's," he said. "Africa was his particular heaven." Then he flung his cigarette away, jumped out of bed and resumed his mad pacing, throwing furious glances toward the north—the general direction, it should be explained, of Joan's bedroom. "All right," he snapped. "I'll talk. I was a damned fool to do it in the first place. Temperamental little coquette, that's what she is, blast her beautiful face!"

"My dear Cheney," murmured Ellery, "what on earth are you talking about?"

"Talking about what a moon-eyed jackass I've been, that's what! Listen to this, Queen, for the prize story of adolescent 'chivalry' of all time," Alan said, gnashing his strong young teeth. "There I was, in love—in love, mind you!—with this, this . . . well, with Joan Brett. And I'd caught her snooping about this house for months, looking for something, God knows what. Never said a word about it—to her or anyone else. Self-sacrificing lover, and all that sort of tripe. When the Inspector grilled her about that fellow Pepper's story of Joan's monkeying around with the safe the night after my uncle's funeral . . . hell, I didn't know what to think. Put two and two together—the missing will, the murdered man. It was pretty horrible . . . I felt that she was involved somehow in the ghastly business. So—" He fell to muttering beneath his breath.

Ellery sighed. "Ah, love. I feel the quotations creeping upon me, but perhaps I'd better not . . . So, Master Alan, you, the noble Sir Pelleas, disdained by the scornful Lady Ettarre, did ride away on the broad back of your white stallion, bent on the chivalrous quest . . ."

"Well, if you're going to make a joke of it," snarled Alan. "So—well, I did it, yes, I did. The damned fool thing of playing the gallant knight, as you say—ran away purposely to make it look fishy—divert suspicion to myself. Huh!" He shrugged bitterly. "And was she worth it? What's the answer? I'm glad to spill the bloody story and forget it—and her."

"And this," murmured Ellery, rising, "this is a murder investigation. Ah, well! Until psychiatry learns to take into account all the quirks of human motive, crime detection will remain an infant science. . . . Thank you, Sir Alan, a thousand times, and don't despair, I charge you. And a very good day!"

*   *   *

Mr. Ellery Queen perhaps an hour later sat in a chair opposite Lawyer Miles Woodruff, in that gentleman's modest suite among the canyons of lower Broadway, puffing—this was the sign of an especial occasion—one of Lawyer Woodruff's perfectos and making unimportant conversation. Lawyer Woodruff, in his bluff red way, it appeared, was experiencing a form of mental constipation; he was grumpy, yellow-eyed and liverish, and he spat inelegantly, from time to time, into a glittering cuspidor chastely perched on a round rubber mat by his desk; and the sum and substance of his plaint was that he had never, in all his crowded years as an attorney, encountered a testamentary situation which presented such head-splitting difficulties as the tangled business of Georg Khalkis's estate.

"Why, Queen," he exclaimed, "you've no *idea* of what's facing us—no *idea*! Here the scrap of burnt new will turns up, and we have to establish duress or else Grimshaw's estate will rake in the gravy of . . . Oh, well. Poor old Knox is mighty sorry, I'll wager, that he consented to act as executor."

"Knox. Yes. Having his hands full, eh?"

"Something terrible! After all, even before the exact legal status of the estate is determined, there are certain things which must be done. Itemizations galore—Khalkis left a lot of piecemeal stuff. I suppose he'll shift it all on to my shoulders— Knox, I mean—that's what usually happens when an executor is a man of Knox's position."

"Perhaps," suggested Ellery indifferently, "now that Knox's secretary is ill and Miss Brett is temporarily out of employment . . ."

Woodruff's cigar waggled. "Miss Brett! Say, Queen, there's an idea. Of course. She knows all about Khalkis's affairs. I think I'll broach it to Knox. I think *I'll* . . ."

Having sowed the seeds, Ellery very shortly took his departure, smiling in great contentment to himself as he walked at a brisk pace up Broadway.

*　*　*

Whereupon we find Lawyer Woodruff, not two minutes after his door closed on Ellery's broad back, engaged in conversation via telephone with Mr. James J. Knox. "I thought that now that Miss Joan Brett has nothing further to do at the Khalkis house—"

"Woodruff! A dandy suggestion! . . ."

The upshot of it was that Mr. James J. Knox, with a rich sigh of relief, thanked Lawyer Woodruff for his *splendid* inspiration, and had no sooner hung up than he called the number of the Khalkis house.

And, when he succeeded in getting Miss Joan Brett on the wire, and quite as if the idea had been original with *him*, he asked her to come to work the very next day . . . for a period of service to endure until the settlement of the estate. Mr. Knox further suggested, in view of the fact that Miss Brett was a Britisher and had no permanent residence in New York City, that she come to live in his, Knox's, house for the duration of her service with him. . . .

Miss Brett demurely accepted the offer—at a stipend, it should be noted, respectably lustier than she had received from the *ci-devant* American of Greek lineage whose bones now lay peacefully in the vault of his fathers. At the same time she wondered how Mr. Ellery Queen had managed the affair.

CHAPTER 24

Exhibit

On Friday, October the twenty-second, Mr. Ellery Queen—informally, to be sure—visited with the aristocracy. That is to say a telephone-call from Mr. James J. Knox solicited Mr. Queen's immediate presence at the Knox residence on a communication of possible interest. Mr. Queen was delighted, not only because he admired refined society but for less subtle reasons as well, and he proceeded with alacrity in a handsome taxicab to Riverside Drive, where at a structure of awesome proportions he alighted, paid off his suddenly obsequious cabby, and strode with dignity into the grounds of what even in a city fabled for its realty values must be considered an estate.

He was ushered, without too much ceremony, by a tall thin old flunkey into the Presence after a decent interval of waiting in a reception-room which might have been plucked bodily out of a Medici *palazzo*.

The Presence, for all his flamboyant surroundings, was working at a very modern desk in his—Ellery had this on the authority of the venerable ramrod butler—in his "den." The den was as modern as the desk. Black patent-leather walls, angular furniture, lamps out of a maniac's dream . . . the very essence of modern riches at homework. And, seated primly by the Presence, notebook propped on a praiseworthy knee, was Miss Joan Brett.

Knox greeted Ellery cordially, tendered a Circassian-wood box filled with pale cigarettes six inches long, waved his visibly impressed visitor into a chair which looked uncomfortable but was not, and then said, in his deceptively soft and hesitant voice: "Fine, Queen. Glad you could come so soon. Surprised to find Miss Brett here?"

"Staggered," said Ellery gravely. Miss Brett worked her lashes and adjusted her skirt to an infinitesimal degree. "Very fortunate for Miss Brett, I'm sure."

"No, no. I'm the lucky one. Jewel, Miss Brett is. Own secretary's down with the mumps, or colic, or something. Unreliable— very. Miss Brett's assisting me in personal matters as well as the Khalkis business. That Khalkis business! Well, sir, I will say it's a pleasant relief having a good-looking young lady to look at all day. Very. Own secretary's a lantern-jawed Scot who last smiled on his mother's bony knee. 'Scuse me, Queen. A few details I want to clear up with Miss Brett here, and then I'll be free.... Make out the cheques for those bills that are due, Miss Brett—"

"The bills," repeated Miss Brett submissively.

"—and the stationery you had sent up. In paying the bill for the new typewriter, don't forget to add on the small charge for that single replacement key—and send the old machine to the Bureau of Charities—hate old machines ..."

"Bureau of Charities."

"And when you find a moment or two, order the new steel files you suggested. That's all now."

Joan rose and went to the other side of the room, where she sat down in the crispest secretarial fashion at a small modish desk and began to typewrite. "Now, Queen, for you ... Damned annoying, these details. Illness of my regular secretary has inconvenienced me greatly."

"Indeed," murmured Ellery. He was wondering why Mr. James J. Knox was relating to a comparative stranger these boring items of personal information, when Mr. James J. Knox would come to the point, and whether Mr. James J. Knox was not concealing a serious perturbation beneath this chatter.

Knox fiddled with a gold pencil. "Something occurred to me to-day, Queen—I've been upset, or I would have recalled it before. Completely forgot to mention it in my original account to Inspector Queen in his office at Headquarters."

Ellery Queen, you lucky devil! thought Ellery Queen. This is what comes of canine persistence. Prick up your lucky ears . . . "And what was that?" he asked, as if it really did not matter.

A story unfolded, related in a nervous Knoxian manner which gradually disappeared as the tale grew in stature.

It seemed that on the night of Knox's visit to Khalkis, accompanied by Grimshaw, a peculiar thing had occurred. This phenomenon took place directly after Khalkis had made out, signed, and handed to Grimshaw the promissory note which Grimshaw had demanded. It appeared that Grimshaw, while he stowed the note away in his wallet, had evidently decided that the moment was ripe for the pressing of a further advantage. Whereupon, putting his request on the basis of a "good will" payment, he had coolly demanded a thousand dollars of Khalkis—for, he said, his immediate needs in advance of expected payment of the principal represented by the promissory note in his wallet.

"No thousand dollars were found, Mr. Knox!" said Ellery sharply.

"Let me get on, young man," said Knox. "Khalkis said at once that he didn't have the money in the house. Turned about and asked me to lend it to him—promised to repay it the next day. Well, pshaw . . ." Knox flipped his cigarette deprecatingly. "He was good for it. I'd drawn five one-thousand-dollar bills from my bank earlier in the day for personal expenses. Took 'em out of my wallet, handed one of 'em to Khalkis, and he turned it over to Grimshaw."

"Ah," said Ellery. "And where did Grimshaw put it?"

"Grimshaw snatched it from Khalkis's hand, took from his vest pocket a heavy old gold watch—must be the one found in Sloane's safe—opened the case at the back, folded the bill into a small wad and stored it in the case-back, snapped it shut, put the watch back into his vest pocket. . . ."

Ellery was gnawing a fingernail. "Heavy old gold watch. You're certain it's the same?"

"I'm absolutely sure of it. Saw a photo of the watch from Sloane's safe in one of the newspapers earlier in the week. That was the watch, all right."

"By the Luck of Eden Hall!" breathed Ellery. "If this isn't . . . Mr. Knox, do you recall the numbers of the bills you drew from your bank that day? It's most essential that we investigate the interior of the watch-case at once. If that bill is gone its serial-number may provide a trail to the murderer!"

"Exactly what I thought. Find out in a minute. Miss Brett, get Bowman, head cashier at my bank, on the wire."

Miss Brett very impersonally obeyed, handed the instrument to Knox and returned quietly to her secretarial chores. "Bowman? Knox. Get me the serial-numbers of the five one-thousand-dollar bills I drew on October first . . . I see. All right." Knox waited, then reached for a scratch-pad and began to scribble with his gold pencil. He smiled, hung up, and handed the scrap of paper to Ellery. "There you are, Queen."

Ellery fingered the scrap absently. "Ah—would you like to go down to Headquarters with me, Mr. Knox, and help me to inspect the interior of the watch?"

"Should be delighted. Fascinated by the detective things."

The telephone-bell rang on his desk, and Joan rose to answer it. "For you, sir. The Surety Bond. Shall I—?"

"I'll take it. 'Scuse me, Queen."

While Knox conducted a dry, pointless—as far as Ellery could see—and thoroughly boring business conversation, Ellery rose and strolled back to the other desk with Joan. He gave her a significant glance and said: "Er—Miss Brett, would you mind copying these serial-numbers on your typewriter?"—an excuse for bending over her chair and whispering in her ear. She took the pencilled notation from him very demurely, placed a sheet of paper in the carriage of her machine, and began to type. Meanwhile, she murmured: "And why didn't you tell me Mr. Knox was the unknown man who came with Grimshaw that night?" reproachfully.

Ellery shook his head in warning, but Knox had not faltered in his conversation. Joan quickly tore the sheet from her machine, saying in a loud voice: "Oh, bother! I'll have to write out the word 'number,'" and, placing a fresh sheet in the carriage, began to copy the numbers with a rapid touch.

Ellery murmured: "Any news from London?"

She shook her head, stumbled a little in her flashing finger-pace, cried: "I'm still not accustomed to Mr. Knox's personal typewriter—it's a Remington and I've always used an Underwood and there isn't another machine in the house ..." concluded her task, tore the sheet out, handed it to Ellery and whispered: "Is it possible that *he* has the Leonardo?"

Ellery gripped her shoulder so hard that she winced and went pale. He said with a smile in hearty tones: "That's splendid, Miss Brett. And thank you," and whispered, as he tucked the notation into one of his vest pockets: "Be wary. Don't overplay your hand. Don't be caught snooping about. Trust me. You're a secretary and nothing more. Don't say a word to anyone about the thousand-dollar bill ..."

"That's quite all right, I'm sure, Mr. Queen," she said clearly, and winked with the wickedness of a harpy.

*   *   *

Ellery had the pleasure of riding downtown in Mr. James J. Knox's town-car seated side by side with the great man himself, and chauffeured by a stiff-necked Charon in sober livery.

Arrived before Police Headquarters in Center Street, the two men got out, toiled up the broad stepped approach, and disappeared within. Ellery was amused to note the awe with which the multi-millionaire regarded the universal cordiality extended by police, detectives and hangers-on to his own son-of-Inspector-Queen person. He led the way to one of the file-rooms. There Ellery commandeered, on the strength of his wholly fictive authority, the file in which the evidence on the Grimshaw-Sloane case was stored. He disturbed nothing but the old-fashioned gold watch; this he took from the steel case, and he and Knox examined it in the deserted room for a moment without speaking.

Ellery experienced in that instant a portent of impending events. Knox seemed merely curious. And Ellery pried open the back of the watch-case.

There, folded into a tiny wad, was what proved to be, on unfolding, a thousand-dollar bill.

Ellery was plainly disappointed; the possibility he had held out in Knox's den had vanished with the materialization of the bill. Nevertheless, because he was a thorough young man, he checked against the list in his pocket the serial-number of the bill from the watch, and discovered that the bill he had found was in truth one of the five which Knox had listed. He snapped the watch-case shut and restored it to the file.

"What do you make of it, Queen?"

"Not a thundering lot. This new fact doesn't alter the existing circumstances as they relate to the Sloane solution," replied Ellery sadly. "If Sloane murdered Grimshaw, was Grimshaw's unknown partner, our finding of the bill still in the watch-case merely means that Sloane knew nothing of the bill's existence. It means that Grimshaw was holding out on his partner, that Grimshaw never really intended to tell him about the thousand dollars he had managed to extort from Khalkis, or to share it with Sloane—witness the curious place in which he secreted the bill. Now Sloane, murdering Grimshaw, took the watch for purposes of his own but never thought of looking into the case, since he had no reason to suspect that anything was there.

Consequently, it is still where Grimshaw put it. Q.E.D.—and rats!"

"I take it you aren't particularly impressed with the Sloane solution," said Knox shrewdly.

"Mr. Knox, I scarcely know what to think." They strolled down the corridor. "Nevertheless, sir, I should appreciate one thing . . ."

"Anything you say, Queen."

"Don't breathe a word about the thousand-dollar bill to anyone—on general principles. Please."

"Very well. But Miss Brett knows—she must have over-heard me telling you about it."

Ellery nodded. "You might caution her to keep quiet about it."

They shook hands and Ellery watched Knox stride away. He walked restlessly up and down the hall for a few moments, then made for his father's office. No one was there. He shook his head, descended into Center Street, looked about, then hailed a taxicab.

Five minutes later he was in Mr. James J. Knox's bank. He asked to see Mr. Bowman, the head cashier. He saw Mr. Bowman, the head cashier. Flashing a special police identification card which was his by right of audacity, he demanded that Mr. Bowman produce at once the list of serial-numbers of the five one-thousand-dollar bills Knox had drawn on October the first.

The number of the bill from Grimshaw's watch matched one of the five numbers the bank official supplied.

Ellery left the bank and, perhaps feeling that the occasion warranted no celebration, eschewed the more expensive motor vehicle and took the subway home.

CHAPTER 25

Leftover

Saturday afternoon in Brooklyn . . . to make it worse, thought Ellery ruefully as he walked through long residential streets under bare Brooklyn trees—Saturday afternoon in *Flatbush* . . . At that, he thought, as he paused to study a house-number, it was not so bad as quipping vaudevillists painted it. There was something about it, a peace and sobriety—a *very* peaceful peace and a *very* sober sobriety. . . . He visualized Mrs. Jeremiah Odell's voluptuous Broadway figure in these almost bucolic surroundings, and chuckled.

Mrs. Jeremiah Odell, it appeared when he turned into a little stone walk which led by five wooden steps to the porch of a white-frame house, was at home. Her golden eyebrows shot up when she opened the door in answer to his ring; it was apparent that she thought him a house-to-house canvasser, and with the hardened abruptness of the experienced housewife began to retreat with the obvious intention of shutting the door in his face. Ellery slid his foot over the sill, smiling. It was not until he produced his card that the healthy belligerence faded and something like fear replaced it on her large handsome face.

"Come in, Mr. Queen. Come in—I didn't recognize you at first." She wiped her hands nervously on her apron—she was

wearing a stiff and flowered housedress—and fluttered before
him into a dark cool foyer. A French door stood open at their
left; she preceded him into the room beyond. "I—You want to
see Jerry—I mean Mr. Odell, too?"

"If you please."

She went out quickly.

Ellery looked about him with a grin. Marriage had done
more for Lily Morrison than alter her name: the connubial state
had evidently touched a nascent spring of domesticity in Lily's
large round breast. Ellery stood in a very pleasant, very conventional, very clean room—it would be a "front room," of course,
to the Odells. Fond but unaccustomed feminine fingers had
contrived those flaming cushions; a new respectability had dictated the selection of those gaudy prints on the wall—the almost Victorian lamps scattered about. The furniture was heavy
with plush and carving; Ellery could close his eyes and see the
flushed Lily of Albert Grimshaw's environment standing beside
the solid figure of Jeremiah Odell in a cheap furniture store and
selecting the heaviest, richest, most ornate things in sight. . . .

His chuckling reflections were cut short by the entrance of
the master of the household—Mr. Jeremiah Odell in person,
who had, from the grimy state of his fingers, apparently been
scrubbing the inevitable automobile in his private garage
somewhere in the rear. The Irish giant did not apologize either
for his fingers or his collarless, old-shoey appearance; he
waved Ellery into a chair, sat down himself while his spouse
elected to stand stiffly by his side, and growled: "What's up? I
thought this damned snooping was over. What's eatin' you people now?"

The lady, it seemed, was not going to sit down. Ellery remained standing. There were thunderclouds on Odell's beetling
features. "Just a chat. Nothing official, you know," murmured Ellery. "I merely want to check up—"

"Thought the case was closed!"

"So it is." Ellery sighed. "I shan't take more than a few

moments . . . For my own satisfaction I am trying to clear up some of the unimportant but still unexplained points. I should like to know—"

"We ain't got a thing to say."

"Dear, dear." Ellery smiled. "I'm sure you have nothing to say which can possibly have an *important* bearing on the case, Mr. Odell. You see, the important things are completely known to us . . ."

"Say, is this one of them dirty police tricks, or what?"

"Mr. Odell!" Ellery was shocked. "Haven't you read the papers? Why should we want to trick you? It's simply that at the time you were questioned by Inspector Queen you were evasive. Well, conditions have altered materially since then. It's not a question of suspicion anymore, Mr. Odell."

"All right, all right. What's on your mind?"

"Why did you lie about visiting Grimshaw that Thursday night at the Hotel Benedict?"

"Say—" began Odell in a direful voice. He stopped at the pressure of his wife's hand on his shoulder. "You keep out of this, Lily."

"No," she said in a trembling voice, "no, Jerry. We're not tackling this the right way. You don't know the bu—the police. They'll hound us till they find out . . . Tell Mr. Queen the truth, Jerry."

"That's always the wisest course, Mr. Odell," said Ellery heartily. "If you've nothing on your conscience, why should you persist in not talking?"

Their eyes clashed. Then Odell lowered his head, scraping his big black jaw with his hand; sluggishly he mused, taking his time, and Ellery waited.

"Okay," said the Irishman at last. "I'll talk. But God help you, brother, if you're pullin' a fast one! Sit down, Lily; you make me nervous." Obediently she seated herself on the sofa. "I was there, like the Inspector accused me. And I went up to the desk a few minutes after a woman—"

"You were Grimshaw's fourth visitor, then," said Ellery thoughtfully, "beyond a doubt. Why did you go, Mr. Odell?"

"This Grimshaw rat looked up Lily soon as he came down the river. I didn't know this—didn't know Lily's life before I married her. Not that I'd 'a' given a damn, y' understand, but she thought I would, and like a fool she never told me what she'd been before I met her . . ."

"Very unwise, Mrs. Odell," said Ellery severely. "Always confide in your soul-mate, always. That's a fundamental of the perfect marital relation, or something."

Odell grinned for an instant. "Listen to the lad talk . . . Thought I'd run out on you, hey, Lil?" The woman said nothing; she was staring into her lap, pleating her apron. "Anyway, Grimshaw looked 'er up—I don't know how he got a line on her, but he did, the sneaky weasel!—and he forced her to meet him at this Schick guy's joint. She went, because she was afraid he'd spill the beans to me if she got balky."

"I understand."

"He thought she was workin' some new kind o' racket—wouldn't believe her when she said she'd gone straight and wanted none o' his kind of trash. He was sore—told her to meet him in his room at the Benedict, blast his lousy soul to hell!—and she beat it out, and then she came home an' told me . . . saw it was goin' too far."

"And you went to the Benedict to have it out with him?"

"That's the ticket." Odell looked glumly at his big scarred hands. "Talked turkey to the snake. Warned him to keep his dirty paws off my wife or I'd take it out of his hide. That's all. Just put the fear o' God into him and walked out."

"How did Grimshaw react?"

Odell looked embarrassed. "Guess I must've scared hell out of him. He went white around the gills when I grabbed him by the neck—"

"Oh! You manhandled him?"

Odell bellowed with laughter. "You call that manhandlin',

Mr. Queen—grabbin' a guy by the neck. Say, you ought to see how we muss up those big steamfitters in our trade when they get too much 'smoke' in 'em . . . Naw, I just shook him up a little. He was too yellow to pull a rod on me."

"He had a *revolver*?"

"Well, maybe not. Didn't see none. But those birds always do."

Ellery looked thoughtful. Mrs. Odell said timidly: "So you see, Mr. Queen, Jerry didn't really do anything wrong."

"On the other hand, Mrs. Odell, both of you would have saved us a lot of trouble by taking this attitude when you were originally questioned."

"Didn't want to run *my* neck in a noose," rumbled Odell. "Didn't want to be collared for killin' the mutt."

"Mr. Odell, was anybody in Grimshaw's room when he let you in?"

"Not a breathin' soul but Grimshaw himself."

"The room itself—did it show signs of a scrap, or whisky-glasses—anything which might have indicated that someone else was there?"

"Wouldn't notice it if there was. I was pretty riled."

"Did either of you see Grimshaw after that night?"

They shook their heads at once.

"Very well. I warrant you won't be disturbed again."

*   *   *

Ellery found the subway journey to New York irksome; there was little to think about, and he found no solace in a newspaper he had purchased. When he rang the bell on the third floor of the Queens' brownstone habitation on West Eighty-seventh Street, he was frowning; not even the sight of Djuna's sharp Romany face popping out of the doorway erased the frown—and Djuna was normally his spiritual tonic.

Djuna's crafty little brain sensed the disturbance, and he went about quelling it in his own cunning way. He took Ellery's hat, coat and stick with a flourish, made a few experimental faces which usually evoked an answering grin—but now did not—darted from the bedroom into the living-room again and set a cigarette between Ellery's lips, struck a match with ceremony . . .

"Somethin' wrong, Mr. Ellery?" he asked plaintively, at last, when all his efforts proved vain.

Ellery sighed. "Djuna, old son, everything is wrong. That, I suppose, should encourage me. For, 'It's a different song when everything's wrong,' as Robert W. Service said in unambitious doggerel; on the other hand, I can't seem, like Service's little soldier, to pipe the tune of bucking up and chortling. I'm a very unmusical beast."

To Djuna this was the most arrant nonsense, but Ellery in a quotative mood betokened certain inevitables, and Djuna grinned his encouragement.

"Djuna," continued Ellery, slumping back on his spine, "attend. Messer Grimshaw had five visitors that hideous night; of the five we have now accounted for three: the late Gilbert Sloane, his worthy helpmeet, and fearsome Jeremiah Odell. Of the two visitors outstanding, so to speak, we are convinced, despite the man's denial, that Dr. Wardes was one. If we could clear up the Dr. Wardes situation, which might have an innocent enough explanation, that would leave the fascinating remainder of *one* unknown visitor, never identified; who, if Sloane were our murderer, came second in the quintuple line."

"Yes, sir," said Djuna.

"On the other hand, my son," continued Ellery, "I confess to checkmate. This is rank verbiage. I have discovered nothing yet which so much as casts aspersions on the general validity of the Sloane solution."

"No, sir," said Djuna. "I got some coffee in the kitchen—"

"I *have* some coffee in the kitchen, you ungrammatical little worm," said Ellery severely.

It was, taking it all in all, a most unsatisfactory day.

CHAPTER 26

Light

The day, as Ellery was to discover, had not yet ended. For, with a telephone call from his father an hour later, the tree which had been planted by Mrs. Sloane's uneventful visit some days before blossomed and bore fruit with a horticultural fecundity as astonishing as it was unexpected.

"Something's come up," said the Inspector briskly over the wire, "which is queer enough, and I thought you'd like to hear about it."

Ellery was not sanguine. "I've been disappointed so many times—"

"Well, as far as I'm concerned this development doesn't alter the Sloane solution." The old man grew brusque. "Look here—do you want to hear this, or don't you?"

"I suppose so. What's happened?"

Ellery heard his father sneeze, cough and clear his throat—an unfailing sign of disapproval. "You'd better come down to the office. It's a long story."

"Very well."

It was with no great enthusiasm that Ellery went downtown. He was heartily sick of subways, and he had a slight headache, and the world seemed a poor place. He found his father, furthermore, in conference with a Deputy Inspector, and he was compelled to wait forty-five minutes outside. It was a snappish Ellery who slouched into the old man's office.

"What's the world-shaking news now?"

The Inspector kicked a chair toward him. "Get a load off your feet. Here's the low-down. Got a little social call from your friend—what's his name?—Suiza this afternoon."

"*My* friend? Nacio Suiza. And?"

"And he told me that *he* had been in the Khalkis Galleries the night of Sloane's suicide."

Fatigue fled. Ellery sprang to his feet. "No!"

"Keep your shirt on," growled the Inspector. "Nothing to get excited about. It seems that Suiza had to work on a prospectus of the pieces in the Khalkis art-gallery—said it was a long and tedious job, and he thought he'd get a head start on it by working that night."

"The night of Sloane's suicide?"

"Yes. Listen, will you, younker? Now he got there, let himself in with his passkey, and went upstairs into that long main gallery there—"

"Let himself in with his passkey. How could he, when the electric alarm was working?"

"It wasn't. Showed that someone was still in the place—generally, the last man out saw that the alarm was in place and notified the protective agency. Anyway, he went upstairs and saw a light in Sloane's office. There was something about the prospectus he wanted to ask Sloane—knew Sloane was probably working there. So he went in and, of course, found Sloane's dead body; exactly as we discovered it later."

Ellery was strangely excited. His eyes were fixed hypnotically on the Inspector as he stuck a cigarette between his lips from force of habit. "*Exactly?*"

"Yes, yes," said the Inspector. "Head on the desk, gun under the hanging right arm, on the floor—everything kosher. This was a few minutes before we got there, incidentally. Of course,

Suiza got panicky—can't say I blame him—he was in a tough spot. He was careful not to touch anything, realized that if he was found there he'd have some tall explaining to do, and beat it fast."

"By the non-existent beard of Napoleon," muttered Ellery with glazed eyes, "if it's only possible!"

"If what's possible? Sit down—you're going off half-cocked again," snapped the Inspector. "Don't get any false notions, Ellery. I put Suiza on the grill for an hour, shooting questions at him about how the room looked, and he came through one hundred per cent. When the news of the suicide came out in the papers, he was a little relieved but still nervous. He said he wanted to see if anything further would develop. When nothing did, he saw it couldn't hurt to talk, and his conscience bothered him anyway, so he came to me with the story. And that's the kit and boodle of it."

Ellery was smoking in furious puffs, and his mind was far away.

"Anyway," the Inspector went on a little uneasily, "it's beside the main issue. Just an interesting sidelight which doesn't affect the Sloane-suicide solution in the slightest."

"Yes, yes. I agree with you there. It's obvious that since Suiza was not suspected of being implicated, he would not have come forward with the story of his visit to the scene of the— suicide unless he were innocent. That's not what I'm thinking about . . . Dad!"

"Well?"

"Do you want *confirmation* of the theory that Sloane committed suicide?"

"How's that? Confirmation?" The old man snorted. "It's not a theory, either—it's a fact. But I guess a little more evidence won't hurt. What's on your mind?"

Ellery was taut with a singing excitement. "It is perfectly true," he cried, "that on the basis of what you have just related there is nothing in the Suiza tale that invalidates the Sloane solution. But now we can *prove* suicide more completely by asking Mr. Nacio Suiza just one little question . . . You see, Dad, despite your conviction that Suiza's having visited that office doesn't alter the facts, there remains a tiny loophole, an infinitesimal possibility. . . . By the way, when Suiza left the building that night, did he set the alarm to working?"

"Yes. Said he did it mechanically."

"I see." Ellery rose quickly. "Let's visit Suiza at once. I shan't be able to sleep unless I satisfy myself on that one point."

The Inspector nursed his lower lip. "By ginger," he muttered, "you're right as usual, you bloodhound. Stupid of me not to have thought of asking that question myself." He jumped up and reached for his overcoat. "He said he was going back to the Galleries. Let's go!"

* * *

They found an oddly disturbed Nacio Suiza in the deserted Khalkis Galleries on Madison Avenue. Suiza was less immaculate than usual, and there was a crinkle in his smooth hair that should not have been there. He met them opposite the closed and barred door to Gilbert Sloane's office, explaining with flat nervousness that the room had not been used since Sloane's death. This was all talk, verbal camouflage to conceal a very genuine perturbation. He seated them in his own curio-spattered office and blurted: "Is anything wrong, Inspector? Something hasn't . . ."

"Don't get your wind up," said the Inspector mildly. "Mr. Queen here has a couple of questions."

"Yes?"

"I understand," said Ellery, "that you walked into Sloane's office next door on the night of his death because you saw a light in there. Is that correct?"

"Not exactly." Suiza folded his hands tightly. "My intention was merely to speak to Sloane about something. As I walked into the gallery I knew that Sloane was in his office because the light was shining through the transom . . ."

The Queens jerked as if they had been sitting on electric-chairs. "Ah, the transom," said Ellery with a queer inflection. *"Then the door to Sloane's office was closed before you walked in?"*

Suiza looked puzzled. "Why, certainly. Is that important? I thought I mentioned that, Inspector."

"You did not!" snarled the Inspector. His old nose had fallen appreciably nearer his mouth. "And in running out you left the door open?"

Suiza faltered: "Yes. I was panic-stricken, didn't think . . . But what was your question, Mr. Queen?"

"You've already answered it," said Ellery dryly.

*   *   *

The shoe was on the other foot. A half-hour later the Queens were in the living-room of their apartment, the Inspector in a vile temper, muttering to himself; Ellery in the gayest of moods, humming and prancing up and down before the fire which a bewildered Djuna had hastily lighted. Neither man said a word after the Inspector made two telephone calls. Ellery calmed, but his eyes were glowing as he flung himself into his favourite chair, feet propped on a firedog, and studied the weaving of the flames.

Djuna answered a wild bell-ringing and admitted two red-faced gentlemen—District Attorney Sampson and Assistant District Attorney Pepper. He took their coats in growing wonderment; both men were nervous, both barked a greeting, both took chairs and joined in the glaring petulance which all at once pervaded the room.

"Here's a pretty state," said Sampson at last, "here's a pretty state of affairs! You seemed damned sure over the wire, Q. Are you—?"

The old man jerked his head toward Ellery. "Ask him. It was his idea in the first place, drat him."

"Well, Ellery, well?"

They all looked at him in silence. Ellery flipped a cigarette into the fire and, without turning around, drawled: "Hereafter, gentlemen, have faith in the warning-note of my subconscious. My premonition of screwiness, as friend Pepper might say, is justified by events.

"But all this is beside the point. The point is simply this: The bullet which killed Sloane penetrated his head and emerged, taking a trajectory line which led through the door of the office. We found the bullet imbedded in a rug hanging on the gallery wall opposite the office-door, and *outside* the office. Obviously, then, the door was open when the bullet was discharged. When we burst in on the Galleries the night of Sloane's death, we found Sloane's office-door open, which was in perfect tune with the *locus* of the bullet. Now, however, Nacio Suiza comes forward with the story that we were not the first to enter the Galleries after Sloane's death; but that he, Suiza, had been a previous visitor. In other words, any condition relating to the door of Sloane's office when we arrived must be re-adjusted and examined in the light of this previous visit. The question then arose: Was the condition of the door the same when Suiza got there? If he had found it open, we would be no further advanced than before."

Ellery chuckled. "But Suiza found the door *closed*! How does this alter the situation? Well, certainly when the bullet was fired the door must have been open, otherwise the bullet would have struck the door, not the rug opposite the door outside the room. Then the door must have been closed *after* the bullet was fired. What does this mean—that Sloane fired the bullet into his own head and then for some ungodly reason went to the door, closed it, returned to the desk and sat down in precisely the same position as when he had pulled the trigger? Ridiculous; not only ridiculous but impossible: for Sloane died instantly, as Dr. Prouty's autopsy report pointed out. This also banishes the possibility that he shot himself in the gallery and dragged himself back into his office, closing the door as he returned. No! When the revolver was discharged, Sloane died at once, and moreover the door was open. But Suiza found it closed . . .

"In other words, since the door was found closed by Suiza after Sloane's instantaneous death, and since the bullet couldn't have penetrated the door, which we noted in our preliminary investigation is made of steel—the only conclusion we can logically make is that *someone closed the door after Sloane's death and before Suiza got to it.*"

"But, Mr. Queen," objected Pepper, "isn't it possible that Suiza wasn't the only visitor—that somebody was there and went away before he came?"

"Excellent suggestion, Pepper, and that is precisely what I am pointing out: that there was a visitor before Suiza—and that visitor was Sloane's murderer!"

Sampson massaged his lean cheeks with irritation. "I'll be hanged! Look here, Ellery, it's still possible, you know, that Sloane did commit suicide, but that the visitor Pepper postulates might have been an innocent man, like Suiza, who's too scared to admit he was there."

Ellery waved his hand airily. "Possible, but deucedly farfetched to evoke *two* innocent visitors in a limited time. No, Sampson, I don't believe any of you can deny that we now have sufficient grounds to cast grave doubt upon the theory of suicide and support the theory of murder."

"It's true," said the Inspector in despair. "It's true."

But Sampson was tenacious. "All right, let's say Sloane was murdered, and his murderer closed the door on going out. It seems to me a damned stupid thing for him to do. Didn't he notice that the bullet had punched a hole clean through Sloane's head and gone out through the open door?"

"Sampson, Sampson," said Ellery wearily, "think about it for a moment. Can the human eye follow the course of even a retarded bullet? Naturally, if the murderer had noticed that the bullet had completely penetrated Sloane's skull he would not have closed the door. The fact that he did close the door, then, proves that he hadn't noticed it. Please remember that Sloane's head fell forward on his desk in such a way that its *left* side, the side from which the bullet emerged, was resting on the blotter. This position would have concealed the bullet-outlet entirely and the blood to a great degree. Besides, the murderer was probably in one devil of a hurry; why should he raise the dead man's head and investigate? After all, he had no reason to *expect* that the bullet would penetrate and emerge. It's not the usual thing for a bullet to do, you know."

They were silent for a space, and then the old man grinned wryly at his two visitors. "He's got us by the short hair, boys. It looks open and shut to me. Sloane was murdered."

They nodded gloomily.

Ellery spoke again, briskly and without the note of personal triumph which had marked his explanation of the fallacious Khalkis solution. "Very well. Let's re-analyse. If Sloane was murdered, as we now have excellent reason to believe, Sloane did not kill Grimshaw. It means that the real murderer of Grimshaw killed Sloane and made it appear a suicide, as if Sloane by shooting himself was thereby making tacit confession that he had been in truth Grimshaw's murderer.

"To return to some original theses. We know from former deductions that the murderer of Grimshaw, in order to have been able to plant the false clues against Khalkis, must have had knowledge of Knox's possession of the stolen painting; I proved that long ago when I showed that the entire Khalkis solution depended upon the murderer's assurance that Knox would not come forward. *Alors*. The only outsider who had this knowledge, also as proved in that dreary past, was Grimshaw's partner. Q.E.D.: Grimshaw's partner is the murderer; and since Sloane himself was murdered, Sloane could not have been Grimshaw's partner. Therefore the murderer is still at large and actively engaged in his pretty occupation of plotting. Still at large, I might point out, and in possession of Knox's story.

"Now," continued Ellery, "to reinterpret the clues against Sloane—clues which, since Sloane was murdered and was therefore innocent, can only have been additional plants manufactured and left by the real murderer.

"In the first place, since Sloane was innocent, we can no longer question the validity of his statement as to what happened on the night he visited Grimshaw at the Benedict. For while as a suspect his testimony was open to suspicion, as an innocent man he must perforce be believed. Therefore Sloane's statement that he was the *second* visitor that night is probably true; the unknown actually did precede him, Sloane said; the unknown must therefore have been Grimshaw's companion, the man who walked into the lobby by Grimshaw's side, the man who accompanied Grimshaw into Room 314, as the elevator-boy testified. The sequence of visitors then is: the unknown—the bundled man; after whom came Sloane, then Mrs. Sloane, then Jeremiah Odell, then Dr. Wardes."

Ellery brandished a lean forefinger. "Let me show you how logic and the exercise of the brain provide an interesting deduction. You will recall that Sloane said he was the *only* person in the world who knew that he, as Gilbert *Sloane*, was Grimshaw's brother; not even Grimshaw knowing his brother's changed name. Yet whoever wrote the anonymous letter did know this fact—the fact that Sloane, as Sloane, was Grimshaw's brother. Who wrote the letter? Grimshaw, not having known the name of his brother, couldn't have told anyone; Sloane by his own now reputable testimony never told anyone; therefore the only person who could have discovered the fact is someone who *saw them together*, heard that they were brothers, and already knew or later discovered by meeting Sloane and remembering his voice and face, that Grimshaw's brother was Gilbert Sloane. But here's an amazing thing! Sloane himself said that the night he went to Grimshaw's room at the Benedict was the _only_ occasion since he had changed his name—a matter of many years—on which the two brothers were face to face!

"In other words, whoever discovered the fact that Gilbert _Sloane_ was Albert Grimshaw's brother, must have been present, in the flesh, that night of Sloane's visit to Grimshaw's room. But Sloane himself told us that Grimshaw was alone when they were talking. How, then, could someone have been present? Very simply. If Sloane did not _see_ this person, and this person still was present, it means that he was merely not visible to Sloane. In other words, hiding somewhere in the room; either in a clothes-closet or in the bathroom. Remember that Sloane did not see anyone emerge from Room 314, despite the fact that Grimshaw's companion had entered with Grimshaw only a few moments before. Remember too that Sloane said he knocked on the door, and his brother opened it _after a few moments_—Sloane's own words. We may presume then that when Sloane knocked Grimshaw's companion was still in 314, but that, wishing to avoid being seen, he slipped either into the closet or the bathroom with Grimshaw's permission.

"Now," continued Ellery, "visualize the situation. Sloane and Grimshaw talk, and our unknown mysterioso is listening, all ears from his place of concealment. He hears, during the conversation, Grimshaw say maliciously that he'd nearly forgotten _he had a brother_. The concealed gentleman, therefore, knew that Grimshaw and his visitor were brothers. Did he recognize Sloane's voice and know that he was hearing _Gilbert Sloane_? Perhaps he could even see—did he recognize Sloane's face? Or did he later meet Sloane and recognize his voice, putting two and two together and inducing what Sloane thought only he himself in all the world knew? We have no way of telling, but one thing is certain: the unknown must have been in Grimshaw's room that night, must have overheard the conversation, must have learned by induction that Gilbert Sloane and Albert Grimshaw were flesh-and-blood relations. For this is the only line of reasoning which explains how someone discovered the apparently unknowable fact."

"Well, at least this is getting somewhere," said Sampson. "Go on, Ellery. What else do you see with that necromantic brain of yours?"

"Logic, not necromancy, Sampson, although it is true I am anticipating future events by a sort of consultation with the dead. . . . I see this, clearly: the unknown, hidden in the room, being the one who accompanied Grimshaw directly before Sloane came in, was Grimshaw's partner—the 'partner' Grimshaw himself specifically referred to the next night in Khalkis's library. And this unknown, Grimshaw's partner and murderer— as proved before—was the only one who could have written the anonymous letter to the police revealing the Sloane-Grimshaw brothership."

"Sounds right," muttered the Inspector.

"So it would seem." Ellery folded his hands behind his neck. "Where are we? The letter was, therefore, one of the planted clues against Sloane to frame him as the murderer, with this distinction from those that had gone before—that is, it was not manufactured, but the truth. Nothing directly incriminating, of course, but a choice titbit for the police when combined with other and more direct evidence. Now, this brothership clue having been planted, it is reasonable to assume that the basement key we found in Sloane's humidor was also a plant; and Grimshaw's watch in Sloane's safe, too. Only Grimshaw's murderer could have had that watch; Sloane having been innocent, Grimshaw's murderer placed the watch where it would be immediately found after Sloane's apparent suicide. The remains of the burnt Khalkis will must also have been a plant to implicate Sloane, for while it is probable that Sloane stole the will and put it into the coffin in the first place, thinking to be rid of it forever, it was indubitably the murderer who found it in the coffin while burying Grimshaw, and took it out and away with him on the excellent assumption that he might be able to make use of it later—as he did, observe, in the plot against Sloane after the Khalkis solution failed."

Pepper and Sampson nodded.

"Now as to motive," Ellery went on. "Why was Sloane selected to be framed as Grimshaw's murderer? This has interesting facets. Of course, Sloane having been Grimshaw's brother, having changed his name because of the family disgrace brought on by Grimshaw's criminal career, having stolen the will and hidden it in the Khalkis coffin, being a member of the household and a physical possibility on all counts for the planting of the Khalkis clues—all these circumstances would give the murderer admirable reason for selecting Sloane as an 'acceptable' criminal to the police.

"Yet, if Mrs. Vreeland's story is true that Sloane was in the graveyard on that Wednesday night when Grimshaw's body must have been buried in Khalkis's coffin, Sloane must have been there for some reason not connected with the burial of the body, since he hadn't killed the man in the first place.— Don't forget that Mrs. Vreeland didn't see him carrying anything.... Very well. Why was Sloane skulking about the court and graveyard that Wednesday night?" Ellery stared reflectively into the fire. "I have had an arresting thought. For if Sloane that night had observed some suspicious activity, had followed the murderer unseen into the graveyard, had actually witnessed the burial and seen the murderer appropriate the steel will-box.... Do you see where we tend? On the basis of these not fanciful assumptions, we can infer what Sloane would do later. He knew the murderer, had seen him burying Grimshaw. Why didn't he reveal this information to the police? Excellent reason!—the murderer had in his possession the will which cut off Sloane as a legatee. Is it far-fetched to reason that Sloane later approached the murderer with a proposition: that he would keep silent about the murderer's identity, provided the murderer returned to Sloane, or destroyed on the spot, the pestiferous new testament? This would provide the murderer with an additional motive: for now he would have all the more reason to choose Sloane as the 'acceptable' criminal, killing him and making him appear a suicide, and thereby obliterating the only person alive who knew the murderer's identity."

"But it seems to me," objected Sampson, "that the murderer in this event, when Sloane approached him, would be forced to give Sloane the will. And that doesn't jibe with the facts, because we found the will burnt in the next-door basement furnace, and you claim *the murderer* left it there for us to find."

Ellery yawned. "Sampson, Sampson, when will you ever learn to use the grey matter in your noodle? Do you think that our gentle homicidal maniac is a fool? All he had to do was to threaten Sloane. He would say: 'If you tell the police I killed Grimshaw, I'll give the police this will. No, Mr. Sloane, I'll keep the will to make sure *you* keep your mouth shut.' And Sloane would have no recourse but to accept the compromise. As it is, the moment he went to friend murderer he sealed his own fate. Poor Sloane! I'm afraid he wasn't very smart."

* * *

What followed was swift, painful and annoying. The Inspector, much against his will, was forced to communicate Suiza's story and its implications to the newspaper reporters. The Sunday papers touched on the matter, the Monday papers blazed with the news—Monday being an extraordinarily weak day for news in the journalistic profession—and the whole of New York City knew directly thereafter that the much-maligned Gilbert Sloane had been not a murderer-suicide after all but, the police now felt, an innocent victim of a clever murderer—diabolical was the word the tabloids used. The police, they went on to inform the public, were therefore still searching for the real murderer, who now had two killings on his bloody conscience, where before he had had only one.

Mrs. Sloane, it should be noted, shone in a belated glory. Her precious family honour was repolished, and it now glittered brightly in the tardy but welcome sunlight of public *apologia* made by the press, the police and the District Attorney. Mrs. Sloane was not an ungrateful lady; she sensed that behind Nacio Suiza's story there had been the fine intellectual hand of Ellery Queen, and embarrassed that young man by gushing effusions to the delighted gentlemen of the press.

As for Sampson, Pepper, Inspector Queen . . . the less said about them the better. Sampson attributes several of his silvery hairs to this period in his official career, and the Inspector has always maintained that Ellery, by his "logic" and persistence, drove him nearly to the grave.

CHAPTER 27

Exchange

On Tuesday, October twenty-sixth, exactly one week after Mrs. Sloane had inadvertently begun the chain of events which led to the snapping of the Sloane solution, Mr. Ellery Queen was awakened at ten o'clock in the morning by the clamour of his telephone-bell. The caller was his father. A tense situation, it seemed, had arisen that morning regarding the exchange of cablegrams between New York and London. The Victoria Museum was getting ugly.

"Conference in Henry Sampson's office in an hour, son." The old man seemed old and weary this morning. "Thought you might like to be present."

"I'll be there, Dad," said Ellery; and added softly, "Where's that Spartan spirit of yours, Inspector?"

Ellery found in the District Attorney's private office an hour later a bristling assemblage. The Inspector was angry and morose; Sampson was irritable; Pepper was silent—and, sitting there as on a throne, his hard old face set in adamantine lines, was the eminent Mr. James J. Knox.

They barely acknowledged Ellery's greeting; Sampson indicated a chair with a flirt of his hand and Ellery slipped into it, eyes dancing with anticipation.

"Mr. Knox." Sampson strode up and down before the throne. "I've asked you to come down here this morning because—"

"Yes?" asked Knox in his deceptively soft voice.

"Look here, Mr. Knox." Sampson took another tack. "I haven't been taking active part in this investigation, as you perhaps know—too busy with other affairs. Mr. Pepper, my assistant, has been handling things on my end. Now, with all respect to Mr. Pepper's capacities, matters have reached the pass where I am forced personally to take official cognizance of the situation."

"Really." Knox's word was neither a sneer nor an accusation. He seemed to be waiting mentally crouched for the spring.

"Yes," said Sampson, almost with a snarl. "Really! Do you want to know why I've taken things out of Mr. Pepper's hands?" He stopped before Knox's chair and glared. "Because, Mr. Knox, your attitude is brewing a serious international complication, that's why!"

"My attitude?" Knox seemed amused.

Sampson did not reply at once. He went to his desk and picked up a sheaf of white half-sheets clipped together—Western Union cablegrams, their messages pasted on to the paper in thin strips of yellow.

"Now, Mr. Knox," continued Sampson in a choking voice— he was making *opéra bouffe* efforts to control his tongue and temper, "I'm going to read you a number of cablegrams, in sequence. This series of messages represents correspondence between Inspector Queen here and the Director of the Victoria Museum in London. At the end there are two cables from neither of these gentlemen, cables which, as I pointed out, may very well result in an international mess."

"Really, you know," murmured Knox, smiling faintly, "I can't see why you think I'm interested in this thing. But I'm a public-spirited citizen. Go ahead."

Inspector Queen's face convulsed; but he caught himself and sank back in his chair, his pale face as red as Knox's necktie.

"The first one," continued the District Attorney in a fiercely conversational voice, "is Inspector Queen's original cablegram to the Museum after learning your story—at the time the Khalkis solution was exploded. Here is what the Inspector cabled." Sampson read the uppermost cablegram loudly, very loudly.

IN LAST FIVE YEARS (it ran) WAS VALUABLE
LEONARDO DA VINCI PAINTING STOLEN FROM YOUR
MUSEUM?

Knox sighed. Sampson went on after a baffled moment of hesitation. "This is the Museum's reply after the lapse of some time." The second ran:

SUCH PAINTING STOLEN FIVE YEARS AGO. FORMER
ATTENDANT KNOWN HERE AS GRAHAM REAL NAME
PROBABLY GRIMSHAW SUSPECTED OF THEFT BUT NO
TRACE EVER FOUND OF PAINTING. OBVIOUS REASONS
CAUSED SUPPRESSION OF THEFT. YOUR INQUIRY
LEADS US TO BELIEVE YOU KNOW WHEREABOUTS OF
LEONARDO. COMMUNICATE AT ONCE. KEEP
CONFIDENTIAL.

"All a mistake. All a mistake," said Knox genially.

"You think so, Mr. Knox?" Sampson was purple. He slapped the second cablegram over and read the third.

This was Inspector Queen's reply:

IS THERE ANY POSSIBILITY STOLEN PAINTING WAS
NOT BY LEONARDO BUT BY PUPIL OR CONTEMPORARY
OF SAME AND THEREFORE WORTH ONLY FRACTION OF
CATALOGUED VALUE?

Reply from the Director of the Victoria Museum:

PLEASE ANSWER QUESTION PREVIOUS CABLE WHERE
IS PAINTING? SERIOUS ACTION CONTEMPLATED IF
PAINTING NOT RETURNED AT ONCE. AUTHENTICITY OF
LEONARDO VOUCHED FOR BY MOST EMINENT BRITISH

EXPERTS. VALUE ON DISCOVERY PLACED AT TWO
HUNDRED THOUSAND POUNDS.

Inspector Queen's reply:

PLEASE ALLOW US TIME. NOT SURE OF OUR GROUND.
WE ARE TRYING TO AVOID UNPLEASANT NOTORIETY
AND COMPLICATIONS FOR YOUR SAKE AS WELL AS
OURS. CONFLICT IN OPINION SEEMS TO INDICATE
PAINTING WE ARE INVESTIGATING NOT A GENUINE
LEONARDO.

Museum's reply:

CANNOT UNDERSTAND SITUATION. IF PAINTING
UNDER DISCUSSION IS QUOTE DETAIL FROM BATTLE
OF THE STANDARD UNQUOTE LEONARDO WORK IN
OILS SUPPOSED TO HAVE BEEN EXECUTED BY THE
MASTER AFTER PALAZZO VECCHIO FRESCO PROJECT
WAS ABANDONED IN FIFTEEN HUNDRED AND FIVE
THEN IT IS OURS. IF AVAILABLE FOR AMERICAN
EXPERT OPINION ITS WHEREABOUTS MUST BE
KNOWN TO YOU. MUST INSIST RETURN IRRESPECTIVE
OF AMERICAN CONCEPTION OF ITS VALUE. THIS WORK
BELONGS TO VICTORIA MUSEUM BY RIGHT OF
DISCOVERY AND ITS PRESENCE IN THE UNITED STATES
IS RESULT OF THEFT.

Inspector Queen's reply:

OUR POSITION DEMANDS MORE TIME. PLEASE HAVE
CONFIDENCE.

District Attorney Sampson paused significantly. "Now, Mr.
Knox, we come to the first of the two cables which may very
well result in headaches for us all. It comes as a reply to the cable I just read to you and is signed by Inspector Broome of
Scotland Yard."

"Very interesting," said Knox dryly.

"Damned right it is, Mr. Knox!" Sampson glared and resumed his reading in a trembling voice. The Scotland Yard cable ran:

VICTORIA MUSEUM CASE IN OUR HANDS. PLEASE
CLARIFY POSITION NEW YORK POLICE.

"I hope," choked Sampson, flipping over the white half-sheet, "I *sincerely* hope, Mr. Knox, you begin to see what's facing us. Here's Inspector Queen's reply to *that*."

The cable said:

LEONARDO NOT IN OUR POSSESSION. INTERNATIONAL
PRESSURE AT THIS TIME MAY RESULT IN COMPLETE
LOSS OF PAINTING. ALL ACTIVITY HERE CONDUCTED
IN EXCLUSIVE INTERESTS OF MUSEUM. GIVE US TWO
WEEKS.

James Knox nodded: he twisted about to face the Inspector, who was gripping the edge of his chair, and said with bland approval: "Excellent reply, Inspector. Very clever. Very diplomatic. Good work."

There was no answer to that, Ellery noted with growing amusement, although he possessed the delicate good sense to keep a straight face. The Inspector swallowed hard, and Sampson and Pepper exchanged glances whose vitriol was surely not intended for each other. Sampson went on, in tones so tight the words could barely be made out: "And here's the last cable. Just arrived this morning, also from Inspector Broome."

This cable ran:

REQUEST FOR TWO WEEKS TIME GRANTED BY
MUSEUM. WILL DEFER ACTION UNTIL THEN. GOOD
LUCK.

There was silence as Sampson flung the sheaf of cablegrams back on his desk and faced Knox, arms akimbo. "Well,

Mr. Knox, there you are. We've put *our* cards on the table. For God's sake, sir, be reasonable! Meet us halfway—at least let us get a look at the painting in your possession, let us have it examined by impartial experts. . . ."

"Shan't do any such nonsensical thing," replied the great man easily. "No necessity for it. My expert says it's not the Leonardo, and he ought to know—he gets enough money from me. To hell with the Victoria Museum, Mr. Sampson. These institutions are all the same."

The Inspector jumped to his feet, unable to contain himself. "Big bug or little bug," he shouted, "I'll be eternally blasted, Henry, if I let this—this . . ." He strangled. Sampson gripped his arm and pulled him into a corner; he whispered rapidly to the old man. Some of the colour left the Inspector's face, and artfulness replaced it. "Sorry, Mr. Knox," he said contritely, returning with Sampson. "Lost my temper. Why don't you be a regular scout and return that dingus to the Museum? Take your loss like a good sport. You've dropped twice that in the market before this without batting an eyelash."

The smile flew out of Knox's face. "Good sport, eh?" He got heavily to his feet. "Is there any reason under God's good sun why I should return something for which I paid three quarters of a million dollars? Answer that, Queen. Answer that!"

"After all," said Pepper with swift tact before the Inspector could frame a retort, "after all your collector's enthusiasm can't be at stake, sir, since according to your own expert the painting in your possession is virtually worthless as a work of art."

"And you've compounded a felony," put in Sampson.

"Prove it. Just try to prove it." Knox was angry now; his jawline was taut and ridged. "I tell you the painting I bought isn't the one stolen from the Museum. Prove that it is, by God! If you push me, gentlemen, you'll find yourselves with a nice scrap on your hands!"

"Now, now," began Sampson helplessly, when Ellery asked

in the mildest voice imaginable: "By the way, Mr. Knox, who is your expert?"

Knox wheeled in his tracks. He blinked a moment, then he laughed shortly. "My business entirely, Queen. I'll produce him when I feel it's necessary. And if you people get too frisky, I'll deny even owning the damned thing!"

"I wouldn't do that," said the Inspector. "No, sir, I wouldn't do that. We'd charge you with perjury, too, by Christmas!"

Sampson pounded his desk. "Your stand, Mr. Knox, puts me and the police in a serious predicament. If you persist in this childish attitude, you'll force me to turn the case over to the Federal authorities. Scotland Yard won't stand for any nonsense, and neither will the United States District Attorney."

Knox picked up his hat and stamped toward the door. There was finality in that broad back.

Ellery drawled: "My dear Mr. Knox, do you intend to fight the United States government and the British government, too?"

Knox turned on his heel; he jammed his hat on his head. "Young man," he said grimly, "you can't *imagine* whom I'd fight for something that cost me three quarters of a million. That's no chicken-feed even for Jim Knox. I've fought governments before—and won!"

And the door slammed.

"You should read your Bible more often, Mr. Knox," said Ellery softly, looking at the shivering door. "'God hath chosen the weak things of the world to confound the things that are mighty. . . .'"

But no one was paying attention. The District Attorney groaned: "We're in a worse mess now than we were before. What the devil can we do now?"

The Inspector tugged at his moustache fiercely. "I don't think we ought to dilly-dally anymore. We've been yellow long enough. If Knox doesn't give up that damned blob of paint within a few days, you ought to put the matter into the hands of the Federal D.A. Let *him* have it out with Scotland Yard."

"Have to take possession of the painting by force, I guess," said Sampson glumly.

"And suppose, my masters," suggested Ellery, "suppose Mr. James J. Knox conveniently can't find it?"

They chewed upon that and found it, to judge from their expressions, a bitter morsel. Sampson shrugged. "Well, *you* generally have an answer to everything. What would you do in this extraordinary mess?"

Ellery looked at the white ceiling. "I should do—precisely nothing. This is one situation in which the policy of *laissez faire* is justified. To press Knox now would be merely to aggravate him; he's essentially a hard-headed business man, and if you give him some time. . . . Who knows?" He smiled and rose. "Give him at least the two weeks' grace you yourselves have been granted by the Museum. Undoubtedly the next move will be Knox's."

There was sad reluctance in their nods.

But Ellery, once again in this case of consistent contradictions, was entirely wrong. For the next move, when it came, proved to be from another source . . . a move, moreover, which far from settling the case seemed to complicate it more than ever.

CHAPTER 28

Requisition

The blow fell on Thursday, two days after James J. Knox had signified his entire willingness to come to grips with both the United States and Great Britain. The idleness or activity of the great man's boast was destined never to be tested in the crucible of the courts. For on Thursday morning, as Ellery lounged in his father's office at Police Headquarters gazing out of the window at the sky most unhappily, Mercury in the form and figure of a weazened telegraph messenger delivered a communication which was to ally the bellicose one with the forces of law and order in no uncertain manner.

The telegram was signed by Knox, and conveyed a cryptic intelligence:

> PLEASE HAVE PLAIN CLOTHESMAN PICK UP PACKET
> FROM ME WAITING AT THIRTY-THIRD STREET OFFICE
> WESTERN UNION STOP OBVIOUS REASON CANNOT
> COMMUNICATE WITH YOU BY MORE DIRECT MEANS.

They looked at each other. "Here's a pretty howdy-do," muttered the Inspector. "You don't think he's taking this way of sending that Leonardo back to us, do you, El?"

Ellery was frowning. "No, no," he said impatiently. "It can't be that. The Leonardo, if I recall correctly, is some four feet by six in size. Even if the canvas has been cut and rolled it would hardly be a 'packet.' No, it's something else. I'd advise you to attend to this at once, Dad. Knox's message strikes me as—well, peculiar."

They waited in a sweat of anxiety while a detective went to the designated telegraph office. The man returned within the hour carrying a small parcel, unaddressed, and bearing Knox's name in one corner. The old man tore it open. Inside there was an envelope with a letter, and another sheet of paper which proved to be a message from Knox to the Inspector—all done up in cardboard as if to disguise the contents of the packet. They read Knox's note first—short, curt and businesslike. It ran:

INSPECTOR QUEEN: Enclosed you will find an anonymous letter I received this morning through the regular mail. I am naturally afraid the writer may be watching, and I take this roundabout method of delivering the letter to you. What shall I do? Perhaps we can catch this man if we are circumspect. Obviously he is still unaware that I told you the whole story of the painting several weeks ago. J. J. K.

Knox's note had been laboriously written in longhand.

The letter in the envelope which Knox had enclosed was a small slip of white paper. The envelope was of a cheap and common variety, such as may be purchased for a penny in any neighbourhood stationery shop; and Knox's address was typewritten. The letter had been routed through a midtown post office, and its postmark revealed that it had been mailed probably the night before.

There was something peculiar about the sheet of paper inside the envelope on which the message to Knox had been typed. One whole edge of the paper presented a fuzzy ragged appearance—as if the original sheet had been twice the size and for some reason had been torn none too carefully down the middle.

But the Inspector did not stop to examine the paper itself; his old eyes were goggling at the typed message:

> JAMES J. KNOX, ESQ.: The writer of this note wants something from you, and you will give it to him without a murmur. To show you whom you are dealing with, look at the reverse side of this sheet—and you will find that I am writing on the back of half the promissory note which Khalkis gave Grimshaw in your presence that night several weeks ago. . . .

Ellery exclaimed aloud, and the Inspector ceased his oral reading to turn the sheet over with shaking fingers. It was incredible . . . but there it was—the scrawly large handwriting of Georg Khalkis.

"It's half the promissory note, all right!" cried the Inspector. "Plain as the nose on your face! Torn down the middle for some reason—only half of it's here, but there's the Khalkis part of his signature, by jingo—"

"Queer," muttered Ellery. "Go on, Dad. What does the rest of the letter say?"

The Inspector licked dry lips as he turned the sheet over and resumed his reading:

> You won't be foolish enough to go with this to the police, because you have that stolen Leonardo and if you go to them you will have to confess the whole story of the respectable Mr. James J. Knox's possession of a work of art cribbed from a British museum and worth a cool million. Laugh that off! I am going to milk you properly, Mr. Knox, and you will be given specific instructions soon as to the exact manner of the first milking, so to speak. If you show fight it will be just too bad, because I will see to it that the police learn of your possession of stolen goods.

The letter was unsigned.

"Garrulous cuss, isn't he?" murmured Ellery.

"Well, I'll be a fireman's red hat," said the Inspector, shaking his head. "He's a cool one, whoever wrote that letter. Blackmailing Knox because he owns the stolen painting!" He put the letter cautiously on the desk and began to rub his hands with glee. "Well, son, we've got the rascal! Got him hog-tied. He thinks Knox can't talk to us because we don't know about this pesky business. And—"

Ellery nodded absently. "So it seems." He eyed the sheet of paper in an enigmatic manner. "Nevertheless, it would be wise to verify Khalkis's handwriting. This note is—I can't tell you how important, Dad."

"Important!" chuckled the old man. "You're sort of overstating it, aren't you? Thomas! Where's Thomas!" He ran to the door and crooked his finger at someone in the anteroom. Sergeant Velie thundered in. "Thomas, get that anonymous letter from the files—the one we got which told about Sloane and Grimshaw being brothers. And bring Miss Lambert back with you. Tell her to fetch some samples of Khalkis's fist with her—she's got a few, I think."

Velie went away and returned shortly in the company of the sharp-featured young woman with the dash of grey in her black hair. He handed the Inspector a packet.

"Come in, Miss Lambert, come in," said the Inspector. "Little job for you. Take a squint at this letter and compare it with the one you looked over some time ago."

Una Lambert went silently to work. She compared the Khalkis handwriting on the reverse side of the paper with a sample she had brought with her. Then she examined the blackmail note under a powerful magnifying glass, frequently turning to the note Velie had brought for comparison. They waited impatiently for her decision.

She put down both notes at last. "The handwriting specimen on this new note is that of Mr. Khalkis. As for the typed notes, both were unquestionably typed on the same machine, Inspector, and probably by the same person."

The Inspector and Ellery nodded. "Corroboration, at any rate," said Ellery. "The author of the brothership note is undoubtedly our man."

"Any details, Miss Lambert?" demanded the Inspector.

"Yes. As in the case of the first note, an Underwood full-size typewriter was used—the same machine. There is an astonishing dearth of internal evidence, however. Whoever typed both these notes was very careful to remove all traces of his personality."

"We're dealing with a clever criminal, Miss Lambert," remarked Ellery dryly.

"No doubt. You see, we evaluate these things on several counts—spacing, margins, punctuation, the heaviness with which certain letters are struck, and so on. There has been a deliberate and successful effort here to eliminate marks of individuality. But one thing the writer could not disguise, and that was the physical characteristics of the type itself. Each character on a machine has its own personality, so to speak; and they're virtually as distinctive as fingerprints. There's no question but that both notes were written on the same machine, and I should say—although I won't be responsible for guaranteeing it—that the same hands typed both of them, too."

"We'll accept your opinion," grinned the Inspector, "in the proper spirit. Thanks, Miss Lambert. . . . Thomas, take this blackmail note down to the laboratories and have Jimmy give it the once-over for fingerprints. Although I suppose our chap is too cagey for that."

Velie returned shortly bearing the note and a negative report. There were no fingerprints on the freshly typed side of the paper. On the reverse, however, where Georg Khalkis had scrawled his promissory note for Grimshaw, the fingerprint expert reported a distinct impression of one of Georg Khalkis's fingers.

"That makes the promissory note authentic on two counts, handwriting and fingerprints," said the Inspector with satisfaction. "Yes, my son, whoever typed this note on the reverse of the promissory note is our man—the man who killed Grimshaw and took the promissory note from his body."

"At the very least," murmured Ellery, "this confirms my deduction that Gilbert Sloane was murdered."

"So it does. Let's go over with this letter to Sampson's office."

The Queens found Sampson and Pepper closeted in the District Attorney's private office. The Inspector triumphantly produced the new anonymous letter and transmitted the experts' findings. The lawyers brightened at once, and the office became warm with the promise of an early—and correct—solution of the case.

"One thing is sure," said Sampson. "You keep your flat-feet out of this, Q. Now there'll be another note or message of some kind from the chap who sent this one. We want somebody on the scene when that happens. If your Number Twelves go pounding about Knox's shebang, they might scare off our bird."

"There's something in that, Henry," confessed the Inspector.

"How about me, Chief?" asked Pepper eagerly.

"Fine. Just the man. Go up there and wait for developments." The District Attorney smiled very unpleasantly. "We'll be killing two birds with one stone in this way, Q. We'll nab the writer of the note—and we'll be able, by having our own man in Knox's house, to keep tabs on that damned painting!"

Ellery chuckled. "Sampson, your hand. In self-defence I'll have to cultivate Baptista's shrewd philosophy. 'For to cunning men,' he said, 'I will be very kind!'"

CHAPTER 29

Yield

B ut if District Attorney Sampson was cunning, so too, it appeared, was the tenuous criminal figure toward whom District Attorney Sampson's cunning was directed. For a full week nothing whatever happened. The writer of the anonymous note had apparently been swallowed up in some unpublicized convulsion of nature. Daily, Assistant District Attorney Pepper reported from Knox's *palazzo* on the Drive that there was no word from the murderer-blackmailer—no word and no sign of life. Perhaps, thought Sampson, and said so encouragingly to Pepper—perhaps the man was wary, was scouting the ground suspiciously because he scented a trap. Pepper was therefore to keep under cover as much as possible. Pepper, after a conference with Knox—who remained oddly undisturbed by the dearth of developments—determined to take no chances; for several days he remained in the house itself, never setting foot outside, even at night.

And, Pepper reported to his superior one afternoon by telephone, Mr. James J. Knox continued to preserve canny silence concerning the Leonardo—or what was supposed to be the Leonardo. He refused to be drawn out, or to commit himself. Pepper said further that he was strictly watching Miss Joan

Brett—very strictly, Chief. Sampson grunted at that; he inferred that the assignment had its not unpleasant moments for Mr. Pepper.

On the morning of Friday, the fifth of November, however, the Armistice flew to fragments in a burst of fire. With the very first post of the day, the Knox mansion stirred into frenzied life. Wile and guile had produced their yield. Pepper and Knox stood in Knox's black patent-leather den and examined with exultant triumph a letter, just delivered by the postman. Hurried conference; and Pepper, hat pulled low over his eyes, was packed off through a side servants' entrance, the precious missive tucked away in an inner pocket. He leaped into a waiting taxicab previously summoned by telephone and was driven at a furious clip to Center Street. He burst in upon the District Attorney with a shout. . . .

Sampson fingered the note Pepper had brought, and there was the hot gleam of the manhunt in his eyes. Without a word, he snatched the letter and his coat, and the two men dashed out of the building and made for Police Headquarters.

Ellery had kept his vigil like an acolyte—an acolyte with a penchant for chewing his fingernails in lieu of more solid nourishment. The Inspector was toying with his mail. . . . When Pepper and Sampson burst in, there was no need for words. The story was plain. The Queens leaped to their feet.

"Second blackmail letter," panted Sampson. "Just came in this morning's mail!"

"It's been typed on the back of the other half of the promissory note, Inspector!" cried Pepper.

The Queens examined the letter together. As the Assistant District Attorney had pointed out, the note had been typed on the supplementary half of the original Khalkis promise-to-pay document. The Inspector produced the first half and fitted the two together at the juncture of the ragged edges—they matched perfectly.

The second blackmail letter, like the first, was unsigned. It ran:

> First payment, Mr. Knox, will be a tidy $30,000. In cash, no bills larger than $100. Payable in a neat little package, to be left to-night, not before ten P.M., in the Checking Room of the Times Building in Times Square, addressed to Mr. Leonard D. Vincey, with instructions that package be given to caller of that name. Remember, you can't go to the police. And I'll be on the lookout for tricks, Mr. Knox.

"Our quarry has a marked sense of humour," said Ellery. "Quite droll, the tone of his letter and the device of anglicizing the name of Leonardo Da Vinci. A very happy gentleman!"

"He'll laugh on the other side of his face," growled Sampson, "before the night's over."

"Boys, boys!" chuckled the Inspector. "No time for gassing." He barked into his inter-office communicator, and a few moments later the familiar figure of Una Lambert, the handwriting expert, and the slight form of the Headquarters fingerprint chief were bending over the letter on the Inspector's desk, intent on whatever message it might unintentionally reveal.

Miss Lambert was cautious. "This one was written on a different typewriter from the one used for the first blackmail note, Inspector. This time it's a Remington full-size machine, quite new, I'd say, from the condition of the characters. As for its author—" She shrugged. "I shouldn't like to be pinned down to it, but it probably was typed, from the superficial internal evidence, by the same person who wrote the other two. . . . An interesting little thing here. A mistake in typing the figures representing thirty thousand dollars. The typist, despite his cockiness, was evidently quite nervous."

"Indeed?" murmured Ellery. He waved his hand. "Let that go for the moment. As for identification, it's not necessary to *prove* identical authorship by the characters themselves. The very fact, Dad, that the first blackmail note was typed on one half of the Khalkis promissory note, and the second on the other half, proves it quite adequately."

"Any prints, Jimmy?" asked the Inspector, not too hopefully.

"Nope," said the fingerprint expert.

"All right. That's all, Jimmy. Thanks, Miss Lambert."

"Sit down, gentlemen, sit down," said Ellery with amusement following his own admonition. "There's no hurry. We have all day." Sampson and Pepper, who had been fidgeting like children, meekly obeyed. "This new letter presents certain peculiarities, you know."

"Hey? Looks legitimate enough to me," ejaculated the Inspector.

"I'm not referring precisely to legitimacy. But observe that our murderer-blackmailer has a nice taste in figures. Doesn't it strike you as odd that he demands *thirty* thousand dollars? Have you ever encountered a blackmailing case in which such a sum was demanded? It's generally ten, or twenty-five, or fifty, or a hundred thousand."

"Pish!" said Sampson. "You're quibbling. Can't see anything odd about it."

"Shan't argue. But that isn't all. Miss Lambert pointed out an interesting thing." He picked up the second blackmail letter and flicked a fingernail at the figures representing thirty thousand dollars. "You will note," said Ellery as the others crowded about him, "that where these figures are typed, the writer made a common typist's error. Miss Lambert's opinion is that the writer was nervous. On the surface it seems the reasonable explanation."

"Of course," said the Inspector. "What of it?"

"The error," said Ellery equably, "consists in this: having just depressed the shift-key for the dollar-sign, it was necessary to release the shift-key in order to strike the figure 3, which occurs always on the lower bank of characters. Now, from the evidence we have before us, it is apparent that the writer had not entirely released the shift-key when he struck the 3, and this resulted in a first impression which was unclear, compelling the typist to backspace and retype the 3. Most interesting—most interesting."

They studied the figures, which presented the following appearance:

"What's interesting about it?" demanded Sampson. "I may be thick, but I can't see that it indicates anything except what you've just said—the typist made an error, and corrected it without erasing. Miss Lambert's conclusion that the error was the result of haste, or nervousness, is quite in keeping with the facts."

Ellery smiled and shrugged his shoulders. "The interesting element, my dear Sampson, is not the error—although that titillates my grey cells a bit, too. It's the fact that the Remington typewriter used in composing this note *hasn't a standard keyboard*. I suppose it's relatively unimportant."

"Hasn't a standard keyboard?" repeated Sampson in a puzzled way. "Why, how do you arrive at that?"

Ellery shrugged again.

"At any rate," interrupted the Inspector, "we mustn't arouse the suspicions of this rascal. We'll nab him when he shows up for the money at the Times Building to-night."

Sampson, who was eyeing Ellery with a trace of uneasiness, shook his shoulders—as if to rid them of an impalpable burden—and nodded. "Have to watch your step, Q. Knox must make a pretence of depositing the money as ordered. You'll take care of all the arrangements?"

"Leave those to me," grinned the old man. "Now, we'll have to talk this business over with Knox, and we'll have to be careful about how we get into his house. Our man may be on the watch."

They left the Inspector's office, commandeered an undistinguished police car, and were driven to the side-street servants' entrance to the Knox mansion uptown. The police chauffeur was circumspect, completely circling the block before pulling up before the side-entrance; there were no suspicious-looking characters about, and the Queens, Sampson and Pepper hurried through the high fence-gate and into the servants' quarters.

They found Knox in his glistening den, masterfully unruffled, dictating to Joan Brett. Joan was demure, particularly with Pepper; Knox excused her, and when she had retreated to her desk in the corner of the den, District Attorney Sampson, the Inspector, Pepper and Knox discussed the plan of attack for the evening.

Ellery did not join in the whispering of the cabalists; he wandered about the room, whistling, and contrived to saunter over to Joan's desk, where she sat quietly typing, without seeming purpose. He peered over Joan's shoulder, as if to examine what she was doing, and whispered in her ear: "Keep that very innocent schoolgirl expression, my dear. You're doing splendidly, and things are really perking up." "Indeed?" she murmured without moving her head; and Ellery, smiling, straightened and strolled back to join the others.

Sampson was saying shrewdly—a hard bargainer, Sampson, when he was master of a situation!—to James Knox: "Of course, Mr. Knox, you realize that the tables have turned. After to-night you will be under very heavy obligation to us. We're placed in the position of protecting you, a private citizen, whereas you repay us by refusing to turn over this painting . . ."

Knox threw up his hands suddenly. "All right, gentlemen. I give in. This is just about the last straw, anyway. Got a bellyful of that damn' painting. This blackmail mess. . . . Take the cursed thing and do what you want with it."

"But I thought you said it *wasn't* the painting stolen from the Victoria Museum," said the Inspector calmly. If he was relieved he did not show it.

"I still say so! That painting's mine. But you can have it for expert examination—anything. Only if you find I told the truth, please return it to me."

"Oh, we'll do *that*," said Sampson.

"Don't you think," put in Pepper anxiously, "that we ought to worry about this blackmailer first, Chief? He might—"

"You're right there, Pepper," said the Inspector with complete good humour. "The good old collar first, by jiminy! Here. Miss Brett." The old man crossed the room and stood over Joan; she looked up with an inquiring smile. "Suppose you be a good little girl and take a cable for me. Or—wait a minute. Got a pencil?"

Submissively she provided pencil and paper. The Inspector scribbled hastily for several moments. "Here, my dear—copy that message right off. It's important."

Joan's typewriter began to click. If her heart leaped at the words she was typing, her face gave no sign. For the message trickling out from beneath her fingers was:

Inspector Broome

   Scotland Yard London Confidential

Leonardo in possession of reputable American collector who paid £150,000 in good faith without knowledge it was stolen. Some question as to whether one under observation is painting belonging to Victoria Museum but can now guarantee restoration to museum at least for examination. Few details to be cleared up on this side. Will notify within twenty-four hours date of delivery.

                Inspector Richard Queen

When the message had been passed around for approval—Knox merely glanced at it—the Inspector returned the sheet to Joan, and she telephoned the cable at once to a telegraph office.

The Inspector outlined again the exact plans for the evening; Knox nodded with weary understanding; and the visitors
donned their coats. Ellery, however, made no move toward his
overcoat. "Aren't you coming along, son?"

"I'll venture to impose upon Mr. Knox's sadly abused hospitality for a few moments longer. You run along with Sampson
and Pepper, Dad. I'll be home shortly."

"Home? I'm going back to the office."

"Very well, I'll be at your office, then."

They looked at him curiously; he was smiling, perfectly at
ease. He waved them gently toward the door, and they went out
without speaking.

"Well, young man," said James Knox, when the door had
closed upon them, "I don't know what your game is now, but
you're welcome to stay if you like. The plan seems to be that I
go to my bank personally and pretend to draw the thirty thousand. Sampson seems to think our man may be watching."

"Sampson thinks of everything," smiled Ellery. "You're very
kind."

"Not at all," said Knox abruptly, and shot a peculiar glance
at Joan, who was sitting at her machine typing with the deaf-
and-dumb air of the perfect secretary. "Only don't seduce Miss
Brett. I'd be blamed for it." Knox shrugged and left the room.

Ellery waited for ten minutes. He did not speak to Joan, nor
did she pause once in her rapid manipulation of the keys. He
passed the time very idly—looking out of the window, in fact.
Then he saw Knox's tall gaunt figure stride out under the *porte-
cochère*—the window at which Ellery watched was in an ell of
the main building, and every detail of the façade was visible to
his eye—and climb into his waiting town-car. The car rolled
away down the drive.

Ellery came alive instantly. So, for that matter, did Miss Joan
Brett. Her hands dropped from the keys and she sat and looked
at him expectantly, with a little wicked smile.

Ellery came briskly over to her desk. "Heavens!" she cried

in mock horror, shrinking away from him. "You're not going to take Mr. Knox's acute suggestion so *soon*, Mr. Queen?"

"Perish the thought," said Ellery. "Now some questions, my dear, while we're alone."

"I'm simply enchanted by the prospect, sir," murmured Joan.

"Considering your sex. . . . Look here, milady. How many menials are employed in this voluptuous establishment?"

She looked disappointed, and pursed her lips. "A queer one, m'lord, a jolly queer one to ask a lady who's anticipating a struggle for her virtue. Let me think." She counted silently. "Eight. Yes, eight. Mr. Knox has a quiet household. He doesn't entertain often, I think."

"Have you learned anything about these servants?"

"Sir! A woman learns everything. . . . Fire away, Mr. Queen."

"Are there any recently employed servants here?"

"Horrors, no. This is a very hoity-toity establishment, *du bon vieux temps*. I understand that each of the servants has been with Mr. Knox at least five or six years, and some of them for as long as fifteen."

"Does Knox trust them?"

"Implicitly."

"*C'est bien!*" Ellery's voice was crisp. "*Maintenant, Mademoiselle attendez. Il faut qu'on fait l'examen des serviteurs—des bonnes, des domestiques, des employés. Tout de suite!*"

She rose and curtsied. "*Mais oui, Monsieur. Vos ordres?*"

"I shall step into the next room and close the door—that is," said Ellery rapidly, "leaving only the merest crack through which to observe these people as they come in. You are to ring for them, one by one, on one pretext or another, and keep them here in my line of vision sufficiently for me to examine their faces thoroughly. . . . By the way, the chauffeur won't respond, but I've seen his face. What's his name?"

"Schultz."

"Is he the only chauffeur employed here?"

"Yes."

"Very well. *Commencez!*"

He stepped quickly into the next room and stationed himself at the thin crack he had left open. He saw Joan ring. A middle-aged woman in black taffeta whom he had never seen before entered the den. Joan asked her a question, she replied, and then the woman left. Joan rang again; and three young women in dainty black maids' costumes entered. They were followed in quick succession by the tall thin old butler; a small pudgy man with a smooth face, snugly attired; and a large and perspiring Gallic gentleman decked out in the spotless finery of the conventional chef's rig. When the door closed upon this last man, Ellery stepped out of his hide-away.

"Splendid. Who was the middle-aged woman?"

"Mrs. Healy, the housekeeper."

"The maids?"

"Grant, Burrows, Hotchkiss."

"The butler?"

"Krafft."

"The little chap with the stoical face?"

"Mr. Knox's personal valet, Harris."

"And the chef?"

"Boussin, a Parisian *émigré*—Alexandre Boussin."

"And that's all? You're certain?"

"With the exception of Schultz, yes."

Ellery nodded. "All total strangers to me, so that's . . . You recall the morning of the receipt of blackmail letter number one?"

"Perfectly."

"Who has stepped into this house since that morning? Outsiders, I mean?"

"A number have stepped in, as you say, but not a breathing soul has got beyond the reception room downstairs. Mr. Knox hasn't consented to see anyone at all since then—most of them have been turned away at the door with a polite 'Not at home,' by Krafft."

"Why is that?"

Joan shrugged. "Despite his nonchalant and sometimes bluff exterior, I really believe Mr. Knox has been nervous since that first blackmail note came. I often wondered why he didn't employ private detectives."

"For the very good reason," said Ellery grimly, "that he doesn't want anyone—or *didn't* want anyone—smeared with the familiar police tar-brush to set foot in this house. Not with that Leonardo or Leonardo copy floating about."

"He hasn't trusted anyone. Not even old friends of his, or acquaintances or clients of his many business interests."

"How about Miles Woodruff?" asked Ellery. "I thought Knox had retained him to attend to the legal end of the Khalkis estate."

"So he did. But Mr. Woodruff hasn't been here in the flesh. Although there are daily conversations over the telephone."

"Is it possible?" murmured Ellery. "Such luck—such miraculous, astounding luck." He grasped her hands tightly, and she uttered a little scream. But Ellery's intentions, it seemed, were purely platonic. He squeezed those dainty hands with an almost insulting impersonality, and said: "This has been a fruity morning, Joan Brett, a fruity morning!"

* * *

And despite Ellery's assurance to his sire that he would return to the Inspector's office "shortly," it was not until mid-afternoon that he strolled into Police Headquarters, smiling at some comforting inner sense of well-being.

Fortunately, the Inspector was immersed in work and had no opportunity to ask questions. Ellery lolled about for a decent interval, rousing out of his lethargic daydreaming only when he heard the old man instruct Sergeant Velie specifically about the rendezvous of detectives at the Times Building basement for that evening.

"Perhaps," said Ellery—and the old man seemed surprised

to see him there—"perhaps it would be more feasible to meet at Knox's place on the Drive to-night at nine."

"Knox's place? What for?"

"For reasons. By all means have your bloodhounds sniffing about the scene of the potential capture, but the official party should really convene at Knox's. We don't have to get to the Times Building until ten, anyway."

The Inspector began to bluster, saw something steely in Ellery's eye, blinked and said: "Oh, very well!" turning to his telephone to call Sampson's office.

Sergeant Velie stalked out. Ellery rose with an unexpected burst of energy and followed the man-mountain out. He caught up with Velie in the corridor outside, grasped his hard arm, and began to speak very, very earnestly—almost in cajoling tones.

It was notable that Sergeant Velie's normally frigid features were suddenly possessed of animation—an animation characterized by a growing disturbance as Ellery whispered urgently. The good sergeant shifted from one foot to the other. He floundered about in a morass of indecision. He shook his head. He bit his big lips. He scratched his stubbly jaw. He looked pained and wracked by conflicting emotions.

Finally, unable to resist Ellery's blandishments, he sighed unhappily, growled, "All right, Mr. Queen, but if anything goes flooey it'll mean my stripes," and walked away as if he were very glad indeed to escape this tenacious flea on the hide of his duty.

CHAPTER 30

Quiz

Cautiously, in furtive pairs, they converged that night under cover of a moonless sky on the Knox house. By the stroke of nine o'clock—all of them having slipped through the servants' quarters off the side street—they were assembled in Knox's den: the two Queens, District Attorney Sampson, Pepper, Joan Brett and Knox himself. Black shades had been drawn; not a chink of light was visible from the outside of the mansion. They were all subdued, on edge, holding themselves in check.

All, that is to say, save Ellery, who, comporting himself with the gravity and decorum that the occasion seemed to warrant, nevertheless contrived to give the impression that *he* wasn't worried over the outcome of this portentous evening—no indeed!

There was nervous talk. "Got the package, Mr. Knox?" The Inspector's moustache hung limply in tattered wisps.

Knox produced from a drawer of his desk a small bundle wrapped in brown paper. "Just dummy stuff. Paper cut to bill size." His voice was even, but there was strain beneath those tight features.

"For heaven's sake," burst out the District Attorney, after a fog-hung silence, "what are we waiting for? Mr. Knox, you'd better get started. We'll follow you. The place is surrounded already and he can't get—"

"I dare say," drawled Ellery, "that the necessity for visiting the Check Room of the Times Building to-night no longer exists."

This was another dramatic moment—just such a moment as Ellery had seized upon weeks before with smugness in giving out his Khalkis solution. But if he was apprehensive that again he faced ridicule, it did not show in his face. He was smiling quite pleasantly, as if all the tumultuous preparations, the police cars parked in the vicinity of Times Square, the gathering of the clans, were a matter for mild amusement.

The Inspector jerked his little body six inches higher. "What do you mean by this, Ellery? We're wasting time. Or is this another of your fancy tricks?"

The smile left Ellery's face. He looked at them, standing and weighing him with their bewildered eyes. The smile left, and something sharp took its place. "Very well," he said grimly. "I'll explain. Do you know why it would be futile—in fact, ridiculous—for us to go downtown?"

"Ridiculous!" snarled the District Attorney. "Why?"

"Because, Sampson, it would be wasted effort. Because, Sampson, your man won't be there. Because, Sampson, we've been neatly tricked!"

Joan Brett gasped. The others gaped.

"Mr. Knox," said Ellery, turning to the banker, "will you please ring for your butler?"

Knox complied; his forehead was corrugated into stony lines. The tall thin old man appeared at once. "Yes, Mr. Knox?"

But it was Ellery who replied, sharply: "Krafft, are you familiar with the burglar-alarm system in this house?"

"Yes, sir . . ."

"Inspect it at once."

Krafft hesitated, Knox gestured curtly, and the butler went

out. No one said a word until he hurried in again, his composure gone, eyes bulging. "It's been tampered with—it doesn't work, sir! And it was all right yesterday, sir!"

"What!" cried Knox.

Ellery said coolly: "Just as I expected. That's all, Krafft. . . . Mr. Knox, I think I can prove to you and to my doubting colleagues the precise extent to which we have been outwitted. I do think, Mr. Knox, that you had better take a look at that painting of yours."

Something stirred within Knox. A spark shot out of his hard grey eyes. He showed fear, and on the heels of fear an instantaneous decision. Without a word he sprang forward and dashed out of the room. Ellery followed quickly and the others streamed after.

Knox led the way to a large, long, quiet room on an upper floor—a gallery hung with rich oil paintings draped in dark velvets. . . . No one had eyes at this moment for things aesthetic. Ellery himself was on Knox's heels as he hurried down the gallery to a far corner. He stopped suddenly at a panel in the wall fumbled with a wooden curlicue. . . . A large section of the apparently solid wall slid without sound to one side, disclosing a black aperture. Knox thrust his hand in, grunted, peered wildly into the darkness of the interior. . . .

"It's gone!" he cried, his face ashen. "It's been stolen!"

"Precisely," said Ellery in a matter-of-fact voice. "A clever ruse, quite worthy of the genius of Grimshaw's wraithlike partner."

It gives me more personal pleasure than I can say to inject at this point in the story of The Greek Coffin Mystery *my customary challenge to the wits of the reader.*

Pleasure, I should explain, because the problems of this mystery provided me with perhaps the knottiest tangle I have ever tried my hand at unsnarling. It is a joy—a very real joy to one who is constantly beset by the jeers of paying customers: "Is that *a puzzler?" they demand. "Heavens, I solved it right off!" — it is a joy to say to such as these: "Now, my masters, you may solve to your heart's content. You'll be properly fooled nevertheless!"*

Perhaps I am over sanguine. At any rate the thing is done, and, ungentle reader, you now have in your possession all the facts pertinent to the only correct solution *of the trinitarian problem: the identity of the individual who strangled Albert Grimshaw, shot Gilbert Sloane to death, and stole James Knox's painting.*

I say with all good will and a fierce humility: Garde à vous, *and a pox on headache!*

ELLERY QUEEN

CHAPTER 31

Upshot

A nd Ellery said: "You're positive, Mr. Knox, that the painting has been stolen? You placed it in this panel yourself?"

The colour had crept back into the banker's face; he nodded with a slight effort. "Last time I looked at it was a week ago. It was there. No one else knew. No one. Had the panel built in long ago."

"What I want to know," said the Inspector, "is how this thing stacks up. When was the painting stolen? How did the thief get in, and how did he know where the painting was, if what Mr. Knox says is true?"

"The painting wasn't stolen to-night—that's a cinch," said the District Attorney softly. "Why then isn't the burglar-alarm operating?"

"And it was working yesterday, Krafft said, and probably the day before," put in Pepper.

Knox shrugged. Ellery said: "Everything will be explained. Please come back with me to Mr. Knox's den, all of you."

He seemed very sure of his ground, and they followed him in meek silence.

Back in the patent-leather room, Ellery set to work with

cheerful briskness. First he shut the door, asking Pepper to stand by and see that there were no interruptions; then he went without hesitation to a large grille set low in one wall of the den, near the floor. He tinkered with this for a moment, succeeded in removing the grille, laid it on the floor, and thrust his hand into the aperture beyond. They craned; there was a huge-coiled radiator inside. Ellery ran his fingers rapidly over the individual coils, like a harpist strumming his strings. "Please observe," he said with a smile, although obviously they could observe nothing of the sort, "that while seven of the eight coils are burning hot, this one—" his hand came to rest on the last coil—"this one is stone cold." He bent over again and manipulated some contrivance at the bottom of the cold coil. In a moment he had unscrewed a disguised cap, and he stood up with the tall heavy coil in his hand. "Comes off, you see," he explained affably. "Clever plumbing, Mr. Knox," and upended the coil. On the bottom there was a barely visible metal thread. Ellery twisted vigorously, the bottom began to move, and to their astonishment screwed off completely, providing a glimpse of an asbestos-lined interior. Ellery placed the cap on a chair, raised the coil, and shook it with energy. His hand was ready . . . as a roll of old stained canvas slipped out of the tube.

"What is it?" whispered the Inspector.

Ellery with a flirt of his wrist flipped the roll. It unfurled.

It was a painting—a massive, turbulent scene in rich oils, a battle-scene centring on a struggling group of fierce medieval warriors fighting for possession of a standard, a proud rich flag.

"Believe it or not," said Ellery, draping the canvas over Knox's desk," you are now gazing upon a million dollars' worth of paint, canvas and genius. In other words, this is the elusive Leonardo."

"Nonsense!" said someone sharply, and Ellery swung on his heel to confront James Knox, who was standing rigidly a few feet off, staring at the painting with a mouth-line of marble.

"Indeed? I found this *chef-d' œuvre*, Mr. Knox, while I took the unpardonable liberty of snooping about your house this afternoon. You said this was stolen from you? Then how do you account for the fact that it is hidden in your own den when it is presumably in the possession of a thief?"

"I said 'nonsense' and I mean 'nonsense.'" Knox laughed shortly. "I see I didn't credit you with enough intelligence, Queen. But you're still wrong. What I said was true. The Leonardo has been stolen. I thought I could conceal the fact that I had *two* of them—"

"Two?" gasped the District Attorney.

"Yes." Knox sighed. "I thought I'd put something over. What you see here is the second one—I've had it a long time. It's the work of either Lorenzo di Credi or a pupil of his, my expert isn't certain—at any rate, not a Leonardo. Lorenzo imitated Leonardo perfectly, and presumably Lorenzo's pupils followed their master's style. The thing must have been copied from the original Leonardo after the ill-fated mural fresco in 1503 in Florence. Hall of the Palazzo Vecchio. The—"

"Don't want any lecture on art, Mr. Knox," growled the Inspector. "What we want to know—"

"Your expert thinks, then," said Ellery smoothly, "that after the fresco project was abandoned by Leonardo—the central group was painted, as I remember from my Fine Arts, but when the heat was applied the colours ran and the paint scaled off—that this oils was done by some contemporary who copied Leonardo's own oils painting of the central group?"

"Yes. Anyway, this second painting is worth a mere fraction of the original Leonardo. Naturally. When I bought the original from Khalkis—yes, I admit I bought the real one and knew it all the time—I already owned this contemporary copy. I didn't say anything about it, because I figured ... well, if I was forced eventually to return the painting to the Victoria Museum, I'd give back this valueless copy with the story that that was the one I'd purchased from Khalkis—"

Sampson's eyes glittered. "We've got plenty of witnesses this time, Knox. How about the original?"

Knox said stubbornly: "That's stolen. I hid it in the deposi-
tory behind the panel in my gallery. For God's sake, you don't
think—The thief evidently didn't know anything about this
copy, which I've always kept hidden in the dummy radiator-
coil. He stole the original, I tell you! How he did it, I don't know,
but he did. I know it was crooked of me to intend to palm off the
copy on the Museum and retain the original secretly, but—"

The District Attorney drew Ellery, the Inspector and Pepper
aside and they conversed in whispers. Ellery listened gravely,
said something reassuring, and they returned to Knox, who was
standing in miserable solitude by the colour-splashed canvas on
the desk. As for Joan Brett, she was pressed up against one of the
patent-leather walls, wide-eyed, motionless, breathing in gusts
that stirred her breast.

"Well, sir," said Ellery, "there seems to be a slight difference
of opinion here. The District Attorney and Inspector Queen feel
that—under the circumstances, you understand—they cannot
accept your unsubstantiated word that this is a copy of the
Leonardo rather than the Leonardo itself. None of us here qual-
ifies as a connoisseur, and I believe expert opinion is called for.
May I—?"

He did not wait for Knox's slow nod, but stepped to the telephone, called a number, spoke briefly with someone, and then
hung up. "I have called upon Toby Johns, perhaps the most celebrated art-critic in the East, Mr. Knox. You know him?"

"Met him," said Knox shortly.

"He will be here very soon, Mr. Knox. Until then, it will be
necessary to compose our souls in patience."

*   *   *

Toby Johns was a dumpy little old man with brilliant eyes, im-
peccable attire and a serenely assured air. He was admitted by
Krafft, who was sent away at once; and Ellery, who had a speaking acquaintance with him, introduced him to the others. Johns
was especially jovial with Knox. Then, as he stood waiting for

someone to explain, his eyes focused sharply on the painting on the desk.

Ellery anticipated the instant question. "This is a serious matter, Mr. Johns," he began quietly, "and please forgive me if I ask that nothing said in this room to-night goes any further." Johns nodded, as if he had heard such requests before. "Very well, sir." Ellery tossed his head in the direction of the painting. "Can you fix the authorship of that canvas, Mr. Johns?"

They waited in palpable silence as the expert beamed, adjusted a ribboned glass to one eye, and stepped over to the desk. He spread the canvas carefully on the floor, flat, examined it; then instructed Ellery and Pepper to hold it taut in the air while he turned the soft rays of several lamps on it. Nobody said anything, and Johns worked without comment. Nor did the expression on his fat little face change. He went over every inch of the painting with painful attention, seeming to be particularly interested in the faces of the figures grouped nearest the standard. . . .

After a half-hour's work, he nodded pleasantly and Ellery and Pepper laid the canvas over the desk again. Knox expelled a soft grudging sigh; his eyes were fixed on the expert's face.

"There is a peculiar story attached to this work," said Johns at last. "It has a distinct bearing on what I am about to say." They were hanging on his every precise word. "We have known for many years," Johns continued, "indeed for several centuries, that there were two paintings of this particular subject, identical in every detail except one. . . ."

Someone muttered something beneath his breath.

"Every detail except one. One is known to have been painted by Leonardo himself. When Piero Soderini persuaded the great master to come to Florence and make a battle-piece to decorate one of the walls in the new council-hall in the Palace of the Signory, Leonardo chose as his subject an episode in the victory won by the generals of the Florentine republic in 1440 over Niccolò Piccinino near a bridge at Anghiari. The

cartoon itself—the technical term applied to the original sketch—
on which Leonardo worked preliminarily is often called, in fact,
The Battle of Anghiari. This was the great mural competition, incidentally, in which Michelangelo also participated, working on a
Pisan subject. Now, as Mr. Knox probably knows, Leonardo did
not complete the mural; it was halted after the detail of the battle
for the standard had been executed. For the paint ran and scaled
after the baking process was applied to the wall, virtually ruining
the work.

"Leonardo quit Florence. It is presumed that he was disappointed with the failure of his labour, and painted an oils version of his original cartoon as a sort of artistic self-justification.
At any rate, this oils was rumoured, but 'lost,' until a very few
years ago, when a field-worker for the Victoria Museum of
London recovered it somewhere in Italy."

They kept horribly quiet, but Johns seemed not to notice.
"Now," he said with vocal zest, "many contemporary copies of
the *cartoon* were made, notably by the young Raphael, Fra Bar-
tolommeo and others, but the cartoon itself seems to have been
cut up after serving as an example for the copyists. The cartoon
disappeared; and the original mural in the signory hall was
covered by fresh Vasari frescoes in 1560. Consequently, the discovery of—so to speak—Leonardo's own copy of the original
cartoon was a find of cosmic proportions in the world of art.
Which brings us to the queer part of the story.

"I said a moment ago that there are two paintings of this
subject extant, identical in every respect but one. The first was
discovered and exhibited very long ago; its authorship was never
definitely established until the Victoria discovery of six years or
so ago. Now here's the rub. The experts had never been able to
decide whether the first one found was a Leonardo; in fact, it
was commonly believed to have been the work of Lorenzo di
Credi, or of one of Lorenzo's pupils. As in all controversial matters in the art-world, there was much scoffing, sneering, and

backbiting; but the discovery of the Victoria's painting six years ago cleared the matter up.

"There were certain old records. These records said that there were two oils of the same subject: one by Leonardo himself and one a copy—the records were vague on the copy's authorship. Both, the legend ran, were identical except for one thing: a shade of difference in the flesh-tints of the figures immediately surrounding the standard. The legend had it that the Leonardo possessed the darker flesh-tints—a subtle distinction enough, since the record insisted that only by placing the two paintings side by side could the Leonardo be determined beyond any doubt. So you see—"

"Interesting," muttered Ellery. "Mr. Knox, did you know this?"

"Of course. So did Khalkis." Knox teetered on his heels and toes. "As I said, I had this one, and when Khalkis sold me the other, it was a simple enough matter to put them together and see which one was the Leonardo. And now—" he scowled—"the Leonardo's gone."

"Eh?" Johns looked disturbed. Then he smiled again. "Well, I suppose it's none of my business. At any rate, the two were together long enough for the Museum, to its vast relief, to determine that the one their field investigator had found was the real Leonardo. Then the other one, the copy, disappeared. Rumour had it that it was sold to a rich American collector who had paid a tidy sum for it despite the fact that it was established as the copy." He shot a quizzical glance at Knox, but no one said anything.

Johns squared his trim little shoulders. "Consequently, if the Leonardo in the Museum should be lost sight of for some time, it would be difficult—I should say impossible—to decide whether either one, examined by itself, was the original. With only one to judge by, you could never be certain. . . ."

"And this one, Mr. Johns?" asked Ellery.

"This," replied Johns with a shrug, "is certainly one or the other, but without the companion-piece . . ." He stopped and smote his forehead. "Of course! I'm being stupid. This *must* be the copy. The original is in the Victoria Museum overseas."

"Yes, yes. Quite so," said Ellery hastily. "If the paintings are so much alike, Mr. Johns, why is one valued at a million and the other at only a few thousand?"

"My dear sir!" exclaimed the expert. "Really a—what shall I say?—a very childish question. What is the difference between a genuine Sheraton and a modern replica? Leonardo was the master; the author of the copy, probably a pupil of Lorenzo, merely duplicated the masterpiece from Leonardo's finished work, as the legend goes. The price-difference is the difference between the *chef d'œuvre* of a genius and the perfect copy by a tyro. What if Leonardo's brush-strokes were exactly imitated? You wouldn't say that a photographic forgery of your signature, Mr. Queen, has the same authenticity as the signature itself?"

Johns was working his little old body into a gesticulating frenzy, it seemed; and Ellery, thanking him with proper humility, herded him toward the door. It was not until the expert, his equanimity partially restored, had departed that the others came to life.

"Art! Leonardo!" said the Inspector with disgust. "Now it's more messy than before. The detective racket is going to pot." He threw up his hands.

"It isn't really so bad," said the District Attorney thoughtfully. "At least Johns's story substantiates Mr. Knox's explanation, even if no one knows which is which. Now we know at least that there *are* two paintings in existence, not one as we thought all along. So—we'll have to look for the thief of the other painting."

"What I can't understand," said Pepper, "is why the Museum didn't say anything about the second painting. After all—"

"My dear Pepper," drawled Ellery, "they *had* the original. Why should they bother their heads about the copy? Not interested in the copy. . . . Yes, Sampson, you're perfectly correct. The man we're seeking is the man who stole the other painting, who wrote the blackmail letters to Mr. Knox, who used the promissory note as notepaper and therefore must have been the framer and murderer of Sloane and, as Grimshaw's partner, the killer of Grimshaw and the framer of Georg Khalkis."

"An excellent summation," said Sampson sarcastically. "Now that you've added up all we know, suppose you tell us what we *don't* know—that is, the identity of this man!"

Ellery sighed. "Sampson, Sampson, you're always on my trail, trying to discredit me, trying to expose my foibles to the world. . . . Would you really like to know the name of your man?"

Sampson glared, and the Inspector began to look interested. "Would I really like to know, he asks me!" cried the District Attorney. "Now *that's* a smart question, isn't it? . . . Of course I want to know." His eyes sharpened and he stopped short. "I say, Ellery," he said quietly, "you don't *really* know, do you?"

"Yes," said Knox. "Who the devil is it, Queen?"

Ellery smiled. "I'm glad you asked me that, Mr. Knox. You must have run across it in your readings, because a number of illustrious gentlemen have repeated it variously—La Fontaine, Terence, Coleridge, Cicero, Juvenal, Diogenes. It's an inscription on the Temple of Apollo at Delphi and has been attributed to Chilo of Thales, Pythagoras, and Solon. In Latin it is: *Ne quis nimis*. In English it is: *Know thyself*. Mr. James J. Knox," said Ellery in the most genial voice in the world, "you're under arrest!"

CHAPTER 32

Elleryana

Surprised? District Attorney Sampson professed not to be. He maintained all of that hectic night that he had had a lurking suspicion of Knox from the beginning. On the other hand, his immediate thirst for elucidation was significant. Why? How? He even looked worried. Evidence—where was the evidence? His busy brain was already marshalling the prosecutor's case . . . and was heckled by the disturbing conviction that here was a sturdy nut indeed to crack.

The Inspector said nothing. He was relieved, but he persisted in stealing furtive glances at his son's uncommunicative profile. The shock of the revelation, Knox's instant and sickening physical collapse and then his almost miraculous recovery, Joan Brett's gasp of unbelieving horror. . . .

Ellery dominated the stage without an excess of exultation. He refused with mulish shakings of the head to explain while Inspector Queen summoned aid from Headquarters and James J. Knox was led quietly away. No, he would say nothing that night; to-morrow morning . . . yes, perhaps to-morrow morning.

On Saturday morning, then, the sixth of November, the actors in this intricate drama foregathered. Ellery had insisted that it was no more than just to explain not only to officialdom but to those harassed persons connected with the Khalkis case—and, of course, to the clamorous gentlemen of the press. The Saturday morning papers ran bulging headlines announcing the great man's arrest; it was rumoured that a personal inquiry from some dignitary close to the President had been addressed to the Mayor of New York City—which was probably true, for the Mayor kept his wires humming all morning, demanding an explanation of the Commissioner, who knew less than he; of District Attorney Sampson, who was gradually becoming frantic; of Inspector Queen who shook his weary old head and merely said to all official interrogators: "Wait." The painting from Knox's radiator-coil had been put in Pepper's charge for custody by the District Attorney's office until the trial; Scotland Yard had been notified that the painting would be required as evidence in the legal battle which loomed, but that it would be forwarded with due precautions as soon as a jury of his peers decided Mr. James J. Knox's fate.

Inspector Queen's office was far too small to contain the swollen assemblage of potential critics insisted upon as an audience by Ellery. A select group of reporters, the Queens, Sampson, Pepper, Cronin, Mrs. Sloane, Joan Brett, Alan Cheney, the Vreelands, Nacio Suiza, Woodruff—and in a most unobtrusive manner of entrance the Police Commissioner, the Deputy Chief Inspector and a very uneasy gentleman who kept running his finger under his collar and was identified as the Mayor's closest political friend—were consequently grouped in a large room at Police Headquarters especially set aside for the meeting. Ellery, it appeared, was to preside—a most unorthodox proceeding, and one at which Sampson chafed and the Mayor's representative looked bleak and the Police Commissioner scowled.

But Ellery was not to be ruffled. The room had a dais, and on this dais he stood—like a schoolmaster about to address a classroom of staring children; there was a blackboard behind him!—very erect and dignified, his *pince-nez* freshly polished.

At the rear of the chamber Assistant District Attorney Cronin whispered to Sampson: "Henry, old boy, this'd better be good. Knox has retained the Springarn outfit, and what they won't do to a lousy case I shudder to think!" Sampson said nothing; there was nothing to say.

Ellery began quietly, outlining in swift prose all the facts and deductions of former analyses for the benefit of those who were unfamiliar with the internal mechanism of the case thus far. After explaining the incidents surrounding the arrival of the blackmail letters, he paused and moistened his dry lips; drawing a deep breath, he plunged into the heart of his new argument.

"The only individual who could have sent the blackmail letters," he said, "was someone who knew that James Knox had in his possession the stolen painting, as I've just pointed out. The fact that James Knox had in his possession the stolen painting was fortunately kept a secret. Now, who besides the investigating party—ourselves—knew this? Two persons, and two persons only: one, Grimshaw's partner, who by former analyses has been proved the murderer of Grimshaw and Sloane, who furthermore knew that Knox had the painting by virtue of his partnership with Grimshaw and by virtue of Grimshaw's own admission that this partner, and this partner only, knew the whole story; and the second, of course, was Knox himself, something that none of us considered at the time.

"Very well. Now the fact that the blackmail letters were typed on halves of the promissory note absolutely proved that the sender of the letters was the murderer of Grimshaw and Sloane—that is, Grimshaw's partner—for the murderer was the only one who could have possessed the promissory note taken from Grimshaw's body. Please bear this in mind; it is an important block in the logical structure.

"Further. What do we find on examination of the typewritten blackmail notes themselves? Well, the first blackmail note was typed on an Underwood machine, the same machine used by the murderer to send the anonymous letter, incidentally, which revealed Sloane to be Grimshaw's brother. The second blackmail note was typed on a Remington. In the typing of this second note was the salient clue. For the typist had made a mistake on the figure 3 in the group-figure $30,000; and from the error it was apparent that the upper-register character of the 3-key was not the usual standard-keyboard character. Let me show you graphically how the figures $30,000 appeared in the note itself, and that will help to explain the point I am making."

He turned and rapidly chalked on the blackboard the following symbol:

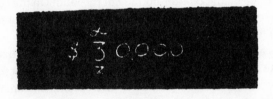

"Now please observe," said Ellery, turning about, "that the typist's error consisted in not entirely releasing the shift-key after depressing the dollar-sign character, with the result that the following key which he depressed—that on which the 3 appears—left a broken, split impression on the paper. Naturally, the typist back-spaced and retyped the 3, but that is not important; what is important is that the split impressions of the 3-key remained. Now what happens when this common typing error is made—the error of not completely releasing the shift, or capital, key when you want to strike a lower-register letter? Simply this: the space where the lower-register letter is intended to be remains blank; a little above this blank space you get the imprint of the *lower* portion of the upper character; a little below this blank space you get the imprint of the *upper* portion of the lower character. You can see the effect from the rough scrawl I've made on the blackboard. Is that clear so far?"

There was a general bobbing of heads.

"Splendid. Suppose we think for a moment about the key on which the figure 3 appears on all standard-keyboard typewriters," continued Ellery. "Naturally, I refer to American typewriters. What have we? The figure 3 on the lower register, and the symbol of 'number' on the upper register. Let me show you." He turned to the blackboard again and chalked the following symbol: #. "Simple, eh?" he said, turning back. "But I want you to note that the error in the second blackmail letter does not indicate a standard-keyboard at least to the extent of that single 3-key. For where the decapitated symbol above the back-spaced 3 should be the lower half of this 'number' sign, it is—as you can see on the board—nothing of the kind! On the contrary, it's a very queer symbol indeed—a little loop at the left and a curved line going to the right, leading from the loop."

He had his audience as surely as if they were chained to him. He leaned forward. "Obviously, then, as I said before, the Remington typewriter on which this second blackmail note was typed had a peculiar symbol above its 3 where the usual sign for 'number'"—he jerked his head toward the # on the blackboard—"should be. Obviously, too, this loop-and-curve mark is merely the lower half of some complete symbol. What can the upper half be? What is the general shape of the whole?" He straightened quietly. "Think about it for a moment. Look at that chalk-mark above the 3 I've scribbled on the blackboard."

He waited. They strained their eyes. But no one answered. "It's really most conclusive," said Ellery at last. "I'm amazed that none of you—reporters especially—catch it. I say that that loop-and-curve can be the lower half of only one symbol in the world which might conceivably be placed on a typewriter—and that is the sign which resembles a script capital 'L' with a horizontal dash running across its ascender . . . in other words, the symbol for the English pound-sterling!"

There was a little murmur of wonderment and appreciation. "Very well, then. We had only to look for a Remington typewriter—an American machine, of course—which had on the upper register of the 3-key the symbol for the English pound. Compute the mathematical probabilities of an American Remington typewriter having just such an alien sign on precisely that one key—I believe you'll find it to run in the millions. In other words, if we could find a typewriter with such a symbol on just such a key, I would have every mathematical and logical right to maintain that there was the typewriter used in typing the second blackmail note."

Ellery gestured largely. "This preliminary explanation is essential to a comprehension of what is to follow. Please attend closely. I discovered, while talking to James Knox during the period when Sloane was still considered a suicide and before the receipt of the first blackmail letter, that Knox had in his possession a new typewriter on which one key had been replaced. I learned this accidentally when I visited Knox and he was instructing Miss Brett to make out a cheque to pay a bill for a new typewriter. He cautioned her to be sure to add on the small charge for the *single replacement key*. Further, from Miss Brett I discovered in the same approximate period that this machine was a Remington—she mentioned that specifically; and I learned that it was the only typewriter in the house, the old one Knox having in my presence instructed Miss Brett to send to the Bureau of Charities. Miss Brett began to type a memorandum of some serial-numbers for me; she stopped short, threw away the sheet, and exclaimed: 'I'll have to *write out* the word "number."' The emphasis, of course, is mine And although at that time it meant nothing to me, I nevertheless had the basis for knowing that Knox's Remington, the only machine in the house, had no symbol for 'number'—otherwise why did Miss Brett have to *write out* the word 'number'?—and that on this machine one key had been replaced. Now, since there was one key replaced on this new typewriter, and since the number-sign was missing, it must by strict logic have been the number-sign key, on which the 3 is the lower-register character, that had been replaced! Elementary logic. Now, I had to discover only one further fact, and my argument would be complete; if, on this replaced key, I found an English-pound symbol above the 3, where the 'number' sign should be, then I could say with perfect justification that this Remington typewriter was probably the one which had been employed in typing the second blackmail note. Naturally, I had only to glance at the machine's keyboard to settle this point after the receipt of the second blackmail letter. Yes, the symbol was there. In fact, District Attorney Sampson, Assistant District Attorney Pepper and Inspector Queen will recall that, had they known what to look for, they should have seen this without actually looking at the typewriter itself; for at the time Inspector Queen wrote out a cablegram to Scotland Yard in Knox's den, one of the words in his message contained the figures for 'hundred and fifty thousand pounds,' and when Miss Brett had copied the Inspector's pencilled message on the typewriter, lo and behold! she had used not the word 'pounds' but the symbol of the script capital 'L' with the horizontal cross-bar! Even if I had never seen the machine itself, the mere fact that Miss Brett was able to type a pound-sign in the cable, coupled with the other facts in my possession, would have made the deduction inevitable.... The proof, as mathematically certain as any inferential proof could be, stared me in the face: the machine used to type the second blackmail letter had been Mr. James J. Knox's."

The reporters were sitting in the front row; their notes grew like Alice in Wonderland. No sound was audible except heavy breathing and the scraping of pencils. Ellery ground a cigarette beneath his sole with a bland disregard of Headquarters regulations and the ordinary proprieties. "*Eh bien,*" he said pleasantly, "*nous faisons des progrès.* For we know that from the time he received the first blackmail letter Knox permitted no visitors of any description in his house, not even Mr. Woodruff, his temporary attorney. This means that the only persons who could have used Knox's machine in the typing of the second note were: Knox himself, Miss Brett and the menial members of Knox's household. Now, because the letters had both been written on halves of the promissory note—which in turn could only have been in the possession of the murderer—this means that one of the above mentioned group was the murderer."

Ellery forged ahead so rapidly that a slight movement from the rear of the room—really, it should be noted, from the seat in which Inspector Richard Queen was crouched—went unnoticed, and a grim smile lifted Ellery's lips at this deliberate stifling of a possible criticism. "Let us eliminate," he said quickly. "Let us take the last category first. Was the writer possibly one of the servants? No; for none of the servants had been in the Khalkis house during the period of the first investigations— accurate lists were kept by one of the District Attorney's men— and therefore none of the servants could have planted the false clues against Khalkis and later Sloane; an essential characteristic, this planting business, of the murderer."

Again an irritable movement from the rear, and again Ellery's instant resumption of his remarks. "Could it have been Miss Brett?—you'll forgive me, Miss Brett," Ellery said with an apologetic grin, "for bringing you into this argument, but logic is no respecter of the gallantries. . . . No, it couldn't have been Miss Brett, for while she *was* in the Khalkis house during the period when the false clues were planted, on the other hand she couldn't have been Grimshaw's partner, another necessary qualification of the murderer. How do we know that she couldn't have been Grimshaw's partner, aside from the obvious grotesquerie of the thought? Very simply." He paused, sought Joan's eyes, found something in them consoling, and continued rapidly: "Miss Brett confessed to me that she has been for some time, and is now, an operative of the Victoria Museum." Whatever he was about to say was drowned in a wave of excited exclamations. For a moment the meeting seemed doomed to eruption; but Ellery rapped on the blackboard, quite like a schoolmaster, and the hubbub died away. He went on without looking at Sampson, Pepper or his father, all of whom were regarding him with mingled expressions of reproach and anger. "As I began to say, Miss Brett confessed to me that she was employed by the Victoria Museum as an under-cover operative, and gained access to the Khalkis household originally for the sole purpose of tracing the stolen Leonardo. Now Miss Brett told me this after Sloane's apparent suicide and before the arrival of the first blackmail letter. At this time she showed me some steamship tickets—she had purchased passage back to England. Why? Because she felt that she had lost the trail to the painting, and was no longer needed on a detective hunt which had become too involved for her. What did this purchase of passage out of the country mean? Obviously, that she did not know where the painting then was—otherwise she would have remained in New York; her very intention to return to London was proof of her lack of knowledge. Yet what was the prime characteristic of our murderer? That he *did* know where the painting was!—in Knox's possession, to be exact. In other words, Miss Brett couldn't have written the second blackmail note—or the first either, for that matter, since both were written by the same person.

"Very well. If Miss Brett and the servants are eliminated as suspects, then only Knox himself is left as the writer of the second letter, and therefore as Grimshaw's partner and murderer.

"How does this check? Knox satisfies the characteristics of the murderer: he was in the Khalkis house during the period when the false clues were planted against Khalkis, for one thing. On the other hand, to digress a moment, why did Knox come forward and explode his own false clues by confessing that he was the third man—after he had gone to all the trouble of making it appear that there *wasn't* a third man? For a very good reason: Miss Brett had already exploded the theory of the third man by her tea-cup story in his presence . . . so he had nothing to lose and everything to gain by seeming to come to the assistance of the investigation—a daring move to support his pretended innocence. He also fits into the mould of the

Sloane case: he could have been the person who accompanied Grimshaw into the Hotel Benedict and in this way learned that Sloane and Grimshaw were brothers, whereupon he sent the anonymous letter to us as a jog toward framing Sloane; as the murderer, moreover, he possessed the will he took from Khalkis's coffin and could therefore have planted it in the basement of his empty piece of property next door and put a duplicate key in Sloane's humidor; and, finally, as the murderer he would possess Grimshaw's watch and could have placed it in the safe behind Sloane after killing his second victim in the Khalkis Galleries.

"Why, however, did he write letters to *himself* and trump up a seeming theft of his own painting? For an excellent reason: the Sloane suicide had been publicly discredited, and he knew the police were still seeking a murderer. Also he was being pressed to return the Leonardo—and by writing the letters to himself he made it appear that the murderer, still at large, and whoever he was, was at least not Knox, and that some outsider had written the letters—for of course he would never have written the letters at all had he thought they would be traced back to his own typewriter.

"Now, in stealing the painting from himself he furthered the illusion by making it appear that this fictitious outsider had deliberately lured the police from the house in order to steal the painting; he tampered with his own burglar-alarm in advance and expected, no doubt, after we should have returned from the Times Building empty-handed, that this tampered burglar-alarm would prove to us that the painting had been stolen while we were away on the vain hunt. It was a clever plan; for the stealing of the painting eliminated his obligation to return it to the Museum, while he secretly retained it thereafter, safe on all counts."

Ellery smiled toward the rear of the room. "I see the honourable District Attorney biting his lips with vexation and worry. My dear Sampson, it is evident that you are anticipating the argument of Mr. Knox's lawyers. For undoubtedly his bat-tery of legal lights will attempt to show, by producing samples of Knox's own customary typewriting style, that these differ from the style exhibited in the two blackmail notes which you will charge he wrote to himself. Don't worry about it: it will be evident to any jury that Knox would *deliberately* alter his habit-ual typewriting style—spacing, punctuation, the heaviness with which he strikes certain letters, and so on—in typing these blackmail notes to strengthen the illusion of their having been typed by someone other than himself. . . .

"As to the paintings themselves. There are two possibilities: that Knox had both to begin with, as he claims, or that he had only one—the one he purchased from Khalkis. If he had only one, then he lied about it being stolen, because I found one in his house after he claimed it was stolen. And when he saw that I had found it, he hurriedly utilized the history of the two paint-ings to make us believe that he had had two all the time, and that the one we found was the copy, the original having been taken by this mythical thief. By this means, it is true, he sacri-ficed the painting, but saved his own skin—or so he thought.

"On the other hand, if he really did have the two paintings to begin with, then the one I found is either the Leonardo or the copy, and there is no way of telling which until we find the other canvas that Knox has inevitably hidden somewhere. But whichever painting is now in the District Attorney's posses-sion, there is still another in Knox's possession—provided he had the two all the time—and this other Knox cannot proffer because he has already committed himself as to its having been stolen by an outsider. My dear Sampson, if you can find that other painting somewhere on Knox's premises, or find it elsewhere and can prove that Knox placed it there, the case against him will be even more airtight than it is now."

Sampson, to judge from the expression on his lean face, would have liked to argue this statement; he apparently did not consider the case more airtight than a sieve. But Ellery did not permit him to voice what was in his mind; he went on without pause. "To sum up," he said. "The murderer had to possess three major qualifications. One: he had to be able to plant the clues against Khalkis and Sloane. Two: he had to be the writer of the blackmail letters. Three: he had to be in the Knox house in order to be able to type the second letter. This third qualification includes only the servants, Miss Brett and Knox. But the servants are eliminated on Qualification One, as I showed you. Miss Brett is eliminated on Qualification Two, as I showed before. Only Knox is left, and since Knox fits all three qualifications perfectly, he must be the murderer."

*   *   *

One would not have said that Inspector Richard Queen basked in the sunshine of his son's public triumph. When the inevitable questioning, congratulations, arguments and journalistic disturbances were over—it was notable that there were several shaking heads among the reporters—and the Queens found themselves alone within the sacrosanct walls of the Inspector's office, the old man permitted such expression of his inner feeling to escape as had hitherto been sternly repressed; and Ellery felt the full blast of his father's displeasure.

Not that Ellery himself, it is important to note, presented the picture of a self-satisfied young lion of the hour. On the contrary, his lean cheeks were hardened into long lines of tension, and his eyes were tired and feverish. He smoked cigarette after cigarette without enjoyment, and avoided his father's eyes.

The old man was grousing in no uncertain terms. "By ginger," he said, "if you weren't my son I'd boot you out of here. Of all the wishy-washy, unsatisfying, ridiculous arguments I ever heard that performance of yours downstairs was—" He shuddered. "Ellery, mark my words. There's going to be trouble. This is one time when my faith in you is, is—well, you've let me down, drat it! And Sampson—why, Henry's no nincompoop; and when he walked out of that room I saw, plain as day, that he felt he was facing the toughest courtroom battle of his career. That case won't stand up in court, Ellery; it just won't. No evidence. And motive. *Motive*, damn it all! You didn't say a word about that. Why did Knox kill Grimshaw? Sure, it's fine to use that blasted *logic* of yours to show by mathematics or something that Knox is our man—but motive! Juries want motives, not logic." He was spluttering all over his vest. "There'll be hell to pay. Knox in gaol with the biggest lawyers in the East to defend him—they'll punch holes in your pretty case, my boy, till it looks like Swiss cheese. Just about as full of holes as—"

It was at this moment that Ellery stirred. All during the tirade he had sat patiently, even nodding, as if what the Inspector was saying he expected and, while he did not precisely welcome it, felt it was not insurmountable. But now he sat up straight, and something like alarm flickered over his face. "As full of holes as what? What do you mean?"

"Ha!" cried the Inspector. "That gets a rise out of you, does it? Think your old man's an idiot? Maybe Henry Sampson didn't see it, but I saw it, by George, and if *you* didn't see it, the more fool you!" He rapped Ellery's knee. "Look here, Ellery Sherlock Holmes Queen. You said that you'd eliminated the servants on the count of one of 'em possibly being the murderer because they hadn't, any of 'em, been in the Khalkis house during the period when the false clues were being planted."

"Yes?" said Ellery slowly.

"Yes. That was fine. Great. True. I agree with you. But, my precious half-wit son," said the old man with bitterness, "you didn't go far enough, you see. You eliminated each of the servants as the murderer, but why couldn't one of 'em have been *an accomplice of an outside murderer?* Put that in your pipe and smoke it!"

Ellery did not reply; he sighed, and let it go at that. The Inspector dropped into his swivel-chair with a snort of discontent. "Of all the stupid omissions. . . . You of all people! I'm surprised at you, son. This case has addled your brain. For one of the servants could have been hired by the murderer to write the second blackmail letter on Knox's machine, while the outside murderer was safe somewhere else! I'm not saying this is true; but I'll bet dollars to doughnuts that Knox's lawyers point that out, and then where is your whole argument which eliminates everybody until only Knox is left? Bah! Your logic is rotten."

Ellery nodded in humble agreement. "Brilliant, Dad, really brilliant. I hope—I trust that no one else thinks of it at this time."

"Well," said the Inspector grumpily, "I guess Henry didn't, or he would have shot right up here and squawked his head off. That's one consolation, anyway.... See here, El. Evidently you've known all along of the loophole I've just pointed out. Why don't you plug it now—before it's too late and costs me my job, and Henry's too?"

"Why don't I plug the hole, you ask." Ellery shrugged, and stretched his arms far over his head. "—Lord, I'm weary! ... I'll tell you why, long-suffering ancestor. For the simple reason that—I *daren't*."

The Inspector shook his head. "You must be going dotty," he muttered. "What do you mean—you daren't? Is that a reason? All right—say it's Knox. But the case, boy, the case! Give us something more definite to work on. You know I'll back you to the limit if you're convinced you're right."

"How well I know that," grinned Ellery. "Fatherhood is a wonderful thing. There is only one thing more wonderful, and that is motherhood.... Dad, I can't say another serious word now. But I'll tell you this, and you may accept it for what it's worth, considering the unreliable source.... *The biggest thing in this unholy mess of a case has yet to happen!*"

CHAPTER 33

Eye-opener

I t was during this period that a rift of serious width opened between father and son. The Inspector's psychology is understandable: freighted down to the gunwales with worry, emotionally awash, the primitive emerged and threatened for several hours to bare its teeth at the slightest quiver of Ellery's for the most part silent figure. The old man, sensing something wrong, unable to put his precise little finger on anything material, reacted characteristically: he stormed and ranted and made the lives of his subordinates unbearable, while all the time his wrath was directed obliquely against the bowed head of his son.

Several times that day he made as if to leave the office. It was only at such moments that Ellery lived again; and scenes of increasing irritableness were enacted between the two.

"You mustn't leave. You must stay here. Please."

Once the Inspector rebelled, and went away; and Ellery who had been sitting hunched over the telephone, tense as a setter on the point, was overcome with nervousness and bit his lip until blood came. But the Inspector's resolution was weak; and back he came, red-faced and growling, to keep the incomprehensible vigil with his son. Ellery's face lightened at once;

and he sat himself down at the telephone again, no less strained than before, but now content to devote all his faculties to the apparently herculean task of waiting, waiting. . . .

Telephone calls came in with monotonous regularity. From whom they were, what they signified, the Inspector did not know; but each time the buzzer sounded Ellery snatched at the instrument as if he were a man condemned to death and this the instrument of his reprieve. Each time he was disappointed; listening soberly, nodding, saying a few noncommittal words, and hanging up again.

At one time the Inspector called for Sergeant Velie; and discovered that the usually reliable sergeant had not reported to Headquarters since the previous evening; that no one knew where he was; that not even his wife could account for his absence. This was serious, and the old man's nose lengthened and his jaw snapped in a manner that boded ill for the sergeant. But he had learned his lesson and said nothing; and Ellery, who perhaps nursed a tiny spark of resentment against his father for having doubted him, did not enlighten him. In the course of the afternoon the Inspector found it necessary to call upon various members of his staff on matters connected with the Grimshaw case; and to his deepening astonishment he discovered that several of these, too, among whom were numbered his most trusted men—Hagstrom, Piggott, Johnson—were also unaccountably missing.

Ellery said quietly: "Velie and the others are out on an important mission. My orders." He could no longer bear the old man's agony.

"*Your* orders!" The Inspector barely did not utter the words loud. His mind was shrouded in a fog of red rage. "You're trailing somebody," he said with an effort.

Ellery nodded; his eyes were on the telephone.

Hourly, half-hourly, cryptic telephoned reports came in to Ellery. The Inspector grasped his surging temper at last with firm hand—the danger of open revolt was now past—and

waded ferociously into a sea of routine matters. The day lengthened; Ellery ordered luncheon to be sent up; they ate in silence. Ellery's hand never far from the telephone.

* * *

At dinner they ate again in the Inspector's office—without ap-
petite, mechanically, in a frightened gloom. Neither man had
thought to touch the light-switch; the shadows clustered thickly
and the Inspector let his work go in disgust. They just sat there.

And then, behind locked doors, Ellery found his old affection, and something sparked between them, and Ellery began to
speak. He spoke swiftly, certainly, as if what he said had crystallized in his mind after many hours of cold experimental thought.
And as he spoke, the last vestige of the Inspector's pique vanished, and an expression of such amazement as rarely visited
that case-hardened old countenance broke through his deep
face-lines. He kept muttering: "I can't believe it. It's impossible.
How can it be?"

And, at the conclusion of Ellery's recital, for an instant
apology crept out of the Inspector's eyes. No more than an instant; the eyes glittered, and from that moment too he watched
the telephone as if it were a sentient thing.

At the normal closing-hour, the Inspector summoned his
secretary and issued mysterious instructions. The secretary
went away.

Within fifteen minutes the report was casually circulated
through the corridors of Police Headquarters that Inspector
Queen had left for the day—had gone home, in fact, to muster
his strength for the battle that was imminent with James J.
Knox's lawyers.

But Inspector Queen still sat in his darkened office, waiting
with Ellery at the telephone, which was now connected to the
central police operator on a private line.

Outside, at the curb, a police car with two men in it had
been stationed all afternoon, motor running.

Waiting, it seemed, with the same iron patience that was enforced upon the two men high in the grey stone building behind locked doors and in darkness.

*   *   *

It was past midnight when the call finally came.

The Queens leaped into action with muscles coiled for the kill. The telephone rang shrilly. Ellery snatched the receiver, shouted into the transmitter: "Well?"

A man's rumbling rejoinder.

"On our way!" yelled Ellery, dropping the telephone. "The Knox house, Dad!"

They dashed out of the Inspector's office, struggling into their coats as they ran. Downstairs to the waiting automobile. Ellery's strong voice shouting instructions, and the car, too, leaped into action . . . turning its black nose north and shooting uptown with its siren screaming.

But Ellery's instructions brought them not to James Knox's mansion on Riverside Drive. For it turned into Fifty-fourth Street—the street of the church and the Khalkis house. The siren had been choked several blocks away. The car stole on its rubber feet into the dark street, slid without noise to the curb, and Ellery and the Inspector jumped out quickly. Without hesitation they made for the shadows surrounding the basement entrance of the empty Knox house next door to Khalkis's. . . .

They moved like ghosts, making no sound. Sergeant Velie's gigantic shoulders pushed up out of a black patch beneath the crumbly steps. A flashlight touched the Queens briefly, snapped off on the instant, and the sergeant whispered: "Inside. Got to work fast. Boys all around the place. Can't get away. Quick, Chief!"

The Inspector, very calm and steady now, nodded; and Velie gently pushed the door to the basement open. He paused a moment in the basement vestibule, and from nowhere another man popped up. Silently the Queens accepted flashlights from his hand, and at a word from the Inspector, Velie and Ellery muffled them with handkerchiefs, and then the three men crept into the deserted basement. The sergeant, evidently familiar as a cat with the terrain, led the way. The small cloudy light from their torches barely lightened the darkness. Like marauding Indians they glided across the floor, past the ghostly furnace, and up the basement staircase. At the top of the steps Velie paused again; a few whispered words with another man stationed there, and then the sergeant beckoned silently and led the way from the stairs into the blackness of the lower-floor hall.

As they tiptoed into the corridor, they all halted with noiseless abruptness. Somewhere ahead there were cracks of feeble light at the top and bottom of what was evidently a door.

Ellery touched Sergeant Velie's arm lightly. Velie turned his big head. Ellery breathed a few words. And although it was not visible, Velie grinned a deprecating grin in the darkness, his hand went to his coat pocket, and out it came grasping a revolver.

He permitted his torch to flash for the merest space—and instantly other dark shadows converged on the spot, moving with caution. A hushed colloquy between Velie and another man, who from his voice was Detective Piggott. All exits, it appeared, were covered.... The party, at a signal from the sergeant, crept forward to the source of the tiny light. They stood still. Velie drew a deep breath, motioned Piggott and another detective—Johnson, it was, from his slight figure—to his side, roared: "*Now!*" and the three men, Velie's iron shoulders in the centre, crashed against the door, splintered it like matchwood, and lunged into the room beyond. Ellery and the Inspector plunged through precipitately; they spread out, uncovered now brilliant flashlights which swept the room, catching something, all trapping in that infinitesimal moment the frozen figure—their quarry—in the centre of the dusty unfurnished room—a figure who had been studying in the rays of a small torch two identical canvases spread out on the floor....

For that same moment there was silence; and then, so suddenly that it might never have existed, the spell shivered. From the chest of the muffled figure came a snarl, a whimper, a choked cry that was animal; it twisted about like a panther, a white hand flashed toward a coat-pocket, and there appeared out of nowhere a bluish automatic. And a very private sort of hell broke loose.

It broke loose as the dark figure fixed a feline glare on the tall form of Ellery Queen, singling him out with a magical directness from among the clustered bodies in the doorway. Very quickly a finger tightened upon the trigger of the automatic and squeezed; and in the same breath there came the coughing roar of many police revolvers. And Sergeant Velie, his face a furious mask in its steely whiteness, hurled himself forward with the speed of an express train on the dark figure. . . . It crumpled to the floor, grotesquely like a form composed of *papier-mâché*.

Ellery Queen, with a soft groan of surprise, opened his eyes wide and toppled to his father's frozen feet.

* * *

Ten minutes later the torches illuminated a scene as still as its predecessor had been frenzied. The solid figure of Dr. Duncan Frost was crouched over a recumbent Ellery, who was lying on a litter of detectives' overcoats on the dirty floor. Inspector Queen, as white as a drifting cloud, as cold and hard and brittle as porcelain, stood over the physician with eyes fixed immovably on Ellery's bloodless face. No one said a word, not even the men who surrounded the crazily shapeless figure of Ellery's assailant on the floor in the centre of the room.

Dr. Frost twitched his head. "Poor shot. He'll be quite all right. A slight flesh-wound in the shoulder. There, he's coming to now."

The Inspector sighed windily. Ellery's eyes fluttered open, a spasm of pain contracted them, and his hand groped for his left shoulder. It met a bandage. The Inspector squatted beside him. "Ellery, old son—you're all right, you feel all right?"

Ellery contrived a smile. He shook himself and struggled to his feet, assisted by gentle hands. "Phew!" he said, wincing. "Hello, Doctor. When did you arrive?"

He looked about, and his gaze coagulated on the thick cluster of silent detectives. He lurched toward them, and Sergeant Velie moved aside with a childish, muttering apology. Ellery clutched Velie's shoulder with his right hand, leaned heavily, stared down at the body on the floor. There was no triumph in his eyes, but a vast moodiness which blended well with the flashlights, the dust, the grim men, and the grey-black shadows.

"Dead?" he asked, wetting his lips.

"Four slugs through his guts," grunted Velie. "Dead as he'll ever be."

Ellery nodded; his eyes shifted and focused on the two stretches of painted canvas, lying very humbly in the dust where someone had tossed them. "Well," he said with a wry humourless grin, "at least we've got *them*," and looked down at the dead man again. "A bad break, a very bad break for you, Mister. Like Napoleon, you won every fight but the last."

He studied the dead open eyes for a moment, shivered a little, and turned to find the Inspector at his side; a little old man who watched him with haggard eyes.

Ellery smiled feebly. "Well, Dad, we can let poor old Knox go now. He's been the willing victim, and he's served his purpose. . . . Here's your case lying harmlessly in the dust of Knox's floor. The lone wolf of the whole affair—blackmailer, thief, murderer. . . ."

They stared down together at the dead man. The dead man on the floor looking back at them quite as if he could see— indeed there was the indelible imprint of a daring and malicious grin on those snarling features—was Assistant District Attorney Pepper.

CHAPTER 34

Nucleus

"There's no earthly reason, Mr. Cheney," said Ellery, "why you shouldn't be treated to a proper explanation—you, of course, and—" But the bell rang then, and Ellery stopped as Djuna ran to the door. Miss Joan Brett appeared at the door of the living-room.

Miss Joan Brett seemed as astonished to see Mr. Alan Cheney as Mr. Alan Cheney was to see Miss Joan Brett. Alan rose and gripped the tortured walnut of the Queens' excellent Windsor chair; and Joan clutched the jamb as if she suddenly needed something to lean on.

This was, thought Ellery Queen as he rose from the sofa on which he had been lying, his left shoulder swathed in bandages—this was the proper ending. . . . He was a little pale, and for the first time in weeks wore an expression of serenity. The trio who rose with him—a strangely abashed father; a District Attorney from whose eyes the horrified amazement of the previous night had not yet fled; a wan and plucky nabob, Mr. James J. Knox, none the worse, it appeared, for his brief incarceration—these gentlemen bowed deeply and received no answering smile from the young lady in the doorway, who seemed mesmerized by the equally frozen young man hanging on to his chair.

Then her blue eyes wavered, and they sought the smiling ones of Ellery. "I thought . . . You asked me—"

Ellery went to her side, took her arm possessively, and piloted her to a deep chair into which she sank with a faltering embarrassment. "You thought—I asked you to . . . What, Miss Brett?"

She caught sight of his left shoulder. "You've been hurt!" she cried.

"To which," said Ellery, "I reply in the accepted words of the shiny hero, 'A mere nothing. A scratch.' Sit down, Mr. Cheney!"

Mr. Cheney sat down.

"Come on!" said Sampson impatiently. "I don't know about the others, but you certainly owe *me* an explanation, Ellery."

Ellery draped himself over his sofa again and managed with one hand to light a cigarette. "Now we're comfy," he said. He caught the eye of James Knox, and they both smiled at some secret jest. "Explanation. . . . Of course."

Ellery began to speak. And while his words crackled through the next half-hour like an accompaniment of popping corn, Alan and Joan sat with folded hands and did not once look at each other.

"The fourth solution—there were four, you know," began Ellery: "the Khalkis solution, in which Mr. Pepper led me about by the nose; the Sloane solution, which we might term a deadlock between Pepper and me, since I didn't believe in it although I couldn't support my disbelief until Suiza came along with his story; the Knox solution, in which I led Mr. Pepper about by the nose—so far a tie, you will observe; and the Pepper solution, which was the proper one—the fourth, I say, and final solution which has amazed all of you but actually is as plain as the good strong sunlight which poor old Pepper will never see again. . . ." He was silent for a moment. "Certainly the revelation of an apparently reputable young man, an Assistant District Attorney, as the prime mover in a series of crimes engineered with profound imagination and supreme insouciance must be confounding if you don't know how and why he did it. Yet Mr. Pepper was snared by my old and remorseless ally, Logic, the *logos* of the Greeks and the bane, I trust, of many plotters to come."

Ellery flicked his ashes all over young Djuna's spotless rug. "Now, I confess that until the events which centred on Mr. Knox's broad acreage on the Drive—the blackmail letters and the theft of the painting—until these events I had not the slightest inkling of where the guilt lay. In other words, had Pepper stopped with the murder of Sloane, he should have gone free. But, in this as in other less celebrated crimes, the criminal fell victim to his own cupidity. And he wove with his own fingers the web in which he was finally ensnared.

"Consequently, since the series of events in the Knox house on the Drive was the salient one, let me begin there. You will recall that yesterday morning I summed up the major qualifications of the murderer; and it is necessary to repeat those qualifications now. One: he had to be able to plant the clues against Khalkis and Sloane. Two: he had to be the writer of the blackmail letters. Three: he had to be in the Knox house in order to type the second blackmail letter."

Ellery smiled. "Now, this last qualification, as I expanded it yesterday morning, was misleading—deliberately so for reasons which will be evident later. My astute sire pointed out privately to me just where I was 'wrong' after that charming little pseudo-explanation I gave at Police Headquarters. For I purposely chose, from the phrase: 'in the Knox house,' to mean a *member* of the Knox household, whereas obviously 'in the Knox house' is a much more comprehensive term. For 'in the Knox house' means *anyone*, whether of the Knox household or not. In other words, the typist of the second letter did not necessarily have to be one of the regular occupants of the house; he might merely have been an outsider who gained access to the Knox house. Please bear this in mind.

"We begin, therefore, from this thesis: that the second letter, from the surrounding circumstances, must have been written by someone who was in the house at the time of the writing; and this someone was the murderer. But my intelligent sire pointed out that this wasn't necessarily true, either; why, he asked, couldn't the writer of the note have been an *accomplice* of the murderer, who was hired by the murderer perhaps to write the letter while the murderer himself stayed away from the Knox house? This would mean, of course, that the murderer couldn't gain legitimate access to the Knox house, or else he would type the letter himself. . . . That was a subtle question, and a perfectly proper one—which I deliberately avoided taking up yesterday morning because it didn't suit my purpose, which was to trap Pepper.

"Very well! If we can prove now that the murderer *couldn't* have had an accomplice in the Knox house, it would mean that the murderer himself typed the second letter and was in Mr. Knox's den when he did so.

"To prove, however, that there was no accomplice in the case, we first have to establish the innocence of Mr. Knox himself, otherwise the logical problem is insoluble."

Ellery expelled cigarette-smoke lazily. "Mr. Knox's innocence is most simply established. Is this a surprise to you? Yet it is ridiculously apparent. It is established by means of a fact in the possession of only three people in the world: Mr. Knox, Miss Brett and myself. Consequently, Pepper—as you will see— being ignorant of this essential fact, made his first slip in the chain of plots and counterplots.

"The fact is this: during the period when Gilbert Sloane was considered generally the murderer, Mr. Knox *voluntarily*— mark that—informed me, in Miss Brett's presence, that on the night he and Grimshaw visited Khalkis, Khalkis had borrowed a thousand-dollar bill from him—Knox—to give to Grimshaw as a sort of advance blackmail payment; that he, Knox, had seen Grimshaw tuck this bill, folded, into the back of his watch-case, and that Grimshaw had left the house with this bill still in his watch. Mr. Knox and I went at once to Headquarters and found the bill still there—the very same bill, because I checked up at once and discovered that it had been issued, as Mr. Knox had said, to him on the day he had mentioned. Now, the very fact that this thousand-dollar bill was traceable to Mr. Knox, which he knew better than anyone, meant that if *Mr. Knox had killed Grimshaw, he would have used every means in his power to keep that bill from falling into the hands of the police*. Certainly it would have been simple for him, had he strangled Grimshaw, to have removed the bill from Grimshaw's watch then and there, since he knew that Grimshaw had it, and precisely where. Even had he been connected with the murderer in a remoter capacity—as an accomplice—he would have seen to it that the bill was removed from the watch-case, since the watch was in the possession of the murderer for quite some time.

"But the bill was still in that watch when we looked into its case at Police Headquarters! Now, if Mr. Knox had been the murderer, why hadn't he removed the bill, as I said a moment ago? In fact, why had he, aside from not having removed the bill, actually come to me of his own free will and told me that the bill was there—when I, in common with the other representatives of the law, did not even dream of the bill's existence? You see, his action was so wholly at variance with what he would have done had he been the murderer or the accomplice that I was compelled to say at that time: 'Well, no matter where the guilt lies, it certainly isn't in the direction of James Knox.'"

"Thank God for that," said Knox huskily.

"But observe," continued Ellery, "where this conclusion, which at the time meant so little to me, being a negative finding, led. For only the murderer, or his possible accomplice if there was one, could have written the blackmail letters—since they had been typed on the halves of the promissory note. Since Mr. Knox was not the murderer or accomplice, he couldn't have typed the letters, despite the fact that they were written on his own distinctive machine, as I pointed out yesterday by the pound-sign deductions. Therefore—and this was rather startling—the person who typed the second letter used Mr. Knox's machine deliberately! But for what purpose? Only so that, by leaving the clue of the mistyped 3 and the suggestion of the pound-symbol—which naturally now had been left on purpose—only that by so doing, I say, a trail would be left to Mr. Knox's machine and it would therefore appear that Mr. Knox wrote the letter and was the murderer. Another frame-up, then—the third, the first two of which had been unsuccessfully directed against Georg Khalkis and Gilbert Sloane."

Ellery frowned thoughtfully. "We now ascend into more acute reasoning. For see! It must be evident that the real criminal, in framing James Knox for the murders and the potential theft, considered James Knox a possibility in the minds of the police! It would be folly to make James Knox appear the criminal if the real murderer knew the police would not accept James Knox as the criminal. Therefore the real murderer could not have known the thousand-dollar-bill story. For had he known it, he would never have framed Mr. Knox. At this point, then, one person could certainly be eliminated as a mathematical possibility, on top of the fact that she was an accredited investigator of the Victoria Museum—which fact, of course, did not necessarily absolve her from suspicion, although it was a tenable presumption of innocence. That was this beautiful young lady, whose blushes I observe are continually deepening— Miss Brett; for she was present when Mr. Knox told me about the thousand-dollar bill, and if she had been the murderer or even the murderer's accomplice, she would not have framed Mr. Knox or permitted the murderer to frame him."

Joan sat up straight at this; then she grinned weakly and sank back. Alan Cheney blinked. He was studying the rug at his feet as if it were some precious sample of weaving worthy of a young antiquarian's strict scrutiny.

"Therefore—a plethora of therefores," continued Ellery, "of the people who could have typed the second letter, I had eliminated both Mr. Knox and Miss Brett, either as murderer or accomplice in each instance.

"Now, would the only other members of the official household—the servants—have among their number the *murderer himself?* No, because not one of the servants could physically have planted the false clues against Khalkis and Sloane in the Khalkis house—a carefully kept list of all people who visited the Khalkis house does not anywhere reveal any of Mr. Knox's servants. On the other hand, could one of Mr. Knox's servants have been an *accomplice* of an outside murderer, being utilized merely because he had access to the Knox typewriter?"

Ellery smiled. "No, as I can prove. The fact that Mr. Knox's typewriter was employed in the frame-up against him indicates that the use of his typewriter was intended by the murderer from the beginning; for the only concrete evidence the murderer intended to leave against Mr. Knox was that the second letter would be found to have been written on Mr. Knox's machine; this was the kernel of the frame-up plot. (Please note that even if the plotter did not know in advance the *specific* manner in which he would incriminate Mr. Knox, he at least was intending to use some peculiarity of the typewriter.) Well, then, it certainly would have been to the murderer's obvious advantage, since he was framing Mr. Knox by means of his typewriter, to have typed *both* letters on that machine. Yet *only the second* was typed on that machine—the first having been written on an Underwood outside of Mr. Knox's house, Mr. Knox's Remington being the only machine *in* his house. . . . If therefore the murderer did not use Mr. Knox's Remington for the typing of the first letter, it clearly indicates that *he did not have access* to Mr. Knox's machine for the typing of the first letter. But all the servants *did* have access to Mr. Knox's machine for the typing of the first letter—they all had been with him, in fact, a minimum of five years. Therefore, one of them could not have been an accomplice of the murderer, or the murderer would have had him type the first letter on the Knox machine.

"But this has eliminated *either as murderer or accomplice* Mr. Knox, Miss Brett, and all the servants of the household! But how is this possible since the second letter *was* written from the Knox house?"

Ellery flung his cigarette into the fire. "We know now that the writer, though somehow in Mr. Knox's den to have written the second letter, was not in Mr. Knox's den—or house—when he wrote the first letter—otherwise he would have used the machine for the first letter also. We know too that no outsider was admitted to the Knox house after the receipt of the first letter—that is, no outsider *except one person*. Now, while it's true that anyone could have written the first letter from outside, only one person could have written the second—the only one who gained access to the house before the receipt of the second letter. And now another point became clear. For why, I asked myself all the time, had that first letter been *necessary at all*? It was garrulous, and it seemed to serve little purpose. Blackmailers generally make their strike the first time they write—they don't indulge in long-winded, pleasantly cocky correspondence; they don't *establish* their position as blackmailers in one letter, and then wait for a second to demand money. The explanation here was psychologically perfect; that first letter was *essential* to the murderer; it served some purpose. What purpose? Why, to get him access to the Knox house! Why did he want access to the Knox house? To be in a position to type the *second* letter from Knox's machine! Everything matched. . . .

"Now who was the only one who gained access to the house between the receipt of the first letter and the receipt of the second? And strange as it seemed, incredible, extraordinary as I found it, I couldn't blink the fact that this visitor was our own colleague, our fellow-investigator—in short, Assistant District Attorney Pepper, who had spent several days there (and, as we instantly recall, at his own suggestion) for the ostensible purpose of *waiting* for the second letter!

"Clever! It was devilishly ingenious.

"My first reaction was natural—I could not bring myself to believe it. It seemed impossible. But staggering as this revelation was to me, particularly since it was the first time I had even considered Pepper a possibility," continued Ellery, "the course was clear. I could not reject a suspect—now no longer a suspect, but from logic the criminal—merely because imagination refused to credit the result of reason. I was forced to check. I went over the whole case from the beginning to see if, and how, Pepper matched the facts.

"Well, Pepper himself had identified Grimshaw as a man he had defended five years before; naturally, as the criminal, he would do this to forestall cleverly the possible chance discovery of this former connexion between him and the victim after he had had the opportunity of recognizing the victim and had refrained from doing so. A small point, and not at all conclusive, but significant nevertheless. In all likelihood this connexion began at least five years ago in a lawyer-client relationship, with Grimshaw coming to Pepper after he stole the painting from the Victoria Museum, asking him perhaps to keep an eye on things while he, Grimshaw, was in prison, and during the period when the painting, still unpaid for, was in Khalkis's possession. As soon as Grimshaw was released from prison, he naturally would have gone to Khalkis to collect. Undoubtedly it was Pepper who was the man behind the scenes, behind all the events that followed, keeping himself always unidentified and in the background. This business of Grimshaw and Pepper being connected may possibly be clarified by Jordan, Pepper's former law-partner, although Jordan is probably an entirely innocent man."

"We're looking him up," said Sampson. "He's a reputable attorney."

"No doubt," said Ellery dryly. "Pepper wouldn't ally himself openly with a crook—not Pepper.... But we are looking for confirmation. How does the matter of motive emerge in a consideration of Pepper as Grimshaw's strangler? ...

"After the meeting of Grimshaw, Mr. Knox and Khalkis that Friday night, and after Grimshaw received the promissory note payable to bearer, Mr. Knox left with Grimshaw, went away, and meanwhile Grimshaw remained standing before the house. Why? Possibly to meet his confederate—a not fanciful conclusion from Grimshaw's own statements about his 'single partner.' Pepper, then, must have been waiting for Grimshaw in the vicinity. They must have withdrawn into the shadows and Grimshaw must have told Pepper everything that had transpired in the house. Pepper, realizing that he no longer needed Grimshaw, that Grimshaw was even a danger to him, that with Grimshaw out of the way he could collect from Mr. Knox without having to divide the spoils—must then have decided to kill his partner. The promissory note would have provided an additional motive, for, made out to bearer, and with Khalkis still alive, remember, it represented a potential half-million dollars to the holder of it; and there too was Mr. James J. Knox still in the background as another source of blackmail later on. Undoubtedly Pepper killed Grimshaw either in the shadows of the basement entrance to the empty Knox house next door, or in the basement itself, for which he must already have provided himself with a duplicate key. At any rate, having Grimshaw's dead body in the basement, he searched the corpse, appropriated the promissory note and Grimshaw's watch (with the notion perhaps of using it later somewhere as a plant), and the five thousand dollars Sloane had bribed Grimshaw with the night before to get out of the city. At the time he choked Grimshaw to death, he must have had some plan in mind for the disposal of the body; or perhaps he intended to leave it permanently in the basement. But when the next morning Khalkis unexpectedly died, Pepper must have realized instantly that here was an unexampled opportunity to bury Grimshaw's body in

Khalkis's coffin. He then played in luck; for on the day of Khalkis's burial, Woodruff himself called the District Attorney's office for assistance, and Pepper asked—you mentioned that yourself, Sampson, once when you were chiding Pepper about being too interested in Miss Brett—to be put in charge of the will-search. Here, then, was another psychological indication to Mr. Pepper.

"Now, having perfect access to the Khalkis premises, he saw how simple matters would be for him. On the Wednesday night after the funeral, he took Grimshaw's body out of the empty Knox basement, where he had crammed it in the old trunk, carried the body through the dark court into the darker graveyard, dug up the earth above the vault, opened the horizontal door of the vault, leaped in and opened Khalkis's coffin—and immediately found the will in the steel box; until then it is probable that he himself did not know where the will had gone. Knowing that the will might come in handy later for the purpose of blackmailing still another figure in the tragedy, Sloane—Sloane being the only one who had motive for the theft of the will in the first place and its insertion in the coffin before the funeral—Pepper then must have appropriated the will, another potential instrument of blackmail. He crammed Grimshaw's body into the coffin, put back the lid of the coffin, climbed out, dropped the door of the vault, refilled the shallow pit, took away what tools he had used plus the will and the steel box, and left the graveyard. Incidentally, here is another tiny confirmation of the Pepper solution. For Pepper himself told us that it was on this night—Wednesday night, in the wee hours—that he saw Miss Brett on her marauding expedition in the study. Then Pepper by his own admission was up late that night; and it is not far-fetched to assume that he went through the ghastly business of the burial after Miss Brett left the study.

"Now we can fit in Mrs. Vreeland's story of having seen Sloane entering the graveyard that night. Sloane must have become aware of suspicious activity on Pepper's part in the house,

followed him, seen everything Pepper did—including the
burial of the body and the appropriation of the will—and realized that Pepper was a murderer ... of whom, however, at that
time, in the darkness, Sloane probably did not know."

Joan shuddered. "That—that nice young man. It's incredible."

Ellery said severely, "This should teach you a stern lesson,
Miss Brett. Stick to those you're sure of.... Where was I? Yes!
Now, Pepper felt perfectly safe; the body was buried, and no
one would have any reason to look for it. But when the next day
I announced the possibility of the will having been slipped into
the coffin and suggested a disinterment, Pepper must have
thought very rapidly indeed. He could not now prevent the
murder from being discovered without going back to the graveyard and taking the body out again; in this case he would have
the problem of disposing of it all over again; a risky business all
around. On the other hand, he might be able to make capital of
the discovery of the murder. So, having the run of the Khalkis
house, he left clues about which would point to the dead man—
Khalkis, I mean—as the murderer. He had had a sample of my
particular brand of reasoning, and deliberately toyed with
me—leaving not obvious clues but subtle ones which he felt
sure I would see. There were two reasons why he probably selected Khalkis as the 'murderer': the first, it would be just such
a solution as would appeal to my imagination; second, Khalkis
was dead and could not deny anything that Pepper suggested
by his plants. And, to make it perfect—if the solution were accepted, no one alive would suffer; for remember that Pepper
was not a habitual murderer, hardened to killings.

"Now, as I pointed out in the beginning, Pepper could not
have planted those false clues against Khalkis unless he *knew*
that Mr. Knox, possessing the stolen painting, must perforce
keep quiet and not admit having been the third man that
night—part of Pepper's false trail to Khalkis being the fact that
only two men were involved in the negotiations at the house
that night. But, to have known that Mr. Knox possessed the

painting, he must have been Grimshaw's partner, as shown many times before; must therefore have been the unknown who accompanied Grimshaw to his hotel room the night of the multiplicity of visitors.

"When Miss Brett inadvertently burst the Khalkis bubble by recalling and pointing out the discrepancy in the tea-cups, Pepper must have felt very badly. But at the same time he would have assured himself that it was no fault of his plotting—there had always been the off-chance that someone would notice the condition of the cups before he had had the opportunity to tinker with them. On the other hand, when Mr. Knox unexpectedly told *his* story, revealing himself as the third man, Pepper realized that all his work was undone, and moreover that I now knew the clues to have been deliberate falsifications left to be found. So Pepper, in the admirable position of knowing at all times everything I knew—how he must have chuckled to himself when I was being smug, oratorical and, in a word, myself!—Pepper decided then and there to make capital of his unique position by arranging succeeding events to bear out my own expressed theories. Khalkis being dead, the promissory note he held, Pepper knew, was valueless to him. What other source of revenue was open? He could not blackmail Mr. Knox with regard to possession of the painting, because Mr. Knox had unexpectedly balked him by telling his story to the police. True, Mr. Knox had said the painting was comparatively valueless, a copy, but Pepper chose not to believe that, feeling that Mr. Knox was merely cleverly covering himself up—as indeed you were, sir; there Pepper shrewdly guessed that you were lying."

Knox grunted; he seemed too pained to speak.

"In any event," Ellery went on blandly, "the only source of revenue left to Pepper was eventually to steal the Leonardo from Mr. Knox; he felt sure Mr. Knox had the Leonardo, not the copy. But to do this he had to have a clear field; the police were everywhere, looking for the murderer.

"Which brings us to the Sloane affair. Why did Pepper

choose Sloane as the second straw-man? We have facts and inferences enough to answer that question now. Indeed, I touched
on it some time ago to you, Dad—remember that night?" The
old man nodded in silence. "For if Sloane saw Pepper in the
graveyard and knew now that here was the murderer of Grimshaw, Sloane possessed knowledge of Pepper's guilt. But how
could Pepper have known that Sloane knew? Well, Sloane had
seen Pepper take the will out of the coffin; even if he didn't actually see it he could infer it later from the fact that the will and
box were gone when the coffin was opened at the disinterment.
Sloane wanted that will destroyed; he must have gone to Pepper, accused him of murder, and demanded the will as the price
of silence. Pepper, faced with the terrible menace to his own
safety, must have bargained with Sloane; he would keep the will
as a weapon to insure Sloane's silence. But inwardly he would
plan to be rid of Sloane, the only living witness against him.

"So Pepper arranged the 'suicide' of Sloane to make it appear that Sloane had been the murderer of Grimshaw. Sloane
fitted all the motives nicely; and with the burnt will in the basement, the basement key in Sloane's room, and Grimshaw's
watch in Sloane's wall-safe, Pepper laid a beautiful trail of evidence against his victim. Incidentally, Dad, your man Ritter was
not at fault for having 'missed' seeing the will-fragment in the
furnace of the empty Knox house. Because when Ritter
searched, the scrap wasn't there! Pepper burnt the will later,
carefully leaving the Khalkis handwritten name of Albert
Grimshaw unsinged, and put the ashes and the scrap in the
furnace sometime after Ritter's little investigation. . . . As for
Sloane's revolver being used for the killing of Sloane, undoubtedly Pepper secured it from the Sloane rooms in the Khalkis
house at the time he planted the key in the humidor.

"So he had to kill Sloane to keep him from talking. At the
same time he knew the police would ask: 'Why did Sloane commit suicide?' The obvious reason would be that Sloane knew he
was to be arrested on the basis of the clues which had been

found. Pepper asked himself: How could Sloane know this, presumably, in a police explanation? Well, he might be warned. All this, you understand, is Pepper's probable reasoning. How leave a trace to the presumable fact that Sloane had been warned? Ah, the simplicity of it! Which brings us to the mysterious telephone call which we established had emanated from the Khalkis house the evening of Sloane's 'suicide.'

"Do you remember that?—the basis on which we believed Sloane had been tipped off of our intentions? And remember that Pepper, in our presence, began to dial Woodruff on the telephone to make an appointment for the purpose of authenticating the burnt will-fragment? Pepper remarked, as he hung up after a moment, that the line was busy; a moment later he dialled again and this time actually spoke to Woodruff's valet. Well, the first time he merely dialled the number of the Khalkis Galleries! Knowing the call could be traced, it was perfect for his plans; when Sloane answered Pepper merely disconnected by replacing his receiver without saying a word. Sloane must have been a much puzzled man. But this was enough to establish a call from the house to the Galleries; and particularly clever since it was done under our very eyes, the dial-instrument permitting him to connect with the Galleries without asking for the number aloud. Another little psychological confirmation of Pepper's guilt, then, since no one, particularly those who had reason to warn Sloane, would admit having put in the call.

"Pepper immediately got out of the Khalkis house, presumably to hunt up Woodruff and substantiate the will-scrap. But before going to Woodruff's he stopped in at the Galleries— Sloane probably admitted him—and killed Sloane, merely rearranging a few details to make the thing look like suicide. The incident of the closed door which ultimately exploded the Sloane-suicide plot was not an error on Pepper's part; he didn't know that the bullet had gone clear through Sloane's head and out the open doorway; Sloane fell on the side of his face from which the bullet had emerged, and naturally Pepper did not handle Sloane's body more than was necessary, if he handled it at all. No sound came from the bullet's striking in the main room outside, because it hit a thick rug on the wall. And so, a victim of circumstances, Pepper did the logical thing when he left—almost the instinctive thing for a murderer to do: he closed the door. And thereby inadvertently upset his own apple-cart.

"For almost two weeks the Sloane theory was accepted—the murderer seemingly had seen the jig was up and had committed suicide. Pepper felt that he now had a clear field for the theft of the painting from Mr. Knox; his plan must have been, now that the police had their murderer nicely filed away, to steal the painting from Mr. Knox in such a way as to make it appear, not that Mr. Knox was the murderer, but that he had stolen the Leonardo from himself in order not to have to return it to the Museum. But when Suiza came forward and gave evidence which pricked the Sloane-suicide theory, and this fact was made public, Pepper knew that the police still sought a murderer. Why not make Mr. Knox out to be not only the thief of his own painting but the Grimshaw-Sloane murderer as well? Where Pepper's plan went awry—and not through any fault of his—was that he had every reason to believe Mr. Knox a theoretical possibility as the murderer. That would have been so—although the business of motive was a hard nut to crack—had Mr. Knox not come to me with his story of the thousand-dollar bill at a time when I had no reason to repeat the story even to my father—since in that period the Sloane theory was the accepted one. So Pepper went blithely ahead framing Mr. Knox for the murders and the theft, not knowing that at last I had him cornered—although I didn't know it was he at the time. The moment Mr. Knox was framed with the second letter, however, I, knowing him to be innocent, spotted the second letter as a frame-up and deduced, as I've already shown, that Pepper himself was the culprit."

"Here, son," growled the Inspector, speaking for the first time. "Have a drink. Your throat is dry. How's the shoulder?"

"Middling. . . . Now you can see why that first blackmail letter *had* to be written from the outside, and furthermore how the answer points again to Pepper. Pepper could not gain legitimate access to Mr. Knox's house for a period long enough to discover where the painting was hidden and to write the second letter; but by sending the first letter he got himself posted in the house as an investigator. Please remember that this was at his *own* suggestion to you, Sampson; another little gram on the scales of Pepper's guilt.

"Sending the second letter from Mr. Knox's own typewriter was the penultimate step in Pepper's frame-up. The ultimate step, of course, was the theft of the painting itself. During the period when he was posted in the house, Pepper searched for it. He had no inkling, naturally, of the existence of two paintings. He found the sliding panel in the gallery-wall, stole the painting, smuggled it out of the house, and secreted it in the empty Knox house on Fifty-fourth Street—an ingenious hiding-place! Then he proceeded to send the second blackmail letter. From his standpoint the plot was complete—all he had to do now was to sit back righteously as one of Mr. Sampson's alert guardians of the law, help pin the guilt on Mr. Knox as writer of the letter if perchance I failed to catch the significance of the pound-sign; and eventually, after everything had blown over, to cash in on the painting either through a not-too-scrupulous collector or a 'fence.'"

"How about that burglar-alarm business?" asked James Knox. "Just what was the idea?"

"Oh that! You see, after he himself stole the painting," replied Ellery, "and then wrote the letter, he tampered with your burglar-alarm system. He expected that we would go to the rendezvous in the Times Building, and then come back empty-handed. We should then have realized, he planned, that we had been tricked, that the purpose of the letter was to lure us away from the house *while the painting was being stolen*. Now, that was to be the obvious explanation; but when we should have pinned the guilt to you, Mr. Knox, we would have said: 'See! Knox tampered with his own burglar-alarm to make us *think* the painting was stolen tonight by an outsider. When actually it was never stolen at all.' A complex plan which requires assiduous concentration for complete comprehension. But it illustrates the remarkably subtle quality of Pepper's thinking processes."

"That's all clear enough, I think," said the District Attorney suddenly; he had been following the course of Ellery's explanation like a terrier. "But what I want to know is about that business of the two paintings—why you arrested Mr. Knox here—all of that."

For the first time a grin spread over Knox's rugged features; and Ellery laughed aloud. "We were continually reminding Mr. Knox to be 'a good sport'; how good a sport he turned out is the answer to your question, Sampson. I should have told you that the entire rigmarole about the 'legend' of two authentically old paintings being differentiated only by a distinction in flesh-tints—all pure bombast and melodrama. On the afternoon of the arrival of the second blackmail letter, I knew everything by deduction—Pepper's plot, his guilt, his intent. But I was in a peculiar position: I had no shred of evidence with which you might convict him if he were immediately accused and arrested; and furthermore that precious painting was in his possession somewhere. If we exposed him, the painting would probably never be found; and it was my duty to see that the Leonardo was restored to its rightful owners, the Victoria Museum. On the other hand, if I could trap Pepper into such a position that he would be caught red-handed *with the stolen Leonardo*, his mere possession of it would serve as evidence for conviction, and would, moreover, secure the painting!"

"Do you mean to say that that stuff about the flesh-tints and all that was made up?" demanded Sampson.

"Yes, Sampson—my own private little plot, in which I played with Mr. Pepper as he had played with me. I took Mr. Knox into my confidence, told him everything—how and by whom he was being framed. He then told me that after he had bought the original Leonardo from Khalkis, he had had a copy made, confessing that his intention had been to return this copy to the Museum if the police pressure became too strong, with the story that this was the one he had bought from Khalkis. It would of course in this event be recognized at once by experts as a rank copy—but Mr. Knox's story would be unassailable and he would probably go scot-free. In other words, whereas Mr. Knox had the copy in the dummy radiator-coil, the original was in the panel, and Pepper had stolen that original. But this gave me an idea—an idea which was to utilize a little truth and a great deal of romancing."

Ellery's eyes danced at the recollection. "I told Mr. Knox that I was going to arrest him—purely for Pepper's benefit—accuse him, outline the case against him, do all the things necessary to convince Pepper that his frame-up against Mr. Knox had been completely successful. Now, if I do say so, Mr. Knox reacted splendidly; he wanted his little revenge on Pepper anyway for attempting to involve him; he wanted to compensate for his own originally illicit intention to palm off a copy on the Museum; so he agreed to play the victim for me. We called in Toby Johns—this was all Friday afternoon—and together concocted a story which I felt sure would force Pepper's hand. A dictaphone record of this entire conversation, by the way, in which all the details of the fabricated plot were discussed openly, was made in the event we failed to make Pepper snatch the bait . . . just to provide evidence that the Knox arrest was not intended seriously, but was part of a greater plot to trap the real murderer.

"Now, look at the position Pepper was in when he heard the expert's beautifully phrased cock-and-bull story, interspersed with resounding historical references and contemporary

Italian art-names, about the 'legend' of the 'fine distinction' between the two paintings—all of it, naturally, pure bilgewater. There has never been more than one old oils of this precise subject—and that is the Leonardo original; there never was a legend; there never was a 'contemporary' copy—Mr. Knox's was a modern daub made in New York and recognizable as such by anyone familiar with art; all this was my own contribution to the fascinating little counterplot. . . . Now Pepper learned from Johns's dignified lips that the only way he could determine which was the Leonardo and which the 'contemporary copy' was by actually placing the two side by side! Pepper must have said to himself what I wanted him to say: 'Well, I have no way of knowing which one I own; the real one or the copy. I can't take Knox's word for anything. So I'll have to put the two of them together—fast, because the one we have here, which will probably be kept in the D.A.'s files, won't be here long.' He would think that if he did put them together and, after determining which was the Leonardo, returned the copy to the files, he was in no danger—not even the expert himself, by his own admission, could tell which was which if they weren't together!

"It was really a stroke of genius," murmured Ellery, "and I congratulate myself upon it. What—no applause? . . . Naturally, if we had been dealing with a man of art, an aesthete, a painter or even a dilettante, I should never have risked Johns telling this ridiculous story; but Pepper, I knew, was the veriest layman, and he had no reason but to swallow the story whole, particularly since everything else seemed genuine—Knox's arrest, imprisonment, the blazoned newspaper stories, the notification of Scotland Yard—oh, precious! I knew that neither you, Sampson, nor you, Dad, would see through the fish-story, because, with all respect for your individual capacities as man-hunters, you know as little about art as Djuna here. The only one of whom I had reason to be fearful was Miss Brett—and I had told her that afternoon enough about the plot so that she showed the proper surprise and horror when Mr. Knox was 'arrested.' Incidentally, I must congratulate myself on still another score—my acting; wasn't I the deceptive little devil, though?" Ellery grinned. "I see my talent isn't appreciated. . . . At any rate, with nothing to lose and apparently everything to gain, Pepper just couldn't resist placing those two paintings side by side for a bare five minutes' comparison. . . . Precisely as I foresaw.

"At the time I accused Mr. Knox in his own house, I already had Sergeant Velie—a very reluctant officer, I will confess, since he is so attached to my father that even the thought of treason makes his huge carcass tremble—searching Pepper's apartment and office on the remote chance that he had secreted the painting in one of the two places. Of course, it wasn't in either, but I had to be certain. Friday night I saw to it that Pepper was given the painting to take down to the D.A.'s office, where it would be available to him at any time. He naturally lay doggo that night and all day yesterday; but, as you all know now, last night he smuggled the painting out of the official files and proceeded to his hiding-place in the empty Knox house, where we nabbed him with the two—the original and the worthless copy. Of course, Sergeant Velie and his men had been on Pepper's trail all day, like bloodhounds; and I was getting frequent reports about Pepper's movements, since we didn't know where he had the Leonardo concealed.

"The fact that he shot for my heart"—Ellery tenderly patted his shoulder—"and fortunately for posterity merely winged me, proves, I think, that in that agonizing instant of discovery Pepper recognized at last that I had turned the tables.

"And that, I believe, spells *finis*."

They sighed and stirred. Djuna appeared, as if by prearrangement, with tea-things. For a few moments the case was forgotten in chatter—in which neither Miss Joan Brett nor Mr. Alan Cheney, it will be noted, took part—and then Sampson said: "I've got something that will bear clarification, Ellery. You've

gone to heaps of trouble in your analysis of the events surrounding the blackmail letters to take into account the possibility of an
accomplice. Splendid! But—" he stabbed at the air triumphantly
with his forefinger in the approved prosecutor-manner—"how
about your original analysis? Remember you said that the first
characteristic of the letter-writer was that in order to have
planted the false clues against Khalkis in the Khalkis house he
must have been the murderer?"

"Yes," said Ellery, blinking thoughtfully.

"But you didn't say anything about the possibility that it
might have been an *accomplice* of the murderer who planted
those clues! How could you assume it was the murderer and
discard even the possibility of an accomplice?"

"Don't excite yourself, Sampson. The explanation is really
self-evident. Grimshaw himself had said he had only one
partner—right? We showed from other things that this partner
had killed Grimshaw—right? Then I said that, the partner having killed Grimshaw, he had the greatest motive for trying to
pin the guilt on someone else, in that first case Khalkis—so, I
said, the murderer planted the false clues. You ask me why
there isn't the logical possibility that an accomplice planted the
false clues? For the simple reason that, in killing Grimshaw, the
murderer was *deliberately getting rid of an accomplice*. Would
he kill an accomplice and then turn right around and take another one for the purpose of laying a false trail? In addition, the
planting of the Khalkis clues was a wholly voluntary action on
the part of the plotter. In other words, he had the world to
choose from in selecting an 'acceptable' murderer. Then he
would certainly choose the most expedient. Having got rid of
one accomplice, the taking of another would be a clumsy and
unsatisfactory expedient. Therefore, giving the clever criminal
credit for his cleverness, I maintained that he had planted the
false clues himself."

"All right, all right," said Sampson, throwing up his hands.

"How about Mrs. Vreeland, Ellery?" asked the Inspector

curiously. "I thought that she and Sloane were lovers. That doesn't jibe with her story to us about seeing Sloane in the graveyard that night."

Ellery waved another cigarette. "A detail. From Mrs. Sloane's description of her visit to the Benedict, trailing Sloane, it was evident that Sloane and Mrs. Vreeland had been conducting an *affaire de cœur*. But I think you will find that, as soon as Sloane realized that the only way he'd ever inherit the Khalkis Galleries would be through his wife, he decided to cast off his paramour and devote himself thereafter to the cultivation of his wife's good graces. Naturally, Mrs. Vreeland being what she is — and a spurned lady-love at that — reacted in the usual way and attempted to hurt Sloane as much as possible."

Alan Cheney woke up suddenly. Out of a clear sky — he sedulously avoided looking at Joan — he asked: "And how about this Dr. Wardes, Queen? Where the devil is he? Why did he skip out? Where does he fit into the case, if he fits in at all?"

Joan Brett was examining her hands with interest.

"I think," said Ellery with a shrug, "that Miss Brett could answer that question. I've had a suspicion all along. . . . Eh, Miss Brett?"

Joan looked up and smiled very sweetly — although she did not look in Alan's direction. "Dr. Wardes was my confederate. Really! And one of Scotland Yard's cleverest investigators."

This was, one felt, excellent news to Mr. Alan Cheney; he coughed his surprise and studied the rug more carefully than before. "You see," continued Joan, still smiling sweetly, "I didn't say anything about him to you, Mr. Queen, because he himself forbade me to. He had disappeared to trail the Leonardo out of official sight and interference — he was quite disgusted with the way things had gone."

"Then of course you wangled him into the Khalkis house by design?" asked Ellery.

"Yes. When I saw I was beyond my depth, I wrote of my helplessness to the Museum, and they went to Scotland Yard,

who until then had been ignorant of the theft—the directors
were *very* keen to keep the affair quiet. Dr. Wardes actually has
a medical licence and has acted as a physician on cases before."

"He did visit Grimshaw that night in the Benedict, didn't
he?" asked the District Attorney.

"Certainly. That night I was unable to follow Grimshaw myself; but I passed the word along to Dr. Wardes, and he followed
the man, saw him join an unidentifiable man . . ."

"Pepper, of course," murmured Ellery.

". . . and dallied about the lobby of the hotel when Grimshaw and this Pepper person took the lift. He saw Sloane go
up, and Mrs. Sloane, and Odell—and finally he went up himself,
although he did not enter Grimshaw's room, merely reconnoi-
tred about. He saw them all leave, excepting the first man.
Naturally, he couldn't tell you these things without disclosing
his identity, and he was unwilling to do that. . . . Discovering
nothing, Dr. Wardes returned to the Khalkis house. The night
after, when Grimshaw and Mr. Knox called—although we didn't
know it was Mr. Knox then—Dr. Wardes was unfortunately out
with Mrs. Vreeland, whose acquaintance he was cultivating on
a—a—what shall I say?—a hunch!"

"Where's he now, I wonder?" said Alan Cheney indifferently, addressing the design on the rug.

"I do believe," said Joan to the smoke-filled air, "that Dr.
Wardes is now on the high seas, homeward bound."

"Ah," said Alan, as if that were a highly satisfactory reply.

*   *   *

When Knox and Sampson had gone, the Inspector sighed, took
Joan's hand in a fatherly way, patted Alan's shoulder, and departed on some errand of his own—presumably to face a horde
of hungry journalists and, what was even more agreeable, some
very superior superiors who had experienced a marked defla-
tion of spirits with the lightning zigzags of the Grimshaw-
Sloane-Pepper case.

Left alone with his guests, Ellery began to pay scrupulous attention to the dressings of his wounded shoulder. He was a most ungentlemanly host; Joan and Alan, in fact, rose and rather stiffly attempted to take their leave.

"What! You're not going already?" Ellery exclaimed mercifully, at last. He crawled off the sofa and smiled idiotically at them; Joan's ivory nostrils were quivering ever so slightly, and Alan was now engaged in tracing a complex pattern with one scuffing toe on the rug in which he had been so completely absorbed for an hour. "Well! Don't go just yet. Wait. I have something that you especially will be interested in, Miss Brett."

Ellery hurried mysteriously out of the living-room. No word was spoken during his absence; they stood like two belligerent babies, furtively looking each other over. They sighed together as Ellery emerged from the bedroom, a large roll of canvas tucked under his right arm.

"This," he said to Joan with gravity, "is the thingamajig that has caused all the fuss. We no longer require the sadly abused Leonardo—Pepper being dead, there will be no trial...."

"You're not—you're not giving it to—" Joan began slowly. Alan Cheney stared.

"Precisely. You're going back to London, aren't you? So allow me to offer you the honour you've earned, Lieutenant Brett—the privilege of taking the Leonardo back to the Museum yourself."

"Oh!" Her rosy mouth framed the ellipse, a little tremulously; and it did not seem with too much enthusiasm. She accepted the roll of canvas and passed it from her right hand to her left and back again, quite as if she did not know exactly what to do with it—this hoary daub over which three men had lost their lives.

Ellery went to a sideboard and produced a bottle. It was a brown old bottle with a nice wink and gleam to it; he spoke in a low voice to Djuna and that priceless supernumerary bustled into his kitchen, to return shortly with siphon and soda and other implements of the bibulous art. "A Scotch-and-soda, Miss Brett?" asked Ellery gaily.

"Oh, *no!*"

"Perhaps a cocktail?"

"You're very kind, but *I* don't indulge, Mr. Queen." Confusion had been superseded; Miss Brett was her old frosty self again, for no logical reason apparent to the less subtle male eye.

Alan Cheney was regarding the bottle thirstily. Ellery busied himself with glasses and things. Soon he had an amber effervescent fluid bubbling in a tall glass; and he offered it to Alan with the air of one man of the world to another.

"Really excellent," murmured Ellery. "I know you have a fancy for these things . . . What, you—?" Ellery managed to exhibit an enormous astonishment.

For Mr. Alan Cheney, under the judiciously stern eye of Miss Joan Brett—Mr. Alan Cheney, the confirmed toper—was actually refusing this aromatic concoction! "No," he muttered doggedly. "No thanks, Queen. I've quit the stuff. Can't tempt me."

A ray of warm light seemed to touch the features of Miss Joan Brett; one with a poor sense of word-values might say that she was beaming; the truth was that the frost melted magically away, and again for no logical reason she blushed, and looked down at the floor, and her toe too began a scuffing movement; and the Leonardo, which was catalogued at one million dollars, began to slip from under her arm, ignored as completely as if it had been a gaudy calendar.

"Pshaw!" said Ellery. "And I thought—Well!" He shrugged with unconvincing disappointment. "You know, Miss Brett," he said, "this is quite like one of those old stock-company melodramas. Hero leaps to the upper deck of the water-wagon—turns over a new leaf at the end of the third act, and all that sort of thing. In fact, I hear that Mr. Cheney has consented to supervise the business end of his mother's now considerable estate—eh, Cheney?" Alan nodded breathlessly. "And he'll probably manage the Khalkis Galleries too when this legal flurry blows over."

He babbled on. And then he stopped, because neither of his guests was listening. Joan had turned on shocking impulse to Alan; intelligence—or whatever it is called—bridged the gap between their eyes, and Joan blushed again and turned to Ellery, who was regarding them ruefully. "I don't think," said Joan, "that I shall be going back to London after all. It's—It was nice of you. . . ."

And Ellery, when the door had closed upon them, surveyed the prostrate canvas on his floor—to which it had slipped from Miss Joan Brett's soft underarm—and sighed, and under the slightly disapproving gaze of young Djuna, who even at that tender age exhibited stern evidences of teetotalism, sipped his Scotch-and-soda all by himself . . . a not unpleasant ritual, if one should judge by the oxlike contentment which spread over his lean face.